Books by Mary Summer Rain

Nonfiction

Spirit Song

Phoenix Rising

Dreamwalker

Phantoms Afoot

Earthway

Daybreak

Soul Sounds

Whispered Wisdom

Ancient Echoes

Bittersweet

Mary Summer Rain on Dreams

The Visitation

Millennium Memories

Fireside

The Singing Web

Beyond Earthway

Trined in Twilight

Pinecones

Love Never Sleeps

Tao of Nature

Woodsmoke

In Your Dreams

Children's

Mountains, Meadows and Moonbeams

Star Babies

Fiction

The Seventh Mesa

Ruby

Books on Tape

Spirit Song

Phoenix Rising

Dreamwalker

Phantoms Afoot

The Visitation

Ruby

a novel

Mary Summer Rain

HAMPTON ROADS
PUBLISHING COMPANY, INC.

Cover design by Jane Hagaman
Cover photograph by Jane Hagaman, used by
permission of Richard Silman

Hampton Roads Publishing Company, Inc.
1125 Stoney Ridge Road
Charlottesville, VA 22902

434-296-2772
fax: 434-296-5096
e-mail: hrpc@hrpub.com
www.hrpub.com

If you are unable to order this book from your local
bookseller, you may order directly from the publisher.
Call 1-800-766-8009, toll-free.

Library of Congress Cataloging-in-Publication Data

Summer Rain, Mary, 1945-
  Ruby : a novel / Mary Summer Rain.
    p. cm.
  Summary: "When antiques dealer Sadie Brennan's niece enters into a trauma-induced state
of muteness, Sadie and her niece Savannah must solve the mystery of a homeless woman in
Chicago named Ruby"--Provided by publisher.
  ISBN 1-57174-434-7 (6x9 tp : alk. paper)
  1. Women detectives--Illinois--Chicago--Fiction. 2. Antique dealers--Fiction.
3. Homeless women--Fiction. 4. Chicago
(Ill.)--Fiction. 5. Mute persons--Fiction. I. Title.
  PS3569.U382R83 2004
  813'.54--dc22
                                        2004028317

To Possibilities yet undreamed of
And to their even more undreamed of Probabilities.

One

Bay Port, Maine–Thursday

Leaden clouds stealthily prowled across the surprised face of the early October moon. They advanced in great growing billows, each dark mass rearing larger than the one before as they swelled and loomed higher with gathering energy. Cells of turmoil began joining forces in the night sky.

The winking play of light and shadow that flickered over the small harbor inlet flashed unmistakable portents of an approaching storm.

Those crew members who were still on board fishing boats at this late hour sharply honed their attention to the familiar markers of the imminent sea change. The queasiness of increasing anxiety rippled through their every nerve.

On the grassy hillside beyond the wharf, people in their neatly clustered homes repeatedly pulled curtains aside to peer out at the sky. The highly charged air sparked growing apprehension within the quickening hearts of the shore dwellers restlessly pacing before their unshuttered windows.

One minute the watery surface danced with reflected points of lustrous moonlight, the next it was ominously dark and mysterious.

The waters of Bay Port began to lose their glassy surface as the breeze became a wind that blew them into ever deepening ripples—ripples threatening to become chop soon.

The alternating light and shadows flashed across the bobbing vessels moored in the slips hugging the crescent cove.

The light and shadows spilled across the rigging of the boat known by the locals as *Destiny II*, a fishing boat badly in need of paint and care. The once shiny gold lettering on the bow and stern had seen better days. Now they were worn by years of lashing waves and blowing spindrift. The vessel's name was as much in need of refurbishing as the rest of its deteriorating exterior. Its tired appearance mirrored the owner's declining interest and growing lack of attention.

Light and shadows played across the faces of the two people in its wheelhouse.

The light reflected off the woman's brimming tears.

The shadows hid the man's rising level of frustration.

"But everything was going so well for us," the woman repeated for the third time. "We had plans." The mistiness of her green eyes caught the moonlight for a moment before it was obscured by another tumbling bank of clouds. "I can't believe how out of the blue this is. How can you just suddenly say that it's over? Oh God," she sighed, an irrepressible sob bringing a hitch to her words. "I . . . I just can't believe you're saying this. This can't be real. It can't be happening." Her voice lowered when she expressed a new thought that speared her mind like a javelin cast into her heart. "It's another woman, isn't it? It has to be."

Paul Hollander released a long sigh of his own. He'd been dreading the day when he finally had to let her know how he'd been feeling about their relationship, their future. That his crazy, unrealistic dream of having his own fishing fleet was never going to pan out. That their idyllic plans to get married, buy that prim little house on the hill with the white picket fence, and raise a couple of kids was just some rose-covered-cottage pipe dream they'd fashioned from nothing more realistic than pixie dust. For six years it'd kept them both going. Barely. And for the last five months of that time he'd been the only one who'd realized that "barely" was never going to get it. He'd been the only one who took the time for periodic reality checks.

He gently raised his hands to the woman's trembling shoulders and slid equally shaking fingers down her arms. Though it might not have been visibly obvious, he was as upset as she was.

"Sadie," he said as tenderly as he could, "listen to me. We need to face the fact that I'm never going to have that fleet. I can barely support myself, much less a wife and family with the kinds of catches I've been bringing in over the last two years." A burst of blinding light from the sky made him hesitate before adding, "You deserve better."

The woman wasn't letting the approaching storm distract her. "But the Prudhoe Bay?! Prudhoe Bay, for god's sake? Why, that's the most absurd thing I've ever heard. Even for you, don't you think that's a little extreme? Way over the top? And, I'd like to know," she said with a voice heavy with incredulity and suspicion, "what's so almighty wrong with me being a pipeline inspector's wife? What's your change of job got to do with us? What's it got to do with you and me?"

Paul didn't know how to tell her that, somewhere along the line, he'd found himself adrift from the secure shore of their shared love. He'd never been good with words, especially words he knew would hurt someone. He'd practiced over and over for the time when this conversation would eventually take place. He'd spent countless sleepless nights pacing the plank floor of his efficiency apartment above the tackle shop. He'd repeated his spiel to the wind as he fished. And once he'd reconciled himself to the idea that the fire of their relationship had died to little more than a fading ember, that it was over, his mind continually spun in desperation over finding the right way to voice his feelings so as not to sound crass, heartless. Now that the dreaded moment of truth had come, he found himself verbally stumbling and tripping over his thoughts. As desperately as he tried, he couldn't manage to keep them straight. They were as tangled as a drying fishing net whipped by a nor'easter. He hadn't counted on the intense emotionality of the confrontation scrambling his well-rehearsed phrasing. His frustration grew when he realized his mind was a blank. He hated that he couldn't find the words, words he'd mentally repeated over and over to himself like a mantra in preparation for this dreaded moment.

Deeply dismayed over how badly things were going, he made another stab at an explanation. "It's just that . . . we . . . I . . . I—"

Stung by her lover's burning words, Sadie abruptly pulled away from Paul's grasp. "You love someone else," she cut in. "Oh, for heaven's sake, Paul. Oh God, why can't you just come out and say it? You've fallen for another woman," she said, while spewing out her words, "and this Alaskan pipeline thing is just an excuse to go away with her!"

Agitated that the situation wasn't going anything like he'd envisioned, Paul quickly countered. "No! No, it's not an excuse," he defensively attempted to reassure. "I told you, my brother offered me the job. All year long he's been bugging me to stop banging my head against a wall trying to make a go of this stinkin' boat." He flung his arms out for emphasis. "My God! Open your eyes! Look around, Sadie. You and I both know this is a piece of floating shit! The dream blinded me to what was right in front of my eyes. You and I, Sadie, you and I both ignored the facts. We were in denial with hearts full of unrealistic hope, always holding onto that thin thread that my luck would one day turn around tomorrow. Tomorrow or the next day. Always the tomorrows, Sadie. Always the tomorrows and the days beyond that. We've been living for the tomorrows that aren't ever gonna come. And all the while, I've just poured money into repairs and could never get ahead." In exasperation, Paul raked his hands through his hair. "Anyway," he softened, "like I said, my brother offered me the job last month and, after spending sleepless nights giving it a lot of deep thought, I, well . . . I went ahead and accepted the position."

Sadie's eyes widened in disbelief. This latest news hadn't made things better. "He'd been bugging you all year? All year? And you've never said anything to me about it? You never thought it was important enough to share with me, discuss together?" She was incredulous over this latest news that'd only served to further exacerbate the situation. "And this new job offer, you just . . . just took it?"

"Yes! I took it because I finally came to my senses and—"

"Oh, really," she broke in. "You came to your senses. I thought our relationship was sense, Paul."

"Let me finish. Please, at least give me that."

The woman pursed her lips and looked to the window before gaining the courage to shift her gaze back in the general direction of the man standing before her. She couldn't bring herself to look directly into her lover's eyes. "I'm listening."

"Okay. So anyway, I realized he was right, Sadie," he admitted with a sigh. "I've been banging my head against a wall and that's no secret to anyone around here. People are whispering, making comments behind my back. I've become the village fool. It's just finally time to move on. You've got to believe me when I say there's no other woman involved. Never has been. It's as simple as that." He thought that sounded lame but the words had already spilled out. He knew this wasn't a simple situation to deal with. Nothing about this conversation was simple.

The first drops of rain dappled the windows of the pilot house.

The man inside hated himself for hurting the only woman he'd loved. The only woman he'd fallen out of love with. The only woman he still cared enough for to hide the truth that would break her heart even more. The fact was, he just didn't feel the same about her. Even if he could remember the right words now, it was far too late. His heart would never let him speak them.

Sadie Brennan couldn't hold back the tears that had been building behind her eyes. Though she tried to contain them, they overflowed their rims like a river cresting its banks after a week of torrential rain. She slowly backpedaled from Paul when he reached out to stroke her cheek.

"Don't *touch* me," she whispered with venom dripping from her voice. She shot her hands up between them in a warning gesture. "Don't you *dare* touch me."

Paul's stomach knotted to see her reaction to him. Her response, so full of repugnance, clenched his stomach, his heart, like an iron fist. His guts twisted to witness love so quickly turning to hatred and revulsion. Sick at heart over the pain he'd caused, he resigned himself to the fact that he'd done a thoroughly lousy job of handling the situation. He'd made a completely bumbled mess of it. He knew he'd bungled the whole thing and there was no way to rectify anything, no way now to erase the last forty minutes and start over. It was irrevocable. Recognizing this, he hopelessly abandoned further attempts to justify himself, make apologies, or soften the harsh impact of his crushing words. Feeling the futility, and heartfeltly wishing he were someplace else, he simply closed his eyes.

When he opened them again he was alone.

The parting. It'd been different from how he'd repeatedly run it through his mind. It'd ultimately happened a lot differently from how he'd envisioned it playing out. But then, he thought, nothing ever happens according to how one imagines it. It'd been harder than he'd ever dreamed. Right then he didn't like himself very much, although he did find that he was left with a sense of deep relief to have it over. The one thought that offered a small measure of solace was the knowledge that Sadie would get past this, she'd recover. Sadie, he knew, was a survivor.

Sadie didn't feel much like a survivor at this moment. She felt as though her fragile life had been viciously shattered and there were no shards of her future remaining; no time, except for her next sobbing breath.

Her clothing had gotten soaked through while she made her halting way from the end of the pier to where her panel van had been parked. The rain had been blowing across the weathered planks of the wharf in chilling sheets by the time she'd pulled herself together enough to see her way through the blur of flowing tears.

Once she was inside the vehicle, the heater felt too good for how she felt inside. How, she wondered, could it be remotely possible for anything to feel good right now?

Numb from the chilling rain and the shock of what had just occurred, Sadie listened to the rhythmic thrump-thrump of the windshield wipers. They sounded like the labored throb of a heart about to burst.

Sadie put the vehicle in gear and eased out onto the slick street that hugged the harbor. The headlights fought to push their beams through the curtain of pelting rain. In a mental haze, she followed the narrow bayside road as it curved itself around the feet of the small village. Now, because of the recent events, her eyes were not enviously drawn to the trim Cape Cod homes tucked on the picturesque hillside. Now her visions of living in one of them were dashed. Now they were empty. They were as empty as a midsummer's abandoned cocoon, empty because she'd abruptly found herself without any plans at all. Only the moment. Just the moment.

The van slowed as it rolled past the eclectic array of shops separating the residential area from the wharf. It eased into the parking space in front of the quaintly appointed storefront of Harbor Heirlooms.

The engine was cut.

The thrumping heartbeat was silenced.

Rain pelted the vehicle.

The view through the windshield was obscured. The woman inside slumped down in the driver's seat and, feeling defeated, let her head loll toward the shop. Her thoughts were jumbled as her gaze roamed over the fancy gold lettering on the colonial blue clapboard. Now what? she found herself wondering. Would she keep the antiques business? After all, she'd worked hard for six years getting it up and going. It'd become the place that renowned dealers frequented and recommended to their more discriminating clients. People came from all over New England to see what rare treasures they could add to their private collections. They came for the pure joy of doing business with the knowledgeable proprietress whom they could always count on as being friendly and fair. They came for the scenic ambiance of the village's postcard setting. Always, they came to mix business with leisure.

Sadie shifted her gaze to the adjoining candle and book shop that her friend had cleverly named Wick 'n' Wit. Glancing at the elaborately scripted lettering on the newly painted Chinese red clapboard, her thoughts naturally turned to its wildly Bohemian owner.

Tina Glaston had been her best friend since childhood, after they'd discovered they were neighbors in one of Chicago's most affluent residential areas. Only one year apart in age, they'd become fast and faithful companions through the thin times of grade school and the thick times of high school. College didn't pull the friendship apart because they made sure they attended the same university. Through those trying years, they'd depended on the support of each other's shoulders when each endured the joys and sorrows of the love affairs that came and went in their lives. After graduating, Tina had been eager to accompany Sadie to Maine to set up shops when Sadie had made the decision to follow Paul on his new fishing endeavor.

Now the Wick 'n' Wit stood dark. Sadie had been on the boat so long she'd lost track of time. She knew Tina would be in her back apartment.

Now what, Ms. Tina Glaston? Now what, old friend of mine? Sadie asked herself. If I scrap the shop, what of you?

Sadie exhaled a long-drawn-out sigh. "Yeah, right," she mumbled with resolve, "as if I'm going to throw everything else away in my life; as if I'm going to let everything else crumble around me. No thanks, Paul. No thanks. You've ruined quite enough for now."

The mental and emotional numbness had chilled her as much as the soaking rain. After disgustedly yanking the keys from the ignition, she ducked through the driving downpour and let herself into her own shop. Slamming the door behind herself, she slumped against it as if seeking a barrier between herself and life on the outside.

Safe. It was so safe inside. It felt like a welcoming sanctuary offering respite from the cruel elements of the weather and the world. Inside, all was as it should be, except for the sound of rainwater dripping off her clothing. She swiped her forehead and pushed from her face the long, wet strands of auburn hair.

Her legs felt like rubber, knees weak.

Not trusting her strength, she remained propped against the door.

Eyes scanned the shadowy interior. Early American brass candlesticks and burnished colonial pewter pitchers winked their buff polished surfaces with each flash of lightning that speared through the gleaming multipaned windows. More reflected winks came from the crystal faces of baroque mantle clocks and elaborately framed wall mirrors. The eighteenth-century grandfather clock ticked soulfully, then rang out to announce the hour from its rich, hand-rubbed cherry wood casing. Each clear gong sounded solid and true as thick Persian rugs mellowed their lingering vibration.

Sadie stood transfixed. Habit had her counting the number of chimes. Eleven. She waited to move until the last of the ringing reverberation melted into the plush carpet fibers and, like ghosts, drifted out through the paneled walls. Providing a welcoming sense of comforting predictability, the clock settled back into the familiar tick-tock of its etched brass pendulum.

Taking a small measure of solace from the soothing comforts of home, Sadie was drawn away from the door. Moving as though she were caught in a bad dream, she shuffled off to the left, past the aisle of heavily carved mahogany display cases filled with valuable jewelry pieces, cloisonné, and rare pocket watches. Silently, she moved in a mental fog through the shadows to the narrow, partially concealed staircase leading up to her living quarters. Only after gaining the top step did she think to reach for the light switch.

The soft spreading aura from Tiffany lamps chased away the shadowed gloom with a warming glow.

After tossing her wet sweater onto the tapestry chaise, she set the gas logs in the fireplace blazing. She lit them as much for emotional warmth as for physical comfort.

Her mind felt abysmally overwhelmed. Resting her forehead on the Italian marble mantle, she closed her eyes. She knew she needed to think it all out. So much had to be sorted and understood; yet, at the moment, the gears of her mind seemed to be jammed as tight as a springtime ice floe. Paul's words had frozen them in place. They required time to thaw.

When she eventually raised her head, emerald green eyes met with those looking out from the framed photograph on the mantelpiece. Paul on the fishing boat. Paul happy, smiling. He was beaming with his first big catch. It'd been a momentous day she'd captured on film for posterity, to one day show their children, perhaps their grandchildren. It'd been a day, they then believed, that verified the inevitability of their shared dreams. Looking at the photograph now, she recalled how incredibly carefree they were back then. They both glowed with ecstatic love for each other and their life together. Their future seemed bright and full of promise. It was a future so full of hopes and dreams that there was no room allotted for disappointments or the slightest probability of failure. Back then they believed that nothing could darken their days.

Instinctively, Sadie's hand rose to touch the picture. A fingertip tenderly traced the line of the man's smile. "When, Paul? When did it all change?" she whispered. "When did you let your heart be so cruelly blown adrift? Or did you knowingly choose to chart a different course? How was it that you—?"

Sadie was startled out of the private moment by the shrill telephone ring that pierced the room's stillness. Irritated, she listened to its harshness, its rudeness, for interrupting her intimate interrogation of the mute perpetrator. She glanced at the annoying phone, figuring that Paul was probably on the other end. Of course, he was. He was calling to apologize, to say it was all a terrible mistake. He was calling to admit that he'd had a temporary lapse of sanity. He was most likely feeling enormous remorse for hurting her. He'd come to his senses now, devastated that he'd broken her heart. And now wanted to rectify things, ask her forgiveness; maybe even beg for it. Well, she'd just let it ring. He wasn't going to get off that easily.

Unaware she was doing so, she counted the rings. She reached sixteen, then twenty-three. When she couldn't bear to listen any longer, she squared her shoulders, strode across the room in measured strides, and yanked the receiver to her ear. "You think you can just make everything go away with a phone call? Try to take everything back as if nothing was ever said? Well . . . it doesn't work that way! You—"

"Hey! Hey, whoa!!" came the concerned voice on the other end. "What the hell's going on, girlfriend? What did I do now?"

Half-relieved and more than a bit embarrassed, Sadie collapsed into the billowy plushness of the imported sofa. Hearing her friend's voice was a balm that disarmed her explosive mood. "Tina. I, ahh . . . I just got in."

"Well, isn't that a breaking news flash. When you didn't come right back after dinner out at the boat I put your shop to bed. I had my own customers and had to get back. I got worried about you after the weather turned wicked, spent more time watching out the window for your van lights than helping my people. Sounds like you've been through more than one storm tonight, honey. Wanna talk?"

Sadie unconsciously traced her finger along the outline of the sofa's Chinese peony print. "No," she replied as an evasive tact. "I'm soaked. I need to get out of these wet clothes. You know, take a hot bath and maybe read for a while before heading to bed. Thanks, anyway."

The perceptive woman on the other end of the line wasn't so easily convinced that all was well. It'd been a long time since anyone had successfully pulled the wool over her eyes.

"You sure? You answered that phone like a snapping turtle. It's me you're talking to. My vibes were spiking before you even picked up. I don't need a fortune-teller to tell me that something's up."

After all she'd just been through, Sadie managed to roll her eyes and mentally snicker over the vision of Tina consulting a jewel-bedecked gypsy. "Since when do you need a fortune-teller? You *are* a psychic. I can never keep anything from you."

"Yeah? Well? Then get a clue, girl. How about it? You need to talk or something? I sense you really need to talk."

"No. No, really I don't. What I need right now is a relaxing, hot bath."

Tina wasn't deterred. "Like I said," she repeated, "you need to talk?"

"Stop playing the analyst. All I need is a good, long soak."

"You sure?"

"I'm sure. I'll be fine."

"Okay then, see you in the morning. You can tell me all about it over coffee."

"Right. See you then."

After hanging up the receiver, Sadie let the bathroom fill with rolling steam while running her much-needed bath. Before stepping into the claw-foot tub, she lit a cluster of heavily scented votive candles that were ceremoniously placed around the rim, then switched off the light. The mood was set for relaxation. It was set, yet didn't quite manage to fully pull off the desired effect this night. As long as her thoughts were of Paul and his revelation of an hour before, Sadie knew she wouldn't reap any of the usual therapeutic benefits from the curling steam and glowing wicks.

Her mind shifted to recall Tina's statement about the fortune-teller and how ridiculous the idea had struck her. Even now, in her emotionally distressed state of mind, she felt a twinge of amusement over her friend's comment. Unbidden, snippets of their shared childhood memories came flooding to the forefront of her mind.

Tina. Tina, the neighborhood Know-It-All whom nobody could keep secrets from. Tina had always won every coin toss. When just a precocious youngster with twin braids swinging behind her back, she'd been annually punished for peeking inside the gift wrap of her hidden birthday presents. Though she was guiltless of gift snooping, she always knew what was inside the bright wrappings. She never could explain how she knew, she just did. And now the corners of Sadie's mouth tipped up in a wry smile. "Tina, honey," she said to the flickering candle flames, "you should've kept your mouth shut back then. You should've learned to stay mum about what you knew." That comment slipped to thoughts of the Tina of today, who'd matured with experience into the graceful wisdom of discernment, gauging when to reveal what she foresaw, when to remain silent about her many inner knowings.

Sadie's reveries were suddenly jarred back to the present by the unexpected appearance of her friend.

"Tina to the rescue!" the newcomer announced, while flamboyantly making a sweeping entry through the bathroom doorway. Her silk caftan swirled with a flourish around the long, slender legs. The waist-length blond braid swung in emphasis of the wearer's exuberance. "Lavender oil," she announced, holding high the full vial. Balancing a tray with the other hand, she added with a flair, "and chamomile tea with honey to soothe away her Ladyship's distress!"

Sadie's eyes glinted with appreciation. "You're something else. You don't have to wait on me like that. It's late. I said I'd be okay."

Tina doubted that. "Oh, right. Besides," she added with a wink, "I don't wait on people. I take care of them. You, sweetie, definitely need attending to. And, in case you've forgotten, I might remind you that it's never too late to care for a friend." After setting the teapot on the vanity counter, she spun around to face Sadie and fluttered her hands. "Up, up. Time to get out of there and let me massage away all that pent-up stress that's messing you up. I didn't get certified in therapeutic treatments for nothing. My God," she dramatically exclaimed, "your stress level is off the scale! It's spiking off of you like static electricity!"

Wisely, Sadie relented without a word of objection. It wouldn't have done any good if she had objected. Tina was an experienced masseuse and, if truth be told, a massage was probably just the ticket to help ease away the tension still crouching in her muscles.

Tina tossed Sadie a fluffy towel before picking up the tray of tea and oil. Ceremoniously carting them out, she didn't hesitate to take charge and voice her instructions.

"You hurry up and get that mass of hair dried. I'll be waiting out here with your tea. You need to talk, girl. You know, get it out in the open or the massage won't do you a whit of good. Mmm-mmm, honey," she hummed, "won't do a damn bit of good unless you release those angry and vicious feelings first. Obviously . . ." the voice trailed off, "you got yourself some mighty hefty man problems. Big man problems. Huge. Believe me, those are the absolute worst a woman can have. And you know I know because when Ronnie and I got divorced . . ."

The hair dryer blew away the sound of Tina's familiar ramblings. Sadie had heard them all before. Her friend had fallen overboard for a dashing fisherman when they'd first relocated to the village of Bay Port. He'd charmed her with flowers and whispered passionate, honey-dipped words. He'd swept her off her feet with a torrid affair that had them racing pell-mell up the chapel aisle with the swiftness of a harpoon in flight. It was over just as fast and had left Tina with a bitter taste in her heart when it came to entertaining the thought of another love-entangled relationship. She'd grown to like her independent life just as it was now. She immensely enjoyed that independence.

Sadie shuffled into the living area.

The lamp lights were off. Aromatherapy candles were winking on the coffee table. Quiet flames danced in the fireplace.

"Okay," Tina firmly informed. "The mood's all set. Come an' tell your girlfriend all about it." She poured steaming, golden liquid into a bone china cup and placed it before her friend.

Sadie gratefully took the proffered cup and settled on the sofa across from Tina. She released an extended sigh before beginning. "You're not going to believe this."

"Try me."

"He called it quits. He's found someone else."

The expected response of outrage didn't come. Normally, a friend hearing this news would drop her jaw and then sympathetically commiserate with the wounded party with, "What? Ohh, the bastard!" But Tina was discerning. Her response could never be clumped in with the "norm" of anything.

"Wait a minute," she immediately shot back. "Did he say that? I mean, did he actually come right out and *say* that he loved someone else?"

Sadie shook her head. The candle glow glinted off the auburn highlights of her natural curls. Her friend's question took her off guard and she instinctively felt defensive.

"He didn't have to," she subtly bristled. "The guilt was all over his face, in his voice, his body language. He kept trying to smooth it over. He kept trying to comfort me with weak apologies and stupid excuses."

Tina was silent for a few minutes. Thoughtful. When she spoke, her words were well chosen. They were deliberate and clear. "You're wrong. You've misinterpreted him."

Sadie recoiled. "No, I didn't," came the swift defense.

"Yes, you did!" Tina was adamant. "You jumped to conclusions by making your own assumptions. You let your mind misread the whole thing. You heard what your mind shouted at you instead of hearing his words. You listened to your own snap conclusions instead of listening to what he was saying. Then, bam!" she said, clapping her hands together for emphasis. "Your emotional reflexes kicked into gear and took over from there."

Sadie, not liking how her friend had sized up the situation so quickly, frowned in disappointment after hearing the startling analysis. It was unexpected. It threw her off balance. She'd wanted Tina to share her outrage, to empathize with her over how selfish and insensitive men were, to help release her anger by jointly ripping the emotionally

devoid male gender to shreds in a heated bout of verbal lashing. She'd
expected Tina to join in the harangue against men and bolster her own
hostility. When the anticipated response didn't come, Sadie was perplexed.

"What are you saying, Tina? What do you mean? How could I
have misinterpreted him? He's taken up his brother's offer to start a
new life with someone else. He's going far enough away so I'll never
see him with her. Isn't it obvious? What's to misread in that?"

Tina sighed as she pensively rested back into the plush sofa pil-
lows. She raised a questioning brow in response. "You tell me."

Sadie wasn't in the mood for Tina's guessing games, yet her heart
quickened with the remote possibility that her friend could be right.
She didn't want it to be so, but then again, Tina was always right,
wasn't she? Didn't she have an incredibly accurate sixth sense? Didn't
she have a strong gift for these types of things? And hadn't she repeatedly proven that her initial impressions were rarely off the mark?

Sadie's mind was caught fast in a web of tangled thoughts stuck to
crosshatched emotions. "I'm sorry," she halfheartedly said. "I'm just
so confused right now. I can't seem to sort any of this out." Her gaze
drifted to the softly burning fireplace flames. "I want to be angry. I
know that that must sound awful but, if I'm honest with myself, that's
what I feel." Then she looked into her friend's sky-blue eyes. "Do you
think I'm a terrible person for wanting to be angry right now?"

"Not if you know what you're supposed to be angry about. It
seems to me that it'd be awful for anyone to be angry over a false
assumption they'd made."

Sadie gave that some thought. She really didn't want to be wrong
or think that she'd misread the situation with Paul. "If it's as you say
. . . that is, if he really isn't in love with someone else . . . what's wrong
with me? Where'd I mess up?"

Notorious for never beating around the bush, Tina was painfully
straightforward and cut to the bottom line without mincing words.
"Right there. You just answered your own question. You made a serious assumption that was wrong. You assumed he was involved with
someone else. You were so incredulous, blindsided, by Paul's decision
to leave, your mental reflexes pulled out a false scenario from your
own cache of defense mechanisms. Then you emotionally clutched at
that altered truth because you wanted to, felt you needed to. You
wanted to do that because your imagined scenario gave his leaving a

more acceptable reason, a reason you could better understand and, ultimately, psychologically cope with."

Sadie's brows knit together. "But how could I have done that? You know me, I never make assumptions. I don't jump to unsubstantiated conclusions. I know better than that."

"Ahh, but here's the bitter twist to that. When the heart's involved, we're not always the mistress of our own mind, are we? Aren't there those certain extenuating situations when first responses are engaged for the purpose of protecting that tender heart of ours from injury? When, without intended malice or conniving forethought, the mind instinctively reacts by charging forward to save the damsel from distress by concocting an alternate scenario and then raising high the banner of a different color? For all to see? The old protective shield?"

Mollified, Sadie's gaze ruefully lowered to the liquid surface of her cup. "And," she whispered, "that shield becomes the false truth that comes between the damsel and the real truth. It's a heart shield." She released a halfhearted chuckle. "God, Tina, your explanations are always so visual." She raised her eyes to again lock on her friend's. "What makes you always come up with such clear images?"

Tina, avoiding the deterring question, wagged her finger in friendly admonishment. "You're changing the subject. Let's not do that right now, okay? It tends to hamper the progress you're making here."

As a further stall tactic, Sadie gave her full attention to slowly draining her cup.

Tina took the cue and quickly refilled it. "Let's not stall out, either," she gently encouraged. "Keep going."

"Going where?" came the slightly belligerent response.

"Excuse me? You still haven't pinpointed what you misinterpreted. When you do that, you'll know what your mind was attempting to protect your heart from, what your heart didn't want to face . . . acknowledge and feel."

Sadie felt her insides begin to squirm. She didn't want to do this "eye-to-eye thing with truth." She felt like fidgeting; instead, she nervously glanced up at the mantel clock. "I thought I already admitted to falsely assuming he'd had another lover. If there's more to it, why do I have to dig deeper right now?"

"Because you need to, that's why. Because there's no better time than the present. Otherwise, you're going to waste time stewing over the wrong kettle. You need to do this right now because you need to walk right up to the truth, look it square in the eye, and then get yourself clear of it. You need to deal, Sadie. You need to deal with it."

Partially unconvinced and mostly unwilling, Sadie released a long, irrepressible sigh. "Look, I really appreciate you wanting to help, but right now the only thing I need to do is just go to bed, get some sleep. I've dealt with enough for one night. I can't handle any more."

"Can't or won't handle?" Tina chuckled at her friend's naive ruse. "Who are you trying to kid? Sleep will be the last thing you get tonight. I think you know that already. Unless you talk this out right now and move past it, you'll end up pacing the floor till sunup."

Sadie, of course, knew her friend was right on the money. She hated it when that happened. She shifted her gaze to the window where the driving rain lashed at the panes like a sea monster wanting inside. Her eyes were as green as a hidden tropical lagoon when she returned her attention to her friend. "Your visual analogy was a sympathetic one, you know."

"Really. How's that?"

"It's not only the heart that's meant to be protected by that falsely colored shield the mind created. It's also the ego."

Tina's brow rose. "Well, that's true," she agreed, while leaning forward. "You must be sorting things out rather nicely if you came to that. You must've figured out the second half of your assumption."

Lightning flashes illumined the room with explosive bursts of blinding brightness.

The two women winced with the sudden glare.

Thunder rumbled and sent a vibration shuddering beneath their feet.

Sadie absently glanced over at the flickering firelight. "You were right, you know. He never actually said he loved someone else. That idea, that whole thing, came from me. That was my assumption. It was pure assumption. It was easier on my fragile ego to believe there was another woman rather than knowing he didn't love me anymore. That was something I wasn't prepared to face."

"Oh, honey," Tina cooed, while moving over beside her friend. She gently lifted a stray strand of auburn hair from the other's face.

Sadie's head slowly tilted. Misting eyes locked onto Tina's. "How long did you know?" she reticently asked, not sure she wanted to hear the answer.

Tina's blue eyes misted in turn. "Know what?"

"Please, don't pretend you don't know what I'm talking about. How long have you known that he didn't love me anymore?"

The answer was difficult to finally voice. For someone like Tina, the act of speaking something aloud somehow made it more real, defined it more clearly, brought it forward to manifest more fully in reality. Steeling herself to keep from flinching, she said, "For about three months. I'm sorry."

Sadie flushed with the news. "So," she pushed, "so, why didn't you tell me? Why didn't you come to me when you first suspected something? You're my friend. Why'd you let me believe everything was rosy when it wasn't? God," she sighed with a berating undertone, "I feel so stupid. I feel so damn stupid now."

Tina rested her hand over Sadie's. "I didn't want to mention anything before this because, contrary to whatever you may think, Sadie, I'm not always right about the things I sense. You know how careful I am about these things. I never just spew out my initial insights until I've had a chance to be sure, taken the time to gather verifying evidence.

"At first there were just little things here and there that I picked up on, things related to Paul's behavior that were inconsistent with how I'd come to know him over the years. I felt he was acting a bit distant, like he was trying to pull away from your relationship, even from me because I'm your closest friend. He didn't seem to be quite as easygoing as usual. There appeared to be some sort of new edge to his mannerisms. There was a sharpness to his behavior verging on avoidance or something. I thought he avoided eye contact. I don't know, for a while I couldn't really put my finger on it, maybe like a new impatience or curtness that wasn't there before. I felt that something was really bothering him and it was affecting the way he related to the both of us. Then, just last month I figured it out.

"God, Sadie," Tina emphasized, "don't you think I agonized over whether or not to say anything to you? I spent countless nights pacing the floor trying to come to a decision about it. I kept asking myself the same questions over and over. I found myself overwhelmed by all kinds of self-doubts. What if I was wrong about him? What if I was just imagining things? I hated the thought of you two breaking up. I really, really hated it. Half of me denied what I was sensing and the other half couldn't overlook what I was seeing and hearing from him. I thought his manner seemed to be growing evasive and his tone becoming more clipped as time went on.

"Like I said, even his eye contact wasn't what it used to be. You know, how he'd always look people square in the eye? He stopped doing that. He began averting his eyes when we spoke. Still, after all those signs, I couldn't bring myself to broach the idea with you because, in my heart, I didn't want it to be true. I figured it'd be best to stay out of it and let the situation run its course. If I was wrong then no harm was done by remaining quiet about it. If I was right, well then, in the end it was ultimately up to you two." Unsure of how her friend had taken her admission, Tina lowered her head to study her nervously entwining fingers. The long braid swung down in front of her. "Are you angry with me, Sadie? Do you hate me for keeping quiet?"

Sadie reassuringly squeezed her friend's hand. "No. No, of course I don't hate you. I'm not even angry with you. I'm angry with myself for not seeing it coming, ignoring those subtle signs that I thought I saw, as well." She paused before finishing. "The eye contact thing, I definitely noticed how he was looking everywhere but in my eyes. I guess I was in denial. I was in denial right up to when I lashed out at him in the wheelhouse and was finally forced to face that denial head-on. Even then I chose not to. Still," she hesitated. "Still—"

"Still, you're hurt. You're hurt just the same. That's natural. You can't figure out what happened so don't even bother trying. In the end, it'll drive you crazy." Tina bent forward to look directly into Sadie's lowered gaze. "Relationships are funny things, honey. It's not unheard of for someone to drift away, to fall out of love. It doesn't mean that you did anything wrong. It doesn't mean that you've changed in any way. It only means that the two of you weren't on the same page. It happens all the time to couples."

Sadie shrugged at the generalized excuse. It sounded oversimplified, like a catch-all rationalization. She wanted it to be more defined. She wanted it to be more black and white, more individualized.

Tina's empathy was deeply sincere as she continued the attempt to comfort her friend. "I mean, look at Ronnie and me. Didn't we have a great relationship for a while? Weren't our hearts on fire for each other in the beginning? My God, we swore we were honest-to-God, dyed-in-the-wool soulmates. Our passions could set the beach ablaze like a bonfire on crabbing night. We believed that the sun rose and set on each other's precious heads. We'd convinced ourselves that the moonlight shone for us and us alone. We were smitten with each other."

Remaining mute, Sadie simply nodded in remembrance of the torrid affair.

"Then, bam!" Tina exclaimed, clapping her hands together for emphasis again. "Nothing went right between us. And I do mean nothing. We were always arguing over something; big things and little things, it didn't matter. We just stopped seeing eye-to-eye anymore. One thing led to another, so we mutually agreed to call it quits. It wasn't necessarily the fault of one or the other, it just didn't work *together* anymore. The flame fizzled out, is all. It happens. Sadie, it happens to the best of us. No matter how often we make ourselves blue in the face blowing on that ember to keep love alive, it can die out anyway. A relationship isn't going to survive if only one of you is always struggling to keep that flame going. That's the time for a reality check, for both parties to take a step back, catch your breath, and just respectfully let it fade out. You watch it go out with acceptance of its reality, its finality."

"But what'd I do?" Sadie softly questioned. "How did I change?"

"You weren't listening to me. You're already blaming yourself and you can't go there. That's a dark place to go. It's nobody's fault, remember? There's no blame to be found or cast. Fading feelings of love don't necessarily come from someone changing a thing. They can just happen all by themselves." She firmly grasped Sadie's chin. "Do you hear what I'm saying? You didn't *do* anything!"

Silence.

"Sadieee?"

Sadie seemed ambivalent. "I heard you."

"Also," Tina wisely interjected, "you're not the only one hurting here. Don't you think it tore Paul's heart out to have to break this off? He still cares for you, you know. Drifting out of love doesn't also mean that you stop caring for the other person. Don't you think that what he said tonight—however badly he managed to say it—was the hardest thing to ever pass his lips?

"I'm serious, Sadie. Think about that. Think about what he let you do. He let you think he loved someone else instead of coming right out and saying that his love for you wasn't as strong anymore. He went ahead and let you think the absolute worst of him, that he was a cheating cad, because he knew that that one idea would hurt you less than the truth."

The sudden realization of the gross error Sadie had made dropped like a two-ton anchor into her gut. Clutching her stomach, she started to rise from the couch.

"Oh! Oh my God! I need to call him. I falsely accused him when he was only trying to let me down easy."

"Later," Tina said, putting out her hand. "You can do that tomorrow."

For the moment, Sadie relented and sat back down.

The two were silent for several long minutes.

When Tina next spoke, her voice was gentle. "There's . . . there's more," she hesitantly informed.

"More what?"

"More to this story. There's more you haven't thought of yet. You've only focused on the part that directly involved you. There's a second half to all of this."

Sadie squirmed in frustration. "Now what? What're you talking about? What second half?"

"That assumption about the other woman he let you believe was only a part of his own pain. He has an equally devastating cross to bear. He's also smarting from deep disappointment over his failed fishing dream. He's facing the fact that he personally failed at something he'd dreamed of doing since he was a boy."

Sadie's brows furrowed as her friend spoke of the elusive second half of the situation.

"Not only is he dealing with a failed love, he's also having to contend with the hard reality of a failed life dream. Right now—"

Sadie was crying. The tears began to fall from her eyes one at a time, then rolled down her cheeks in rivulets until she couldn't hold back the torrent that was soon pouring like an overflowing rain barrel.

Tina embraced her friend. She held her until she was all cried out.

Sadie suddenly jumped to her feet. "I've been so blind! I've been so selfish that I never even thought of his own heartbreaking disappointment."

Though Tina halfheartedly agreed, she asked, "So now we're going to wallow in a bit of self-indulgence, are we? Maybe throw in a cup of self-deprecation for good measure? That'll get you nowhere fast. It'll only end up exponentially exacerbating the whole situation if you try doing that. You need to keep it as simple as you can without making matters worse. You had just temporarily lost sight of the greater picture, that's all."

Sadie thought about what her friend had said. She saw the point and felt duly chastised. "Okay, okay," she relented, while beginning to pace the floor. She was visibly shaken. Her hands trembled while running them through her mass of drying curls. "So, even forgetting about all that self-deprecating bullshit that goes nowhere, I've still got to call him," she moaned, wiping her face with the sleeve of the chenille bathrobe. "I have to call him to apologize and . . . and tell him how sorry I am that he has to move on to something else. I've got to let him know that I, well, that I understand."

Tina went to her friend's side and gently gripped the trembling shoulders. "Later. You don't need to do that right now. Though you may think you do, you don't. Right now I'm going to give you that massage. Mentally and emotionally, you just came a long, long way." She wiped a corner of Sadie's eye. "Look at you, you're all cried out. Believe me, a massage is just what you need to work out the last of tonight's tension and help you sleep." She smiled warmly. "Listen to Tina. Tina knows about these things."

Sadie didn't quite agree. She was persistent. "No. No, I'll never sleep if I don't get this out of the way," she said, crossing the room to the phone. "I know I won't rest until I do this first. I have to get this out of the way before I can even think about relaxing."

Tina let her friend assuage her conscience and, without another word, returned to the couch. She watched that friend anxiously punch in the phone number, and then disappointedly wait through the seven rings until Paul's message recorder kicked in. She heard her friend's attempt to haltingly apologize for her earlier misunderstanding and then ask if they could talk again in the morning.

Sadie gently set down the receiver and let her eyes drift over to the woman sitting on the couch. "I had to do that," she whispered. "I hated leaving a message, but I had to let him know that I no longer believed he was involved with someone else. I had to let him know that I understood and shared the pain of the decision to abandon his fishing dream." She paused then as her eyes shifted to the window and lingered there. The wind was whipping autumn leaves against the pane. "Where do you suppose he is?" she asked in a faraway voice. "He can't still be out on the boat, can he? Do you think he's still out on the boat?"

Tina shrugged. "No telling where he might be. I think it's a good guess that he's either still out there or went over to Jack's Place to toss back a few. You know how old Jack loves to be a sympathetic sounding board for his customers." Tina fluttered her hands. "Paul will be okay. He's a survivor."

Sadie turned to face her friend. "Odd you should say that. He always said the same thing about me. He'd say, 'Sadie, my love, you're a survivor. You could get through anything life threw at you.'"

"Well," Tina agreed with a capricious grin, "there you go. You're both right. You'll both come through this. You'll see."

Sadie thought on that idea. She didn't know if her friend was being a clear-seeing psychic or simply trying to make her feel better. She decided that she didn't want to know which one it was. She managed a meager reciprocal smile and gave in to her friend's therapeutic offer. "I think I'm ready for that massage now."

Before the massage was finished, she fell asleep to the soft drone of Tina's voice expounding on the frivolous soulmate concept. She never felt the soft flannel sheet and light blanket being pulled up over her shoulders. She never heard her friend quietly slip from the room.

During the night, the storm blew out to sea.

The choppy waters of the inlet returned to a mirrored calm of reflected starshine.

Moonlight bathed the quaint harbor village in a soft, silvery glow.

The woman sleeping above the antique shop on the wharf never saw any of it. She never heard the calm return to the harbor. And she never heard the pickup, loaded with all of the driver's meager belongings, follow the curve of the bayside road for the last time.

Two

Friday

The storm of the previous night had spent its raging energy and the waters of the harbor now danced with mirrored light. The new sunrise spilled its golden glow over a picture-perfect morning. It was a dawn so brilliantly clear and vibrant that it could be mistaken for one of those retouched scenic postcards found packed in the souvenir racks of every tourist shop. Just beyond the rain-washed wharf, surface reflections from the water's sparkling ripples played across the gleaming windows of the Wick 'n' Wit. The popular book and candle shop bustled with browsing customers.

Three matronly women, members of the Ladies Bay Port Cooking Club, were examining the new shipment of holiday recipe books. You could almost hear their stomachs growling while their eyes twinkled with the anticipation of filling their kitchens with the sumptuous aromas of pumpkin pies and savory custard tarts baking in the ovens.

Their heads were together while the trio pored over a volume generously illustrated with Halloween party specialties. Although they kept their voices down, it couldn't hide their animated chatter, their exhilaration over the delectable find.

A clutch of out-of-towners eagerly tested the exotic fragrances of the aromatherapy candles and exclaimed over the interesting array of essential oils as they milled here and there in the various sections of the shop.

A young couple quietly discussed which book on Celtic lore to purchase. They'd pulled five volumes from the shelf and clearly needed to narrow their choice to one or two.

An elderly gentleman lounged on one of the comfortable chintz settees, his world centered within the glossy pages of a regional book generously illustrating the captivating natural attributes of Maine. Enrapt in the vivid pictorial, the man appeared to successfully maintain his unwavering literary focus. After peering over the reading glasses perched low on his nose to give a perfunctory glance at a couple of unruly children, he returned to the book and ignored the whirlwind of activity spinning like mini-tornados about him while the two boisterous youngsters were being chased down by their embarrassed mother.

And the proprietress, pleased with the brisk business, was torn between which group of customers to give her attention to first.

Her dilemma vanished when a new movement caught her eye. She spied her neighbor quietly slip through the interior door adjoining her place with the antique shop. Tina's eyes brightened. She gave her full attention to the newcomer.

"Sadie!" she softly exclaimed in a tone intentionally balanced between empathy and cheer. "How are you doing this morning?"

Instead of making a verbal response, Sadie quickly scanned the shop. Her attention was immediately drawn to the two squealing youngsters who were enjoying their game of Catch Me If You Can with their harried mom.

"Looks like you have your hands full," she finally said, avoiding Tina's question.

Tina sarcastically chuckled in her friend's ear. "Not *my* hands," she said, inclining her head toward the commotion. "Those little rug rats are *her* problem."

Together they watched the problem move out into the sunlight and thump down the wooden planks of the nearest pier. Looking at one another, they shook their heads and rolled their eyes. Both were relieved to see the atmosphere of the shop return to its normal state of reserved, yet comfortable ambiance. Book lovers had a natural respect for the printed word; booksellers held that respect a notch higher.

Although Tina knew that her friend must be terribly sad, she couldn't suppress the bursting excitement of her news. In a flood of words, she whispered, "So, how do you feel this morning? Do things look any brighter in the light of day?" Not waiting for answers, her energy carried her forward. "Oh! I've got to tell you about something I did last night. Honey, you are not going to *believe* this. After I left you I got my runes out and, no matter how many times I did them for you, they kept giving the strangest message. It was the oddest thing I've ever experienced with them. Over and over they kept repeating the same thing! They—"

Tina's words were cleanly sliced by the sharp ping of the customer bell on the counter beside the cash register.

Irritated at the ill-timed interruption, Tina put her hand on Sadie's arm. "Let me just go take care of these folks and then we have to talk." She began moving away from her friend's side, then, as an afterthought, spun back around. "Don't go anywhere," she warned. "This is important. We really have to talk."

Sadie opened her mouth to object.

Tina hushed her. Eyes were half warning, half pleading. "I mean it, Sadie. This is important. It's really important. Please, do yourself a big favor and stick around until my customers are gone. We have to talk."

While Tina rang up the candle sales, the elderly man decided to purchase the regional tome that'd so effectively enraptured him.

With their decision finally made, the young couple lined up behind him, two books happily in hand.

The members of the cooking club brought up the rear. They'd decided that trying to choose a single volume was far too difficult. No matter which one they picked, they'd always be thinking and wondering about those left behind on the shelf. They'd bought them all.

Standing at the front window, Sadie was watching a small group of people board the tour boat that scheduled trips out to an island lighthouse and back. Her thoughts were pulled to their carefree mood, their lightheartedness, their anticipation of experiencing a new adventure by the sea. The sounds of their excited chatter carried by the light breeze almost made her smile, for they were filled with expectation. Their joy at being on a vacation away from their mundane day-to-day routines was clear on their countenances, in their voices, and through the eagerness of their mannerisms. These thoughts were suddenly disrupted by the metallic sound of the door lock clicking home. She turned toward the sound.

Tina was facing the "Closed" sign to the window.

"What're you doing?" Sadie asked with a questioning frown creasing her forehead. "This is one of our best sale days. How come you're closing?"

"*You're* closed," Tina smugly reminded beneath her breath. The loss of today's sales was the furthest thing from her mind this morning. She had more pressing matters to address before this day grew any older. Touching Sadie's arm, she inclined her head and cryptically whispered, "Come into the back. I've got something to show you."

Sadie had more important things on her mind this morning than her friend's psychic mumbo-jumbo. She didn't want to be distracted from her urgent plans. Halfheartedly making an effort to conceal her impatience, she reluctantly followed her friend's lead past the rows of bookshelves and into the private apartment at the back of the shop.

"I can't stay," she informed. "I just peeked in to let you know that I'm okay this morning. I've got my day pretty well planned out and need to get going. What's all this about?" she asked. "Is this going to take long? If it is, maybe we can do this some other time because, like I said, I was just on my way out to the—"

"He's not on the boat," came the clipped reply. "He's not in his apartment either. He's already gone." Tina turned and looked her friend in the eye. "What, don't tell me you expected him to hang around? Whatever for?"

Sadie's mouth fell open as they entered the private apartment. This was the last thing she expected to hear. Suddenly, all her plans evaporated like the summertime morning dew. "What? Gone where? And what do you mean by 'whatever for'? Paul and I needed some kind of finalization here. We needed to tie up loose ends. You know, say all those things that were left unsaid." Her hands shot up in frustration. "I don't know, maybe release emotions, cry on each other's shoulders or something. Closure. Something!"

"Closure! Now you're reaching. Now you are really reaching, girl.

There's no such animal. You know that. Pgghh, *closure*, she says. There's never closure," she reminded while setting a purple velvet bag onto the kitchen table.

"Well, I think that there can be . . . sometimes. And another thing—"

Ignoring Sadie's rambling prattle, Tina patted the seat of a chair, indicating that it was time for her friend to take a seat.

Sadie stared at the chair in disbelief. She remained standing.

"What?" Tina asked. "You expected him to hang around after last night? C'mon, sit. We have some serious exploring to do. You and I have a mystery to unravel. Stop being belligerent. Sit."

Sadie stood her ground and remained firmly rooted to the floor. "I can't. I . . . I'm not in the mood for frivolous hoodoo right now." She began restlessly pacing the floor in irritation. "God, Tina, get a clue! A six-year relationship has just been flushed down the toilet and you expect me to calmly sit and play games?"

Tina, understanding Sadie's broken heart, was not in the least offended by the harshly demeaning words. "I'm going to pretend I didn't hear you make that disparaging reference to my runes. And about Paul," she advised without hesitation. "If you calmed yourself enough to give the whole thing some deeper, more serious thought, you'd realize that his leaving was for the best, for both of you." A brow raised then. "Did you really expect this thing to drag on? And on?"

Begrudgingly, Sadie slowly shuffled toward the chair. She allowed her body to slump into it. "Well, not drag on, exactly," she defensively admitted, before pausing to correct herself. "Well, yeah," she revised, "I guess I did expect him to hang around. At least long enough for us to talk all this out. You know, face to face, so we'd both be clear on things. Yeah," she reiterated, "yeah, I did expect him to be here this morning. It was cowardly to slither off into the night like he did. There were things I needed to say to him. Out of respect for our long relationship, he needed to give me the time to say them."

"'Slither off'? You're overreacting."

"No, I'm not. He did slink away."

Tina's expression didn't conceal her suspicions. "Whatever. But don't forget, sometimes people can end up saying too much without intending to. They end up making matters worse, if you know what I mean. Besides," she reminded, "you had your say last night."

Incredulous, Sadie went on the offensive. She straightened her back and blurted, "On his voice mail? That's it? That's all the say I get to have in this? You can't be serious!" She leaned far forward across the table to get into her friend's face. "Tina! You can't be serious!"

Tina's response was lightning quick. "See what I mean? Look, for heaven's sake, look at yourself. You're already getting indignant and defensive just talking with me about it. Believe me, girlfriend, an honest-to-goodness face-to-face meeting with him is not in anyone's best interest right now. It'd only end up being a confrontational encounter that neither of you need or want to have." Tina's eyes lowered for a second before returning to firmly fix on her friend's. "I think somewhere in that brilliant brain of yours you already know that. Don't let your emotions make things worse. Be smart, let the dust settle. Let time do its healing thing. You both need some space. Apart."

Recognizing some threads of truth in those words of wisdom, Sadie's shoulders fell as her disposition softened somewhat. "But on a message machine? That's it?" She sighed. "That's all I get?"

Tina shrugged. "Guess so. For now, at least. It's enough, isn't it? You let him know that you realized he didn't have anyone else in his life. Wasn't that the main point you wanted to get across?"

Sadie reticently admitted that it was. "Well, yes." Then, quickly reconsidering, she added, "No! No, I also wanted to offer him some sympathy over his lost dream and—"

Tina's sky-blue eyes rolled to the ceiling. "Oh right, Sadie. You think that that man wants your sympathy, for god's sake? Do you really think he wants anybody's? Don't be insensitive. Sympathy is the last thing he wants from anyone. Jeez, Louise," she exclaimed in disbelief, "anyone who's had dreams shattered will tell you that sympathy is the last thing they want to hear from people because it only adds fuel to the feelings of defeat."

"Well, *comfort*, then," Sadie said, altering her choice of words. "I at least wanted to let him know that I understood how he felt about having to ditch his fishing dream, having to sell the boat, and start all over doing something else." Her attempt to justify her intention sounded weak at best, even to herself.

"Honey . . ." Tina began with a sigh, preparing to delve deeper into the issue's philosophy. Before continuing further, she squared herself in the chair and took a deep breath. It was discomforting to see her friend in such emotionally distressing turmoil and she wanted to help Sadie understand the important paradoxical aspect to the concept of trying to help others. She paused to exhale a long breath.

"Sometimes," she began again, "no matter how good our intentions are, they don't turn out like we'd anticipated. For whatever reason, they aren't received as well as we'd hoped by the recipient. Know what I'm saying? Sometimes when we rush to apply a well-intended balm to a wound, it can end up being more irritating than the soothing effect we thought it was going to achieve. That paradox can work the same way with emotional or psychological wounds. In that case, a cooing commiseration can make the wound worse. It acts like an irritant scratching at the rawness. So there are times when we need to just let nature do the healing without our good-intended intervention. Get my drift?"

Now it was Sadie's turn to sigh. "I'm not an idiot. Of course I get your drift, but . . ."

Tina narrowed her eyes. "But what? There's no 'but' here. This just happens to be one of those situations, is all I mean to convey."

Sadie wasn't so sure.

Tina reached across the table for her friend's hand. When she gained it, she again looked into the sea-green eyes.

"Look, Paul did what he had to do in order to extricate himself from everything here as cleanly as he could. Emotionally, he had no choice. The quicker the better. You would've done the exact same thing."

"Ohh, no," Sadie denied with a slow shake of her head. "No, I wouldn't have. I'd have at least spent a couple of days talking things out to make sure there were no misunderstandings. If the tables were turned, I would've made sure we parted friends."

"Sadie, you two *are* friends. You still are. There's no hatred or animosity left between you two. The message you left him assured him that you understood. He's got to feel comforted by that. Now he doesn't want to hang around and cause the parting to be a lingering one. A clean and quick break is the best thing for you both."

Sadie thought on that. She thought for a while. "Well . . . maybe. I suppose a shred of logic can be found somewhere in that. I guess I wanted to assuage my own guilt for initially jumping to conclusions the way I did." Sheepishly, she further admitted, "I wanted him to still be here for my own reasons, to smooth over my rashness, my overreaction."

"Maybe you needed that, but I think it's obvious that he didn't."

"Obviously not."

Tina patted her friend's hand before letting go. "Okay, so you need to move forward now. Right?"

A doubtful mutter could be heard coming from across the table.

Tina expectantly peered over at her friend. "Right?"

No response.

"Dammit, Sadie! Don't *do* that. Don't be in denial and don't choose to wallow in your own mire of self-pity. Forward is the only productive direction open for you now. The runes say so."

Sadie's brow arched in doubt. In a voice dripping with sarcastic skepticism, she said, "Oh, really."

Tina scowled. "Quit that," she scolded. "You just quit that right now. I told you that I had something important to tell you. Now get serious and get rid of that snotty attitude you have going. You need to listen up."

"I thought we *were* being serious."

"We were. And we still are. This is just as serious." Tina underscored that seriousness with a hard, warning glare. "Maybe more so," she added.

Sadie defiantly exaggerated the motion of straightening to attention in her chair like a good little schoolgirl in class. The gesture was meant to convey an unspoken truce even though she couldn't imagine how Tina's new issue could be more serious or be of greater import than what she'd been currently dealing with. Yet, she also knew from past experience that she was about to become privy to one of her friend's prognostications—one gained from her most dependable manner of divination. "Okay, Venerable Priestess of the All-Knowing Oracle Runes," she half-teased, "let's have it. I'm all ears."

Tina rolled her eyes to the ceiling, then stared hard into her friend's eyes. She wagged a chastising finger. The red lacquered fingernail shook in stern emphasis before Sadie's nose. "Tsk, tsk. Don't you go poking fun at me, Missy. Shame on you. This is not something to take lightly."

"I'm not poking fun. I said I'm all ears, didn't I?"

Tina gave a side glance. "You'd better be listening. At least I think you will be when I get through showing you what I found out."

Sadie thought her friend was dramatizing a bit too much. Maybe purposely doing so in an effort to distract her from Paul's sudden departure. She gave her the benefit of the doubt and again squared herself firmly in the chair. She leaned forward. "Okay. Seriously. I'm all ears and ready to be enlightened. What do the Forces say?"

Once more, Tina suspiciously eyed her friend before giving her full attention to the bag of runes. These were not the mass-produced type that were commercially manufactured and sold in every metaphysical shop. These were a set of runes which she'd personally carved many years ago when she'd been spiritually guided to meticulously wood-burn the uniquely different symbols into the flat pieces of mahogany. She'd seen each of them in a vision, their meanings clear and always proving true. She had come to implicitly trust their message. She trusted them as much as an angel whispering the words into her ear.

"Okay," the gifted woman somberly instructed. "Now listen up. First I'm going to randomly pull out the runes and do the layout as usual. I'll do it twice. Then you're going to randomly choose each rune for the layout. Twice." She looked to her friend for confirmation.

Sadie reluctantly nodded her agreement.

Without looking down, Tina began picking out pieces of wood from the bag. Before she was finished, she locked eyes on her friend. "We're going to do this over and over until you're convinced."

Furrowing her brows after hearing the mildly cryptic statement, Sadie asked, "Convinced of what, exactly?"

"That's just it," Tina whispered. "I don't know what, exactly."

Suspecting that Tina was intentionally being mysterious in order to distract her, Sadie didn't have to play-act at being the skeptic.

"What do you mean, you don't know what? Since when can't you decipher their meaning? Don't they *tell* you what the *What* is?"

Tina's tone held no pretense. She had no reservations admitting that this was one time when she was at a complete loss when it came to interpreting the runes.

"They do and they don't," she said. "That's what I was trying to tell you earlier," she reminded, while slowly pulling another polished piece of wood from the bag. "I'm telling you, this has been just too bizarre. Even for me, this is just too weird. I have to admit that it's been extremely vexing."

In a friendly kind of way, Sadie doubted that. "Nothing's weird in your life. Your whole life's based on weird. Weird is normal for you. You're the queen of weird."

Tina managed a wry grin. "I'll definitely take that as a compliment, my friend."

Sadie returned the grin. "Good. It was meant as one. It was also meant to express my shock over the fact that *you* think something is actually weird. I mean, if *you* of all people think it's weird, it's gotta be really out there."

"Mmm. Maybe. We'll see if what I kept getting last night repeats itself today. We'll see if it comes up when you do the layout, as well."

Sadie had to privately acknowledge that her curiosity was sparked. The hoodoo element of the situation had effectively shifted into a bona fide seriousness that succeeded in drawing her attention away from her misery. Her growing anticipation paused in a held-breath hesitation while she watched her friend place the final symbol piece in the center of the layout.

Tina pensively stared at the message. She was silent.

Sadie couldn't stand the suspense any longer. "Well? What's it say? Is it the same as last night or not? Read it to me."

Perplexed, Tina leaned forward and brushed the loose strands of hair from her face. "Yeah," she whispered, "it still gives the same message."

"You know," Sadie interjected, "you never told me what you asked the runes. You never told me what your question was. Don't you usually have a specific question in mind before you pick the pieces out?"

Tina nodded. "Sure. I asked what comes next for you. After I returned home last night, I felt so bad about the rotten deal between you and Paul. Your pain was a touchable thing. I was very concerned for you both.

"You know, Paul's right when he says that you're a survivor, but this latest thing between you two . . . well, I just didn't know how you were going to get over this. It's pretty big. It's a huge bump in your path. I just didn't know. So I got out the sacred runes and I asked. Then I asked again. It was as though, no matter how many times I tried, I couldn't change destiny . . . your destiny. After the fifth layout I finally gave up trying anymore."

"Trying for what?" Sadie asked.

The question was unexpected. Tina thought her explanation had been clear. "Trying to extract a variant message, of course."

Somewhat confused, Sadie needed more clarification. "But if a message is true, I mean, if the message is *meant* to be, won't it always say pretty much the same thing each time you do a layout for the same question? Know what I mean? Even if different symbols do happen to appear in each layout, won't they still always point in the same general direction as far as intent?" Her brows knit in puzzlement. "I don't think I'm getting your drift. I'm missing something. Why is this time so different? What's so weird about it?"

"What's weird about it is that the *same symbols* keep showing themselves. Not just different ones that'd mean the same, but the exact same *pieces.*"

Sadie felt her cheeks flush after hearing this oddity. The hair on the back of her neck prickled. Her eyes were magnetically drawn to the mysterious symbols spread out in the familiar pattern on the tabletop.

"Okayyy," she hesitantly uttered. "Okay. So, what's it saying? What does it keep showing? What's coming next for me?"

Tina released a long, extended sigh while her shoulders lifted and dropped. "I need to forewarn you, though. You're not going to like my answer."

"Why not?"

"Because I can't give you one. I don't know the answer."

Sadie rolled her eyes. "If I'm not mistaken, haven't we already been down that road? It's got to show *something,* for heaven's sake. Am I gonna die? Oh, God, I'm gonna die. That's why you're being so evasive and not telling me what it says. Oh, jeez. Oh, Jesus, I'm gonna die."

Tina's head tilted in utter disbelief over how quickly her friend had jumped to the wrong conclusion. "Oh, for god's *sakes,* get *real,* Sadie! The Death symbol is never in the layout. Look!" she said, stabbing her finger on the table. "You know what the Death symbol looks like. Do you see it anywhere? Good grief, Sadie, you really do need to stop envisioning the worst all the time."

"Well, what am I supposed to think? You say these things keep giving the same message over and over but then you can't tell me what they mean! You *always* know what they mean. You can always read them. Why not now?"

Tina raised her hands. "Calm down. It's not that I can't *read* them, it's more like . . . well, it's more like I can't make *sense* out of the message. The message itself is weird. It's just so weird, is all."

Suddenly Paul had vanished from the forefront of Sadie's mind. In an instant, her full attention had been pulled into the drama of the mysterious runes.

"How? You keep using that word. How is it weird? You can tell me that much, can't you? What the hell's so peculiar about this whole thing?"

"It's weird—extraordinary, really—because, well, because you're not a religious person."

Sadie was not anticipating that response. She was taken off guard by it. "Religious? That's a new one. What's that got to do with anything? Besides," she countered with a defensive huff, "I'm religious."

"No," Tina attempted to clarify. "What I meant was, you're not *religion* religious. You're a *spiritual* person. There's a huge difference between the two. Know what I'm saying?"

"Well, yeah. I'm certainly not one to see the image of Jesus in a tree or hear St. Clementine talking in my ear, but I believe in Higher Powers. I mean, I don't belong to a church because I think the underlying concept of church can be found all around us." She rolled her eyes again. It seemed to her that she was doing a lot of that. "Why am I telling you all this? You already know what I believe."

Now it was time for Tina to raise a brow. "That's just it, girlfriend. You do believe in Higher Powers, but you're a little lacking in the scope of your belief's overall *reach*."

"Ahh, now I get where you're going with this—the same place we always end up when we discuss spiritual ideas. You mean the reach to include the feminine variety of deities. Is that where you're going with this? It is, isn't it?"

The psychic nodded.

"I never said that there weren't any, either," Sadie immediately quipped back. "I'm just not quite the spiritual feminist that you are."

Tina indulgently leaned back in her chair. She spent a few minutes in pensive thought before responding to her friend's slightly critical comment.

"How many times have we been over this idea? You don't have to be a feminist to understand this one basic reality of the spiritual realm, Sadie. We've talked quite extensively about this through the years. Historically, cultures the world over have consistently revered a wide variety of female deities. The concept certainly isn't new to recorded history or to you."

Sadie didn't want to get into the depths of this discussion again, at least not right now. "I know," she playfully teased in an effort to bring it to a speedy end. She grinned and gave a tongue-in-cheek response. "The concept is older than God."

Tina didn't think her friend's witticism was particularly amusing. "Now you're being sarcastic," she replied. Then quickly added, "Which God? You said the concept is older than God. Which God are you referring to? Which God does the practice of revering female deities predate, Sadie?"

Knowing she'd been bested, Sadie responded with a shrug that conveyed she really didn't care all that much about the answer to the posed question. Instead of making a reply, she glanced down at the layout of runes and intently studied the odd markings on the individual pieces. An unexpected shiver coursed up her spine with an attention-grabbing ripple. Then, unable to let it pass, she softly replied, "I didn't mean to be. The sarcasm, I mean. I didn't mean to be flip." And pointing to the arrangement of wooden pieces on the table, she inquired, "Is there a specific deity or someone like that in these? Are the runes what brought us to this subject?"

Tina straightened in her chair. Maybe her friend was ready to be serious. She evaded the direct question. "As I said earlier, I can't say what it's pointing to. All I know is that there's someone extremely important—*uniquely* special—showing up in your immediate future."

Sadie piped in, "Paul. He's going to come back into my life."

"Nope. It's not Paul."

"How can you be so sure if you say that you don't know?"

"Believe me, this, I know. The runes are definitely not pointing to Paul."

That brought another playful grin tipping the corners of Sadie's mouth. "Maybe it's my true soulmate then."

Once again, Tina was not amused. "Just when I thought you were beginning to take this seriously, you throw in that cockamamie soulmate idea. You are not taking this seriously and you need to, you really do. Besides," she quipped back, "you don't need a man in your life to feel whole again, to have a sense of fulfillment." Glancing down at the layout, she added, "Sometimes there are others who can serve that purpose just as well—better even. What the runes are indicating is *someone*. Someone who is uniquely remarkable—peerless—is going to cross your path. In fact, this extraordinary someone is going to cross your path many times, maybe become a major player in your life, at least for a time."

"How so?"

When Tina didn't immediately respond, Sadie was quick to

answer for her. "You don't know. You can't tell me because you don't know that either, do you?"

Tina shrugged. "All I know is that whatever's going to happen, it won't happen here. It'll be someplace else."

Sadie was sure she didn't care for the sound of that. "Someplace else? But I'm not going anywhere else," she informed. "That can't be right. Could you be misreading that element?"

Tina's head shook with surety. "Not after all these layouts showed the exact same thing. They always show the Journey rune. You're going to be traveling somewhere. You're going to take a trip. Soon."

Sadie couldn't conceal her agitation. Mistakenly interpreting this latest news as though it were some kind of esoteric directive designed to control her life, she visibly bristled with contrariness.

"No, I'm not," she declared with conviction. "I'm staying right where I am. I've absolutely no plans to go anywhere." Then, even surprising herself, she shot her hands out with lightning speed to scramble the wooden pieces before Tina could stop her. "This is silly," she spouted, trying to explain the impulsiveness of the act. She bent to pick up some of the tokens that'd shot onto the floor. "We'll do another layout."

Taken aback by her friend's rash reaction, Tina sighed. "Okay, okay. You don't have to get violent over this. I told you I was going to do two. I'll do it once more and then you're also going to do two layouts." She eyed her friend. "Okay? Isn't that what I said at the outset? Isn't that what you agreed to?"

Nervously, Sadie nodded, then watched closely while Tina cleared the table of remaining tokens and dropped them back into the velvet bag.

The clattering sound of them heightened Sadie's anxiety.

The tension in the air became palpable.

The fabric sack was vigorously shaken.

Then, one at a time, Tina intentionally kept her eyes fixed on Sadie while each piece was individually placed in the prescribed pattern.

"Well?" the observer asked when all was done. "Is this mysterious upcoming travel still showing in my future?"

Tina lowered her gaze. Silently, the Journey piece was pointed to. And, curiously, in the center position again, was the same lone token. It was the one depicting a woman holding a dove.

Neither woman spoke.

Sadie wondered what the odds were of having the same symbol turn up a second time in the center position. Coincidence, she concluded while watching her friend's hand reach over the table. The odds of it appearing in the center probably weren't that unrealistic. Her assuaging thoughts were broken by the voice coming from across the table.

Tina's fingernail was tapping the glossy surface of a different rune. "See this?"

Sadie nodded.

"Do you recall seeing it in the last layout?"

Again the nod came.

"This symbol denotes wealth. Great wealth."

Sadie wasn't particularly impressed to hear this. "So, my family's wealthy. You already know that. Both our families are. We grew up together in the poshest area outside of Chicago. Just because my sister returned to run the old family estate after her husband's death doesn't mean that I want any claim to it. And, I might add, you also know that I don't want anything to do with that pretentious, old-money wealth."

"You need to settle down and stick with the issue. The fact that I'm familiar with your family's wealth isn't the issue here, Sadie. My knowledge of that has no direct bearing. The issue is that the same token appeared a second time."

"So?"

"So . . . what I'm trying very hard to convey is, since you don't want anything to do with your family's wealth, we might have to consider the alternative—the idea that some other source of wealth is intended in the message."

Sadie still wasn't buying it. She remained nonplused. "I only want what I can earn myself. I'm not interested."

Tina promptly emphasized that one's level of interest had nothing to do with it. She reminded her friend that an individual's personal desires or aversions had no altering effect on what a message ultimately conveyed.

Sadie didn't seem to care. "I don't need anyone's money. I don't want it. Tell your runes that I don't want their stinking money."

"Look, girlfriend," Tina sighed with tempered exasperation. "You don't need to get your hackles up over this. I'm not the enemy here. I'm just pointing out the symbols as they appear. All I meant to underscore was that this same symbol showed up in both layouts. Okay?

That's all. That's it. Nothing more. No judgments. No speculation. Just the facts."

Sadie softened. The hackles relaxed. "Okay. Okay. I noticed it."

Clearing the table and dangling the now full pouch of runes before Sadie's eyes, Tina added, "And besides, the Wealth symbol doesn't always point to material wealth. There are other types of riches. It could mean emotional or spiritual fulfillment. You know, like having a wealth of happiness or something. Here," she said, inclining her head to indicate the bag, "it's your turn."

Staring at the bundle as though it contained a coiled cobra, Sadie hesitantly reached for the bag.

She shook it.

Again and again the velvet fabric was energetically shaken and punched to mix up the pieces inside.

When she was satisfied that all was sufficiently redistributed, she confidently began pulling out one wooden piece at a time. Without looking at the tokens, she didn't stop until the well-known pattern was on the table and the final center piece was set in place.

Like Tina had done, Sadie stared at the face across the table. Though she searched, the countenance gave no hint of revelation.

Finally Sadie was forced to lower her gaze to the table.

The hair on her neck bristled like a cactus.

The Journey token was there as before.

In the center was the dove cradled in a woman's hand.

The Wealth piece rested at the same three o'clock position of the layout.

"Oh!" she spouted disbelievingly. "This is nuts! This is just too ridiculous! What the hell are the odds?"

Tina made no comment, nor did her noncommittal expression alter as she keenly watched the other impatiently slide all of the tokens back into the bag and begin to irritably shake them.

Suddenly, Sadie stopped. She gave her friend a suspicious look, then peeked under the table. Like a mime, she transformed the expression on her face from concern to playfulness. She grinned like a Cheshire cat.

"This is some kind of new hoodoo trick you've learned, right? Tell me you discovered a new magic trick. I'm impressed. I really am. How does it work? Magnets under the table or what? Huh? Huh? Tell me how it works?"

Tina's voice was soft, accepting. "How can magnets create repeat results when *you're* the one who's randomly choosing which piece to pull out of the bag each time?"

Suddenly the bag was upturned and all the remaining tokens clanked onto the tabletop. In seeming desperation, Sadie expectantly examined each one, thinking that perhaps the different ones had been removed for this trick. They weren't. The table was full of pieces that hadn't shown up in the previous layouts.

Sheepishly, she slid them all back into the pouch. "Just checking," she said behind a guilty grin. "I knew there weren't magnets on the tokens. I knew that." And again she shook, palpated, and punched the engraved pieces around to thoroughly mix them up within the soft fabric bag.

As before, she stared directly into her friend's eyes while blindly picking out one piece at a time and placing it on the table. From the bag she withdrew her final choice and placed it in the center. She lowered her eyes to rest on the pattern.

A lump caught in her throat. She found it difficult to swallow. "Shit! How can this be, Tina? What's it all mean? Have you ever had a continually repetitive layout like this happen before? Look," she said excitedly, "there's the Journey symbol, and there's the Wealth one. How incredible is this? Why's the woman with the dove always ending up in the center like that? How often have you had something like this happen?"

Tina shook her head. "Never. Like I said, it's too weird. That's why I needed to talk to you so urgently this morning. It's just so extraordinary." She released a weighted sigh. "I gotta tell you, Sadie, it beats all odds. It really beats all odds. It goes way past being a coincidence." She gave her friend a long, hard look. "It means something, Sadie. It means something big. It's trying to tell us something really, really important. Huge."

"But what?"

"Well . . . the Journey rune is always there. For starters, maybe you ought to give that one some deeper thought. Could it be possible to have forgotten about needing to go someplace to check out an antique? That was the first thing I thought of."

Sadie was pensive. "No, I've got nothing pending in that area. There's nothing I need to pick up or even deliver."

Tina tried another possibility. "Is anyone you know ill? Could you be traveling to someone's bedside or funeral?"

That idea wasn't one Sadie particularly wished to think about, but she understood the possibility of the future reality. "Who's to say about a death I may hear about, but there's been no word of anyone being sick or in need of my help." Mystified, she shook her head. "I just can't figure it. And," she added, while tapping the center token with her fingernail, "who's this supposed to be, anyway?"

"Someone very important. That's all I know. The Dove Woman always represents an extremely important individual in one's life."

"Mmmm," Sadie mused, "this is all too puzzling. It's nothing short of being downright bewildering."

"You got that right. It's right up there with the most mystifying things I've ever experienced and, believe me, I've seen a lot of baffling things in my time. I'm wondering if perhaps—"

Tina's voice was cut off by the racket of someone banging on the shop door. "Can't people read a 'Closed' sign when they see one? Anyway," she continued while ignoring the clatter, "I was wondering if perhaps this—"

The banging continued more urgently.

Disgusted with the interruption, Tina shot out of her chair. "Nobody needs to buy a book that bad. I'll be right back just as soon as I send them on their way." She eyed Sadie. "Don't move. I'll just be a minute."

Left alone, Sadie idly glanced about the shop's living area that was decorated in a manner reflecting her friend's eclectic personality and special interests. There was a strong theme of Far Eastern mysticism dominating the overall atmosphere. The unmistakable hint of sandalwood and cloying Oriental spices hung heavily in the air.

Persian rugs dominated the majority of the highly varnished plank flooring.

The walls were covered by massive, floor-to-ceiling bookcases crammed with the owner's private collection of popular and rare philosophy and metaphysical works.

The apartment felt alive with the energy of its own distinctive aura.

Sadie's gaze randomly shifted to the various figurines of her friend's collection of multicultural deities. The scanning gaze paused when it came to the small shrine of a Far Eastern goddess. Smoke from the still burning incense wafted about the gracefully posed figurine and curled about the lady's delicate facial features. In one hand, the deity appeared to be emptying some type of vessel. The woman's countenance was serene, yet held a hidden sorrow. The figurine held her spellbound.

Sadie whispered to the mute image. "What do you know, Kuan Yin? Do you know what all of this means?" Half-expecting some esoteric type of message or vision to emit from the strong aura of the statue's pervasive presence, Sadie was suddenly startled by the voice that came from behind her.

"Told you nobody needed to buy a book that bad. It was Connie, our FedEx lady," Tina announced in a tone that shattered the reverential state Sadie had been drawn into. As she set a package on the table, Tina's seemingly discordant voice continued. "It's for you! It was brought here because your shop was closed up tighter than a drum and Connie's got my habits down, knows I never really close during the day."

Curious, Sadie examined the package and read the return address label. "Huh, it's from my sister. Wonder what it could be? It's not my birthday or anything."

Tina slid back into her chair. "Well, how about that. You going to open it or just stare at it?"

Sadie glanced down at the runes they'd left on the table. She gave her friend a questionable look. "Considering the weirdness of those," she said, "I'm not sure I want to open this."

Tina laughed. "Oh, for heaven's sake, don't even go there. Let's not get superstitious on top of everything else," she suggested, fluttering her hands in front of the package. "Go ahead, you could use some cheering up from family."

Hesitantly, the package was opened.

"It's a sculpture Savannah made in school!" she exclaimed with admiration. "My niece is so talented for her age."

Tina, having met the precocious eight-year-old, agreed. "She's a sweetie, that's for sure."

A folded paper fell from the bubble wrap.

Sadie opened it and read. The joy on her face faded.

"What?" Tina asked. "What is it?"

"My sister. Mira says that Savannah's not doing as well as everyone expected. She's still not talking and appears to be showing signs of becoming more withdrawn."

"Ohhh," Tina cooed with sincere empathy, "I'm sorry to hear that. I'd hoped she was coming out of that by now."

Sadie rested her arms on the table and unconsciously toyed with the tokens. "She took her dad's death real hard, you know."

"Well, sure she did, poor little thing. Obviously, she took it harder than anyone realized. Being in the car with him when the accident happened, she was lucky she came away unhurt. But still, Sadie, that accident happened over two years ago. Your niece is eight years old now. Shouldn't she be pulling out of it?"

Sadie randomly picked a token off the table and rubbed the engraved surface with her thumb. She absently toyed with it, working it like a prayer bead.

"You'd think so, but she adored David. She loved her dad so much. The shock was too great to bear for someone so young and impressionable. She's pulled herself into a shell that nobody can seem to crack." She skimmed her sister's letter. "Mira writes here that Savannah's retreated more into herself. She writes that my niece has stopped talking altogether."

Tina sympathetically moaned. "Oh, poor baby."

Sadie slowly looked up from the letter. A chilling shiver shot through her.

"What?" Tina asked. "You're as white as a ghost. What's wrong?"

"Mira's asking me to come stay with them for a while. She knows how much Savannah loves me and thinks there may be an outside chance that my presence in the house might be a trigger to snap her out of the withdrawn state. She's at her wit's end with this and is grasping at straws."

Tina whispered two words, only two. "A journey."

"Yeah," Sadie murmured, "a journey. Seems I'm about to go traveling after all." Her gaze glided across the table to settle on the center token that beckoned to her. She tapped its surface. "And is this," she asked, "is this *special* person my little Savannah?"

Tina's own gaze remained riveted on the engraving of the woman holding the dove. She couldn't respond because she had no answers to give. And the question went unanswered.

Sadie pushed her chair back from the table. Tossing down the other token she'd been handling like a talisman, she picked up the package containing the sculpture of a cat.

"Well, that's it, then. Guess I'm off. My niece needs me. I've absolutely no idea how I can be of any help pulling her out of her silence, but I'll never know unless I try. Can't really blame my sister for wanting to try everything she can think of."

Tina wholeheartedly agreed. "Sometimes just being there can make a difference. You know, have some type of positive effect on her. Sometimes someone's presence alone can make a world of difference."

"Maybe," Sadie sighed, "maybe." At this point she didn't know what to make of the recent turn of events that seemed to be twisting her life in an increasingly intricate knot. She'd had enough surprises for one morning. She stood. "I gotta go." With the package in hand, she headed toward the door. "By the way," she added, after peeking back from the doorway, "thanks for the reading. It's been loads of fun."

Tina winked and watched her friend disappear into the bookshop. She heard the interior door adjoining their stores open, then close. She felt a great sense of relief now that she'd done her duty by revealing the message of the runes. Now, in her friend's absence, the solitude felt like a respite she hadn't realized she'd needed.

As she relaxed into the calm serenity of the apartment's soothing atmosphere, her eyes roamed the room. Her glance paused momentarily on the primitive stone statuette of the Peruvian deva, large breasts resting on a swollen belly, before her gaze was drawn back to the token Sadie had so haphazardly tossed away after working it like a worry bead. Tina was struck by the curious realization that this was the one piece they never addressed. She recalled how meticulously she'd carved it, giving it extra care to precisely replicate her vision of it. Picking it up now, she pensively traced the outline with her fingertip and wondered why they'd not discussed this one. She thought it more than curious.

Tina intently stared at the image. She stared at it so long that all else in the room faded from her peripheral vision. "No," she softly whispered, "with this other extraordinary sign always appearing in the layout, the token of the Dove Woman becomes secondary. It does not point to Savannah. The Dove Woman is pointing to *this* one." This she knew with all her heart, with every ounce of her being. This she knew, yet not even in her most wild and eccentric imaginings could she begin to guess who the intended sign was meant to represent. The real-time identity of the person meant to correspond to the token of the Primal Mother—the MotherGod—remained a shadowy mystery . . . for now.

Suddenly, the high anticipation that Tina felt for Sadie jolted through her like powerful surges of electricity. Her eyes were magnetically drawn to the apartment doorway, the vivid afterimage of her friend still burning clear and vibrant in her mind.

Again she looked down at the image on the token. She cradled it in the palm of her hand and, for the first time in her life, felt twinges of envy for the mystery and intrigue into which her friend was destined to be drawn.

Envy quickly slipped away as amusement took hold. A smile tipped the corners of Tina's mouth after her gaze shifted to the primitive stone statue, then back to the token resting in her hand. It rested there like a sleeping goddess. The smoothness of the piece felt like tide-washed glass grown warm in the midday sun.

"Hold onto your hat, old friend," she murmured. "You don't know it yet, but you are about to have the most excellent, most amazing, most unbelievable adventure of your life." The smile widened to brighten her face as she playfully imitated the lyrical accent of the Southern fortune-teller she'd once known.

"Why, I do declare, Miss Sadie!" she exclaimed to the vacant chair across from her. "My, ohhh, my! You are charmed, girl. Yesss, ma'am! Y'all surely must be charmed because you, Honey, are about to walk straight into a big ol' magical web of intrigue! Mmm-mmm!" she hummed. "A big ol' web of the most *profound* proportions."

Three

Chicago—Three Days Later

The woman driving the blue commercial van was on the third leg of her journey. She'd opted out of taking the quickest, most direct method of travel for many reasons, two in particular. To begin with, she was never particularly fond of the overall concept of being confined in a seat thousands of feet up in the sky where she voluntarily handed over the control panel of her destiny to complete strangers. That idea alone scared the bejeezus out of her. She felt far more comfortable being in the driver's seat where her confidence in the solid knowns of her own well-honed skills of defensive driving and lightning reaction time assured her safety. She never cottoned to the thought of willingly placing her life in other people's hands no matter how experienced they appeared or claimed to be.

The second reason was time. Considering the collective circumstances, bizarre as they all were, time was of the essence. Not the urgency of time's speed but rather the need of its drawn-out extension and greater, more meaningful, quality. The recent events in her life had happened too fast, way too fast. Consequently, her mind craved additional time to absorb and analyze those events. She'd wanted to give herself more time alone to think things out. Though her well-meaning friend back in Maine didn't believe a road trip was the wisest and safest choice of travel considering how Sadie felt so utterly blind-sided by recent events and could be easily distracted by her deepening thoughts on the matter, the driver herself wholeheartedly disagreed. She'd refuted that argument by expressing how much she was looking forward to taking advantage of the additional time alone to mentally muddle through her current state of affairs.

During the first two days of the journey, her initial efforts to figure things out hadn't been as productive as she'd hoped. They'd been nothing more than a jumble of stray strands of this and that, as the separate subjects fought for her attention and tumbled one into the other. They teasingly somersaulted over one another in their own taunting game of Catch Me If You Can until the issues became too hopelessly entwined to sort out.

The brilliant autumn sunshine that greeted Sadie on the morning of her third day of travel affected her in a surprising way. While gazing out her hotel window at the wooded copse, and without giving more than a moment's consideration or taking time to gauge the pros and cons of her next move, she impulsively decided that today she was going to drastically alter her intended route by avoiding the interstates altogether. Instead, today was going to be spent leisurely cruising the picturesque secondary country roads. She focused her attention on the stand of maples and the bittersweet bushes beneath them. The leaves on the trees and shrubs, she now noted, were nearing their peak colors. Without any pangs of trepidation, she was drawn to the pleasant idea of experiencing that wonderful sense of serenity one feels while passing through the tranquility of nature's spectacular autumn prime.

The inspired idea of veering from her normal travel route struck her as being a novel one for her because she'd never been the daring type, never deviating from her set way of doing things. She'd always traveled with greater assurance by staying on the main thoroughfares. To alter such a tried-and-true habit carried the potential for flirting with the unknown. Not that she was superstitious; yet she had to admit now that a deviation from her norm was just what she emotionally needed. Just the thought of driving through the colorful countryside today felt right.

An unexpected adventurousness rushed to her head. Her heartbeat quickened. The corners of her lips slowly curled up in a satisfying smile while mulling over her unexpected decision. And, filled with renewed excitement, she crossed the room to study her maps. "Yes!" she whispered. "Yes, today is definitely going to be different."

The morning began with a heart full of hope: hope of coming to terms with the shattered relationship, of better understanding Paul's view of things and the complex set of psychological traumas he must be experiencing.

There was the hope and high anticipation of unraveling the enigma of Tina's runes and what message they could possibly convey to her.

There was hope of being able to help Savannah ease out of the silence that she'd so effectively shrouded herself in.

The morning began with bright sunshine beaming down on the dark blue van and into the driver's heart. Yet all of nature's beauty couldn't be exquisite enough to bring the serenity of mind that Sadie needed this day. She'd made the mistake of turning on the radio to yet another talk show and, listening to the host's obvious enjoyment of tweaking the callers' ire and provoking them into argumentative confrontations, she grew more vexed by the minute. She spat out an expletive while angrily reaching over to switch off the chatter that'd so quickly turned her sweet mood sour.

Irritated, she realized that she should've left the radio alone. She audibly admitted to herself that her first mistake of the morning was to turn the damn thing on. "What'd I do that for, anyway?" she berated herself with an irrepressible groan. This last leg of the trip was supposed to be calming and tranquil, setting the stage for deep thought. What she should've done was slip one of her calming instrumental CDs into the player; that way she'd now be reaping the soothing rewards of music conducive to focused rumination instead of having her mood bedeviled by hostile talk show hosts.

Easing the vehicle off onto the grassy shoulder of the narrow ribbon of blacktop, she cut the engine. As she leaned forward against the steering wheel, her line of vision was drawn to the glisten of sunlight bouncing off the surface of a pond.

Birdsong trilled from the surrounding oaks and willows.

Frogs croaked their warning signals that an intruder had encroached upon their private domain.

In an effort to salvage and reclaim the frame of mind she'd set out with, she got out of the van and made her way toward the water's edge. A soft breeze brushed her cheek and teasingly played with the errant strands of her auburn hair. She tossed her head as though she were making an attempt to shake off the negativity the talk show had coated her with.

Emerald-green lily pads, dotted with fading blossoms, clustered about the pond's surface in bobbing groups. Cattails spiked tall along the far side. Willows swayed and hushed in shared whispers.

The frogs grew silent, watchful from their covers of leaf and fern.

A sigh escaped the woman's lips as the peacefulness of the place cast its spell. She could physically feel it wash over her soured mood. She smiled then, thinking it felt much like a warmly soothing balm; no, she reconsidered, just like a mother's lullaby.

She sat cross-legged on the mossy bank and, as she sensed her former agitation drain away like rainwater coursing down a mallard's back, her parched mind and thirsty soul drank in nature's healing nectar. By the time she checked her watch, she was surprised that she'd spent the good part of an hour by the pond. She'd been somewhere far away, lost in a place of reverie without thought. She realized that she hadn't been thinking of anything in particular, just sitting there among the willows and cattails without any conscious thought to detract from the tranquility she was soaking up. It occurred to her that perhaps nature had quietly cast some type of mesmerizing magic over her, drawn her into a secret meditative state. Whatever it was, she now found herself refreshed, both physically and mentally renewed. So much so that she considered tarrying longer before heading back to the interstate to make up for the lost time. She didn't take more than a few minutes to mull over the idea and then concluded that it was a sound decision. Convinced that this was a good place to do some hard thinking about the curious convergence of odd events that had come into her life, she lowered her eyes and glanced about the fertile ground. Randomly picking a miniature purple aster from the mossy grass, she gently touched its delicate blossom.

"Perfection. Such exquisite perfection," she whispered, while holding it up to the sunlight. "How different we humans are from you," she murmured. "We're so far from being the perfect little species that you are," she added before thoughts drifted to her lost relationship with Paul. "No, we sure aren't perfect. Not a single one of us."

And so the traveler began her thought process that differentiated this day from the two unfruitful ones preceding it.

The thoughts about her breakup were as complex as a skein of yarn that the cat has been tearing into—one thread led into others that were entangled with a dozen more. She'd mentally backtracked over all the "what ifs" and delved into the possible scenarios that could have resulted if different decisions had been made along the way.

What if she'd given Paul some of her money to help with boat repairs and supplement his income until he'd gotten better established? No, she reconsidered, he would've never accepted monetary assistance from her, even in the form of an interest-free loan. He had made that clear right from the beginning of his venture. He'd been adamant about that. It wasn't that he was prideful, he'd simply felt that he had to make a go of things on his own. She recalled how, more times than she could count, they'd gone around and around about that. She couldn't see what difference it made using her money since they were planning on getting married anyway. And he could never get past the idea that he had to do it completely on his own.

The "what if" they'd relocated to a different coastal area was explored. Would his business have flourished in a region where the fish were more plentiful? Or was it the fish at all? She didn't think so because other fisherpeople running boats out of Bay Port were seeing good years with full nets every time they went out. No, it wasn't whether or not the fish were plentiful. She wasn't sure what it was that relentlessly plagued Paul's efforts. Efforts. He certainly couldn't be accused of being lazy because he worked hard at what he did. Fishing for one's living was hard labor—backbreaking labor—and he was never one to avoid putting in a long day's work. Time after time, she recalled, he'd go out before daybreak and not come home for days on end, not until his nets were as full as he thought they were going to get on that particular run. She'd seen fishermen who'd lost heart and ended up throwing in the towel too soon. Oh yeah, she'd seen plenty of that. But no, Paul was no screw-up and, though he'd had to quit his lifelong dream, he never lost the heart for it. And that one aspect, she regretfully thought, was the greatest sorrow of it all—he'd never lost the heart for it.

And another thing—wasn't their love for each other strong enough to weather this monster nor'easter that blustered into their lives? Why did their relationship and future plans have to hinge on him being a success as a fisherman? Why was it that they couldn't stay together no matter what either of them did for a living? What made his profession the pivotal criterion for their ongoing togetherness?

It was then that Tina's words echoed in Sadie's mind. "Sometimes people's love for each other just wanes without either party having done anything wrong." And it was then that the whole situation took a nose dive. It was then that the trying-to-figure-things-out thoughts crashed and burned.

She shook her head with the realization that she'd never ever understand it all well enough for everything to be nice and tidy. There'd always be stray elements and odd bits and pieces that dangled without being attached to any form of reason or logic.

Sadie was distracted by a passing shadow and looked up to see a crow land in a brilliant orange sugar maple. It cocked its head and curiously peered down at her.

Shielding her eyes from the glare of the sun to get a better look at the feathered newcomer, she spoke to it. "Well, hello there! How are you doing on this warm autumn day? Huh? What do you know, crow? Just don't bother asking me the same thing because I sure don't seem to know beans about anything lately."

Once again the perched bird tilted its glossy black head this way and that before responding with a coarse voice. "Caawww!" Then it flew off.

"Yeah," Sadie playfully uttered, "sorry, old girl. I didn't turn out to be as interesting as you thought, did I?"

In the distance she heard the bird's voice as it met up with its gaggle of neighbors. Their combined ruckus sounded as though they'd found something far more intriguing to gossip about than a lone woman sitting beside their watering hole.

With the plan of strolling the perimeter of the spring-fed pond, Sadie stood and brushed off her jeans. She figured that as long as she was going to backtrack to the interstate she had a little extra time to idle away in the bucolic spot. No cars had passed since she'd pulled onto the country road and she liked the idea of reaping the solitude that the peaceful area gifted to her.

Stopping now and then to inspect an unrecognized plant or listen to the sounds of a scurrying critter disturbed by her passing, she spent the time mentally drifting from one subject to another. One of those subjects held her attention longer than the others, though: Tina's runes.

She had to admit that she'd never seen her friend quite so confounded over one of her own layouts. Maybe "confounded" wasn't exactly the right word for the reaction she'd seen in Tina; maybe it was more closely associated with a sense of "astonishment" or "incredulity." It'd been a rarity to see her friend display a truly astonished reaction to anything; because she'd experienced so many oddities in her life, there wasn't much that sent her into an actual tailspin. Yet a tailspin is just what the repeated rune layout seemed to elicit in Tina.

Well, sure, Sadie thoughtfully agreed, the fact that the layout always included the same tokens was rather incredible in itself, but she didn't see the big mystery in who the Dove Woman was supposed to represent. Of course it referred to her niece. That was as obvious as the nose on one's face. Why couldn't Tina see it as well? To Sadie, that was by far more of a mystery than any of the rest of it.

Sadie picked up a pebble and tossed it into the pond. Watching the resulting ripple swell in ever-widening circles, she voiced her thoughts.

"See, Tina? It's like the circle of a ripple breaking a pond's surface. Clean and simple. No mystery there. Everything's connected. All the token symbols point to this very normal Journey to see the Dove Woman who's my little troubled Savannah girl." The pond visitor had it all figured out. "And that Wealth symbol that I got so up in arms over simply denotes the family money and estate that my sister still maintains . . . with her high-minded, high-societal aplomb, I might add." Then Sadie treated herself to a self-satisfied grin. "See Tina? No big mystery. Everything correlates just fine. Nothing is left unaccounted for. Nothing's left to tuck away into your magic pouch of esoteric enigmas."

An unexpected vision of the Dove Woman token momentarily superimposed itself on Sadie's line of sight. Though she wasn't unaccustomed to experiencing flashes of insight, the sudden appearance of the image was far more vivid and clear than those of the past. She quickened her pace and headed toward the van. "I'm coming, Savannah. Hush, baby, your auntie's coming to help you."

The interstate system was a far cry from the quiet rural road, but it served to hasten the van's driver into the heart of Chicago. Exiting the freeway, Sadie expertly wove her way through the squalid vicinity of town. It was a shortcut to the posh business district where her sister had her law office. Mira was always appalled whenever she heard Sadie had driven through the Combat Zone area, yet Sadie never let it bother her.

Now she slowed for an amber light. Waiting for it to change, her eyes drifted along the sidewalks and alleyways cluttered with litter.

Winos in ragged, soiled clothing sauntered with unsteady gaits while holding on with a death grip to their paper-covered bottles.

In the shadowed recesses between gutted buildings, drug dealers were doing a brisk business; and the hookers, hardened by always being dealt losing hands, kept a keen eye out for prospective johns.

Halfway down the block, Sadie watched a disheveled middle-aged woman in a winter coat having trouble pushing a heavy shopping cart full of all the belongings she owned. Beside her shuffled an elderly woman in a worn army coat and a red knit hat. Dangling from the old woman's hand was a tapestry carpetbag that looked like an empty knitting bag with a wooden handle. As the two walked into a ray of sunshine, a spear of light glinted off something on the old lady's hat. It momentarily flashed in Sadie's eyes, causing her to blink.

Using the crosswalk, a derelict haltingly staggered in front of the idling van. The man's bloodshot eyes peered at the driver. He shakily raised his bottle of cheap whiskey, then took a hearty swill as if intending to toast everyone he saw.

The corner pawn shop, windows crosshatched with iron bars, didn't appear to be wanting for customers.

The sight of so many homeless people didn't elicit a sense of disgust or revulsion; instead the driver waiting at the light shook her head in sympathy. "How can people live like this?" she whispered. "Dreams of a better life fizzled until all hope was snuffed out like a candle flame. How did all of you people fall through society's cracks? How did our social system push you into its shadows? How did we fail you? How—?"

Sadie startled when the irritated driver waiting one car over blasted his horn to discourage a derelict from trying to wash his windshield with a grimy rag. The man leaning over the fender just shrugged and ambled off toward another car.

The commotion in the street drew the attention of the two women who'd been making their way toward the intersection.

Sadie's eyes again shifted to the pair on the sidewalk.

The elderly lady's attention wasn't fixed on the disturbance in the street; it was focused on the driver of the blue van.

The hair on Sadie's neck prickled. Was that old woman looking at her? Why was that bag lady staring at her like that?

The light changed and traffic crept forward.

Sadie tried to keep her eyes on the person wearing the army coat while she maneuvered the vehicle. As she slowly rolled abreast of the woman, their eyes locked. After Sadie had passed, she couldn't resist turning her head for a last look. The old lady was still staring at the back of the van. "How odd," she muttered, before focusing her concentration on the route to the newer, upscale business district.

Twenty minutes later, after pulling into the parking garage and riding the exterior, scenic elevator to the eighteenth floor of the glass high-rise, she stood before the shiny brass doors and nervously waited for them to open.

The prestigious atmosphere of the building was never particularly intimidating to her. What set the butterflies fluttering in her stomach now was the anticipation of that initial, emotionally cool meeting with her sister. At thirty-eight years of age, Mira positively thrived on being an accepted member of the city's high-society A-list. And she equally adored playing the part of one of Chicago's chosen people whose photographs regularly appeared on the pages of the *Tribune*'s society section. As far as Sadie was concerned, you could take your elitist attitude and put it where the sun didn't shine. Since she'd been a teenager, there was little that could truly impress her; equally true, there were few people she'd been awed or inspired by, except maybe Gandhi and Mother Teresa. Money, new or old, was never an aspect of life that caught her attention. It wasn't that she took money for granted because she'd been born with a silver spoon in her mouth; it was more of an acquired respect for the hard-earned gain of it. She was more readily drawn to what Mira's crowd referred to as "commoners" and down-to-earth individuals than someone who was moneyed and full of pretentious aloofness. To Sadie's way of thinking, those who comprised the aloof, moneyed crowd weren't solidly plugged into reality.

Now, bracing herself for the drastic transition from her world to her sister's, she inhaled a deep breath and slowly released it in a controlled, well-practiced manner as the elevator doors prepared to open on a foyer that screamed of success and money.

The doors silently slid open to reveal the opulent decor of Mira's working domain. The gold letters that were backlit on the wall directly opposite the elevator entrance boldly announced the fact that one had arrived at the law office of Woodward and Woodward. The sign was symmetrically flanked by two lush, eight-foot bamboo plants.

Steeling herself, Sadie stepped out of the elevator and sank into the deep pile of the Chinese red carpet. Immediately, she was drawn toward the glitzy sign on the wall and couldn't restrain the impulse to touch the letters. Doing so, she wondered why her sister kept the double name after the death of her husband? Night and day, the couple had put their brilliant legal minds together to build their concern into one of Chicago's top ten law firms. Maybe she was in denial and couldn't bring herself to change it to just Woodward, keeping the name as a desperate attempt to remain connected to the man she loved. Or, more probable, it was a calculated move on Mira's part, cleverly figuring it advantageously served the business to keep the double name that had become known as the most hard-hitting law firm in the city.

Sadie stepped back and lingered a moment longer. Her head tilted while considering the polished letters. Yes, she thought, Mira would naturally keep the established name to preserve her company's A-list professional standing. Mira was like that. That's how her mind worked.

She passed the intricately carved mahogany plant stands holding Ming vases bursting with fresh flower arrangements. Footfalls hushed in the deep pile, she made her way to the cherry wood reception desk centered on the massive Aubusson rug.

The staid-looking woman sitting behind the desk sported cropped red hair. Today she was dressed in a tailored grey pant suit. Her name was Caitlin Harris, Mira's longtime, devoted secretary. Sadie never knew what to think of Caitlin because she never understood why a woman of forty-two had vowed to stay single all her life. Yet this woman was an extremely independent thinker with extensively diverse interests.

In a chastising and somewhat condescending manner, the secretary arched a questioning brow while watching Sadie approach. "You're late."

The newcomer gave her watch a perfunctory glance. She managed to conceal the fact that she was surprised to see it was later than she'd thought. Without missing a beat, Sadie quipped back, "Nice to see you, as well, Caitlin. However, I don't recall having agreed to a specified time to meet with my sister."

The receptionist pursed her lips and lowered her eyes to the appointment book opened on her desk. "She keeps a tight schedule, you know. She had me put you down for lunch today at one o'clock . . . in red."

"Do you read the riot act to all her clients who're late?"

"It's my job to keep her on schedule."

Refusing to be annoyed, Sadie rolled her eyes. "How about 'Hi! Long time no see! How the hell are ya, Sadie?'"

Caitlin's dour veneer peeled away. She was eager to readily comply with this visitor's request. She quickly flashed a wide, friendly smile. "Hi! Long time no see, Sadie. How the hell are ya?"

Sadie grinned. "That's better. You know, once you shed that uptight secretary attitude, you're actually a likable person. And me? I've been better." Inclining her head toward the door to her sister's private inner sanctum, she added, "Is Her Highness in?"

The secretary's brows knitted together in a frown. "Sounds like you're the one with an attitude on. You two are going to butt heads quicker than usual if you don't tone it down right now."

Sadie nonchalantly took the advice. She shrugged. "What's the use of pretense? It always ends up the same way. The way I see it, one uppity sister and one down-to-earth sister get along like oil and water. Always has been that way and always will. I'm not into pretense. Is she in?"

Caitlin conspiratorially leaned toward the standing woman and whispered a bit of additional advice. "Well, maybe you *could* be a little bit *into* it. Shedding that attitude. You know, for Savannah's sake. Just this one time?"

"Is she in?"

Ignoring the repeated question, the woman in the grey linen suit raised her brow higher as she patiently waited for her answer.

"What?" Sadie replied. "What's the brow action for?"

"You know what."

"Okay!" Sadie relented. "Just this once, though. For Savannah. Now . . . is she in?"

"No."

Sadie threw her hands up. "Oh, great. Oh, fine. Now what am I supposed to do? Hang around in her perfectly feng-shui'ed office? Ohhh, my gawwwd! I might sit in the wrong place and throw everything off balance! Then she'll have to pay a king's ransom to have it rearranged all over again."

Caitlin's smile widened in amusement. "I'm warning you. You better cut that out or you'll be setting yourself up for a rough time at the ol' homestead."

Sadie resolutely sighed. "Yeah, I know. I only said all that because she isn't around to hear it. Actually, I did forget we'd made a tentative date for lunch, but the drive took a little longer than expected. I wouldn't have made it, anyway." The visitor peered down at the full notations in the appointment book. "Did she bump me back to dinner? Are we on for dinner somewhere?"

Frowning, Caitlin softly groaned. "No, I'm sorry. She didn't make other arrangements. But if you don't mind waiting a few minutes, you and I could grab a bite, maybe just run upstairs to Rathskeller's. Unless, of course, you prefer to get on over to the house and see Savannah. Mira's in a long meeting over at the Brerdan, Sanborn, and Talbot office. I don't expect she'll get back home until late, probably early evening at the earliest."

"Actually," Sadie admitted, "us going out sounds nice." She smiled. "Rathskeller's it is. I'll wait."

When Caitlin had cleaned up the last of her paperwork, she locked the door to the inner sanctum, and the two women rode the elevator one floor up. The elegant restaurant catered to professional clientele who frequented it for the famous seared steaks served with portobello mushrooms. The atmosphere attracted those who had spent an exhausting day litigating difficult cases in court and could look forward to winding down in the shadows of subdued lighting and high-backed leather seating that promised patrons an optimum sense of privacy. Candlelight and offerings from the bar added to the anticipation of relaxation.

Caitlin and Sadie were escorted to a quiet corner booth where they ordered drinks to start, then quickly gave the waitress their dinner selections. With that out of the way, they settled back into the soft seats and, after Caitlin made the mistake of asking what was new in Sadie's life, the latter went through the events of her relationship with Paul. Caitlin had genuinely liked the couple and expressed sincere regret over how badly things had turned out.

After their meal was served, Sadie purposely changed the subject and began to recount her experience with Tina's runes. The issue of prognostication wouldn't have been broached with just anyone, but Caitlin had never made a secret of her open mind on matters of the paranormal. She had been interested in various aspects of the human psyche for as long as Sadie had known her. Caitlin had met Tina several times in the past and they'd hit it off like old friends. Now that the warm, relaxing ambiance of the restaurant had melted away the tension of the three-day drive, Sadie felt more than comfortable bringing up the subject. Since she knew that, oftentimes, a third party could have a fresh perspective, it occurred to her that Caitlin might very well have one or more interesting insights about the unusual, repetitive rune layouts. While Sadie gave as detailed an account as she could, Caitlin intently listened to the story.

"So, what do you think?" Sadie asked, while soaking a hunk of garlic bread in peppery olive oil.

No response.

"Ahhh, Caitlin? Did you hear me?"

Thoughtfully, the woman in the suit nodded.

"Well? What do you think?"

The listener unceremoniously swiped a napkin across her mouth and shook her fork for emphasis. A speared piece of savory filet mignon dangled on the end of the tines.

"What I think is that you've had three independent situations in your life converge to create a catalytic moment—at least in relation to the greater scheme of things—and this convergence is just one moment, a blink in time. Know what I mean? This catalytic moment, though, is nothing to scoff at; it's undeniably a hallmark point in your life. Oh, yes," she repeated, "this convergence is most certainly a hallmark occurrence associated with a destined event in your future."

"Which three situations? Catalytic moment for what? Destined event? Slow down. I don't think I'm following you." Sadie smirked. "No. I *know* I'm not following you. What the hell are you talking about?"

Unfazed by her dinner partner's challenged grasp of her own recent history, Caitlin explained.

"The three events that converged to make a hallmark happening are the broken relationship with Paul, the rune thing, and Mira's unexpected message for you to come to Savannah's aid. Good grief," she exclaimed, while continuing to talk after she'd popped the tasty morsel of steak into her mouth, "any *one* of these events would be huge in anyone's life, but these, these all consecutively happened within a span of twenty-four hours!"

Sadie nodded, eager to hear more.

"But even more important, what I think is, either you purposely left something out of your story about the runes or you completely missed a key element of the event." She again pointed with her fork. "If it's the latter, you consciously or subconsciously let something important go way over your head. You either ignored it or chose to be in denial of it."

This was not what Sadie expected to hear from her knowledgeable friend. It took her by surprise. Didn't she have the mystery of the runes all figured out when she'd stopped to ponder it by the pond? Didn't she conclude that there, in fact, *was* no mystery lurking among the layout tokens? Hadn't she anticipated to hear a verification of her conclusion?

Despite the half-chuckle, her voice trembled with disappointment. "Aren't you reading far too much into this? You sound like Tina. She gets so hyped up about her runes that she tends to overreact at times."

Caitlin took a sip of her Burgundy. "You think so?"

Sadie nodded.

"I don't," came the contrary response. "Tina's an intelligent woman, sharper than most. She never struck me as being an alarmist, even when it came to her treasured runes. She's not the type. I believe her opinion is right on the mark." Caitlin effectively suppressed a burp and leaned back in the soft leather seat. "Want to hear what I think?"

Oh, God. The listener smiled. "I've the feeling you're going to tell me whether I want to hear it or not. Shoot."

"Well, you're right. I am going to tell you anyway. I think you're reaching, Sadie. I think you're reaching for something commonplace to hang the seriousness of the situation on. Don't pretend you don't know what I'm talking about so you don't have to look it square in the eye and accept its existence, especially its gravity. Whether or not you want to admit it, your psyche's in a tailspin from the blow Paul dealt you. I suspect that having to also contend with the import of the runes may have been too much to take on at this point. Ergo . . . denial."

Sadie was visibly shaken by the discomforting effect Caitlin's view of the situation had on her. She particularly didn't like the fact that the woman's words made her feel queasy. That usually meant that her subconscious had been confronted with the truth it was attempting to keep interred.

In her heart, Sadie secretly conceded that Caitlin was right. Yet she wasn't ready to openly admit it. "Okay," Sadie said in a not so subtle begrudging tone. "Hypothetically, then, let's say you and Tina are right about the importance of the rune's message. What did you mean by me 'missing something'? What was that all about?"

"Hypothetically? Did I hear you say, hypothetically?" Caitlin echoed. "Sadie, there's nothing hypothetical about any of this. Before we go any further, you've got to realize that you can't make progress unless you accept the facts, the gravity of what's happened."

Sadie dropped her napkin onto her plate and slid the dish aside. Before she could reply, the attentive waitress appeared to ask if she could take the plates away. Would they like to see the dessert menu?

"Absolutely!" Caitlin exclaimed.

"Not for me," Sadie politely declined.

"Oh, come on," Caitlin urged. "They've got red velvet cake to die for! And the triple chocolate torte is absolutely decadent!"

"I don't know. I'm pretty full."

Caitlin winked at the patient waitress. "Go ahead and bring two dessert menus. She'll change her mind once she sees those irresistible photographs."

The waitress eyed the reluctant patron and tilted her head in question.

The reluctant patron sighed. "Oh, all right. You've convinced me. If things are as tempting as she claims, maybe I can be persuaded to try a little something."

The menus were placed before the two women and it didn't take long to voice their orders.

Sadie still wasn't sure she should've ordered the triple chocolate torte topped with fresh raspberry sauce, but assuaged her guilt by deciding a well-deserved treat couldn't hurt after all she'd been through. She'd managed to savor every rich bite without dwelling on how many calories she'd ingested and, when done, both women lingered over steaming cups of the restaurant's dark-roast coffee.

"So where were we?" Sadie asked, knowing her dinner partner wouldn't let her walk out of there without finishing the conversation that was left dangling when the waitress had appeared. "You were saying something about me needing to accept the gravity of the rune's message. Right? Wasn't that where we left off?"

"Glad you didn't forget," Caitlin somberly said. "I would've sworn you were going to try to slink out of here in an attempt to avoid going back there."

Sadie's eyes widened in a playful manner. "Who, me? I could've done that with a hundred other people, but with you? Not a chance."

"You better believe it. So. What about it?"

"Are you talking about that acceptance thing?"

"Don't get funny. Of course we're talking about that acceptance thing. Tina takes her runes very seriously and well she should. This latest sequential layout means something very important. And I'm not talking about those repetitive layouts being a normal kind of importance. Both she and I know they represent something, well," she paused while searching for the right word, "something almost . . . profound. I'm not exaggerating, either. This is hugely profound. *That's* what you've got to let sink into that stubborn head of yours."

Sadie wasn't in the mood to continue repudiating the issue. "That may be, Caitlin. I do trust both of your instincts in things like this, but I have to tell you, there's not a damn thing in my life that comes even close to being described as profound."

One corner of Caitlin's mouth tipped up. "Not *yet*, you mean. The rune's message isn't referencing what's come before. It's not connected to the present time. What it's revealing is what is to come!"

Sadie rested back in her seat while the waitress refilled their coffee cups and removed the empty dessert plates. When the two women were alone again, she leaned forward. The timbre of her voice was pragmatic.

"I drove through the Combat Zone on my way here this afternoon. Let me tell you something. Let me tell you that I didn't see a whole lot of what you could call 'profound' aspects of our world. Society is bursting with bedraggled homeless people shuffling out from shadowy alleyways. When I stopped at a light, it was perfectly clear that pitiful people of all ages and genders have slipped through the proverbial crack in our social system. They've dropped so far down that crevice that they've no hope of ever being in a position of having their self-respect back.

"I saw a couple of bag ladies making their way down the sidewalk.

One was pushing a shopping cart full of everything she owned. The thin elderly woman beside her was wearing an army coat and must've been in her late eighties. Her grey hair was long and bushy, wildly sticking out from a red knit hat. The only thing that woman carried was an empty-looking knitting bag and—"

"Maybe her belongings were in the other woman's cart," Caitlin cut in.

"That wasn't my impression. Anyway—"

"Anyway," Caitlin cut in again, "we already know that our cities are loaded with throngs of street people. Where're you going with this? What's it got to do with what we were discussing?"

Maintaining her reserve without letting the irritation show, Sadie replied. "If you wouldn't keep interrupting me, I'd get to that."

Caitlin apologetically put her palms up. "Okay, sorry."

"What I'm trying to express is that I don't see your so-called 'profound' aspects in the world. Nothing I see is profound. And . . . and to attach such a hugely impressive connotation to the rune's message is just too far off the wall for me to swallow." Sadie tempered her seemingly nonexistent level of acceptance. "Don't get me wrong, though," she added. "I'm not saying that the message isn't important, that it doesn't carry a certain amount of merit to take to heart. I believe—"

"'Merit,' she says," Caitlin quietly snapped in a whispered retort. "Sadie! 'Merit' doesn't even come close! Merit is something a Girl Scout earns those little badges for!"

Just then the waitress appeared with the bill. "Would you ladies care for anything else this evening?"

Hiding their annoyance at being interrupted at this critical point in the discussion, the two seated patrons forced cordial smiles and, in tandem, shook their heads.

Setting down the leatherette folder containing the bill, the waitress politely wished the two an enjoyable evening after again refilling their coffee cups.

Sadie checked her watch. "I should get going. Savannah will have been home from school for some time, and she's probably watching for me to drive up."

"Savannah's probably been watching out her window all day long. Didn't Mira tell you? She had to take Savannah out of school because of her behavior. A private tutor has been going to the house each day to keep the class lessons current."

Sadie hadn't been informed of this development. "Since when does Savannah's silence keep her from school? How long has this been going on?"

"I guess for about six weeks now. Sorry you weren't told. I suppose Mira just forgot about it. She's had a lot on her mind lately with a couple of killer cases—literally."

"But why does Savannah's silence keep her out of school? She loves school."

Caitlin shrugged. "It turns out that her unwillingness to speak is just the tip of things. Savannah's also become socially withdrawn and, well . . . begun displaying some belligerent behavior that seems to be related to social anxiety. Mira's had several conferences with the school psychologist and everyone concerned believes it is best to do the home schooling for a time."

Sadie blew a long breath from pursed lips and slumped in her seat. She waved the waitress over. "I'll have another glass of wine," she said, while motioning to her dinner companion in an unspoken offer for her to do the same.

"You bet. Same for me," Caitlin said.

After the waitress returned with the drinks and the adjusted bill, she quickly left the two women to their conversation.

Caitlin was first to speak. "Savannah's a whole different issue. Can we finish with the rune subject before we get into something else?"

Sadie sighed with resignation. "I believe we left off at the point where you were incredulous that I'd used the 'merit' word in connection to the runes. Okay, I'll give you that. It was a poor choice of word. Let's scrap that. Granted, you and Tina would rather use something more apropos, maybe a term more like 'monumental.' So, okay, maybe the repeated layout portends some type of monumental event. I'll give you that. But to be perfectly honest with you, Mira's not the only one who's got her plate full."

Sadie took a long draw on her drink. "Cait, I just can't have so many separate issues boiling over right now. I came here at the behest of my sister to see what I can do to help my niece. That's got to be my number one priority. I can't do anything about what's happened between Paul and me. And I can't begin to fathom what the runes mean. I'd just be spinning my wheels trying to figure it all out. It'd be nothing but speculation after speculation. That whole thing's got to play itself out in its own time. The way I see it, there's only one thing left to talk about regarding the runes and we may as well get that cleared up right now so I can go see Savannah without having your cryptic statement nagging in my head."

Caitlin frowned. "What cryptic statement?"

"Earlier you made the comment that you'd thought I'd perhaps 'missed' something about the rune layout. Remember that?"

"Ahhh, of course," Caitlin recalled. "That had to do with my sense that there was a hole left in the rune story after you'd relayed the sequence of events to me."

"A hole? What, a hole as in I'd inadvertently left something out?" Sadie was pensive as she attempted to quickly replay the conversation through her head. "I don't think I left anything out. It was pretty much as I said. And," she politely reminded, "you also wondered if I'd *purposely* left something out. What was that all about?"

"That was all about how you interpreted the symbols. As I recall, you're convinced that the Dove Woman represents Savannah. That didn't strike me as ringing true."

"Why not? It made perfect sense to me."

"I don't believe Savannah's in the runes at all."

Sadie finished her drink. "Seriously? If the Dove Woman doesn't point to Savannah then who does it point to?"

"I tend to think that the token isn't the *main* one like you're so convinced it is. I believe the Dove Woman appeared in *conjunction* with the main symbol. The Dove Woman was *pointing* to *another* one that's the *main* subject of the whole message."

"Another one? And this other mysterious token is the real key that you think I missed seeing? That's the one that's your 'profound' player?"

Caitlin responded with a definitive nod. "Absolutely. That's what I think. I'm sure of it. Can you recall seeing any other symbol that looked like a person? It'd be a token that appeared in all the layouts. And," she added, "it probably also kept reappearing in the same layout position each time it showed itself."

Sadie narrowed her eyes as she pressed her mind for an answer. "You've got me going, now," she murmured. As she slowly shook her head, disappointment weighed in her voice. "I'm sorry. I just can't recall seeing something like you describe. I think the Dove Woman was the only human-type figure that kept reappearing."

Disappointed, Caitlin bit her lip. "Bummer. I'm sure it had to be there."

Then Sadie brightened. "Wait a minute! There was a second figure!"

"I knew it! It had to be there! What was it?"

The unexpected answer deflated the growing possibility of the solution to the mystery coming to light. "I don't know."

Caitlin's jaw dropped. "What do you mean, 'you don't know'?"

"Just what I said, I don't know. We never discussed that token. As I recall, when Tina went to the door for Mira's package, my head was spinning with feelings of amazement over the repeated layouts. To be honest, I was overwhelmed. I'd randomly picked up a token from the table and had been toying with it while glancing around the room at her collection of various goddess statues. When she returned I barely glanced at it before tossing it back on the table after my attention was drawn to the package. I remember that the token's image was a rendition of a primitive art piece, a woman with pendulous breasts and belly. It looked like a woman in her final days of pregnancy. As a matter of fact," Sadie recalled, "it looked a lot like the artifact I gave Tina for her birthday one year. It'd been unearthed at an archaeological dig in the Peruvian highlands."

Caitlin's cheeks flushed.

Concerned with her friend's sudden reaction, Sadie grew alarmed. "What? What does that token mean? Who is it supposed to be?"

If the woman in the suit could have had one wish it would have been that she hadn't already drained her glass of wine. Suddenly her throat felt as parched as a summer desert at high noon. In an effort to recover, she looked down at her watch.

"Caitlin!" Sadie impatiently whispered, while leaning far over the table. "What is going on? Do you know what the primitive image means?"

"I know a lot of things, Sadie. I also know that there are a hell of a lot of things that I don't know. But one thing I do know for certain is that I wasn't exaggerating when I used that word earlier."

"What word?"

Caitlin's hazel eyes widened. They sparkled with new intensity. "Profound!" she respectfully whispered back. "*Profound*, Sadie."

Now it was Sadie's turn to blush with the impact of Caitlin's dramatic reaction. She didn't know what to say, how to feel. "What am I supposed to do with this information? What's it all mean? Where do I go from here? Caitlin," she finally asked, "what's going to happen to me?"

Caitlin tilted her head and a grin grew to winning proportions. "Sadie? What you do with the information will be dictated by what's inside you—your heart and soul. What it means will become clear in time. Where you go from here will be wherever you're led. And what's going to happen to you is anyone's guess, but I'd be willing to bet that it'll be determined by destiny." She winked while tucking a hundred-dollar bill into the folder on the table. "I can be a bit more precise about one thing, though. One of the places you *are* going to go from here is to an old friend of mine. She has the wherewithal to provide you with more answers than I can at this point."

After Sadie left a generous tip, the two headed out of the restaurant.

While the elevator descended to the parking garage level, Sadie eventually found the nerve to break the silence that had heavily hung between them. "So," she began, trying to lighten the mood, "who's this amazing Answer Lady you're intending to have me visit?"

Aware of Sadie's leery attitude toward psychics, Caitlin felt a twinge of trepidation. She intentionally overspiced her tone with cheeriness. "Well, let's see. I've known her for years. She's very powerful, and in the Haitian community she's known as—"

"That's enough," Sadie said, slicing off the sentence. "No voodoo woman for me, thank you very much."

Caitlin's reaction was one of exasperation. "God! How'd I know you were going to react like that? Sadie?" She was so irritated she didn't know where to begin. "Sadie, you're profiling."

"No, I'm not. You want to take me to see some bangle-jingling woman in a flowered turban who has a back room full of dolls with straight pins stuck into them. No, thanks."

"See? See, there? You're stereotyping!"

"Am not."

"Are too. You've been watching too many old black-and-white zombie movies. Things aren't like that in the real world. At least, not with all of them. This woman's highly intelligent and—"

"I don't care if she's Einstein reincarnated. The answer's no."

"Gads, you're stubborn," Caitlin spat with a disgusted shake of her head.

"No, just smart."

The elevator doors opened and the two women stepped out.

Not wanting to part ways on a sour note, Sadie turned and rested her hand on her friend's arm.

"Listen. I know you mean well, but all this mystery coming on the heels of my breakup has really been too much for me to deal with right now. Who knows, maybe there is something special in my future, something *profound* even, yet I need to stay focused in the here and now—on Savannah. She's my priority. She's why I'm here."

Caitlin reassuringly patted her friend's hand. "You're right," she halfheartedly agreed. "Sometimes certain things have a tendency to carry us away to Neverland and we get distracted. I didn't mean to be intrusive. Are we okay?"

Sadie smiled. "We're okay, Caitlin. I just can't afford to get sidetracked right now. I'll keep you posted on my progress with Savannah. Maybe I'll bring her by and we'll all go to lunch one day. I think she'd enjoy that."

"I think she would, too." And then they each headed in opposite directions toward their awaiting vehicles.

Caitlin secretly treated herself to a satisfied smile while making plans to phone her Haitian friend for the express purpose of filling her in on the mystery of Tina's cast runes. Marie Claire deRouge, she knew, would need the history behind the enigma before she and Sadie had their meeting.

On the other side of the garage, Sadie grinned as well. She was confident that she'd artfully squelched Caitlin's wild voodoo woman scheme.

Sadie pulled out of the parking garage and headed toward the more rural region of the city's heavily treed outskirts where the homes were compounds spread over extensive acreage. It was an area where high stone walls hid the imposing estates from the prying eyes of the passing commoner. The fortresslike walls of the area were set far back on the manicured grounds winding along the picturesque stretch of Old Mill Road. They served to ensure the complete privacy of the sequestered residents collectively known as Chicago's elite.

The van with the Harbor Heirlooms logo painted on its side turned into a wide drive. A security motion detector flooded the area with bright lights as the vehicle pulled up to an electronic control panel. The driver punched in a code sequence and eased the vehicle forward to wait. When the set of double wrought-iron gates soundlessly opened inward, the van moved through. Sadie suddenly felt queasy. She heard herself moan as the feeling of entering the jaws of a monster swept over her. Her foot remained on the brake while her attention was drawn to the rearview mirror, as she watched the gates swing closed behind her. Slowly the van crept up the narrowly curving lane flanked by old-growth red maples. They sparked memories from her youth when she used to pretend the trees were a grand castle arch and she was Cinderella riding a golden coach to the prince's ball. Now, the returning vision from the past brought a cynical smirk.

"Dreamer," she whispered. "What a stupid little believer in magic you were back then. Sorry, kid," she said to herself, "dreams, miracles, and the fairy godmother are all made of flimsy, whimsical illusion . . . just so much pixie dust and Sandman's sand."

The paved lane curved around to bring the van to the portico in front of the mansion.

Josef, the family's longtime gardener, was waiting on the wide stone steps to greet her and take her bags. Josef and his wife, Greta, were in their early seventies. They'd been a part of the Brennan household for as long as she could remember. Greta used to keep Sadie's childhood secrets and they'd conspire together now and again to hide the fact that Sadie had been naughty. Greta had tucked the youngster in at bedtime more than Sadie's mother had. Josef would regale the child with Swiss folktales while she helped him with the springtime garden plantings and year-round tending chores. Now the couple were a devoted part of Mira's world because the former Brennan compound had become known as the Woodward estate. They doted on young Savannah just as they had Sadie and Mira. Josef opened the van door. "Sadie! My, what a lovely sight for these old eyes!"

Sadie laughed and hugged her old teller of strange tales. She teased him. "And is the Brennan garden still full of fairy whisperings?"

"Oh," he chided, "this old place will always be the Brennan homestead to you, eh?"

"It's where the Brennan sisters grew up. I suppose you're right. I can't quite get used to it being a Woodward place. And, you, you old clever wizard, didn't answer me. Are your garden fairies still whispering in your ear?"

The old man mildly blushed and chuckled. "Ahh, Sadie, now and again they do. Oh yes, they still play about the blossoms and splash in the rain barrels."

Sadie hugged her old gardening mentor. "You're still my favorite man, you know. You were the only man who made me feel like what

I had to say was important. You listened. You listened even when I incessantly pestered you with childish prattle." She kissed him. "I love you, Josef. I hope you've been well. You have been well, haven't you?"

"Hale and hearty, as always."

"And Greta?"

"Just the same. She'll outlive us all." Then a shadow crossed his face.

Sadie frowned. "What's the matter, Josef? Is it something about Greta?"

"Oh, no," he hesitated. "It's just the little one. She's in a sad way," he said, while bending into the van for the bags. "I hope having you here will do your double some good."

Sadie's concerned expression didn't alter, yet she inwardly warmed to Josef's private joke about Savannah being a replica of herself when she was young. Though Sadie's hair color had darkened and the wildness of it had tamed some with age, it was once the identically headturning auburn shade her niece's was now. The green eyes had remained the same along with the rosy Irish blush to the complexion.

Sadie politely tugged on the man's jacket. "I'll take the bags in. Why don't you drive the van around to the garage. And," she felt the need to add, "I'm not sure how much good I can do her, but I'm sure hoping something good will come of my visit."

"And how long will that be for?" he casually inquired.

It was a question Sadie hadn't anticipated. "I hadn't thought about it. I suppose I can stay for however long it takes to see some improvement. I was thinking that I could take her along with me to some antique shops, go to the park down the way, museums, things like that. Do you think she's up for those kinds of activities?"

The gardener winked. "No," he said.

"Oh, no. Are you serious? Is she that bad?"

The old familiar grin curled up to light his face. "Only with Mira. I think the little one would be thrilled to do those things with the auntie she adores. Though she doesn't speak and has become more withdrawn, that child still loves to have adventures."

Sadie's face brightened. "Then adventures she'll have!"

He nodded. "I knew you'd be the good medicine she needed."

Sadie remained reserved. "I think the jury's still out on that one. We'll see."

The old man gave her one of his fey looks. "Yes, indeed. We *will* see."

The van was moved around to the garage after Sadie pulled out her luggage. She hadn't packed much and managed to carry all the bags in one trip up the wide entry steps.

Greta was anxiously standing beneath the Gothic stone arch that framed the entry door. The massiveness of the structure's entranceway made the woman appear diminutive. Though by nature she was of slight build, her great store of energy and vivaciousness belied her physical appearance of seeming frailty. She immediately crossed her hands over her heart at the sight of the woman she'd helped to raise. The grey eyes were moist with emotion. She flung out her arms. "Ohhh, my little *Sadie!*" she cried. "Come give old Greta a great big hug!"

Sadie beamed. Her own eyes misted when she saw her old governess; and little Savannah as well, with her aura of long, bushy auburn hair glowing like a halo, was hesitantly peering out from behind the folds of the elder woman's long grey skirt. The soft fabric shook as the young girl visibly trembled with excitement. Sadie didn't know which element of the scene touched her more because, suddenly, she was overcome with emotion. But then, it was always this way when she returned to the homestead for a visit. Still, the familiar tearful reaction never failed to take her by surprise after all these repeated performances. Those involved never expected it to play any other way.

Sadie dropped her bags and hugged Greta. Then she bent low to be embraced by her niece. The little arms clung so tightly around her neck that she felt she was about to be strangled by the child's exuberant show of love. Or, Sadie wondered, did the extra-tight embrace carry a more weighty reason behind it? Was it a sign of desperation? A cry for help? A signal flag waving an SOS?

"I love you, sugar," Sadie whispered in the small ear just before easing herself out of the circlet of arms. She held Savannah out before her. "My goodness!" she exclaimed. "Have you been sneaking some of Josef's magic beans from the garden shed? Look how you've sprouted up since I was last here!"

Savannah shyly blushed, trying to suppress a giggle that threatened to make a forbidden sound come out of her. She covered her mouth with her hand before burying her head in Sadie's jacket.

"Ohhh," the aunt chided with an added tickle to the ribs, "you're still as silly as ever." She pointed to the baggage on the step. "Come on, you've grown so big you can help me carry my things upstairs. Or has my old room been converted into one of your mom's ta-ta guest rooms?"

Savannah almost let herself laugh when she vigorously shook her head.

Sadie eyed Greta before returning her attention to the girl. "You mean the room's still mine? It's still all mine?"

Showing as much enthusiasm as before, Savannah nodded her head up and down. Then she eagerly picked up twin pieces of luggage to show how strong she'd grown. Proudly, she strode past the two women. Crossing the wide foyer, she abruptly stopped at the staircase and turned. She eyed the newcomer and tilted her head in unspoken question, *are you coming, or what?*

Sadie looked to Greta. "Guess I'm being summoned."

Greta smiled. "That's what it looked like to me. You'd better go get settled in. We'll meet up in the kitchen as usual." The elder gently set her hand on the younger's arm. Her voice was light with relief, full of hope and expectation. "You have no idea how good it is to see you again." Her eyes momentarily shifted to the girl patiently waiting by the stairs. "Having you here holds great promise."

Sadie gave a dubious look. Her hand patted the woman's. "Please, don't expect too much from me. Of course, I'll do everything I can. We'll see."

"I already see," Greta grinned. "She's smiling! This is the first time I've seen a smile on that little face in months!"

"Really?"

The woman's grin grew. "Really!"

Sadie considered that for a moment. She'd felt somewhat embarrassed by the high expectation she felt coming from the elder proudly standing before her. She didn't want the burden of carrying the weight of that expectation. She didn't want to fail them by dashing their hopes. Instead of addressing the fact that her presence had already sparked a positive response in her niece, she changed the subject. "By the way," she said, "I didn't see Mira's car in the garage. I assume she's still at her conference meeting. Has she called?"

Greta's response was a knowing shake of the head.

Sadie snickered. "Same old Mira, huh?"

"Nothing's changed. She'll arrive when she arrives."

"Yeah, well, I've got some unpacking to do, anyway. We'll be down as soon as we're done upstairs. I expect hot chocolate to be on the table when we come down." The latter was added in reference to their unbroken tradition.

In anticipation of that ritual, the governess was already turning to attend to the joyful task. She laughed and waved the younger woman away. "That's one thing you can always count on, Sadie, dear. That's one thing you can surely count on in this place. You go on upstairs and get settled in. Everything's just as you left it. Take your time. We'll see you two whenever you're ready."

Thirty-five minutes later, Savannah and her beloved aunt strolled hand-in-hand into the cozy country kitchen. The Swiss couple were seated at the table, each idly perusing their favored section of the daily newspaper.

The young girl had a gleaming smile on her face.

Sadie, though smiling, appeared troubled.

Greta peered over the paper and raised a brow to emphasize her unvoiced warning about Savannah's state of silence. *Yes, her condition is quite serious, isn't it?*

Josef set down his paper and eyed Sadie. Mirroring the same sentiment as his wife's, he simply pursed his lips.

Sadie responded with a quick look that reflected agreement. Then, like a mime, she purposely brightened her expression. "Ahh," she crooned with pleasure, "look, sugar! Once again Greta timed it perfectly! The hot chocolate's just been poured." She bent down to make eye contact with the child. Their deep, sea-green eyes connected. "How do you suppose she manages to get it timed down to the second like that?"

Without uttering so much as a peep, the girl hitched her shoulders up, then dropped them.

Sadie had the strongest feeling that Savannah desperately wanted to burst out of her silent shell and giggle, that she had the urge to jump up and down like she used to do. Sadie's mind replayed the scene she'd witnessed countless times: a little girl happily skipping about and shouting her announcement to the world, "Magic! Greta and Josef are *magical!*"

The recalled vision from the past evaporated like a sun-touched mist.

Sadie gave the child a dose of emotional support by squeezing the small hand. "Well, know what? I don't know, either. Maybe it's magic, or something. Let's go have some of that hot chocolate before all the marshmallows melt."

The four of them comfortably gathered together at the end of the long pine trestle table that Mira had purchased for the oversized kitchen. Mira had always had a strong attachment to the family homestead. At a young age, she'd thumbed through home decor magazines and envisioned such a table placed in front of their kitchen's brick oven. Once she'd inherited the estate, one of the first changes she made to the house was to realize her long-held vision of how the room should be properly appointed.

Warmth from the oven radiated over the four people seated at the table.

From the oven, the mouth-watering aroma of Greta's specialty braided breads wafted lazily about the room. It pleasingly swirled to blend with the rich scent of the steaming hot chocolate.

The familial atmosphere kept the conversation confined to light subject matters. No one wanted to disturb the emotionally restful ambiance of the room.

Greta and Josef didn't broach the issue of Savannah's present state of silence.

Sadie didn't think it wise to upset her niece by mentioning her recent breakup, nor did she wish to introduce the curious subject of Tina's rune layouts. Instead, while Savannah remained as quiet as a church mouse, the adults spoke of innocuous subjects, such as the weather in both Chicago and Maine, Sadie's recent business transactions, and how wonderfully Tina was getting along with her book and candle business.

During a lull in the conversation, Sadie's thoughts drifted to how everyone seemed to be counting on her to be Savannah's saving grace. Her shoulders felt the new weight of that expectation. She had no idea how to meet the challenge, didn't have the slightest plan or know where to begin. Then thoughts about a jumping-off place came to mind and she casually ran them by those at the table. She carefully chose her wording.

"While I'm here, I'd like to visit the museum. On the drive out here I realized that I hadn't been there in a long while. I've always loved spending leisure hours there. I want to make a point of going there this time."

The Swiss couple, quick to pick up on Sadie's intent, both agreed that it'd be a wonderful thing to do.

Sadie wasn't through. "I also want to take advantage of my time here and connect with two or three of my antique contacts here in the city. Then, if I have the time, do what I do best—hit some of those little mom 'n' pop antique shops. Those owners never really know what they've got. I love finding something of value and then watching their jaws drop when I tell them how much they should be asking for it."

Greta grinned. "Good thing you've got a conscience. Plenty of dealers with your knowledge would buy the item for a song, then sell it for a big return in their own shops. You always did love rummaging about in those little out-of-the-way places and surprising the owners with your big finds. That's such a kind thing to do. I imagine it gives you a lot of pleasure and satisfaction doing good like that."

Sadie shrugged off the compliment. "It's just fun," she said. Then, giving her attention to the silent one at the table, "Wanna tag along with your ol' auntie while I look for treasures among the dusty junk?"

Savannah wasn't sure her mother would allow such a thing, yet the girl felt her heart quiver with excitement at the idea. Almost imperceptibly, she nodded.

Greta and Josef eyed one another.

Encouraged by the positive response, Sadie kept her eyes on her receptive niece. "How about the museum? Wanna go ruminate before a couple of Rubenses or Michelangelos?"

The formerly precocious girl bit her lips to keep from laughing. She gave another nod.

Auntie controlled her own growing excitement over the child's responsiveness to her suggestions. She tried to appear mildly passive. "Okay, we'll do some bumming around together, then. That'd be nice." Sadie's attention turned to the adults. She winked at them. "What's Savannah's schooling schedule look like? Can we play some hooky?"

"*Who's* playing hooky?" came a voice from behind them.

Sadie noticed Savannah stiffen.

Four sets of eyes slid to the doorway.

Greta began to stand. "Mira. I didn't hear you pull in. Would you like to join us? We're having our traditional hot chocolate."

The woman in the severely tailored suit crossed the room. With a condescending smile, she politely declined. "Sit. Sit, Greta, dear. I'll pass. I need a martini," she said, leaning down and kissing her sister on the cheek. "Good to see you, Sadie. Glad you made it okay. Although," she added, while fluttering her fingers, "I still don't understand why you didn't fly out here instead of driving that awful work van. You did drive that van of yours, didn't you?"

Sadie looked toward the seated couple and secretively crossed her eyes at Mira's comment. "Of course I drove that 'work' van. I never know when I might come across an antique to take back with me."

"Whatever," Mira said before shifting her attention to the young girl. "And, how was your day, honey? Did you get all of your homework done?" Not waiting for answers she knew weren't forthcoming, she dramatically sighed. "I'm beat. I've got a complicated case going and it's getting worse by the hour." She turned away from the group and began heading toward the doorway. "I'm going to go make myself that drink." Then, "Sadie," she half-ordered, "come join me in my office for a moment, won't you?" Before Sadie could respond, Mira swung back around. "By the way," she reminded, "nobody answered me. Who's playing hooky?"

The four people at the table instinctively conspired to present a unified front. They gave each other puzzled looks.

"What?" Greta asked.

Josef shrugged. "Say what?"

Mira rolled her eyes in exasperation. "I *said*, who's playing hooky? When I walked in just now you were talking about someone playing some—"

Sadie laughed. "Ohh, no, no, Mira. Cookie! I was suggesting that Savannah and I spend time *baking* some *cookies!*"

The woman near the door suspiciously eyed the group. "Oh. I see. I could've sworn I heard differently. Well," she relented with a wave of her hand, "like I said, I'm tired. I'm going to get that drink. I'll see you presently, Sadie." And she was gone. From the foyer, the group heard her call back. "That bread smells done, Greta!"

When Sadie glanced over at Savannah, the girl was biting her lips again. Sadie winked and raised a finger to her lips. "Shhh. She'll never know you're going to play hooky instead of bake cookies." Seeing the youngster fight to maintain control of her forced sober expression, Sadie got silly. "Of course, we could do both if you like. We could play hooky by baking cookies or we could play hooky and then bake cookies. Or we could bake the cookies first and then go do that play hooky thing. Or we could—"

The girl covered her mouth with her hand to keep from showing the grin that couldn't be controlled.

Greta was chuckling to herself as she rose to check on the bread.

Josef, shaking his head at hearing the familiar humor coming from his favored Brennan family sibling, stood. "Well, I can see this is going to work out just fine," he smiled to Savannah. "You can hide it all you want, little lady, but old Josef can already see the difference that your aunt is going to make." He laughed then. "Hooky. Cookie. That was a good one your auntie pulled on your mama, huh?"

Savannah nodded.

Tending to the task of removing the racks of fresh bread, Greta said, "Savannah, it's time you got yourself up to bed. After your Aunt Sadie's done talking to your mother, she'll go up and tuck you in."

Reluctantly, Savannah rose from the chair and carried her mug to the sink. She gave Sadie a questioning look.

Sadie nodded. "Sure, punkin. I'll be up in a few minutes. I wouldn't dream of not tucking you in."

Satisfied, the girl obediently left the room.

Sadie headed for the office. She hoped to God that it hadn't been turned into a sparse Oriental, feng-shui'ed room. She was spared dashed hopes. The spacious office hadn't been tampered with. Everything was just as she'd remembered growing up. It was just as her father had left it. Out of respect for their father, Mira had left the dark, oversized desk, the wall-to-wall bookcases, and heavy damask draperies.

When Sadie entered, Mira peered over her reading glasses. Setting down her sheaf of papers, she motioned her sister to make herself comfortable in the burgundy leather wingback. Sadie chose the edge of the desk as the perfect place to park herself.

Mira tilted her head. "Still contrary as ever, I see."

"No. I call it 'choice.'"

"Whatever." Without voicing a reprimand about the missed lunch date, she got straight to the point of her letter.

"Listen, I haven't a clue as to how you being here can do anything for Savannah, but her therapist seemed to think it was worth a shot. I know we don't get along famously, but there's no reason we need to be tripping over each other, is there? I'll be gone most of the time and I'll leave dealing with Savannah up to you."

"What, you're giving me carte blanche?"

"Within reason, of course. Savannah's always been attached to you. You two seem to have some kind of invisible connection of some sort. Maybe you know how to utilize that to her benefit."

"Spiritual bond," Sadie corrected. "It's generally called a spiritual bond."

"Excuse me?"

"That 'invisible connection of some sort.' It's a spiritual bond we share."

Mira smirked. "Spiritual, smiritual. I don't really give a damn what you call it. Just try to make it work, will you?"

Toying with the desk items, Sadie said, "I thought I'd take her to the museum. Has she been there recently?"

Moving the items back where they belonged, Mira asked, "How do I know? I'm not her tutor."

"No. No, you're not. You're her mother. And you don't know if she's been to the museum recently?"

Without a hint of guilt, Mira replied. "No, I certainly do not know. I can't keep up with everything the tutor does with her. I'm a busy woman."

"Too busy to know what's going on in your daughter's life?"

Mira impatiently huffed. "Oh, enough! See what I mean? The more we can stay out of each other's hair, the better. You just do whatever it is that you need to do to help Savannah." She reached for the martini glass and drained it. "I'm going to fix another one of these. You want one?"

Sadie shook her head.

"Didn't think so," came the quick reply. "Anyway, I am glad you're here," Mira admitted without choking on her words. "I think there just might be a slim possibility of Savannah responding to you. Stay as long as you like. Maybe through Halloween?" she suggested. "It'd be nice if you could get her interested in something celebratory. You know, maybe play up the spooky aspect of the holiday, get her hyped up about it." Mira snickered. "Hyped. That'd be a laugh. I haven't seen that girl hyped about anything in a long time."

"I'll see what I can do," Sadie said.

Mira rose from behind the desk and strode across the room. The thick pile of the plush carpeting muted her footfalls. When she reached the bar set up on the sideboard of the study, she flipped her hand as though shooing away a pesky fly. "Good. Great. Whatever." It was a dismissive gesture she'd picked up from their mother.

But there was no one left to dismiss. Recognizing an end to the discussion, Sadie had anticipated the detested mannerism and made a retreat back into the kitchen. There, she said her goodnights to Greta and Josef before climbing the grand staircase that curved up to the second floor.

Bypassing her own room, she went right to Savannah's. Standing in the doorway, she thoughtfully leaned against the jamb. Eyes roamed the child's familiar room. A soft glow came from the fairy night-light on the bedside table. Beside it was a replica of the cat statue that her niece had made her. Sadie smiled and tiptoed to the bed. She leaned down to comfort the troubled child lying beneath the rumpled coverlet.

The bed was empty. It wasn't unexpected.

Sadie turned off the night-light and headed toward her own room, where she found the child deep in slumber. It had been a long day and, after smoothing down the fiery wildness of her niece's thick hair, she snuggled in beside her.

*F*our

Tuesday

The weather in Chicago, like that of Maine, was unpredictable during the changing seasons. For Chicago, the chilling winds could fiercely blow off Lake Michigan, bringing sleet or early snow flurries. For Maine, the winds off the Atlantic could be just as fickle. Those residing in both regions were well accustomed to the wiles of nature where large bodies of water lapped against the land. Yet on this particular autumn day, the weather in the windy city was as balmy as late springtime.

People were out in lightweight fall jackets; the more hearty souls went without jackets altogether and had their shirt sleeves rolled up.

Mothers were taking advantage of the mild weather to stroll their babies up and down neighborhood streets.

Park benches were occupied by senior citizens soaking up the warming sunshine, claiming it to be a therapeutic treatment for arthritic bones.

Joggers and bicyclists were out in force, each respectfully dodging the other's space. Schoolyards were full of playful children reluctant to head back to class.

The windows of the blue van with the Maine license plate were rolled down and the light, sweet-scented breeze stirred the hair of the two redheaded occupants. As the passenger idly watched the passing scenery, the driver soon found herself lost in faraway thought.

It hadn't been a difficult task to sneak the young girl out of the house; everyone involved in the conspiracy felt no compunction over having done so. If truth be told, each of the guilty parties would readily admit to feeling more than a bit proud of themselves for pulling one over on the stern mistress of the house. Mira had already left the premises long before everyone else had gathered for breakfast. And when the tutor had arrived with a briefcase full of new lessons, she'd been pleased to have a day off in the middle of the week. In fact, she'd been thrilled to learn that she could expect to take the following week or so off and still be fully paid for her services. Anyone would naturally jump at the opportunity to have a surprise paid vacation, and the child's teacher was certainly no exception. Sadie caught herself grinning at the ease with which their first problem had been hurdled. If only all the rest would resolve themselves so effortlessly.

Now, as she leisurely drove along the scenic tertiary road and noticed the springlike beauty of the autumn day, visions of her once-favorite pastime lazily wove through her mind. Her smile broadened. She made the sudden decision to alter their plans for the day. She decided to make an impromptu detour. They wouldn't be heading straight for the museum as planned. They'd first revisit the heavily treed park that Sadie used to play in when young.

When the driver made the unexpected turn onto a secondary road, she immediately got a response from her young passenger. Savannah had leaned forward and given a quizzical look, as if to ask if perhaps the driver hadn't remembered the way to the museum.

Sadie flashed a reassuring smile. "I know what you're thinking. I didn't forget the way. It's such an incredible day," she said, swinging the vehicle into the park entrance. "I thought it might be nice to spend a little time in the old neighborhood park. Your mom and I used to play here a lot when we were girls. We were about your age when we came here the most often. We'd come and play all day long. Greta would bring us and she'd always have a picnic basket full of her delicious

Swiss specialties. Sometimes she'd even make a surprise treat for lunch, something to barbecue on the park grill." Sadie winked at her niece. "If I'd thought about stopping here earlier, Greta wouldn't have dared to let us out the door without handing us one of her packed baskets." Sadie impishly raised a brow and eyed the child. "Think she'll be upset when she finds out that we didn't give her a chance to do that for us this morning?"

The child made no audible response. Her body language remained unchanged. The stare of her green eyes was broken only by a blink or two of the long-lashed lids.

Although Sadie had already forgotten about the silent treatment she was supposed to expect from the child, she couldn't hide the slight frown of disappointment over the fact that the girl hadn't outwardly shown any sign of excitement with her little surprise detour. This new situation of the child's silence was going to take some getting used to, for her niece had always been full of exuberance, so animated and bursting with life. Her niece had been a nonstop talker, always fearful her thoughts would somehow flee before she could get them voiced. Now, Sadie decided that her best course for dealing with the new situation was to continue talking to Savannah as though she were involved in a normal two-way conversation. She figured that just because the child wasn't speaking back didn't mean that everyone else should remain mute as well. That would be no way to encourage communication and prompt responses from the child.

"Here we are," she said, nosing the vehicle into a parking spot shaded by a brilliantly colored sugar maple.

The two emerged from the van. Sadie offered her hand and the child seemed eager to take it. Hand in hand, the aunt and niece crossed the tarmac of the parking area and stepped onto the soft carpet of well-tended grass.

Sadie, suddenly finding herself flooded with happy childhood memories, pointed to the grouping of swing sets.

"Oh, gosh, Savannah," she exclaimed as the old memories sharply came into focus. She pointed off to the left. "Your mom and I would spend hours and hours on those swings over there. We'd actually tire Greta out with squeals of, 'Higher, Greta! Push us higher!' And poor Greta would have to finally admit that she was 'too pooped out' before finding her own empty swing to rest on for a while." With a chuckle, Sadie shook her head as additional memories filled out the vision.

"Gads, your mom would act really put out whenever Greta did that. She would purse her lips like this," she said, while imitating an exaggeration of the childish gesture, "then she'd pout over having to do the work herself."

Savannah mimicked her aunt's humorous facial expression.

"Yeah, you got it. Just like that. Your mom, of course, never could manage to get herself as high as Greta could push her. I guess she didn't like it that she couldn't do as well herself. Even when young, your mom was always secretly competing with everyone else. She turned everything into her personal competition. Anyway, when Greta rested, I'd usually slow myself down, jump off the swing, and go over to her. I'd give her little pushes on the back and she'd let out these soft, pleased sighs while she gently swung back and forth. I think it felt really good to her. Yeah," she concluded, "come to think of it, I think Greta enjoyed the swings as much as we did." Sadie squeezed the small hand. "I think your mom and I were more work for Greta than she ever let on. We could be quite a handful at times. I bet you aren't that much trouble for her, huh?"

The child made no reply.

"Well," the aunt said, ignoring the lack of response, "I, for one, happen to know that you could never be anything like the little monsters we were. And I hope your mom doesn't give you any baloney about what a perfect child she was. She could cook up some pretty outrageous schemes back then. She was a real rascal. She was forever getting us into hot water and I bet she never told you anything about those delinquent times, did she?"

Silence.

"Well, if you knew some of the mischievous things she did, you'd roll over laughing at them, you'd absolutely bust a gut to hear some of the scampish tricks she cooked up. Someday I'll tell you about all the trouble she got me in with her crazy pranks. You'd never know it to look at her now, but back then she was full of mischief all the time." Sadie raised her hand and daintily crooked her little finger. "She's grown too uppity and ta-ta now to admit that she'd ever been a troublemaker in her youth."

Sadie's peripheral vision caught the motion of the child's hand gesture. She'd crooked her little finger in imitation.

"Oh, yeah, to hear her tell it, she was nothing but the model child."

Sadie hadn't been denigrating her sister. The issue of Mira's haughty airs had been a conspiratorial matter between the aunt and niece for as long as the child had grown old enough to express her own opinions. They both loved Mira in their own ways, but like Sadie, Savannah was developing her own societal viewpoints that greatly opposed those of her mother's. Theirs were in no way shared by the other's elitist worldview.

The swing sets were being used. Only one was vacant. Savannah motioned for her aunt to take it.

"Oh, no, sweetie, you go ahead."

Determined, the girl remained firmly planted to her spot.

"All right. Okay. I'll go first if you want. Maybe one of these other kids will be getting off soon." After positioning herself squarely in the swing seat, she felt the gentle pressure of the child's hands on her back. "Are you pretending to be Greta?" She didn't expect to hear an answer. "That's just the way Greta always pushed us."

The little girl swinging beside Sadie thoughtfully gave up her swing. "Here," she offered, "I'm done. It's time for me to go now, anyway. My nanny's calling me." Due to the park's location, one could always spy nannies clustered together as they visited with one another while watching over their charges. Their conversations were most often about the hottest gossip of their wealthy employers' misdeeds.

Without uttering a word, Savannah smiled her thanks to the girl and sat down.

"There," Sadie said, "now we can both swing for a while. I always thought there was something magical about the motion of a swing. Have you ever thought about it? If you close your eyes, the motion has a mesmerizing effect. Don't you think it feels kind of hypnotic?"

When Sadie looked over at the girl, her eyes were closed.

They soon lost the matched rhythm of their swings and the idea of continuing a conversation lost its former appeal. Sadie didn't feel like shouting and she, too, closed her eyes.

Birdsong filled the air and pleasantly intermingled with the familiar park sounds of children's squeals and laughter. Teeter-totters squeaked. Off to their right, a young man was tossing a Frisbee to his playful black Labrador retriever. The dog proudly barked and yipped as the game caught the attention of amused onlookers.

For Sadie, the autumn scent on the light breeze brought vivid, seasonal images of the fall harvest to her receptive mind's eye. These, in turn, led her to wonder if Savannah would enjoy going to a pumpkin farm to pick out a few pumpkins for decoration and, of course, that very special one they could spend an evening carving together. She'd noticed that the house hadn't been festively outfitted for the holiday yet. That fact was glaringly obvious when Sadie had pulled up to the house the night before. Now the idea of sharing that activity with Savannah seemed like a good one. She didn't know how much Mira decorated for the different holidays any more. At one time, before David's death, she'd put extensive time and exhaustive energy into it and the place would look like the center spread in the holiday issue of *House Beautiful.* Now she thought it'd be more like Mira to completely ignore the once anticipated seasonal trimmings. She certainly wasn't helping her daughter by keeping the place in mourning. Sadie made a mental note to take her niece to the pumpkin farm and also help her choose a costume for the big night of trick-or-treating. And if they couldn't find the perfect outfit, they'd make one. Satisfied with the new plans, she smiled at the thought of immersing her niece in holiday gaiety.

The smile grew wider after she opened her eyes and scanned the bucolic scene of the park. Here in the autumn sunlight, life reflected the good and happier aspects it had to offer.

The smile vanished when her gaze was drawn to a glint that flashed beneath an old-growth oak. Sitting on a park bench, partially shaded by the rustling leaves of the brilliantly colored tree, was the same bag lady she'd seen when passing through the seedy section of the city.

Savannah, noticing a frown crease the smoothness of her aunt's brow, searched for the cause. The curious youngster intently looked back and forth from her aunt to somewhere in the near distance. Zeroing in on what she thought was the source of Sadie's interest, she focused her attention on an old woman sitting beneath a century-old oak that proudly displayed its blazing autumn colors.

The woman's faded army coat, which partially covered her long skirt, had seen better days. A mass of silver hair bushed out wildly from beneath a red knit hat that had something on it that twinkled in the sunlight. On the lady's feet, dirty tennis shoes were riddled with holes, exposing thin green socks beneath. The approach of a mangy, crippled dog caught the girl's attention as it slowly limped into her line of vision. It was pitifully hobbling on three of its legs toward the seated woman.

The girl looked back to her aunt. Her swing was slowing.

Savannah slowed hers as well.

Sadie noticed her niece's imitated response. She'd been so intent on the woman under the tree that she hadn't realized the girl had been watching her. "I didn't mean for us to stop," she said apologetically.

Savannah stared at her.

Sadie looked from Savannah, to the park bench, then back to the girl again. "It's nothing," she said, "let's not stop." Her swing was put in motion again.

The girl followed suit while keeping a sharp eye on her relative. She didn't quite believe her when she'd said it was "nothing." And once she realized that her aunt's attention was again drawn to the lady beneath the tree, Savannah also kept her eyes on the ragtag homeless woman.

Together they slowly swung back and forth.

In silence they watched the old woman call the limping mongrel to her. She appeared to be whispering in its ear while gently massaging its injured leg. The two on the swing set could tell that the woman was sympathetically cooing to the animal as it closed its eyes in obvious pleasure.

Sadie, observing the unfolding drama, was about to ponder the question of which was more pitiful, the homeless lady or the lame dog, when suddenly the dog began to vigorously lick the woman's face. Then, right before her eyes, it excitedly ran in circles before bounding across the park . . . on all four legs.

The blood drained from Sadie's face. Her swing stopped.

Savannah's mouth fell open. Her swing stopped. Awestruck, she looked to her aunt for an explanation.

Her aunt didn't appear to have one.

Their eyes were wide when they locked on each other's before simultaneously shifting back to the woman. They watched her stand, pick up her tapestry bag, then nonchalantly amble away in spanking new white tennis shoes.

Savannah watched her aunt frantically look about the park to see if anyone else had witnessed what they had.

Likewise, the girl checked around the park before catching Sadie's eye. She wanted to ask what it all meant, but couldn't bring herself to voice the question.

Sadie managed a weak smile before responding in a halting manner.

"What? There are, ah . . . there are logical answers to everything, sweetie. They're just . . . they're . . . well, some answers just aren't always right in front of us. They're not so obvious, that's all. Sometimes, it's a matter of properly interpreting what you see. That dog was most likely just fine all along. At some point in time, somebody probably taught it a great trick. You know, how to play injured, like how people teach their dogs to play dead. There's always a good reason for everything. It's important to avoid attributing mystery to things we can't immediately explain. Know what I mean? Anyway, that's important to remember because, at some point down the line, an explanation will become clear. When it does, then we're not embarrassed because we'd placed some sort of spookiness to it."

Sadie glanced at her watch and began striding away from the swings. Anxious to change the subject, she called back over her shoulder, "Come on, honey, let's get to that museum before we run out of time to do it justice. You want to see everything like always, don't you?"

With lightning speed, Savannah eagerly followed. She jumped off her swing and skipped to catch up with her aunt. She was a smart girl. She was a very smart girl. The explanation she'd been given for the seemingly healed dog sounded plausible enough, but there was more. Ohh, yes, there was more.

But the shoes, she wanted to blurt out, *what about her* shoes?"

Back in the van, Savannah continued to urgently stare her question at the driver. With all her might, she tried to convey what she so desperately wanted to ask. Maybe, if she stared hard enough, her aunt would explain where the bag lady's new shoes had come from.

The driver, lost in her own mix of swirling thoughts, was oblivious to the child's pressing body language. Or at least she appeared to be unaware that someone was staring a hole through her. Perhaps it was more like she was grateful for the girl's silent state because, if truth be told, she instinctively knew what the girl's unspoken question was and had no explanation to offer. She had no logical reason for the difference in the woman's footwear. They'd had their eyes on the elderly lady the whole time and neither of them had observed her changing shoes. She'd been sitting with tattered tennis shoes one minute and walked away wearing new ones a few minutes later. No matter how many times Sadie mentally replayed the drama she'd witnessed, the outcome was the same. She even distinctly recalled the size of the woman's carpetbag. It'd been as flat as a pancake the entire time. At no time had there been a bulge indicating something inside. There had been no extra pair of footwear hidden within the satchel.

A blaring horn and the screech of brakes yanked the driver from her mental maze. She slammed the brake pedal to the floor, automatically jutting out her arm in front of her precious passenger.

The meticulously coiffed driver of a silver Lexus glared hard at Sadie while completing her left turn in front of the blue commercial van.

Realizing she'd failed to notice the STOP sign, Sadie felt weak with relief that things hadn't turned out worse. "Oh, God," she nervously exclaimed, while giving her niece a cursory once-over. "I'm so sorry. Are you all right, honey?"

Savannah quickly recovered from the scare. She simply stared at her aunt.

Annoyed with herself for letting her thoughts become a dangerous distraction, Sadie snapped, "I said, are you okay?"

The girl hadn't been physically hurt in the near accident, but her feelings were bruised with the curtness she heard in the question. Not wishing to raise her beloved aunt's ire, she answered with a slow nod of the head.

Sadie pulled over to the curb to settle her rattled nerves. She rubbed the girl's shoulder. "You sure, baby? Are you sure you're okay?"

The nod was repeated.

The driver released a relieved sigh and bent forward. Resting her head on the steering wheel, she apologized for her carelessness.

"I'm so sorry about that, honey. It's not like me to pull dumb driving mistakes like that. It was a stupid thing to do, losing my concentration. I was a million miles away, lost in thought. I've had a lot on my mind lately. Even so, I should have been concentrating on what I was doing. I know better than to mentally drift off like that while driving. So many things are happening all at once. I've got to pull myself together. I've just got to get a grip." She raised her head. "Your aunt's a mess," she whispered with a mild hint of a self-deprecating smile. "I'll be okay." Reaching over to give the girl's knee a reassuring squeeze, she confidently added, "I'll be fine. We'll both be okay. You'll see. Whatever we both need to work through, we'll do it together."

Easing back into the sparse traffic of the suburban side street, Sadie again found reason to berate herself; she'd caught herself quietly thanking her lucky stars that Mira wouldn't be hearing of their close call. After all, her daughter wasn't talking at the moment. Yet, she reasoned in defense of the girl, knowing Savannah, Mira wouldn't have gotten wind of it even if her daughter's Chatty-Cathy mode had miraculously been switched back on. Although only eight, Savannah had already developed an aversion to people who were tattletales.

Once back in the heavy traffic of the main thoroughfare, Sadie vowed to keep her mind focused on driving down South Michigan Avenue. The vow was short-lived. She couldn't keep her thoughts from being pulled back to the strange incident in the park. Her mind kept being drawn back to the perplexing scene. The most baffling element of the whole thing was the issue of the woman's shoes. Those damn shoes. She was sure the old lady had been wearing torn tennis shoes when she'd first seen her. She was just sure of it. Yet, where had the brand new ones come from? Had Savannah seen something she herself had missed? Had her niece seen the woman change shoes and she herself had somehow missed it while her attention had been drawn to the dog? Should she bring up the subject? Then she realized that that idea wouldn't produce any satisfying resolution because the girl wasn't talking. Maybe too many things had happened over the last few weeks. Maybe she should just stop trying to make sense of every little befuddling oddity she saw and, instead, just take one day at a time. An *hour* at a time sounded like it had more possibilities for success. Yes, she'd just take one hour at a time and not clutter her mind with so many widely disparate issues at once. One thing at a time.

"One thing at a time," she softly muttered.

Savannah leaned forward and tilted her head in question.

Sadie caught her niece's eye. "Don't mind me, baby. I'm just talking to myself. People do that a lot when they get older, you know. It's nothing to worry about. Your auntie's not ready for the loony bin yet."

The girl's eyes widened. She suddenly pointed to something past the driver's side window.

Sadie snuck a quick look to her left. "Oops. Looks like we just passed the Art Institute of Chicago. I'll turn around up here." She covered her embarrassment with a light chuckle. "Right about now you must be wondering what's happened to your auntie? You must think your old auntie has turned into a real ditzy lady!"

Savannah's hand flew to her mouth. She didn't think that at all but also wanted to hide the grin caused by her aunt's funny statement. No matter what, she'd never think her aunt was ditzy. That was never a word that could be used to describe her aunt who she thought was the smartest and coolest woman on the entire planet. Oh, no, she didn't think that at all. Everything her aunt had seen in the park had been real, that much she knew was true. Trouble was, she didn't think either of them had any explanation for what they'd witnessed. The child's heart was bursting with happiness to be with her aunt again. She was finding herself feeling emotions that she hadn't felt in a long while. Hope stirred within her. She recognized the possibility that the time had come when she could no longer hold those feelings at bay. It was because of her Aunt Sadie. Excitement tickled the fringes of her self-imposed state of reserve. Most of all, it tempted her with a new motivation. Yes, she silently acknowledged, most of all, her impulse to speak was being tickled like a feather waved under her nose. Quickly, she held her breath for fear of sneezing. She wasn't quite ready to sneeze yet.

Although the Art Institute of Chicago was an imposing structure and could appear intimidating to the first-time visitor, Sadie and her niece were familiar with all of its unique nooks and crannies. As usual, they'd headed straight for their favorite section, the rooms dedicated to Egyptology. It'd been their habit to make that part of the building their first stop. The artifacts of this ancient culture had always been a strong draw for Savannah and this trip proved to be no exception.

Intently, the girl leaned over the glass display cases and, with the depth of interest a scholar would show, studied the papyrus scrolls. She spent a considerable time staring at the hieroglyphics preserved on stone fragments. Each time they'd been to the museum and Sadie had observed her niece doing this, she found herself pondering the same inexplicable question. Why did Savannah have such an affinity for this time period? Of course, the question had been repeatedly asked in the past when the girl had been able to speak, but even then she couldn't give a definitive reason. The only response Sadie ever received was a shrug of the shoulders. The attraction had been a mystery to Savannah, as well.

Sadie hung back to let her niece wander the exhibit at will. She didn't want to rush the girl, who appeared to be lost in the distant past, overcome with a great sense of awe for the long-ago time. Now, while the enrapt Savannah methodically went from one display to another, Sadie quietly followed a few paces behind. Once in a while, when Savannah seemed particularly engrossed with a specific item, Sadie would make some kind of explanatory comment. Though she was a masterful antiques dealer with a wealth of knowledge, this particular era was not within her realm of expertise. However, her own shared interest in it did provide her with a more rounded background than most of the casual museum visitors. She had the complex sequence of the Pharaohnic dynasties down pat and, when appropriate, would offer Savannah various little-known tidbits of information as they strolled throughout the rooms. Of course, the mummy which appeared to be peacefully resting within the elaborately decorated sarcophagus was always the highlight of the Egyptian section. And little Savannah, forever in the habit of increasing her level of anticipation, felt pride in her strength of will each time she managed to savor the viewing of it until last.

Now, as the two stood before the highly decorative coffin, Sadie's thoughts drifted back to the time she'd flown into the city for the express purpose of taking her niece to see the touring Tutankhamen exhibit when it had come to the Art Institute. She recalled how excited the girl had been when she'd phoned her aunt, stumbling over her words in an effort to get out the wonderful news of the upcoming event. When Sadie had told her that she would make the trip to Chicago to take her, Savannah hadn't been able to eat or sleep for days before the scheduled visit. Now, as she watched her niece study the fragile ancient wrappings, she wondered if the girl hadn't spent several past lifetimes living in the Nile region. How else could this magnetic draw be so pervasively strong in the girl? Her musings were broken by the soft sound of a long, extended sigh coming from her niece. Sadie looked down at her and smiled. "Pretty amazing, huh?"

Savannah nodded. Her eyes were misty. It was clear that she'd been mentally transported back to a long ago time. It was hard to tell for sure because whatever thoughts—or memories—flooded the girl's mind were relegated to the sounds of silence. She wouldn't be sharing them anytime soon.

Savannah reached for her aunt's hand as a sign she was ready to move on.

Together they left the exquisite rooms devoted to the era of pyramids and palaces in the sand to head for the second-most-interesting exhibit on their must-see list.

In the Department of Decorative Arts, a wide range of artifacts from primitive cultures on the African continent, the Pacific islands, and pre-Columbian America were displayed. These were also of great interest to Savannah and they'd spent considerable time wandering through this particular section of the museum, where the girl seemed to be magnetically drawn to early renditions of the prevailing deities of the time. These deities mostly consisted of a wide variety of goddess images. When Sadie noticed the transfixed Savannah staring especially long at a specific statuette behind the glass display, she sidled up beside her niece.

"These are particularly rare pieces," she informed. "They remind me of a primitive piece I acquired for Tina's birthday one year." Sadie gave her niece's hand a little tug. "You know how crazy Tina is for goddess figures."

Savannah smiled and rolled her eyes.

"Anyway, when I first saw it, I initially thought it'd come from somewhere around the vicinity of the Yucatan Peninsula. I was way off. One thing I quickly learned in my business is that you can't be right all the time. I'd shown the piece to a friend of mine who specializes in those types of figurines and she'd said it'd originated in the Peruvian Highlands. She'd been quite amazed that I'd had it. Though she never actually asked, I think she wanted to buy it from me. Evidently, it was quite a rare piece." Sadie grinned. "Guess the person I bought it from didn't know what a find he had. At the time, neither of us knew that it would've brought thousands if it'd been offered at auction. That was one time I lucked out. I paid the eight hundred bucks and wrapped it for Tina." The aunt pointed to the figurines in the display case. "This one looks a lot like Tina's." She leaned closer to read the placard placed at the feet of the pregnant statuette. "Look. It's dated 4000 B.C.E. Says it's an image of Putanni, Goddess of Women's Primal Wisdom." She glanced down at the girl. "Mmm, sounds like she was one major deity to me. What do you think? You think she was the big Peruvian kahuna back then?"

Savannah's eyes grew as round as full moons as she nodded. She nodded even though she really wanted to correct her aunt by clarifying that a kahuna was a Hawaiian term for a male priest. Against her better judgment, she let it pass.

Sadie smiled. "Me, too. Well," she caught herself, "not really a kahuna, exactly, because a kahuna is a chief, a male-type person. I guess as long as we're going for accuracy, we should say that Putanni was the supreme goddess over all the others."

Savannah seemed relieved that the correction was made. She was quick to nod her approval before pulling her aunt to another display case. She pointed to a primitive drawing which the placard explained as being the Peruvian culture's image of the Primal Mother.

When Sadie laid eyes on the faded drawing, she experienced a shock of déjà vu. The image was oddly similar to the token she recalled toying with at Tina's. She didn't want to go there. She'd left all that behind in Maine. She was not going to dwell on those stupid runes while she was here. Why had Savannah pointed out this particular image? What drew her interest to it? Wishing to stop the flood of unwanted questions, she tapped her niece's shoulder. "We'd better get moving if you want to get through the gallery section. We've spent more time than usual in these departments."

Savannah detected a hint of something bordering nervousness in her aunt's behavior, yet without being able to express what she'd noticed, or ask what was wrong, she followed close on Sadie's heels. They quickly left the room that she hadn't realized held too many whispered secrets, too many clues to Sadie's future. Savannah knew when something was bothering her aunt and, she silently reasoned, although her dearest relative had come to Chicago for the purpose of helping her, she felt her Aunt Sadie required her own form of aid. Savannah secretly hoped that, together, they'd end up helping each other. She knew that her aunt wasn't the type to whine about her problems, especially to an eight-year-old. She was convinced she'd have to unravel this mystery all by herself. That meant she'd have to keep an extra close eye on her. She'd keep her ears open, to the wall, if necessary. Yes, she'd keep a good watch and be extra aware of everything that her aunt said and did, even pay extra attention to her body language. A surge of excitement rippled through her. The sensation took her by surprise. She hadn't experienced that kind of reaction in a long time. Now, every nerve ending seemed to twitch with anticipation. She suddenly had something in her life to spark her interest and she loved the feel of it—the sensation of purpose. A real-life mystery to unravel. She was determined to discover what was bothering her aunt and help her with it.

Savannah narrowed her eyes and allowed a wry smile to curl the corners of her mouth. She liked the invigorating feel that this new purpose gave her. *Yeah,* she silently vowed, *I'll be the best sleuth ever. Just like Nancy Drew!*

The other museum visitors automatically assumed that the two redheads entering the gallery of the great master painters were mother and daughter. Though in error, that assumption was a natural reaction for anyone seeing the two together. They were used to it, for their shared physical characteristics were so much alike that the child appeared to be a miniature of the older one. They also shared mannerisms, including the gift of gab; the only difference this time was that one readily voiced her thoughts while the other remained mute by choice.

When perusing the rooms of the great masters, the two had developed a routine of viewing. Their pace quickened through the gallery of impressionistic works. The first time they'd been to the museum together, Savannah had plenty to say about the style. She didn't like it. In no uncertain terms, she'd made up her mind about the art technique when she commented that she didn't know what all the fuss was about because it reminded her of art pieces left unfinished. It had no flow, she'd decided. In her words, it was a silly, jerky way to paint.

So as they passed through the impressionistic rooms, neither one bothering to look right or left, Sadie remembered that her niece had once expressed a liking for the works of Toulouse Lautrec. Without breaking stride, Sadie said, "You don't have to look at the Van Goghs, but did you know that he and Toulouse Lautrec knew one another?"

The girl responded with a look of genuine surprise.

"It's true. I believe they even shared living quarters for a time when they were both young, struggling artists waiting for public recognition. You know, waiting for the world to appreciate their talents. When you get older, you may want to read more about some of the tribulations the old masters lived through for their art. Anyway, I read about the two artists' connection in a book about Van Gogh's life by Irving Stone. It's called *Lust for Life.*"

Savannah rolled her eyes.

Sadie grinned. "Yeah, I know. That's a pretty racy title to an eight-year-old, but let me remind you that I mentioned it as suggested reading when you're *older*. Even though you don't care for the impressionists' way of interpreting what they see, it's interesting to understand what some of them went through, the terrible living con-

ditions they put up with for their craft. Van Gogh endured much suffering for his. I wouldn't be too quick to discount all he went through
for his faith in his creations. Don't forget, his style was unique for the
times. In spite of everyone who pleaded with him to change it, he
stayed true to his own way of seeing the world. He had to express it in
his own way. For him, it was that or nothing. There's something to be
said for that kind of unwavering dedication to one's convictions."

By this time, Savannah was heading for a bench in front of a
Rembrandt. They'd come to the rooms she loved best to tarry in. She
was drawn to the masters who, she'd once said, showed depth and
brought out people's emotions. The overall colors of these masterpieces never had the brightness of the later painters, but she thought
that the darker, muted tones were more soothing. She'd once
expressed the idea that she liked how the Rembrandts and Renoirs
were mysterious to her, that their light and shadowy scenes had a way
of drawing the viewer into more than the picture itself. When she'd
innocently expressed these thoughts, Sadie had had her perception of
Savannah's intellect verified—she'd always thought the child was
exceptionally bright.

Now the two sat in silence while admiring the works of those
Savannah considered to be the true masters. Once or twice, the girl got
up to closely inspect an element of the artwork. She'd return to the
bench and continue appraising it. She'd lose herself in the scene.

As Sadie watched her, she wondered if her niece was imagining anything. She wondered if Savannah was placing herself in the scene, creating a complex story line around the picture. It was a pastime the girl
often indulged in. The ability to speculate and extrapolate, she noticed,
was one of her niece's stronger traits. Sadie wished the girl weren't
caught in the uncharacteristic silence. She would've loved to have heard
the intricate tale Savannah wove around this particular piece of art. She
made a mental note to stop at the gift shop to see if they sold prints of
it.

Abruptly, Savannah stood. She pointed to her stomach, then her
mouth.

"You hungry?" Sadie asked, before checking her watch. "I didn't
realize it was so late. We shouldn't have stopped off at the park like
we did. I'm sorry about that. I guess we didn't leave ourselves enough
time to see the whole museum. We need to get you some dinner, huh?"

Savannah nodded.

"But," Sadie said, "we need to check out the gift shop before we leave. There's something I want to see if they have in stock. It won't take long."

The aunt quickened her step as they headed along the corridor toward the gift shop.

The niece skipped alongside, stomach growling in anticipation of being satiated.

When they entered the shop, a commotion was in progress at the sales counter. It involved the clerk and an irate customer wearing worn and dusty cowboy boots.

The two newcomers stopped dead in their tracks. Stunned at the scene being played out before them, they gave each other bewildered looks, then watched the drama unfold.

They observed a second clerk use her transceiver radio handset. She was calling for assistance from museum security.

As the ruckus began attracting a crowd of curious visitors behind them, Sadie and Savannah listened to the agitated, elderly customer berate the clerk while waving an art print beneath the employee's nose. The print seemed to be the subject of the customer's ire. It appeared to be extremely offensive to her.

"*This*, I tell you, is all *wrong!*" the vexed woman shouted. "You've got to believe me. This artist got it all *wrong!*"

The clerk valiantly tried to calm her. "Ma'am," she softly said, "I can't do anything about a print. It's how the original was done. It's famous. It can't be altered. You'll have to—"

The customer fluttered the print faster in the air, then held it in front of the clerk's nose. "Look," she spouted, jabbing a finger at the card stock, "see that arm? That hand? It's a *man's* arm and hand!"

"Yes, ma'am. It's supposed to be a man's hand and arm. It's supposed to be—"

"God?" the customer spat. "You telling me that it's supposed to be *God?*"

The clerk was getting desperate for the troops to arrive. Her customer was getting more agitated by the moment. "Yes, ma'am. It's supposed to be God in the picture. Now if you'll just calm down a minute and—"

The onlookers were pressing forward to get a better view of the commotion. They were interested in seeing what print the woman was so riled up over. They didn't have long to wait.

As if hearing the collective thought of the crowd milling behind her, the angry woman spun away from the clerk to face the gathered patrons. With purpose she strode over to them.

"Look!" she ordered. "Look! Look! *Look!* Do you people *see* this?" she asked, holding up a print of a portion of Michelangelo's Sistine Chapel work. The print was of the selected section called *The Creation of Adam.* "It's all *wrong*, I tell you! He painted it all *wrong!*"

The gaggle of curious patrons was eased aside to make room for a couple of broad-shouldered security men. When they reached the wisp of a woman, they positioned themselves on either side of her and spoke softly.

"It's going to be all right, ma'am. Everything's fine. You can come with us and we'll help you find your way out."

One of the officers wrestled the print from the disgruntled woman's grasp and passed it over to the relieved clerk. It wasn't in salable condition anymore. She tossed it in the trash can behind the counter and finally released her anxiety with a long sigh.

As the security pair gently maneuvered the frail-looking woman past the parting crowd, the old lady cranked up the volume of her protest; she'd raised it several decibels. The looming presence of the burly officers hadn't fazed her. No one, it seemed, was going to intimidate her into silence. She continued to rant about the print that so badly offended her sensibilities.

"It's all *wrong*, I tell you! You people just don't *get* it! The lot of you, you just don't get it! You *never* will! That arm and hand in the picture . . . they're *supposed* to be a *woman's!* God has a *vagina!* God's a *woman*, you idiots! It should be *MotherGod* in that painting. The *Mother*God breathed spirit into Adam!"

The people in the crowd began dispersing, but not before having their say.

"Crackpot," one muttered, shaking his head. "Crazy fruitcake."

"Nut case oughtta be locked up," said someone else.

"You can say that again," an elderly man whispered. "A nice, warm and comfy padded room is what that one needs. Poor lost soul like her shouldn't be left out on the streets."

"Aggh, street trash like that shouldn't be allowed in here where decent folk come to appreciate good culture," another grumbled. "That ilk always find their way in here on Tuesday because Tuesday's a free admission day. They should get rid of free Tuesdays, that's what they should do. I bet that'd keep the place clear of the derelicts."

A group of young men snickered beneath their breaths. "God has a vagina!" one quietly mimicked.

"Yeah, right, lady," another said. "You wish."

Then one fellow elbowed his pal. "Hey, I've got a good one for you. If God has a vagina, the world's in a shitload of trouble when she's PMS-ing!"

Sadie and Savannah ignored the crass comments. They didn't think the punch line was the least bit funny. They were too intent on watching the woman in the army coat and red hat being escorted to the nearest exit. On her feet were a pair of highly polished, hand-tooled cowboy boots that looked as though they'd just come out of the box.

They looked at one another at the same time.

Savannah's eyes were round as full moons.

Sadie gave the child a look of warning. "Don't go there. Don't even go there. I've decided not to check out the gift shop after all. It wasn't that important, anyway. If I recall correctly, we were on a mission to get us something to eat. You choose. A restaurant or home?"

The child remained mute and chose not to communicate with body language.

"Okaaay," Sadie sighed, "I'm for heading home. I don't know about you, but I believe I've had enough bizarre experiences for one day. I'm sure Greta's got the fridge chock full of just about anything we might want. Is home okay with you?"

Savannah tended to agree with Sadie's decision. She didn't feel like going anywhere else but home, either. It had been a most extraordinary day. An understanding smile tipped the corners of her bow mouth. She surreptitiously slipped her hand into her aunt's and, together, they walked out into the amber light of the lowering autumn sun.

After dinner, Sadie played video games with her niece until it was long past her routine bedtime. Mira had left a message that she was going to be late getting home again, and Sadie thought that the hours her sister kept were just fine with her. They were actually going to work out well for everyone concerned. They precluded opportunities for arguments and also kept the mother in the dark regarding her daughter's new hooky playing.

Sadie tucked her niece into bed before retiring to her own room. Though she was beat, she knew she wouldn't be able to sleep until she placed her promised call to Tina.

She made the call from the phone in her room. She let it ring three times before slamming the receiver down. "I can't do this," she whispered. "I can't tell her about the bag lady. Then again, if I don't tell her, she'll sense I'm keeping something from her. She'll bug me until she wheedles it out of me. No, I'm not ready to talk about it."

Unsure of her decision, she paced the floor recalling how she'd promised to call her friend to tell her she'd safely arrived. The call was already a day late in coming.

Exasperated with her dilemma, she picked up the phone and dialed again.

Once more she dropped it in the cradle before it was answered.

She nearly jumped out of her skin when the shrill ring of the phone vibrated on the night stand.

She reluctantly answered it. "Hello?"

"I think we got a bad connection or something," the familiar voice cleverly hedged. "Thank goodness for modern inventions, huh?"

"Modern inventions?"

"Yeah, caller ID. You were supposed to call me last night. I called during the day and Greta said you were out with Savannah. How come you never called when you got in? How did the trip go? Where'd you two go? How is she?"

Sadie sank onto the edge of the bed. She'd forgotten about caller ID and she silently cursed the advancements of technology.

"That was quite an interrogation. Which question do you want me to answer first?"

"Take your pick, we got all night."

"I didn't call last night because we were up late," she lied, "and, well, I guess I just spaced it out. Sorry about that."

"You better be. All sorts of sordid scenarios went through my mind. I worry about you, you know."

"I know. I said I was sorry. Anyway, the trip went fine. I'd taken a detour, cut off the interstate to take a rural route. I stopped by a pond and did some deep thinking. I'm convinced that Savannah is the Dove Woman. It's the only thing that makes any sense."

"Nope. Sorry to burst your bubble, but, more times than not, we short-sighted people can only draw conclusions from the knowns in our lives. The runes are pointing to something unknown, something that's going to enter your life."

Sadie's mind was too overloaded from the personally bedeviling events of the day. "Whatever," she sighed in resignation. "What else was I supposed to answer? I'm so beat my brain is fried."

"Where'd you and your little mute mini-me go today?"

Sadie was so nervous about concealing the homeless woman from her friend that she blurted out the verbal cut-and-paste version to get it over with.

"Well, we started out for the museum and when we neared the park where Mira and I always played in when young, I pulled in. The neighborhood park you and I played in. The one where we first met?"

"Yeah . . ." Tina said with sparked suspicion at her friend's rushed version.

"So anyway, we had a good time on the swings. I told her how Greta used to push Mira and me. Being there again brought back a lot of good memories. Then we went to the museum and came home for dinner."

"Uh-huhhh."

"Savannah's being tutored at home instead of attending school. Mira thought it was best if she was away from so many other kids and could concentrate better through a one-on-one study session in the home where she'd feel more comfortable. She hasn't said a word, but she does occasionally use body language to communicate when she wants to."

"Uh-huhhh," Tina uttered, waiting to hear whatever Sadie was trying to keep herself from revealing.

It wasn't going to be forthcoming without some tugging. Sadie rambled on. "I'm encouraged, though. I'm encouraged because there was a time when I was sure she was bursting at the seams to say something. I think speech is floating right beneath the surface. At least, I hope it is."

Silence.

"Did you hear me?"

Silence. Waiting.

"What?"

"You know what."

The game was up. Sadie knew she'd been tagged, yet still tried for a cover-up.

"I'm tired, Tina. I'm just tired. It was a long three-day drive and then today we spent the whole day on the go. Tomorrow I plan on taking her to Grant Park. You remember, the one with the big Buckingham Memorial Fountain."

Silence.

Sigh. "Why do you always do this to me? I told you how the trip went. I told you what we did, and how Savannah's doing. What's going on with you?"

"Me? I'm just sitting here waiting for you to fill in all the blanks you so conveniently tried to skim over. Admit it. You're squirming right now. Just spill everything and get it over with. I'm all ears."

It was true. Sadie was squirming. She'd been nervous to make the call because her friend was too perceptive for her own good. Secrets were something nobody withheld from Tina Glaston. Nobody understood that more than Sadie. Tina would harp and hound until all the facts were wheedled out of her and in the open.

Sadie wasn't sure where to begin.

Tina patiently waited through the prolonged silence on the other end of the line.

Finally, the story began in a halting manner. "There was this . . . this woman."

"Now we're getting somewhere. I'm listening. Take your time."

And the encounters with the homeless woman were detailed, including the first time Sadie had seen her when passing through the Combat Zone of South Chicago. When the tale was finished, there was a pause on the other end of the line.

"You there?" Sadie asked.

"Mmm, I'm processing."

Sadie waited. Her friend did a lot of processing.

"Okay, let's take this one step at a time. We can't say that the woman actually healed the dog because you can't be certain that it wasn't just doing a hobbling trick. So let's ignore that aspect.

"Now," Tina continued, "the bit about the shoes . . . that's somewhat more complicated. Let's again discount the first time you both noticed the shoe event. I mean, it is possible that the lady managed to change them without either of you observing the act. So . . . so far, the sighting in the park can't positively be associated with any type of unexplainable or paranormal activity. Let's stay together here. Do you agree with my assessment so far?"

Sadie could always depend on her friend to be pragmatic when it came to the unexplained. She used a down-to-earth, analytical approach that always made logical sense of any allegedly nonsensical event.

"I guess so," she relented. "I suppose those two events weren't so odd after all."

"Good. Now. Now, the museum situation is a bit more grey. You say you had your eyes on this woman the entire time?"

"Yes. When we entered the gift shop I naturally checked out the footwear when I realized who the troublemaker was. She wasn't wearing the new tennis shoes from this morning. She was wearing old, scruffy cowboy boots. They were actually full of dust. I remember that so clearly because, when I saw them, it occurred to me that they looked like boots a cowboy had worn rounding up cattle. Yes, the boots were definitely well used."

"Okay. And you said that when she was being escorted out of the shop she was wearing brand new boots. What were your words? Hand-tooled, shiny, new boots that looked like they'd just been taken out of the box?"

"Uh-huh. Yes, they were brand new. I recall thinking that they were so new that a walking crease hadn't even been made on the topside across the toes. Brand new, Tina."

"You mentioned something about some sort of carpetbag or knitting satchel? Could you be more specific on that point?"

"Sure. She always has this bag with her. I don't know, it's like a fabric pouch with a wooden handle. You've seen them. The fabric is plush, somewhere between a velvet and chenille with a flowery tapestry design. What's so odd about it, is that it always looks flat. It always looks completely empty."

"Have you ever seen her without it?"

"Never. She's had it with her every time I've seen her. Each time it's been as flat as a sheet of paper."

Silence.

"Tina?"

"I'm here. Okay, I'm stumped. I need more time to think on that one. What about the things she said in the gift shop? First I want some surrounding details. To start with, how did she sound? What was the quality of her voice. What type of diction did she speak with? How articulate did she sound to you?"

"Gads, you're asking me a lot of things I hadn't given thought to. I don't know. I suppose she sounded articulate. I mean, she certainly didn't slur her words like a drunk or someone strung out on street drugs." Sadie grinned. "She certainly didn't have any reservations about speaking her mind, that's for sure. She was very upset over that print, really obsessing over it."

"And the print was of Michelangelo's *The Creation of Adam*?"

"Yes. The one with God's finger touching Adam's."

"And the woman was claiming that the hand of God was supposed to be a female's?"

"Yes. That was the whole point of her tirade."

"Mmm. You know what? Well . . . let me first ask you this. Did she appear educated to you?"

"Educated! How was I supposed to tell that? She was a raving lunatic!"

"Watch yourself there, girlfriend. Every person walking this planet has ranted over something at one time or another. Let's not prejudge just yet, okay?"

Sadie's shoulders slumped. Of course her friend was right. They'd both been guilty of ranting over things in their pasts.

"Reprimand accepted," she conceded. "I don't think there was anything in her demeanor or speech that gave any clue to her intelligence. Except that she did articulate her words very well. She didn't slaughter them like a lot of street people do. She didn't use slang or street talk. Well," Sadie corrected, "maybe shouting the word vagina could be considered street talk to some people. Other than that, no. Like I said, her words came out extremely clearly and well articulated."

Tina asked, "Since when is voicing the word vagina any more street talk than saying penis? This isn't the Victorian era anymore. The *Vagina Monologues* was a big hit and had a long run. In fact, it's still being produced and drawing more crowds. People have grown up; they're not snickering schoolchildren anymore when it comes to body parts. At least this woman used the correct term instead of slang like you really hear everywhere you go. Was she clean?"

"Clean?"

"Yes, clean. Clean, as in, hygiene. Was her hair tangled and full of nits? You said she was escorted right past you. Was there anything odious about her? Did she smell bad? Unwashed? Did you notice her fingernails? Were they dirty? That army coat. Was it filthy?"

"I said I was tired. You're forcing a lot of recall here."

"Believe me, it's important. Force yourself."

Sadie shut her eyes tight as she tried to recall the physical details of the woman.

"I don't recall getting hit by any offensive odor when she passed me. I suppose that means she wasn't unclean. The hair. There were no tangles because it bushes out full like it'd just been washed and wind-dried. It's quite long. I remember thinking that it was odd for a woman of her age to have such a full head of hair. Most elderly people have scant, thinning hair.

"Anyway, let's see . . . the army coat had seen better days, of course, but it was clean. When she held up the print for the onlookers to see, her fingers were somewhat misshapen with arthritis, but the cuticles and nails were clean."

"Did you ever actually look directly into her eyes?"

"Yessss?" Sadie hedged. "Are you going to tell me that I've been bewitched now?"

"Oh, get real. About the eyes, were the whites clear?"

"Yes."

"What color were the irises?"

No answer was voiced.

"The irises? Their color?"

"I heard you. I'm just trying pin down a word for them. They were grey. No, blue."

"Make up your mind. Which were they?"

"Both. In the park I could see how blue they were. In the museum they were an even deeper, more vivid blue. But when I first saw her walking down the street, they seemed very grey, like an overcast winter sky. Why? What's the color of her eyes have to do with anything?"

"Nothing in particular. I'm just trying to get an accurate overall mental image of her."

Sadie didn't comment. And when there was an extended period of silence between them, she knew her friend was filtering the collected information through her psychic sieve. She respectfully waited for the verdict.

Finally Tina cracked the tension with a statement outlining her determinations.

"My initial sense is that the woman is more intelligent than she appears. She obviously gets around. One time she's in the worst of the worst of South Chicago and then she's seen in an upscale park in one of the wealthiest neighborhoods. Then she appears at the core of culture, the museum. What is she doing showing up in such diverse places? How does she get around? She maintains cleanliness about her person, and is articulate in her speech pattern. And she clearly has some very deep philosophical ideas about the spiritual realm. The only hitch to the whole issue of her is the bit about those cowboy boots. I need to think on that some more. I'll have to get back to you on that one."

"What makes you think she has some deep philosophical ideas?"

Tina laughed. "She believes God has a vagina! Or did you forget about that already?"

"Why is that deep? Wouldn't *radical* be a more fitting term?"

"Radical? Do I need to remind you that multicultural history is rife with female deities, the goddesses who were worshiped and revered for centuries before Christianity became the newborn religion?"

Sadie felt stupid. "I said I was tired. Yeah, all those goddesses. I guess the old woman knows something about them, as well. Or," she began without finishing.

"Or what?"

"Or she could just be an old feminist trying to alter history."

Tina didn't respond to her friend's comments. She was looking down at the MotherGod rune, the token Sadie had held for so long. Tina had placed it on her table. Of their own volition, pieces of the puzzle were drawing themselves together as if they'd had a life of their own.

"Did you hear me?" Sadie asked. "I said she could be an old feminist or, for that matter, even an old—"

"I heard. My guess is that she knows a lot more than you're currently willing to give her credit for. Keep your eyes peeled, girlfriend. I have a feeling that you've not seen the last of your bag lady. I don't think she's as crazy as she may appear. I know you're tired. I'm going to let you go. Sleep tight. And don't forget, call me. Keep me posted."

Sadie promised that she would; then an image of the woman's hat came to mind. "Oh, wait a minute! I forgot to tell you about her hat."

"Hat?"

"Yes. Remember I said that the glint from her hat was what caught my attention in the park? Well, when she passed us in the museum, I got a good look at what caused it. She has a gaudy pin clipped to her knit hat. It's a piece of costume jewelry that catches the light."

"What kind of pin?"

"A large—huge—imitation garnet or something. Cheap stuff. Red-colored glass. It's in a silver filigree setting."

"You sure it's a cheap costume piece?"

"Oh, now who needs to get real? Come on, Tina, the woman's a street person, for Christ's sake. The stone's as big as a silver dollar. If it'd been the real McCoy, she would've been rolled for it the first time she pinned it to her hat!"

"You've got a point. If it's as big as you say, it'd be worth a fortune. If she had something that valuable she wouldn't be homeless. Well, like I said, keep me posted. Sleep tight."

When Sadie finally slipped between the cool sheets and wearily rested her head on the pillow, the last thing she remembered before falling asleep was the twinkling glint from the pin on the old woman's red hat. In her dreamscape, it had transformed into the North Star sparkling among the winking starshine of a clear, crisp autumn night.

And Savannah, excited to have begun her new sleuthing, backed away from her aunt's doorway. Striving to be quiet as a mouse, she tiptoed back to her room.

Five

Wednesday

During breakfast the following morning, Sadie never mentioned her idea of taking her niece to Grant's Park. She'd awakened with an epiphany. She'd take Savannah to the pumpkin farm instead. Grant's Park would always be there; holiday activities wouldn't. The Swiss couple thought the plan was ingenious. And when the child was asked if she'd like to go there, the girl's face lit up. Excitement sparked from rounded eyes. Sadie had struck gold with her idea.

Margaret and Rory Foster had both come from a long line of those who devoted their lives to working the land. Being close to the earth and working the soil had been in their blood from the time they'd carried toy trowels and toddled barefoot behind their mothers in the family vegetable gardens. Their parents, grandparents, and great-grandparents had all been hard-working farmers who had instilled a love for agriculture in their children.

When the young Margaret Harris, known to locals as Maggie, inherited her parents' farm and later married the rugged-looking Rory Foster forty-seven years before, they'd combined their abutting property. By doing this, they'd created one of the largest parcels of farmland outside Chicago. Of their four children, three offspring likewise inherited the drive to work the land and had successful nearby farms of their own. Though their parcels were much smaller than their parents', the three children now had families of their own and, it appeared, those children had the blood of farmers running in their veins. When harvest time arrived, they'd all gather together to help one another bring in the fruits of their labors.

Maggie and Rory worked the land from spring to fall, but for them, their greatest joy and reward for their hard labor came in the autumn when their fields rang out with the laughter and squeals of children. Even the adults who accompanied the youngsters couldn't successfully hide their childlike enjoyment of the annual trip to the pumpkin farm.

For more years than anyone around could remember, the Fosters' was the place to go in the fall to handpick one's holiday pumpkin. The elderly couple grew so many pumpkins that it seemed their fields were dotted with bright orange for as far as the eye could see. They never had to advertise. Only through word of mouth had the Foster place become the state's most famous farm.

Elementary school teachers from dozens of surrounding counties brought scores of classes on afternoon field trips. The small members of girls' and boys' scouting organizations looked forward to their scheduled visit to the Fosters'. Special days were always reserved for physically handicapped and mentally challenged children. On those days, Maggie and Rory would take special joy in accompanying the young ones through the fields and helping to carry their choices back to the parked vans. And, although the public was welcome to stop by anytime, Wednesdays and the weekends were generally reserved for the public at large to roam the fields. Every day of the week, Maggie and Rory would be out among the excited children, helping them choose the perfect pumpkin to carve.

Carefully weaving her way among the orange orbs at her feet, Savannah Woodward was on her third excursion through the fields. Each time she returned, she headed off in a different direction after leaving her precious find with Maggie to save for her at the roadside stand. Her first find was for herself and Sadie to make into a jack-o-lantern. After much deliberation between the two, they'd agreed that they'd discovered the one in a thousand that best suited their requirements. That one, she decided, was special. It would go in the front room window. The second one was smaller; it was destined to be the centerpiece for a seasonal arrangement with gourds and autumn leaves around it on the dining room table.

Now came the hard part. Now came the girl's search for the three most perfect specimens of them all. These three had to be just right. None of them could have any dings or mars on their skins. They couldn't be lopsided shapes nor could they stand crooked. They couldn't have a single imperfection. And, of course, each had to have a proper stem which curved just so.

Intrigued by the elusive perfection her niece appeared to be seeking in her search for the mysterious special pumpkins, Sadie patiently followed the girl. She watched her scrutinize each one she was initially attracted to. If it didn't pass muster, Savannah would gently place it back where she'd found it and continue her quest.

After she had observed the girl reject more than a dozen, curiosity got the best of her.

"Why do these have to be so perfect?" Sadie asked, forgetting the girl was not going to be able to give a satisfactory reply without talking.

Savannah's response was a wide grin bordering on mischievousness. It was a look one gives when concealing a deep secret.

"Okay," Sadie teased, "fine with me if you don't want to share." She pretended to have injured feelings. "I'm just a nobody. I don't need to know."

The girl, who knew teasing when she heard it, snickered over her aunt's silliness.

The mid-morning sunlight bouncing off the girl's hair brought out the brighter red highlights, making Sadie think of the folktales of the Little Wee People which Greta and Josef had raised her on. Savannah's sunlit tresses made her think of those vivid childhood visions of playful pixies, elaborately winged fairies, and impish elves flitting here and there playing peek-a-boo in the Brennan garden while Josef worked and spoke to spirit beings Sadie tried very hard to spy.

Now, seeing the girl meticulously pick her way across the fields and bend to carefully reach through the curled tendrils of the sturdy vines, Sadie thought her niece appeared very much like those little magical beings. She resembled them not only in appearance, but also in personality, in spirit. Silent. Innocent. A sweet and gentle soul, to be sure.

The two had been at the farm for nearly two hours. Forty-five minutes of that time had been spent on scrutinizing dozens of imperfect "mystery" pumpkins.

Sadie was in no hurry. The only other stop she'd planned for this day's outing was the cemetery to visit her parents' grave site. More than a grassy plot, the Brennans' site was a private family mausoleum which visitors could enter for privacy. Each time she made it into Chicago, she made a point of stopping at the vault. At breakfast she'd intended to ask Mira when the two of them could go together, and when she'd discovered her sister had already left for the office, she'd checked with her niece to see if the stop was all right with her. Sadie hadn't wanted to take Savannah anyplace that would unduly upset her or cause her greater psychological distress. When she'd voiced her plans, the child hadn't shown any objections. In fact, she seemed pleased with the idea of visiting the grandparents and great-grands she'd only known through photographs.

Now, watching the child pick her way through the pumpkin patch, she wondered how much time Mira actually spent with her daughter. If the last few days were any indication of the norm, it certainly wasn't much. And if that was true, how detrimental was that to Savannah? How much did Mira's absence contribute to the child's present state? It occurred to Sadie that Mira wasn't around enough to even have in-depth conversations with her daughter. It seemed that the two didn't have much one-on-one contact at all. She told herself that she'd have to remember to talk with Greta about the matter. Greta would be honest with her.

The frantic gyrations of the fairy child pulled Sadie's attention away from her disturbing thoughts. Savannah was frantically waving in an effort to catch her aunt's eye. When Sadie looked her way, the girl was literally jumping up and down. The prizes she'd been questing after were held up high like grand trophies.

Sadie could barely make out the specks of orange in the girl's hands. The miniature pumpkins perched on the tips of the little fingers like gems in raised-prong settings. Why ever would she want something so small? And, being so tiny, why had it been imperative that they be flawless? These questions and more would remain unanswered until the reasons for the perfect mystery pumpkins eventually unfolded. It was one more mystery added to all the others that had marched into her life of late.

"Yeaah!" Sadie exclaimed, while clapping her hands. "Success at last!"

When Savannah ran back to join her aunt, she proudly held the jewels in the palm of her hand. Each prize wasn't more than three inches in diameter.

"Good for you, honey," Sadie praised. "You found the most perfect specimens in the entire field!" Then she narrowed her eyes. "So what are you going to do with them?"

Savannah raised her chin to display an elfin grin of secrecy.

"Okay, sweetie, mum's the word. They sure must be special pumpkins."

The girl nodded in agreement before the two headed back to the roadside stand to pay for their finds. Closer to the edge of the field, Sadie bent to pick up a couple more pumpkins. They were medium-sized and heavy. She grunted with the cumbersome weight. "For house decorations," she huffed and puffed, after seeing the girl's questioning expression. "These are for placing around the house for a festive look. I thought we'd also pick up more gourds and maybe some of those cornstalks out by the road stand. You know, do it up good. What do you think?"

That idea appealed to Savannah. Her grin widened.

Seeing the child's joy, Sadie became irritated with her sister for ignoring such a fun and exciting holiday. It seemed to her that Mira could be doing a lot more with her daughter to help with her condition. Even if the child hadn't had a psychological condition, Mira's routine absence was a detriment to a healthy mother-and-daughter relationship. Yes, she'd definitely bring it up with Greta.

When the two neared the stand, Rory Foster spotted them. He didn't hesitate to rush out from beneath the makeshift sun canopy to lighten Sadie's load. "You ladies have quite a haul," he chuckled.

"And we're not even done, yet," Sadie added, while moving toward the stacked cornstalks lined up against the split rail fencing.

Savannah skipped toward the stacks.

Her aunt began to curiously eye the tied bundles. "What do you think, honey? Think there's much difference between these?"

The girl's palms upturned. Then she made her decision and nodded.

Sadie was afraid of that answer. "Do you really think it makes that much difference?"

Another nod followed the first.

"All right, then. I guess that means we need to do some sorting. This is going to be a bit more difficult than the pumpkins were."

Overhearing the woman's words, Rory, ever the gentleman, moseyed over to offer assistance. He inclined his head to the child. With a nod and a wink, he said, "I agree with the little lady, here. Some cornstalks look like they're as fresh as the day they were harvested and others are, well, others have become bedraggled. You wouldn't want those." He pulled off his straw hat and wiped a kerchief along his forehead. "Unseasonably warm day, today, ain't it?"

The ladies agreed.

After replacing the hat, he set about the task of helping the two. "I probably should pull the ragged ones. See here?" he asked, showing them a particularly brittle bundle to demonstrate what he meant. "These older stalks get real fragile after they've dried out. They tend to fall apart, shred real easy." He set the unsaleable items aside. Peering over his glasses at Sadie, then down at the girl, he asked, "How many are you wanting?"

Savannah looked up at her aunt.

"Four is good. We'll take four."

Both of his wispy, grey eyebrows arched up. "Four? You sure? They're gonna make quite a mess of your car, ma'am. Take up a lot of room, too. You sure you want four?"

Sadie inclined her head toward the parking area. "The blue panel van. That's us. We have plenty of room. As far as the mess, don't worry about that. You wouldn't believe what I've carted around in that vehicle over the years."

Rory flashed an understanding grin. "You came prepared, then. Good for you." He chuckled and shook his head. "Some folks come out here with the idea of picking up a pumpkin or two and then decide a cornstalk would look good on their porch or in the yard. They expect to get these stalks into them teeny compact cars. I'd hate to see what they look like by the time they get 'em home!"

Behind them, Maggie laughed. "Folks need to come better prepared!"

Rory picked out four of the best-looking stalks and asked if he could put them in the van for them.

Sadie thanked him and told him the vehicle was open. Then she and Savannah strolled over to look through the bushel baskets of assorted gourds. They were separated by size and shape. There were smooth ones. Ones full of bumpy nubbins. Round, oval, and curvy shaped ones. Solid colors and ones with stripes. Their sizes ranged from large to miniature. A variety were selected and they returned to the stand to pay Maggie for their choices.

Savannah, noticing Mason jars of homemade pumpkin pie filling and a wide range of preserves which the woman had canned, picked out a jar of blackberry jam and added it to the growing pile of purchases heaped on the counter. She knew her aunt wouldn't mind because blackberry was also her favorite flavor.

"You've made some fine choices," the friendly woman commented.

The girl giggled. She thought Maggie Foster looked just like Mrs. Claus without the traditional red dress.

Mrs. Claus was chatty. "It's always interesting to see what folks pick out. Some spend the entire day looking for that perfect pumpkin, others want the tall, skinny ones. Sometimes the squatty ones are favored. There's something for everyone out there."

"Well," Sadie replied, "you certainly have the largest selection of anyone around. If people can't find it here, it doesn't exist. My dad would bring my sister and me here when we were young. My sister would be one of those people you mentioned who took hours on end looking for the perfect one. Me, I was just the opposite. I was the kind who felt bad for the lopsided ones and ended up carting those types away."

Maggie gave a warm-hearted, knowing smile. "You weren't alone. We still do get those youngsters who don't want the imperfect ones left to freeze in the frosty morning. In the end, most of them find homes." She counted back her customer's change, then looked down at Savannah, who'd surreptitiously slipped one of the miniature pumpkins into her pocket once everything was paid for.

Without bringing attention to what she'd seen the child do, she asked, "And what are you going to be for Halloween, young lady?"

The girl shrugged, a look of indifference on her face. She hadn't thought about a costume before now. She hadn't thought about it because her daddy had always taken her out on Halloween night. She hadn't any interest in going trick-or-treating this year.

"Well," Maggie said, "I'm sure you'll come up with something very special, won't you? You look like the type who uses her imagination when choosing her costume. Huh? I think ol' Maggie's right on that score. No store-bought outfits for you! Well, have fun, dearie, and be safe when you go out." She raised a warning finger. "And remember, don't eat all of your candy in one night the way I once did." Maggie scrunched up her face in an exaggerated grimace and rubbed her midsection. "Had a stomachache for two days after that!"

The van, loaded with the pumpkin patch haul, waited for a line of incoming cars full of excited Girl Scouts, each one of them anxious to find the perfect pumpkin before anyone else snatched it out from under their noses. While Sadie waited for the last car to turn in front of her, she smiled with the mental image of all those girls spilling out of the cars and racing into the fields. No wonder Maggie and Rory loved this time of year so much. Their fields rang with children's laughter from daybreak to dusk. Sadie felt a pang of envy. The old couple's life together was one repeatedly blessed with the joy of reaping great satisfaction from their shared labors. This was the time when their efforts drew laughing children from miles around.

Seeing the scouts brought back more memories from her childhood.

"Savannah? Are you in Girl Scouts? Well," she corrected, "you're not quite old enough for Girl Scouts yet. Are you in Brownies, Campfire Girls, or anything like that?"

Sadie's passenger blankly stared back.

The driver pushed for a response. "You know what I'm asking, honey. Are you in any kind of young girls' organization?"

The small red head slowly shook.

"Have you ever been?"

The response was repeated.

"Would you like to be? It's a lot of fun. Your mom and I were Girl Scouts for quite a few years. We were Brownies before that. Our troops did all kinds of fun things and went tons of places together. Would you like to join something like that?"

Savannah gave a noncommittal shrug before turning her attention to the road.

Sadie was certain her niece would like being with girls her own age, enjoy being a part of a group that went on field trips, went to summer camp, and experienced the thrill of achievement that working on individual skills brought to one's sense of self-worth. She mentally began to tally up the growing list of issues she needed to talk over with Greta. If the answers verified her fears, she'd take her concerns straight to Mira. If it came to that, they'd end up embroiled in a full-blown confrontation, that she was sure of. Yet, confrontation or no, it was clear that her niece's life was a far too solitary one. She needed more social contact with her peers. It appeared that the youngster's life was being groomed to promote an elitist and exclusionary attitude. That, she considered, was definitely detrimental for the child, especially now when the companionship of other girls her age could well serve as an effective means to spur her recovery.

Sadie didn't let the girl's body language deter further questions. The child's pretense—that of appearing interested in the scenery—didn't bring about the desired response. Sadie wasn't about to drop the probing.

"Sports? Do you participate in any sports in school? Gym was my favorite class when I was your age. Do you like gym?"

The girl still made no reply. She acted as though she hadn't heard a single question.

"Savannah, I know you heard me. It's not going to do you any good acting like the scenery is so engrossing that you haven't heard me. I'm not pushing you to speak, I'm simply trying to find out what you enjoy doing. Now, what about gym class, do you like it?"

The girl's head didn't move an inch.

Sadie continued looking at the back of Savannah's head. She purposely muffled the sound of her sigh. She could see where this silent treatment could be exasperating. Curbing her natural instinct to come across as being perturbed, she took another tack.

"When I was your age I lived for gym class. I absolutely lived for it. Don't get me wrong, though. I was terrible at it. I was the ultimate class klutz. If I didn't look down to double-check my shoes now and again, I would've sworn the reason I kept tripping was because I had two left feet! And even though nobody wanted me on their team, I loved the class just the same. Eventually I got better at it, but I never came close to what you'd call Olympic material, if you know what I mean." Sadie gave her niece a side glance and was surprised when she'd caught the girl's eye. Good, she thought, the yakking is working. Now that she had her attention, she didn't want to break the momentum. She yakked on.

"So I put my name down for basketball and then signed up for volleyball, as well. I was never a great player, but I did get to the point where the other players stopped groaning when I was assigned to their team. I liked the team sports better than having to compete in the kinds that depended on one's individual skill, like track. I liked to run well enough, and I could get up a fair amount of speed, but the idea of people watching just me out there, you know, being the focus of the spectators' attention, gave me the heebie-jeebies. It really scared me. Maybe things like that scared me because I didn't have enough confidence in myself. Do you think that's why I tended to stick to the team-type sports?"

Savannah was quick to nod.

The driver smiled. "Me, too."

There was more than one reason for the smile: she'd managed to elicit a response from the child. She'd cracked the shell her niece had hidden herself in. She'd done it by continuing to talk on despite the girl's purposeful act of indifference. She was pleased with the success. And, with that one small success, she realized she was learning. Through trial and error, she was learning how to most effectively communicate with her niece. Even though she knew they had a long way to go, she felt a warm wave of encouragement wash over her. It brought a spark of hope. Given enough time, maybe, just maybe, she could pull her niece the rest of the way out of her shell.

The Holy Sepulcher Cemetery was just ahead. From where the van had slowed for the stoplight, the entrance could be seen up on the right.

The driver gave her passenger a side glance. "Are you sure you're okay with this? If you're not, I thoroughly understand. I don't mind. We can go somewhere else and I can come back by myself another day."

Savannah was sure it was okay with her, but she wasn't sure if she should nod or shake her head. Her aunt hadn't left a clear response open to her. Yes, she wanted to go. No, she didn't want her to have to return another day. Rather than make the wrong reply and confuse matters, she chose the middle ground. She just blankly stared.

Sadie tried again. "Do you want me to come back another time?"
Savannah shook her head.

"So it's okay with you that we stop now?"

Then the nod came.

Sadie smiled as the light turned green and she steered the vehicle toward the opened gate of the cemetery.

Holy Sepulcher was a long-established memorial ground. Most of the grave sites were shaded by century-old maples, willows, and oaks. Brilliantly colored autumn leaves were vividly backlit by the early afternoon sunlight. Slanted light rays speared down onto the manicured grass and peacefully spilled over the markers. It was as though God were spreading a warming blanket over those slumbering below.

The van slowly advanced along the narrow ribbon of sun-dappled blacktop that wove a meandering trail around the maze of headstones. Both occupants of the vehicle couldn't help being affected by the aura of solemnity pervading the air. The place, though beautiful with nature, was heavily weighted with a touchable sorrow. It was a place that prompted folks to speak in hushed whispers. It was high, holy ground.

"There it is," Sadie softly announced, pointing up ahead. "Off to the right. It's that grey marble mausoleum."

The van eased around the curve and stopped at the edge of the tarmac.

The two got out and crossed the span of freshly mowed lawn. They stood before the impressive stone structure.

Savannah's gaze was drawn to the deeply engraved family name over the doorway. She spoke the name in her mind. *Brennan.* It was a nice name. She liked the sound of it. It was her aunt's name and her mother's maiden one. But she also liked Woodward, the name of her own father. She looked up at her aunt.

Sadie had her hand on the cool stone. "This place is pretty old," she informed. "My great-grandpa had this built in the eighteen hundreds. He'd imported Italian marble for it." The hand glided over the slick smoothness. "It still looks good. Weather hasn't changed it much in all these years." Caught by the light breeze, a tendril of weeping willow brushed her cheek. Glancing up, she smiled. "The trees have changed, though. This willow has gotten huge. It could use a little trimming."

Savannah bent her head back to see the top of the towering tree.

She didn't think it needed a single thing. She liked how its fingers gracefully caressed the stone home of her grandparents. She touched her aunt's hand to get her attention.

When Sadie looked down, the girl was shaking her head.

"What, you don't agree with me? You don't think this ol' tree needs a haircut?"

The girl vehemently shook her head.

Sadie regarded the tree. "Well, maybe not," she reconsidered. "Maybe you're right. It is kind of pretty the way it sways around." Then she selected a key from her key ring and unlocked the metal door.

Once inside, she asked whether or not they should close it behind them. She didn't want her niece to feel trapped in a place surrounded by dead people. But the girl was fine with the idea and the door was shut.

The sound of the breeze hushing through the trees was silenced.

The sweetness of birdsong was dampened.

The pair scanned the small room, then raised their gaze to the ceiling. Sunlight caused them to squint.

"My father," Sadie explained, "your grandfather, made changes to the mausoleum. He was the one who added the skylight. He always felt that light should be able find its way inside. He had it done in stained glass." Sadie's eyes lowered to the floor. "See the pretty designs the glass makes on the floor? I think it was a great idea. I'm glad my father did that. It'd be pitch dark in here without the skylight."

The girl followed on the heels of her aunt as she moved from one brass plaque to another. Lovingly, Sadie touched the inscribed name-plates and shared joyful memories about each family member with her niece. When they arrived at her mother and father's plaque, she rearranged the silk flowers that were set in the wall planter, then retreated to the bench in the center of the room.

"I should've brought new silk arrangements," she whispered. "I didn't think to do that, but I suppose those are still good enough. The sunlight that comes in here doesn't fade flowers like it does to those on the outside."

Savannah respectfully remained as still as a rabbit while letting her aunt reminisce and talk on. She knew how important it was to be able to talk to one's parents, even if they were dead. She knew they could still hear every word, just like God did.

When Sadie returned to the present, she thanked Savannah for coming with her and letting her ramble on. She thanked her for the silent time they shared together in this sacred family place. Then they made their way toward the door.

Savannah stepped out into the sunshine.

Before her aunt followed suit, she turned to whisper a last good-bye to her family. Instead of feeling sadness, she felt a smile curve the corners of her mouth. Sunlight streamed down on the bench where they'd been sitting. From the skylight, rays of light fell on the gift of a brilliant orange pumpkin.

"Savannah," she cooed, "what a nice thing to do. Your grandma and grandpa must be so pleas—"

The girl was no longer beside her.

Sadie locked the door, stepped off the stone threshold and onto the grass. In her chest, she felt her heart suddenly lunge. *Where'd Savannah go?* Her head whipped in one direction, then the other. Rushing to check the back of the structure, she cupped her hand over her eyes to shield them from the glaring sunlight. In the distance, Savannah was bent before an old headstone. The tall angel statue towered over her as if giving its blessing.

Sadie released a relieved sigh. "Oh, thank God," she whispered, while heading over to the girl. After closing the distance between them, she whispered, "Honey, I got frantic when I turned around and you weren't there. You need to let me know—"

The sound of a sniffle cut off the words. A small finger was pointed to the dates.

Sadie knelt down before the headstone. "Ohh, isn't that sad. Hannah was only two years old. She was just a little girl."

The small redhead upturned her palms in question.

Thinking the girl was asking what the child had died of, Sadie responded. "I don't know how she died, honey. It doesn't say. It usually doesn't."

A frown marred Savannah's sweet face. She pointed to the blue sky, then to the grave. Hands upturned.

"Are you asking me why God takes people?"

Savannah nodded.

"Well, actually, God doesn't. God isn't the one who causes people to die. Sickness does that, honey. Sickness, wars, accidents, acts of violence, and things like natural disasters take people's lives. It's part

of the reality of life. People are born and people die. Some die when
they're old and others go when they're young. It's just the way it is.
God has nothing to do with it. We shouldn't blame things like death
on God because death is caused by too many other things."

Savannah slowly raised herself from the grave and began wandering toward another. Then another. She traced the engraved letters
while intently studying each headstone. When she gazed off into the
distance, Sadie figured the child was lost in thought. But when the girl's
head swung back and their eyes locked on each other's, the smaller
ones had grown as round as melons.

Alarmed at the girl's look of surprise, Sadie asked, "What's the
matter, honey? What is it?"

Savannah's arm shot out. She pointed off to the left.

Sadie turned toward the indicated direction and saw someone bent
over a grave. The someone wore a faded army coat and a red hat. A
glittering facet of the attached rhinestone had captured a spark of
sunlight.

When there was a lull in the breeze, the trees quieted their shushing and the sound of the woman's whisperings could be heard.
Individual words were not discernible, but the lady's cooing voice was
within hearing.

The two observers looked at one another. They both had questions
that neither could answer. They nonchalantly strolled over to a grave
site that was closer to the woman and, in a meager attempt to use the
waist-high headstone as a shield, the two sidled up against one
another and crouched. Now they could hear better. Two pairs of green
eyes were trained on the woman busily tending to a grave.

The elder, feeling the heat of the afternoon sun, yanked off her hat
and set it in the grass. The mass of grey hair fell loose like a veil over
her shoulders when she bent to kneel. Reaching for the flat carpet
satchel, she stuck her hand inside and pulled out a garden tool.
Immediately it was used to gently jab at the base of every offensive
weed she found.

"I know you don't have any people, Rosamund, dear. Shame on
them, if you did. You have a fine resting place here, but it's been let
go some. Ohh, don't you worry none, dearie. I don't mind. I'm going
to clear it of everything that doesn't belong. See?" she said, raising the
extracted weed like a trophy, "See that? We'll just clean up your nice
grassy blanket and make it all tidy once again." The voice had a touch

of raspiness to it, yet was soft and sympathetic. There were no hints of foreign or regional accent.

The woman wiped her brow.

The weeder went back into the flat bag and out came the grass clippers.

Several tombstones away, two mouths fell open in disbelief. They could've sworn the carry bag had been as flat as a pancake lying on the ground. Where had the pair of clippers come from?

Clip. Clip. Clip, snip, snip.

"There now, dearie. Your quilt's good as new. Rest assured I'll return by and by to straighten out your blanket again."

Gathering up her hat and satchel, the woman took great pains to straighten up and ease her back. She appeared to aimlessly amble about, stopping momentarily here and there to brush off a headstone or shake an accusing finger at a grave.

Intent on their surveillance, the two spies surreptitiously followed at a safe distance, tiptoeing from headstone to headstone.

As she pulled up short at a pin oak tree, the woman's arm shot out. "And *you*, Jake Whitting," she scolded with a hard shake of her finger, "you better be *quiet!* You hear? You skedaddle! You get going to where you belong and quit lollygagging around here! There's nothing for you here! You got things to do. Go on! Git!"

The woman mumbled to herself as she dropped her hat and bag beside another grave. Lowering herself to her knees, she bent to give the lawn caressing strokes.

"Sweet baby," she cooed. "Sweet, sweet baby. Your brother's not gotten away with what he did to you. He may think he has, but I know what he did. Nobody can pull the wool over my eyes. I know what everybody does. Don't you fret, now. In the end, Ruby's going to make sure he gets what's coming to him. You sleep tight, baby. Mama's going to take care of everything." Then she pulled a bountiful bouquet of silk flowers from her bag and planted the wire stems into the soil at the base of the headstone.

Huddling close together, the crouching spies snuck a look at each other. The older of the sleuthing duo whispered, "Did she say her name was Ruby? Is her baby in that grave?"

The smaller spy's shoulders hitched up and down. Evidently she hadn't heard the woman's words clear enough either. The sound of resumed talking pulled their attention back to the action.

"Let's see, now . . . who's next?"

The old woman repeated her backbreaking work of standing, moving to various graves, kneeling, and either pulling tools from the bag to tidy unkempt plots or just speaking to those laid below. At one point, while she was clipping the grass that had grown tall around a headstone, her attention was drawn to a wren that had hopped within her line of vision. One wing drooped at an odd angle.

"Ohhh, poor baby," she cooed in an emotionally painful voice heavy with empathy. "Come to Mama. Mama will take care of you." And the woman cupped the tiny bird in her hands and softly sang to it. Two minutes later, she lowered her hand and spread her fingers to let the bird hop down into the grass. It took five or six hops, tested its wings by stretching them both out, then flew to her shoulder. It chirped, then flew into a red-leafed maple. The woman laughed. "Ohh, yes! You surely are very welcome. I told you Mama would take care of you."

Again, the surveillance team was awestruck by what they'd witnessed. When Sadie turned to whisper something to her niece, she saw a man standing a few feet behind them. He'd been watching them. She straightened up, took Savannah's hand, and gently pulled her away from their hiding place. She was flustered—mortified—over having been caught spying in a cemetery.

When Savannah also realized the game was up, her face flushed with embarrassment. The two headed toward the van.

"Is there something I can help you with?" the man in the coveralls asked, while angling his way over to them. "Maybe locate a site for you?"

They stopped in their tracks. "No, we're fine. We're just leaving."

"I'm the groundskeeper here. If there's anything I can assist with, I'd be more'n happy to help you out."

"No, no. We're just on our way out."

Halfway to the vehicle, Sadie turned.

The man was still watching them.

She'd changed her mind. "There is something," she called, retracing her steps back to the waiting caretaker. "That woman you caught us watching. We didn't mean to be rude, but we've run into her at quite a few places. Do you happen to know who she is?"

He didn't have to turn around to look for who she was talking about. "Well, she's a regular here." He chuckled over that. "I know it sounds strange to say that someone's a regular at a cemetery, sounds like you're talking about a resident, if you know what I mean."

Sadie, anxious for answers, made a quick attempt to be amused before getting serious again. "Do you know who she is? What her name is? Where she lives?"

"Nope. Couldn't help you with any of those things. All I know is that she's here a lot and will spend the entire day cleaning up graves nobody comes to tend. I always figured she felt sorry for those without family." The man's hands went into his pockets. "That lady talks a lot, too. She's always talking up a storm to the residents. She actually talks like she personally knew each one when they were living. You know, like each one had been family to her. Like she was each one's mother." He shifted his weight from one foot to the other. "Never have spoken outright to her so I couldn't tell you exactly who she is. Don't know her name, either." He scratched his head. "S'pose I should at least find that much about her since she's here so much. I've no idea where she lives. She always has that bag with her, that much I do know. Sorry I couldn't be more helpful." He then voiced an afterthought. "Funny thing, though."

"What's that?"

He seemed embarrassed, like he was about to put his foot in his mouth.

"What is it?"

"Well, sometimes it crosses my mind that she's some kind of rich lady."

That was the last thing Sadie expected to hear. "Rich? Why?"

"I mean, rich as in eccentric. Despite that old coat you never see her without, she always has a different pair of shoes on. Never seen a woman wear so many different shoes."

"Yeah, the shoes," Sadie said while squeezing Savannah's hand. "Well, thanks a lot. You've been helpful."

Maybe he'd been more helpful than he believed, Sadie thought. She thanked him again before leading her niece to the van.

Settled in the driver's seat, she watched the caretaker turn his back to them and amble off. A compulsion drew her to scan the grounds one last time before pulling away.

In the distance, something brightly flashed in the sunlight.

Sadie squinted, then shaded her eyes to see better.

But nothing was there.

That evening, a call was placed to the Wick 'n' Wit book and candle shop in Maine. When the proprietress answered, she was hyped.

"Sadie! I've been dying to hear what's new with that woman! There has been something new, hasn't there?"

"Ohh, yes."

"I knew it! I just knew you hadn't seen the last of her. Tell me everything! Don't leave out a thing!"

And so she didn't. Feeling impish, she teased her friend by making her painfully wait to hear the good stuff. She dragged out the recounting of the pumpkin farm visit by detailing every inconsequential tidbit. Then she skated over the juicy part by ending with, "After the cemetery, we came home with our farm goodies and had fun decorating the house."

"Cemetery? *Cemetery!* What cemetery?" came the excited response.

"Oh, did I leave that part out?"

"Sadieee!"

Recognizing when it was time to cut the teasing, she backtracked the story to include everything she could remember about the visit to Holy Sepulcher. She took her time and tried to include all the details. Then she waited for a response. She waited and waited while Tina was doing her processing.

"Gads, I don't know where to begin." Tina inhaled a deep breath and slowly released it. "Okay, what was your first impression when you heard her talking to Rosamund? Do you think she actually *knew* this person?"

"How do I know? She said that she knew Rosamund didn't have any people. I assume that refers to family. I can't interpret her intention for the term 'knew.'"

"What I'm looking for is your *impression* when you heard her say that. You're the one who heard the words, the inflection and emotion in the woman's voice. That's what I'm going for. Did her tone give you the impression that she actually knew the deceased?"

Sadie had to think on that. How had the words struck her at the time?

"I can't be sure, but I think I believed she actually knew the person."

"Okay. Now. When she was chastising the other one. What was the name?"

"I don't recall. It was a Jake something. She was quite perturbed with him."

"When you told me about when she was chastising Jake, her words sounded as though she was scolding him for doing a haunting and—"

"A haunting!" Sadie exclaimed. "Where did that come from?"

"It's obvious. The woman was telling him to 'skedaddle' and to stop 'lollygagging around.'

"You tell me what that's supposed to refer to when it's spoken to a dead person. Come on, Sadie, she told him to be quiet! Isn't that what you said she said to him?"

"Yes, but—"

"There are no 'buts' about anything here. She said what she said because she meant what she meant. What she meant was for the spirit to get on with it, get where it was supposed to be and stop hanging around on Earth. It's as plain as day. What else could she have meant when she reminded him that 'there was nothing for you here'?"

Sadie conceded. "It just never occurred to me at the time," she admitted. "I never realized that she might have been speaking to a spirit. Oh my God, do you think there was a real spirit hanging around out there?"

Sometimes Tina couldn't believe her friend's naïveté. "Have you been living under a rock up until now? Get a clue, girlfriend, you were in a friggin' cemetery! You were in a cemetery and it never crossed your mind that there might be restless souls out there?"

"No. Not really. Maybe if I'd been out there after dark I would've been a bit more skittish and those types of things might've entered my mind."

"You bet they would've. God," she repeated, "I can't believe you didn't realize the woman was trying to send a wayward spirit back home where it belonged!"

"Okay. Okay. So I was dense and didn't get it right away. Can we please dispense with the ravings over my stupidity?"

"Absolutely. We can do that. We need to move on."

Sadie waited and waited for the "moving on" part that took a while to break out of her friend's pondering stage.

Tina broke her silence. "What was the bit about the . . . ahh . . . about a brother? About the woman saying that she knew what he'd done to a baby? Could you run that by me again?"

The event was recapped. "If you're going to ask me about those feelings I had when I heard the woman's words, I can tell you right now that I do recall what I felt with that one. I had the distinct feeling that she wasn't making reference to a real baby, not an infant. I felt she was using a term of endearment for a young woman, one who'd been fatally harmed by her brother."

"According to the old woman."

"Well, yes. According to what the woman said. I suppose it couldn't be proven as fact because she made it sound like he was never charged with a crime, like he'd gotten off scot-free and she was going to correct that at some point."

"Do you recall which tombstone she was addressing at that time?"

"What you're asking is: could I find it again to verify the age of the deceased?"

"You're getting the hang of this. Yeah, could you do that?"

"Probably, but I'm not that interested in checking it out. I don't think it's that important."

"Okay. Then she said what? Something about how she knows what everybody does?"

"Yes. She said, 'I know what everybody does' . . . then something to the effect that, 'In the end, Ruby's going to see that he gets what's coming to him. Mama's going to take care of everything.'"

"Back up. Back up. She said she *knows* what everybody does?"

"Yes. We heard that part real clear. That's what she said."

"There's an awful lot of 'knews' and 'knows' in this story. Doesn't that strike you as unusual? Strange?"

"It didn't then. It does now."

"And what's more interesting to me is the 'Mama' bit. She can't be the mother of everybody out there." Tina suddenly laughed. "Get it? Without meaning to, I made a pun! Did you get it? I said she couldn't be the mother of every *body* out there!"

Although Sadie didn't actually laugh aloud at the unexpected joke, it had brought a smile when she'd first heard it. "Yeah," she admitted, "I got it the first time. It was okay."

Tina didn't want to break the rhythm of their progress. "Joking aside, my intent still remains. Didn't it seem as though she was acting like every grave she visited contained one of her children? Like she was everyone's mother?"

Sadie mentally went over what she'd witnessed. "It did seem like that. Even the caretaker noticed that. He actually came out and said that she always talks to each resident as though she personally knew them, like she was each one's mother." Her breath caught with the realization. "Oh my God! Tina!" she exclaimed, "He verified the feelings I had!"

"Bingo. You rang the bell with that one. Give the lady a prize. You're catching on with this analyzing stuff, but let's not get hung up on one right answer. We have more ground to cover. I thought it was a kick when you said that the caretaker suggested the woman might be wealthy. No way."

Sadie wasn't so sure. "His statement didn't strike me as being that ridiculous. I mean, let's look at this. She's always very clean in person and clothing. She speaks well. She certainly knows her way around the city and manages to get to wherever she wants to go. Her behavioral mannerisms don't particularly shout that she's needy in any way. She appears healthy and well fed. I don't see that, by speaking her mind and wearing a lot of different shoes, it makes her a homeless person. I think that being a wealthy eccentric is very much within the realm of her reality."

"You do, do you?"

"Yes, I do. I think it's a distinct possibility."

"Okay, Inspector Brennan, where does she live? Why don't you look into that one so we can come to an agreement on whether or not she's a rich eccentric or a street person?"

"Now I'm supposed to follow her?"

"Sure. What else do you have to do? You and the kid can play Cagney and Lacey and tail the woman."

"That's not even funny."

"Sadie, it wasn't meant to be. If you want to know if this lady's homeless or not, you need to do a little investigating. You know, ask around. It's not like you're not running into her everywhere you go. The next time you see her, get friendly with the people who are out and about in the area. If you've run into her so often, others have as well. Start asking questions."

"Oh, I don't know. I'm afraid I'm making something out of nothing."

"Nothing? You call *healing* a bird's broken wing *nothing?* Or did you conveniently forget about that? That bird was nothing like the lame dog incident. That bird was a wild wren! Nobody teaches a wild wren to pretend its wing is broken! I hate to say it, but I think you're in denial about what you saw out there today, Sadie. What you saw was a genuine, friggin' miracle!"

Silence.

"You there?"

"I'm here."

"Well, stay with me then. You're on to something big here. Maybe bigger than either of us can imagine."

"Don't exaggerate."

"Who's exaggerating? Humor me. Repeat after me. A woman who heals animals."

Sadie sighed. They'd played this game before. Trouble was, it usually made her see things more clearly. "A woman who heals animals," she repeated.

"Let's keep going. A woman who pulls needed items from an empty bag."

"A woman who pulls needed items from an empty bag."

"A woman who sees through reality's veil and orders wandering spirits home."

Sadie joked. "You're running a little long now."

"Don't break the rhythm."

"A woman who sees through reality's veil and orders wandering spirits home."

Tina kept up the pace. "A woman who believes she's everyone's mother, even the animals."

"A woman who believes she's everyone's mother, even the animals."

"A woman who's footwear miraculously rejuvenates after she performs acts of goodness or righteousness."

Silence.

"Go on. Say it," Tina urged.

A response wasn't forthcoming.

"Sadie?"

"I . . . I never made the connection. You're right. Her shoes do appear to be transformed after she does something good. Why couldn't I put two and two together and see that?"

"Oh, stop. It's not important why you didn't see it. All of us miss the boat at one time or another. It's nothing to wear sackcloth over. Quit it. What's really important is that we keep gathering up the threads of this enigmatic lady of yours. Keep notes if you have to. I do."

Slowly, Sadie repeated the last statement. "A woman who's footwear miraculously rejuvenates after performing acts of goodness or righteousness. Good *God*," she added with a heavy sigh.

Tina had been staring at Sadie's forgotten token. "Maybe."

"What?"

"Nothing. Really, it was nothing. Just doing some mental sorting. So," she quickly asked. "What about her name? Do you think it might be Ruby?"

"Oh, who knows. That's what I thought she said."

"Why do I have the sense I'm losing you here?"

"Maybe because you are. I need some time to think about all this. I don't know. If it weren't for Savannah being with me to witness everything I'd think I was going around—"

"Don't go there, girlfriend. You're fine. You're certainly not seeing things. And you're certainly not going around the bend. I wasn't going to say anything yet, but I think your Ruby—or whatever her name turns out to be—is who your mysterious recurring token is pointing to."

"Okaaay. That's it. Now you're really pushing the envelope. It's not that I don't like talking to you, but I gotta get some shut-eye. Tomorrow we're getting up early to be at the Farmer's Market. Greta's coming along." She paused. "Hopefully, it'll be the first normal day since I've been here."

Tina was understanding. "Okay, hon, sure. While you're there, see if they have some of that special sausage I like. We can't get it here. Freeze it till you're ready to leave."

Sadie promised she'd look for it and they ended their conversation. When she turned to set the phone on the night table, a movement from the dark corridor caught her eye. Disgusted with herself, she shook her head in frustration and mumbled.

"I gotta get more rest. I could've sworn I saw the edge of Savannah's nightie move in the doorway." She looked at her reflection in the mirror. *Get a grip, girl. Get a grip. Things will get better.* Yet, just to be sure, she went to the door to peek down the hallway.

Empty, just as she'd expected it would be.

Six

Thursday

The air was heavy with mingling smoke wafting up from a multi-
tude of sources. Cooking smells, intended to entice, drifted over the
milling throng of market shoppers.

Texas-sized cookers sizzled with racks of ribs generously slathered
with barbecue sauce. Hibachis and flaming woks sent up curling tendrils of mouth-watering aromas that tickled the noses and beckoned
to those passing by, promising tantalizing morsels to sample.

Slow-cookers simmered as their vendors boasted claims of having
the hottest five-alarm chili east of the Mississippi.

Sweet and spicy. Bland and hot. The three-block square Farmers'
Market had it all when vendors from miles around gathered on the
third Thursday of the month. They gathered to create a colorful
patchwork of ethnic diversity with their wide variety of cultural wares.

It hadn't always been that way. At first, when a block of abandoned warehouses had been razed by the city, the local farmers used the vacated space to sell the fruits of their labor. And when two more adjoining blocks had been cleared, there was never vendor space left wanting. Soon the Farmers' Market became an event to look forward to as it exponentially expanded beyond locally grown fruits and vegetables to the fare of other countries.

The residents of Chinatown were the first to establish a tent among the local farmers' booths. By the following month, the Hispanic population was represented. Then the African-Americans put up booths. Eventually the market became a multicultural gathering place where people could browse all day long and sample the exotic culinary delights of many countries they'd never get the chance to visit. Of course, you had to arrive early because by late afternoon the place was bustling with shoulder-to-shoulder visitors, each with a quest to taste-test every free sample and locate that perfect birthday gift for their great-aunt who thought she had everything.

They came by the car- and busload. Senior groups, Garden Club members, and high schoolers on field trips for their sociology class unloaded in the parking area. Each year the monthly event became more popular. Soon they'd need another city block to accommodate the vendors who had signed the ever-lengthening waiting list.

"Ouch!" Greta exclaimed, grabbing onto Sadie for support. They looked behind them to see an elderly man apologize for bumping the back of her legs with his motorized wheelchair.

"Sorry," he mumbled, before maneuvering it around her. With a shake of his head, he sputtered to no one in particular. "They need to expand this place! It's outgrown itself!"

The three watched him bump into another shopper before he disappeared into the milling crowd.

Sadie tightened her grip on Savannah's hand. "He's right, you know. I can't believe how popular this place has become. It never used to be so packed."

Greta rolled her eyes. "The October market is the worst. It's usually not so bad during the other months. Don't know what makes October so popular. Maybe because it's the last of the good weather and folks are wanting to get out and about to see what they can pick up in the way of Halloween party fixins. October's a farmer's last hurrah." She angled her body to avoid running into a woman who was trying to keep her three toddlers gathered together like a trio of chicks around herself. "September's the second busiest month for the market," Greta informed. "There's plentiful harvest produce in September."

Sadie's attention was split between listening to the housekeeper and forming her own thoughts. She found herself growing irritated with the unexpected crowd. She privately entertained the idea of asking Greta if there was somewhere else she'd like to go today, then thought better of it. Greta went to the Farmers' Market every month. It was one of the small pleasures she treated herself to. She would always look forward to it, no matter how crowded it became.

Sadie snuck a furtive glance at the woman with the nimble step keeping pace beside her. Excitement sparkled in her eyes. In each hand she held tightly to her net carry bags. Greta was planning on discovering some wonderful finds to fill them with today. There was no way out of it. It was the Farmers' Market today or nothing. Nothing else would do.

"Smell that?" Greta asked, as her eyes began to have that special twinkle.

Sadie wasn't sure which smell the woman was referring to. The place literally reeked of pungent aromas coming from all directions.

"I smell a lot of things. Which one in particular are you talking about?"

The woman's arm shot out in front of Sadie. "Over there. The Columbians are brewing fresh coffee. Gotta get us some of those dark beans you like so much." And the three veered over to the booth topped by a flapping Columbian flag.

While Greta shifted into her glory role as connoisseur, discriminately sniffing each sample bag of beans, Savannah's interest was piqued by something she spied at the end of the line of tables. She sidled up to the display and shyly ran her fingertips over a wooden flute.

"The villagers make these," Sadie informed the child, while picking up another from the display box. "Would you like one?"

The girl discreetly lowered her hand back to her side and slowly shook her head.

"Well, if you see something here today that you really can't live without, you'll tell me, won't you? Your Aunt Sadie would love buying you something to remember our day at the market." She touched Savannah's chin and raised it so their eyes met. "Okay? Promise you'll tell me if something catches your eye?"

Silently agreeing, Savannah nodded.

"Good." When she looked up, she saw Greta arguing with the vendor. "Oh-ohhh. Maybe we better go see what Greta's up to."

But the experienced woman didn't need rescuing. She came away from the table sporting a beaming smile of satisfaction. Four bags of coffee beans weighted the bottom of one of her net bags. She winked as Sadie reached out to carry it for her. "Gotta know how to haggle if you expect to get the best buy here. These vendors expect to dicker over their prices. Makes both parties think they got a deal." She eyed Sadie. "Do you know how to dicker?"

"Not really," she admitted.

"Well, how do you know you're getting the best deal then?"

"I suppose I don't know."

The woman was aghast. "You mean to tell me that you always pay sticker price?"

Sadie was grinning. "I thought that was what the sticker price was for. It tells you how much the item costs and that's what you pay."

Greta grunted. "That's pathetic. You young'uns gotta stick up for yourselves better than that. The sticker price isn't what you pay, it's where you start dickering down from!"

The grin grew into a genuine smile of amusement. "I'll try to remember that in the future. Does it work for big ticket items like refrigerators in department stores?"

"You bet it does. People are just too naive to try it. You ought to know how to dicker. Don't you do a lot of that in your antique business?" She jabbed the younger woman's arm. "Sure you do. You must do it all the time."

"Well, I guess I do. I never thought of it as dickering, though. It's more like—"

"Dickering is dickering. You want to hang a hoity-toity name on it in order to make it sound more respectable, more dignified. Makes no difference to me what you want to call it. You might call it compromising or negotiating, but it's still dickering, just the same. No matter what color you paint it, underneath it's still plain old dickering."

"Then I guess I do know how to dicker."

"Of course you do. Now, let's get crackin'! We have a lot of ground to cover before this day's over."

Sadie glanced down at her niece and raised her brow. "You heard the lady, we've a lot of ground to cover."

Savannah pursed her lips to keep from laughing while the two tailed close on the heels of the housekeeper.

They watched Greta maneuver through the crowd with aplomb. She knew the layout of the tents and booths like the back of her hand. And well she should, for she'd been going to the market every month for years. She deftly wove her way around shoppers who already had armloads of merchandise. She expertly shouldered her way past a chattering group of elderly women wearing brightly colored djellabahs. They carried their newly purchased sugar cane stalks like walking sticks. The women, it appeared, had made the African-American booth their first stop of the day. The fresh sugar canes went quickly and they made sure they got their choice before the supply was picked over or depleted altogether.

The former irritation of the pressing crowd began to diminish as Sadie's interest was heightened by the vendors and shoppers alike. What a diversity it was. Colorful. And the scented air was adrift with a pleasing blend of accents and dialects from many countries. Sadie's initial discomfort with the masses slipped into growing excitement. Like a fisherwoman's lost bobber, she was riding the crest of a cultural wave. She found the commotion infectious and realized that it was exactly what she needed to return normalcy to her life. Here among the flurry of activity was her respite from the bizarre events of the past days. Here among the enlivened shoppers milling about international tents was her salvation, her chance at sanity. Here, she realized, there were no dark clouds of Paul hanging over her head. Here there was no mysterious old woman with a tacky dime-store pin stuck in her hat.

Sadie's hand was jerked. Grinning wide with her private thoughts, she looked down and saw her niece frowning up at her. She laughed.

"You've been watching me again. I'm laughing because it just dawned on me that this is a good place for me to be right now. I can blend in here. I can blend into this wonderful cultural tapestry and become part of it. The bustle and hubbub is just the ticket to having a normal day, a day of distraction from . . . well, you know, all that business about Ruby."

The girl wasn't as convinced as her aunt appeared to be. She wasn't so sure Ruby should be forgotten because she was positive the old woman was someone very special. Why would her aunt want a day without thoughts of Ruby? This whole thing with the bag lady was becoming a deeper mystery by the day. She was determined to stay on top of things. She concealed her concern by smiling up at her aunt while they tailed Greta over to the Mexico tent.

Ironwood carvings filled the makeshift rows of shelving. On clothing racks pushed outside the tent entrance, brightly colored ponchos were tightly packed together along with handwoven table scarves draped over hangers. Greta urgently made a beeline to the bundles of hanging red peppers and, although plenty hung at shoulder level, she strained to reach high up to unhook the perfect one.

Sadie came to her rescue. "Here, let me get that for you."

"No! Not that one," Greta barked. "That one there! No, no. Yes! There! That one beside it."

"Picky. Picky," Sadie shot back. "I don't see the difference. They all look the same to me."

"Of course they do. That's because you're not a cook! You're not a connoisseur! All your peppers come out of a can!" Greta playfully chided. "I got an eye for this kind of thing because I'm used to using fresh ingredients!" Then she patiently explained the subtle differences between the bundles after her purchase was safely tucked into the bottom of her second net bag. When they turned to venture back into the moving crowd, Sadie panicked. She was no longer holding onto her niece's hand.

"Savannah's gone!" she cried.

Greta reassuringly placed her hand on Sadie's arm. "Not to worry. Don't panic. I know where the little minx is. She'll be down the way in the India tent. She loves that place. You'll see. It's okay."

Sadie thought it far from okay. Greta's calming voice did little to assuage her concern. "Where's the India tent? We need to go get her."

Greta pursed her lips. "I'm telling you, she does this every time. She's perfectly fine. Oh, look," she pointed, "I'm just going over there to get me some of that—"

"No. Not now," Sadie insisted. "First to India, then we can come back to Greece."

The housekeeper wasn't pleased. The aroma of fresh baklava was strong as they bypassed the Greek pavilion. Normally Sadie would've been drawn in as well. She had a passion for baklava. But today that passion couldn't override her deep concern for the child. Greta hadn't seemed overly worried that they'd gotten separated. Did she make it a habit of letting Savannah roam freely about in such crowds? It certainly sounded that way. Was that wise? Especially nowadays when anything could happen to such a beautiful, unattended girl?

The two passed the Syrian booth, where pita bread was being made.

A barker in chaps and properly curled cowboy hat couldn't deter the two scurrying women with his tantalizing smoker packed with sizzling racks of baby-back ribs. On the ground were stacked cases of the man's own brand of barbecue sauce.

"I can't believe this," Sadie grumbled. "I can't believe you let her wander alone through this crowd. What were you thinking to let her go—"

The question was cut short when Sadie turned to chastise the housekeeper and Greta was nowhere to be seen.

Her hands went up. *Oh fine. Isn't this just dandy. Now I have two missing persons.* "Greta? Greta!" she called, while retracing her steps.

Greta, grounded like a three-ton statue, was standing stock still in the middle of the aisle, forcing the crowd to veer around her. It flowed around her like stream water around a boulder. When Sadie came up to her the housekeeper had something of her own to say.

"Sadie? I'm too damn old to go pell-mell at dodge'um cars through this crowd. You may not have realized it, but you were nearly running. Running blindly, I might add. You don't even know where the India tent is." The woman wiped her brow with her sleeve. "I have to sit down a minute."

Sadie apologized while snapping her head this way and that. "Look, over there," she said, inclining her head. "There's a park bench. Let's get you seated and I'll go get Savannah after you point me in the right direction."

"I don't have to sit down!"

"You just said—"

"Well, I know what I just said but that's not what I meant. What I mean to say is that we have no call to go racing about without our heads. The girl's fine, I tell you. You're whipping yourself into a lather over nothing. Now, we can do this *without* getting in a lather over it." She squinted up into the sky. "Lordy, it's going to be a hot one for this time of year." When she lowered her sights to lock eyes with Sadie, she said, "Savannah's fine. Believe me, she's just fine. Now let's go see what she's up to. We don't need to run, either."

Against her better judgment, Sadie resigned herself to keeping a rein on her urge to charge forward. Instead, she respectfully let the elder woman set the pace and lead the way. Eight minutes later, after they had been weaving through the maze of aisles overflowing with merchandise, a banner caught Sadie's attention. The East India Trading Company. She rushed forward and sped through the opened flaps of the triple-sized tent.

The interior was packed with such a wide variety of items that it reminded Sadie of a Pier One store.

Rows of shelving held layer upon layer of bolts of sparkling sari cloth.

Handwoven rugs were stacked along the length of one tent side.

Racks of exotic spices filled the air with pungent scents and mixed with the cloying sweetness of frangipani and sandalwood incense.

A wall of shelving that ran a second length of the tent displayed miniature wooden carvings and brass images of Indian deities.

Glass jewelry display cases held gold-colored metal earrings and wrist bangles of every size and shape.

Sadie, heart pounding with growing panic at not immediately spotting her niece, finally called out. "Savannah? Savannah, are you in here?"

The sound of a dozen sets of brass temple bells suddenly ringing drew her attention to the back of the massive tent. There was Savannah, wafting her hand back and forth over the hanging chimes like Huck Finn with a stick across a picket fence.

Sadie's shoulders visibly slumped with relief. Well, of course, the girl wasn't speaking, so how could she answer? She'd caused the chimes to speak for her. Instead of scolding her, Sadie just smiled at the girl as Greta sidled up beside her.

"Told you," she gloated. "Told you she'd be just fine. She's always fawning over those fancy sandalwood trinket boxes. She especially likes the ones with inlaid stone work."

Sadie didn't take her eyes off her niece. "Well, you could've at least told me where to look once I got in here. This place is huge."

Greta shrugged. "Eh, knowing she was here was enough. Shall we go see what's caught her eye today?"

"Whatever it is, I'm buying it for her."

When the two women came up to the girl, she dreamily closed her eyes and made high drama of smelling the air.

"Yes," Sadie agreed, wrinkling her nose, "it's pretty thick in here. Do you want to take some incense home with you?"

"Not likely," Greta piped in. "Mira would have a hissy fit. No smoke in her house. She can barely stand cooking smoke. Says it compromises the integrity of the fine wallpaper. I think she envisions her draperies languishing under the suffocating cloy of clinging smoke."

That was all Sadie needed to hear. Her eyes conspiratorially slid to meet the girl's.

"I'll tell you what. You choose whichever fragrance of incense you like best, maybe two or three kinds. You leave your mother to me."

Savannah's eyes grew to the size of hubcaps. She looked to seek Greta's permission.

"Ohhh, no, sirree! Not on your life! You leave me out of this. This is between you and your auntie here. If she wants to take on your mother then who am I to interfere? Go on," she encouraged, "go choose some of that smelly stuff you love so much."

The girl set down the trinket box she'd been admiring and raced to the incense section of the tent.

Sadie unceremoniously picked up the trinket box and turned to Greta. She put her finger to her lip. "Shhh. This is our little secret. I'm going to the counter with this. You go keep her occupied till I'm done and I'll join you."

As the tissue-wrapped purchase was slipped into the generous pocket of her jacket, Greta and Savannah rounded a display of carved elephants and headed toward the register. Two packages of incense were proudly held up.

"Two? That's all?"

Savannah nodded. She was sure two was more than enough because her mother would never allow even a single stick to burn all the way through. Once she got a whiff of the scented smoke she'd follow her nose throughout the house to track down the offending source and extinguish it with relish. And then heads were going to roll. And then someone was going to get What For! Savannah wanted to see the sparks fly when that happened. She wanted to see her aunt stick up for her.

The incense went into a plastic East India Trading Company bag and Savannah carried it like a prize. It wouldn't do to put incense in with Greta's coffee beans or red peppers. Everyone knew you didn't carry scented items in the same bag as food.

"Now where to?" Sadie asked.

"Peru."

"What's in Peru?"

"Slippers. Weather's going to be getting nippy soon. I want to sur-prise Josef with a pair of those shearling slippers."

On the way to their destination, they passed a new tent. Greta, overcome with awe, cut away from the trio. "Come look at these!" she exclaimed. "Look at these beautiful Amish quilts!"

Sadie and Savannah made their way over to the side as politely as they could. The afternoon crowd had gotten heavier. Suddenly veer-ing from one's course was a feat in managing finesse as well as avoid-ing stepping on others' toes.

Nearly fifty minutes went by while Greta inspected the quilts and discussed the fine art of intricate stitching with the skilled Amish woman in the booth. They alternated between laughter and seriousness depending on how the conversation swayed. Sadie, hav-ing some interest in the items as a dealer in fine wares, wasn't quite as fascinated as Greta had been. She eased away from the huddled bonnets toward her niece, who'd been patiently sitting on a hand-crafted settee.

"Can't quite get worked up over quilts," Sadie whispered.

Savannah rolled her eyes indicating the same sentiment.

A breeze lifted the ends of their hair.

"Ohh, what's that wonderful smell?" Sadie asked, while sitting taller to crane her neck and look about. "It's roasted nuts! I haven't had those in ages! Greta!" she called. "We're going to go get some roasted nuts. Do you want us to get several to take back with us?"

"I'm coming. We're done here. Wait for me."

Strolling while munching from a shared bag of nuts, Sadie and Savannah exaggerated their pleasure while Greta tried to ignore them. Four full bags were in Sadie's carryall.

"Mmm," Sadie smacked, "aren't these delicious, Savannah?"

The girl playfully imitated her aunt's exaggerated pleasure by rolling her eyes while chewing.

"Ohh, you two! If you don't beat all. Shame on you eating those in front of me like that."

Sadie passed the opened bag beneath Greta's nose. "Have some."

"Now how do you think the Peruvian vendors would take to some-one touching their sheepskin wares with hands full of salty nut oil?"

"Not kindly, I imagine," Sadie sang. "Not kindly at all. Suit your-self," she added, passing the bag down to the child.

Greta pointed to a tent. "Here it is." Then, belligerently, she shook her finger in Sadie's face. "When I'm done in here I'm going to eat a whole bag myself. All by myself!"

The other two grinned at one another. They knew Greta would make good on her word. She'd do it just to get back at them for teasing her.

The Peruvian tent was stifling during this time of day. The afternoon sun poured down liquid heat on the heavy canvas tent top, and the stock of sheepskin rugs and clothing was actually warm to the touch. The woolen serapes and thickly woven blankets lent a sense of intensified warmth to the enclosed area. Little breeze made its way through the tent's narrow seam gaps.

While Greta hemmed and hawed over which style of slippers to purchase for Josef, her companions gravitated toward the displays located near the cooler entryway. They idly scanned the tables of Andean pottery and carved Incan images. Just as Sadie picked up a large piece of pottery, she nearly dropped it when Greta startled her.

"Okay! I'm done! On to the last stop!" Her hand shot out. "Gimme those nuts!"

Carefully setting the item down, Sadie let out a relieved breath. She plucked a bag of nuts off the top of the net bag hung on her arm.

"Where's that? You mean you don't want to shop till you drop?" She checked her watch. "It's just four o'clock. You've only got one more stop?"

"Yep. Remember the Robertsons' place?"

She did. The Robertsons had been long-time friends of Greta and Josef. The couple would take the young Sadie and Mira out to their farm for visits and, while the old friends chatted, the girls would run wild in the fields. Mira was always getting lost in the cornfields.

"Sure I remember them."

"They have a booth here. Still grow the sweetest corn in the state. We're going to get us some and have it while it's still freshly harvested."

Loaded down with bulging shopping bags, the three worked their way to the parking lot and, with a satisfied sigh of a job well done, Greta eased herself into the passenger seat of the panel van.

While Sadie rolled down the windows to let the stifling heat escape, Savannah scrambled into the jump seat behind the driver's side. Her scented prize from the India pavilion was held tightly in hand. It held more than incense. It held expectation, a challenge of two sisters' wills.

Greta dug another bag of nuts out and, without the need for fanfare, nonchalantly made double good on her promise.

"Everybody ready?" the driver asked, turning to check if the one behind her had her seatbelt fastened.

The girl tapped her shoulder to let her aunt know she was ready.

Greta munched and nodded.

"Good. Then, ladies, we are out of here," she announced, shoving the gear into reverse. A second later it went back into park. "Ohmigod."

Without breaking her metered munching, Greta gave the driver a questioning glance.

The driver returned the look. "Do the Guttensteins still have a booth here?"

"The Guttensteins? At one time they did. Not anymore. Old man Guttenstein passed on three years ago. Why?"

"Tina. She wanted me to get her some of that sausage of theirs. Is there a German booth here? I didn't recall seeing one."

"Sure. Sure, there's a Bavarian one. They have a big tent." The housekeeper gave a disbelieving stare. "You mean to tell me that you didn't smell that German sausage cooking? The sauerkraut?"

"Maybe. I guess I did when we went looking for Savannah. It didn't register or I would've gone back after we left the India place. Look," she explained, "I have to get Tina some of that sausage. I promised her I would. Just give me directions and you two wait here for me. I won't be but a few minutes. It's too hot to get back into that crowd."

Greta thought that was a fine idea and gave explicit directions. The Bavarian tent was two booths down from the Mexico one.

Sadie was already out the door as Greta called out. "Remember, it's between the Cajun Queen and the Thailand tents!" Returning her full attention to the bag of nuts, she chuckled before addressing the child.

"Your mama's going to hit the ceiling when she smells that incense of yours. You and your aunt are in for a time with that little bit of mischief." She reached her hand toward the back of the driver's seat. "Let me see what fragrance you picked out." She waited. "Savannah? Savannah, honey, did you hear me?" Then she turned to look at the girl.

The jump seat was empty.

Oh, Lordy. Her head spun back to the opened window.
"Savannahhhh!"

The sounds of the crowd drowned out Greta's frantic call. The girl
nimbly moved through the milling people without seeing them, her
eyes fixed on the bobbing head of auburn hair highlighted by the
afternoon sun. She was closing the distance between them and would
soon be at her aunt's side. That was, after all, why she'd followed her,
wasn't it? Or was it? It suddenly occurred to her that this was a bit
like playing Nancy Drew—tailing her subject. She could keep a safe
distance behind and still watch everything her aunt Sadie did. And so,
she decided, this was the perfect opportunity to play super sleuth.
Could she measure up to Nancy Drew? She was going to give it her
best. Maybe she could even be a spy and then hightail it back to the
van before her subject returned. That idea appealed to her even more.
At any rate, if nothing else, she'd be there to make sure her aunt didn't
get lost at the market. Like Greta, she knew it like the back of her
hand.

An aura of spiciness drifted from the opened tent flaps of the
Cajun Queen where Creole women, hair wrapped in colorful, turban-
like bandanas, carefully tended to catfish frying on the portable grills.

The woman rushing past the sizzling catfish now wished she'd had
more time to explore the entire marketplace. Cajun food wasn't her
favorite cuisine, yet there were certain ethnic dishes she greatly
enjoyed. Controlling the urge to pop inside, she set her sights on the
pavilion beside it.

The Bavarian Bazaar was far more than a tent, double or otherwise. The German vendors occupied an actual building that had been
preserved during the demolition of the other structures on the block.
Evidently, a structural engineer had judged the integrity of the foun-
dation and first-floor walls safe enough to let it stand. Besides updated
finishing work, a new roof had been added.

When the redheaded woman entered, her senses were assailed by
a variety of scents and, though she wanted to tarry a while—browse
the beer steins—she headed straight for the refrigerated meat display.
She'd never seen so many different kinds of sausage in one place and
would've been hard-pressed to pick out the exact one Tina wanted if
it hadn't been for her familiarity with it. A sigh of relief escaped her

lips when she spotted it. There it was, the segmented links couched among dozens of other types of sausage coils. She made her purchase and, willing herself to refrain from looking at the shelves of beckoning steins, headed straight for the exit. She paused long enough to raise her face to the light breeze and offer a prayer to Whomever that she'd remembered her friend's request and had been able to fulfill it.

A shrill squeal pulled her mind back to the market's activity. Her attention was drawn to a clutch of small children racing to and fro in front of the Thailand tent. They were laughing and running in and out of the entrance. Their joy brought a smile to the onlooker's face. The smile froze when three children ran screaming out of the tent, an old woman chasing them in a game of Monster's Gonna Get You. The woman's red hat slumped lopsidedly over the silver hair as she bent to catch a giggling child.

Sadie ducked back into the shadows of the Bavarian doorway. With a pounding heart, she watched Ruby play with the little children. The happiness on their faces glowed like sunlit morning dew. They seemed to know her well. They seemed to love her.

Exhausted, Ruby sat down on a low wooden bench and tiredly mimicked a rag doll. Her head lolled to one side and arms hung loose. The children raced to gather around her. One carefully climbed on her lap.

The old one straightened and began to speak.

The little group sat in a semicircle, intently listening to the woman's soft voice. They listened to the fairytale she began to weave for them . . . in Thai.

The hair on the back of the hidden woman's neck prickled. *Ruby knows Thai?* Slowly, she inched her face out into the sunlight to get a better view of the seated group. Sure enough, the children understood everything the old one said. The storyteller sprinkled her tale with great animation, making the children react in fright or giggles.

Mesmerized by the drama, Sadie couldn't take her eyes from the scene. She watched the woman stand, the children making a circle around her. Then, in slow motion, Ruby began to gracefully move her arms and legs. Tai Chi? Stunned, Sadie realized the woman was doing Tai Chi with the children. Where did she learn that? It seemed that the surprises were never-ending. One after the other, they just kept coming.

She watched until the woman brought her hands together as though in devout prayer, then respectfully bowed low. After the children bowed back, she hugged each child and waved to them as she shuffled away to disappear into the throng of shoppers.

Easing out of the shadows, the redhead hesitantly moved toward the Thailand tent. The large black eyes of the children suspiciously viewed the woman's stealthy approach. One ran inside, only to reappear with her mother in tow.

"Yes?" the mother inquired. "Can help with some thing you look for?"

"Ahh. Yes. Ahh, that old woman who was here. Do you—"

"Woman?" the mother repeated, looking about the throng of passersby.

The child tugged her mother's tunic. "Ruby," she whispered.

"Ahhh," the mother sang with a big knowing grin. "Woman Ruby!"

"Yes," Sadie smiled back with an anxious nod. "Ruby. I saw her with the children."

The mother eagerly bobbed her head. "They love Ruby. She play with them. Tell funny stories. Sometimes give presents. Children all love Ruby."

"I see that. Ruby speaks Thai?"

Again the woman nodded with excitement as she turned to attend to her shop.

Sadie followed close on her heels and was struck by the heavy incense smoke.

"Thai," the woman repeated. "Yes. She speak good Thai." The vendor nervously straightened out a row of enameled temple guardian dogs. She placed her hand on her heart. "I Mei Phan." Then, pointing to the inquiring woman, "You?"

"Sadie. My name is Sadie."

"Say-dee buy mangos? Rice?" Then she pointed to the cone-shaped straw hats. "Hat to keep sun off pretty red hair?"

"No, not today."

Unfazed, Mei Phan moved to the stack of silk and brocade lengths of cloth. "Maybe some cloth? Bananas? Mei Phan make good curry," she added, pointing in the direction of the simmering cook pot.

"Maybe next time."

Mei Phan shrugged. "Okay. Maybe next time you come buy rice."

"So, Ruby tells the children stories?"

The woman nodded.

Sadie gracefully moved her arms around. "And she teaches them Tai Chi?"

Frowning at the poor imitation, the mother's brows knitted together. "Tai Chi? No Tai Chi. Ruby do dance. She teach Siam temple dance to girls."

And the surprises still paraded nonstop before Sadie. She was so shaken she didn't know what to ask next. Her mind drew a complete blank. Suddenly she felt she was about to be overcome by the cloying incense. She sought air. "I . . . I have to go now. Thank you. Have a nice afternoon."

Surprised at her visitor's hasty exit, Mei Phan called, "Nice afternoon you, too!" Then she pursed her lips and looked down at her daughter. "Crazy lady."

Out in the cooling breeze, Sadie's hand went to her chest. Her mind buzzed like drones in a hive. She had to get out of there. The world didn't make sense anymore. She had to get back to the van. Time had passed, yet it felt like it had stood still. Greta and Savannah would be worried.

Making her hurried way to the parking lot, Sadie jostled people for right-of-way and half ran toward the van. The van. A safe place in a world gone crazy.

She and Savannah reached the vehicle at the same time. Both were breathing hard with the effort of racing time.

Sadie gave the girl a curious look. "Where were you?"

Savannah pointed in the direction of the portable toilets.

"Oh. Well, let's get going. Home looks pretty inviting right about now."

After they both climbed in and buckled up, Greta heaved a sigh. "Thank God."

"For what?" the driver asked, while putting the van in gear for the second time.

The housekeeper shifted her gaze back to Savannah who was making outrageous faces behind the driver's back—faces pleading secrecy.

"For what?" Greta echoed. "Oh, for everything, I guess. Mostly for small favors."

Sadie lowered her eyes from the dramatics she'd seen played out in the rearview mirror. "Small favors, huh? I suppose we could all use a few of those now and then." She didn't know what the conspiracy was all about. Just knowing there was one was enough to end her day on a sour note. Nothing seemed to ring of reality anymore. Somewhere along the line, she didn't recall quite when, she'd fallen down the rabbit hole. She thought she heard the tick-ticking of the White Rabbit's pocket watch. If she saw the Mad Hatter run in front of her while pulling out of the market lot, she wouldn't doubt her eyes. The unexpected had become the new norm, she thought. The old norm? Well, who knew where that went? *Probably off to see the Wizard.*

When the van pulled up to the kitchen door entrance, Josef greeted the shoppers with arms out to help carry in the market goods. His eyes lit up when he saw the haul of fresh Robertson's corn.

His wife's eyes twinkled as she secretively carried her special purchase inside.

"I thought we'd do up the corn and have it with the rest of the baked ham tonight. Savannah?" she called to the girl who was already halfway up the stairs with her incense. "You come back down and we'll all shuck the corn together. Okay?"

The girl nodded. She liked pulling the husks off. And she was meticulous in making sure every silk was properly removed.

Greta put Tina's sausage in the freezer. She'd save Josef's gift for later that evening when they were alone.

The corn-shucking had been a great success. With Mira calling to say she'd be late, needing to delegate research among her four paralegals and prep two clients for their upcoming depositions, the four at home had spent a companionable evening. While they worked cleaning the corn, laughter had rung through the kitchen, and dinner conversation had opened itself to the telling of amusing experiences that left everyone in stitches. And, as it turned out, Sadie had been the only one who thought she'd successfully masked the turmoil that roiled inside her.

During the game of Scrabble after dinner, Greta and Josef had noticed how distracted she'd been.

Savannah had kept a keen eye on her aunt all evening. She'd been the perfect spy. Nancy Drew would've been proud of her. And after Sadie had tucked her in bed, she mentally counted to five hundred to keep from falling asleep. Her clandestine job was just beginning. Her eyes were glued to the telephone on her bedside table. When the extension light came on it'd be her cue to move into action.

"I almost didn't call you tonight," Sadie admitted in a low, quivering voice. "Things are . . . well, things are getting out of hand here."

"With Savannah?" Tina asked.

"No. With that woman. I—"

"You mean Ruby?"

"Yes."

Tina waited for her friend to elaborate. When the silence became weighted, she gently prodded for information. "What's going on, honey? You really sound awful. Depressed or something?"

Silence.

"Sadie? Talk to me." Then she heard sniffling. "Are you crying? What's wrong?"

Sadie blew her nose but couldn't manage to stop the tears. "I shouldn't have come. I wasn't ready to take on the job of helping someone else. I need help myself. I feel like I'm being smothered."

"By what?"

"Life!" she cried. "I feel like I've been thrown away and—"

"By Paul?"

"Yes! And I haven't had time to deal with all of that yet. I haven't even had time to think about it, absorb it. Then, there's Savannah. I want to help her so bad and I think maybe I could've, but then Ruby gets thrown into the mix and I can't deal with all of it at the same time. I feel smothered by everything that's happened. I can't keep things sorted out. Everything's getting jumbled together. I feel like I'm going crazy."

"Sadie. Don't go there. You're not going crazy. You just got hit with a lot at once, is all. Listen to me. There's nothing you can do about Paul. That's over and done with. You need to set that issue aside for now. You can process that later. Agreed?"

Agreement reluctantly came through halting sobs.

"Savannah's the reason you're there. Right?"

"Yeah."

"Okay. So you need to focus on her."

"But what about Ruby? She's everywhere I go. I can't get away from her. How can I ignore her when she's always in my face?"

Tina thought on that. "Did you end up going to the Farmers' Market today?"

"Yes. You wouldn't believe how huge it's gotten. It was like some kind of international cultural festival."

"Was she there?"

"Yes. Yes, dammit! That's what I'm trying to tell you! I can't get away from her and it's driving me crazy!"

"Slow down, girlfriend. Just slow down. First of all, you're not crazy. You need to talk it out. Tell me about it."

"Ohhh, God. I'm going crazy," Sadie sobbed.

"Sadie! Snap out of it. Stop it! You're not being rational here. There's nothing crazy about running into someone here and there."

"Here and there? Try *everywhere!*"

"Okay, everywhere. And if it's everywhere then there's a reason for it. Just because you don't see the reason doesn't mean that it's irrational or that you're crazy. How can you think *you're* the crazy one if Savannah's seen her as well?"

The question jammed a wrench of logic into Sadie's spinning thought process. She fell silent.

Tina had hit a bull's-eye. "See what I mean? I have to agree that it is highly unusual to run into her everywhere. That alone leads me to believe that there's some reason behind Ruby's appearances. I've given it a lot of thought and I think that the three of you are tied together somehow. You know, tied together as in destiny."

"The three of us? Ohhh, God," Sadie sighed with a hitch to her breath.

"Quit that! You have to stop making this into some horrible thing! You need to go with the flow. Relax! You've got to relax and let yourself be carried with the current of this thing. You have to stop fighting it. Stay open. Stay open to wherever it leads you. Your problem is that you're fighting it rather than accepting it. It's the fighting that's making you feel crazy. It's frustrating you and it's wearing you down."

Sadie blew her nose instead of commenting.

"Am I right? You know I'm right."

"Maybe."

"You said you saw her again today?"

"Yes, at the market."

"Can you tell me about it? Are you okay talking about it?"

Sadie recounted their day and explained how she'd seen Ruby after she had to go back for Tina's sausage.

"She played with the kids like she was their grandma. She told them stories. She spoke in Thai. Then when she began making those slow motions with the kids following her lead, I thought she was doing

Tai Chi. It kind of looked like Tai Chi. After she left I talked to the Thai vendor and she said that Ruby came often. That the kids loved her. That she speaks fluent Thai and was teaching Siam temple dances to the girls . . . Tina, how can an elderly, white, homeless woman speak fluent Thai? How can she know traditional Thailand temple dances? See what I mean? I'm going crazy."

"How does what *Ruby* does make *you* the crazy one just because you *witnessed* it? Now you aren't making sense. That's not logical."

Sadie hesitated before replying. "Yeah, I know. It didn't make sense to me either after I heard myself say it."

"All right, then. There's still an explanation for everything. You're still assuming she's homeless. That hasn't been established. And as far as her speaking Thai goes, who's to say she hasn't spent time over there. She could've been in the military in Cambodia or she could've been part of a Peace Corps volunteer group. Hell, Sadie, she could've been *raised* over there. Lots of white folks speak other languages and are familiar with different cultures. What's so almighty odd about that? Huh? What's so crazy about that?"

Sadie didn't reply.

Tina pushed her point further. "Remember Janine Dombrowsky?"

A chuckle was audible. "From college?"

"So you do remember her. She could fluently speak four languages."

"And read them. And write them. Don't remind me. She let everyone know how great she was."

"Well, maybe knowing her will shed more light on your shadowy bag lady. Doesn't knowing that lots of people speak other languages take some of the mystery—craziness—out of Ruby's behavior?"

"Yes."

"You've got to settle down, Sadie. For some reason, you're seeing some pretty normal things and taking them all the way to the moon. Keep your perspective. Granted, some of the things Ruby has done do seem out there. We don't have explanations for everything, but stay grounded."

"Grounded."

"Yeah, grounded. You're frustrated and confused because you're mentally trying to deal with too many things at once. You can't do anything about the Paul situation so leave it for now. And, as far as I can see, you can't really do anything about Savannah, either. You certainly can't force her to speak. That has to come on its own, in her own time. Just be there for her. That's all you're there to do. Just be there for her. So that leaves Ruby. Take a day at a time and, if you cross paths with her again, keep your head. Keep perspective. If you and she are supposed to keep crossing paths then stop bucking destiny. Make it an adventure, an intriguing adventure."

"An adventure."

"Sure. Why not?"

"I don't need an adventure. I need some peace in my life."

"Like I said, you need to get grounded. Take a day off from the hustle-bustle of having to go somewhere everyday. Take a day for yourself. You need it. Get away from the house and just veg out someplace where it's quiet. Solitude. Some solitude might work miracles right now."

The idea sounded appealing. "Maybe I do need a little solitude. Maybe tomorrow I could get a day off by myself and pull things together."

"There you go," Tina encouraged. "Just get away by yourself. The pier would be a nice spot. Or maybe Grant Park."

"I'll think about it."

Tina didn't like the noncommittal sound of that. "You need to do more than think about it. You really do need to get away from everything for a day and get grounded. Promise you'll do that tomorrow?"

Sadie hesitated. She took her promises seriously.

"Promise?" Tina pushed.

"Promise."

"Do you feel any better about things?"

"I guess. Like you said, I need to get grounded. But—"

"But?"

"But what about Savannah? What'll I tell her? Her feelings may be hurt. She may not understand that I need a day by myself. What if she takes it personally?"

"Trust me, she won't. She's a sharp little cookie. You need some rest. Goodnight, Sadie. Have a good day tomorrow."

"Goodnight, Tina. And thanks."

"Don't mention it. Thanks for picking up the sausage. I feel guilty that you ran into Ruby because of me."

"Now who's not keeping perspective?"

"Whatever. Remember, I'm just a phone call away."

"Thanks, Tina. Thanks for keeping my head on straight."

Exhausted, Sadie fell into a deep sleep. In that sleep she tossed and turned with dreams of Savannah crying great crocodile tears because her aunt didn't want to be with her tomorrow. And in those dreams she looked into a full-length mirror and froze when she saw Ruby passing behind her own reflection.

Seven

Friday

You have to do it just right, the child mentally instructed her invisible students. *The secret of making it happen on the first attempt comes from practice, a lot of practice. But once you get the hang of it, success takes only a second or two. All it takes is a steady heat source. See here? The light bulb on this bedside lamp is perfect. Now watch!*

Mira sat on the edge of her daughter's bed. Dressed to the nines in a Chanel suit jacket and skirt, she smoothed her long, lacquered fingernails through Savannah's thick mass of hair which was spread across the pillow like wind-whipped flames.

Greta, standing close by, waited for instructions.

"Hey, what's up?" Sadie chirped, peeking her head around the doorway of the girl's room. A shadow of concern darkened her light-hearted mood when she saw the child was still in bed.

Mira visibly stiffened at the intrusive sound of her sister's voice. In a perfunctory manner, she abruptly picked up her Italian leather briefcase and stood. "Savannah has a fever this morning and requires bed rest." After striding across the room, she paused in front of her sister. Her eyes narrowed as her voice took on the tone of a clever litigator addressing a witness with an intimidating statement she knew would be overruled by a judge. It dripped with implied accusation. "I can't imagine how she picked up a bug when she's home all day. Can you?" Without waiting for a response, she inclined her head toward the housekeeper. "Plenty of water and only broth or light soup to eat. Call me if she gets worse. I'll be in court all morning, but you can leave a message with Caitlin." She blew her daughter a kiss before disappearing into the hall.

No one moved until they heard the front door close.

Troubled over the unexpected development, Sadie went to the child. "I'm sorry you're not feeling well, honey." She was about to voice her worry that perhaps the girl had picked up something at the Farmers' Market, then thought better of it when she realized that it was too soon to show up if that was where she'd caught something. Her eyes met Greta's. "Should she see a doctor?"

The elder woman, long experienced in childhood illnesses, dismissed the question with a flip of her hand. "It's nothing serious. She'll be fine. Children get fevers now and again. It'll pass as quickly as it came." She glanced down at the child's closed eyes. "She'll be as good as new for tomorrow's dance classes, you'll see."

"She takes dancing lessons now?"

"Oh, yes, indeed. Every Saturday. Wouldn't miss them for the world."

"Well," Sadie cooed, bending down to pamper her niece. She tucked the blanket around the small shoulders. "I've brought you something to help you get better." And from behind her back, she presented the girl with the carved trinket box.

Savannah's lids shot open. The eyes sparkled a bit too brightly at the sight of the unexpected gift. She remembered herself then. The eyelids fluttered to settle at a sickly half mast. A pained smile slightly upturned the corners of her mouth. Fingers weakly snaked over the top of the blanket to accept the present.

"Here," the aunt said, handing over the box.

The girl released a piteous sigh as she took it and cradled it to her heart beneath the quilt. *Oh, thank you! Thank you! It's beautiful!* She wanted to tell her aunt that she'd always treasure her sandalwood box but, most of all, she wanted to tell her not to worry about her. Instead, she closed her eyes again.

Sadie smiled sympathetically before catching the housekeeper's eye. "We probably should leave so she can go back to sleep," she whispered, while turning to tiptoe away from the bed.

Greta thought that that was an excellent idea. She nodded, motioning that Sadie should go ahead.

The elder woman remained rooted to the floor beside the bed. She looked down at the child's long lashes that fluttered the rims of her closed lids. Her gaze went to the thermometer on the bedside table, then back again to the girl. She didn't speak until Sadie was well out of earshot.

"Okay, Missy," she quietly said. "I know you're not sleeping. I think your mother's on to the hooky playing. And though you've managed to fool her and your auntie with this fever, old Greta's wise to your lightbulb tricks. Your aunt started pulling the same thing when she was your age so it's nothing new to me. I don't know why you chose this morning to pull your little caper, but I suppose you have a good reason. If your aunt goes out today, we're having your favorite barbecued burgers for lunch. If she stays home, well, you're out of luck on that score and you'll be stuck keeping up the charade—with having to stay with the broth."

When the child was left alone again, she pulled the gift from beneath the covers and tenderly ran her fingertips over the intricately carved lid. Pangs of guilt washed through her conscience for having to worry her aunt over the feigned sickness. Well, she reasoned, there was no other way. It had to be done. It was the only way to spare her aunt from feeling guilt over needing a day to herself. She knew that people sometimes needed to be off by themselves. She was no baby who'd pout over being left out. She was a big girl. She understood those kinds of things because they weren't just for grownups. There had been plenty of times when she needed to be alone, even away from those she loved. Her only regret was that her aunt hadn't realized that her niece would've understood that kind of need.

Sadie's first choice for a location in which to reap the needed grounding benefits turned out to be less than satisfactory. She'd chosen one of the larger parks by Lake Michigan and, after being interrupted by children's playful shouting and their errant balls rolling past her feet, she chose an alternate destination and drove the short way down to Navy Pier. After parking, she walked out onto the pier, passing several elderly couples strolling hand in hand. It was a bitter-sweet sight to her. How sweet for a couple's love to have endured so long, yet the thought brought the sting of her own recently broken relationship. Deciding on one of the empty park benches that faced the water, she gave the couples a last lingering glance before wearily seating herself. Her aloneness seemed conspicuous now as her gaze swept out over the watery scene. She squinted. Sunlight danced with a million winking sparkles on the wavering surface. The water would ground her. Whenever she was deeply upset over something, a long, soaking bath never failed to improve her outlook. Just the sound of water had the effect of an emotional elixir for her.

On the horizon, a thin trail of dark smoke gave sign of a freighter heading toward shore. Nearer to port, the breeze carried the sounds of horns blowing from various ships. Some bellowed deeply resonant bass tones as though beginning their sounds from the depths of their wide-bellied hulls. Others voiced their presence through tones higher on the scale, which made the vessels seem smaller in size than the supertankers with the booming voices.

Marking the channel lane, bells on nodding buoys clanged like someone pulling the rope of a bell tower.

Cutting through the air, gulls soared and dived. Others of their kind, already well satiated, lazily glided on the air currents in seemingly effortless flight. One curious bird alighted on the iron rail of the pier. It cocked its head in unvoiced question at the woman sitting on the bench.

"Sorry, fella," the woman cooed in an apologetic tone, while upturning her palms. "I came empty-handed. No morsels for you here. If I'd known this was where I'd end up today I would have brought some gull snacks. Sorry to disappoint you, old boy."

The bird, not quite believing someone would sit on the pier with-out a bag of gull goodies, tilted its head this way and that.

The woman extended her empty hands toward the bird. "See? Nothing there. You're welcome to keep me company if you're not expecting lunch."

The gull took wing.

"Opportunist," the woman whispered before returning her sights to the expanse of water.

Sadie Brennan had so many issues to think about that she didn't know where to begin. They swirled in her mind like a turning kaleidoscope.

Paul. She felt that she hadn't had enough time to process the shock of the sudden broken relationship before the mystery of Tina's runes intruded to complicate matters. The repeat layouts of the tokens had left their mark. They had affected her more deeply than she was initially willing to admit. The Journey piece had been borne out by Mira's letter.

This brought her to the issue of how she was supposed to be of help to her niece. How did one bring another out of a traumatically induced state of silence? What sort of psychological technique would work to reverse it? Would a different sort of dramatic event induce speech? Or would time be all that was needed? What could she personally do to bring the child back to normalcy?

And what about the bag lady? What the hell was Ruby all about? Why did the old woman have such a hold on her? If . . .

Children's excited hollering and laughter broke Sadie's train of thought. Three classes of schoolchildren were making their way up the pier. Teachers and their aides were shouting after the kids who were running ahead of the main group. A field trip to Navy Pier was in progress.

The woman on the bench again cast her gaze over the water and forced herself to return to the mental page she'd been on. Ruby. Was she actually the enigma that Sadie had built her up to be? Were the odd aspects associated with her simply circumstantial elements, coincidences, or even imagined? Considering she hadn't had time to deal with the Paul issue, was her mind in such a fragile state that an overload of events caused her to overreact to the repeat encounters with the bag lady? Was she blowing it all out of proportion? Did she need to step aside and look at the situation from a different angle? Yet Tina didn't seem to think she was overreacting. Tina thought the woman's behavior just as odd. So . . .

Bits of bread flew past the woman on the bench. Children, jostling one another to get the best spot, hugged the rails and tossed their tidbits of food to the circling gulls.

"Don't bother that lady!" a teacher called.

But, of course, the lady had already been bothered when she had been bombarded by incoming missiles of bread. The lady rose from the bench and maneuvered through the throng of children scrambling toward the railing. The teacher apologized for the unruly class of excited youngsters.

"It's okay, I was just getting ready to leave anyway." *Leave*, she thought, *leave for where? Where to now?* And as she walked back down the pier, something piercing the skyline caught her attention. It was a cathedral spire. A place of peace and quiet was what she'd been seeking. A place to be able to think more clearly. A place to ground herself. She smiled. It'd been many years since she'd been inside a church, but as sure as the gulls were flying, she knew that the spire was a sign that beckoned her to a place of solitude.

Our Lady of Sorrows Cathedral was an imposing structure which humbled the buildings that were later put up in its vicinity. Constructed at a time when the city was young, the church spared no expense in striving to create a marvel of Old World architecture that would physically awe and spiritually inspire the new congregation of worshipers that would be drawn to its doors. The six spires surrounding the center bell tower in the steeple could be seen from many vantage points throughout the city. The structure had gained not only regional fame but national recognition as well. Views of both the exterior and interior were featured on postcards. Visiting tourists included the famous cathedral on their list of top ten places to see while visiting Chicago.

Sadie climbed the worn stone steps and stood before the small entry door cut into the massive wooden double doors that were studded with iron nails. This destination felt right to her. She was sure this was where she was going to get some things settled. This was where she was going to get grounded. With feelings of mixed determination and expectation, she heaved a deep breath, pulled on the wrought iron ring, and opened the door.

As she stepped inside, the sounds of the busy street were silenced when the door closed behind her. The scent of hundreds of burning votive candles pleasingly intermingled with the trace of frankincense from a recently swung censor. The combined fragrance soothed her weary soul. She'd entered a hushed aura of sacredness. She felt as though she'd just stepped into a holy womb—a safe shelter from the turmoil of the world, of life.

Her footfalls across the mosaic tiles of the stone floor echoed through the vestibule as she passed recessed alcoves housing life-size statues of the Madonna. These, she thought, reminded her of the many grottos she and Tina had seen in the hilly Italian countryside when they'd flown there after receiving their degrees. Like the offerings of the faithful in Italy, fresh flowers were left before these images as well. Her eyes were drawn to each statue in turn before passing through the medieval-style, stone arch leading into the main cathedral.

Though she'd visited this place in the past, the awe she felt never diminished. The dizzying height of the domed ceiling was breathtaking and one could sit and study its painted scenes for hours. It was nothing on the scale of St. Peter's Basilica in Rome, yet it was clear that had been the architect's loose model.

Sadie, quietly moving up the center aisle, passed a scattering of others who, like herself, had sought respite in the house of God. Some folks were kneeling, lips silently moving while deep in fervent prayer. Others sat with their eyes closed, reaping solace from the profound peacefulness they'd found.

The newcomer randomly stopped midway to seat herself in one of the oak pews. Here there would be no screaming children or reprimanding teachers, no pieces of bread flying past her. With a relieved sigh she rested back against the wooden seat and, letting herself be soothed by the comforting surroundings, closed her eyes. The serenity of the church was a balm on her raw nerves and she found herself relaxing into a state which settled itself between meditation and dozing. It was a restful place to be. It was a state of nonthought where all conscious awareness of oneself was nonexistent. She had no idea how much time had passed before her eyes slowly opened on the wrought iron stands holding tiered rows of red votive candles. Through half-opened lids, she watched the flickering flames, which reminded her of starshine on a moonless night. Why can't life be simple? she wondered. Why does everything have to get so complicated? Why can't we have better vision to understand more of the whys?

"Excuse me," came a whisper to her left.

She started and straightened in her seat. She turned to the sound, and her green eyes locked on the grey ones of a rosy-cheeked priest.

"Are you all right, miss?" came the question weighted with an Irish brogue.

Embarrassed, Sadie nervously touched her hair. "Why, yes. Yes, I'm fine."

The man wasn't convinced. "Are you sure, ma'am? You looked as though you might've been having a bit of an ill spell."

Sadie's face flushed. "Actually, Father, I think I was just about asleep. It's so quiet in here. It's so peaceful. I'd been wondering why life had to be so complicated."

A hand was extended and the woman shook it.

"I'm Father McElveney," he informed, while smoothly easing himself into the pew beside her. "Everyone here about calls me Mac, though. I'm not one for formalities."

"Nice to meet you, Father Mac."

"So you were wonderin' why life has to be so complicated, were you?"

Father Mac was one of those soft-spoken people one felt immediately at ease with. He was the type who emitted unwavering integrity. Sadie imagined that his heart held an untold number of secrets his parishioners had entrusted him with.

"Love?"

"Excuse me?" she asked, realizing that she'd been lost in her own private evaluation of the man. "I'm sorry. What did you say?"

His wispy white brows formed a sharp vee. "You've got a great deal on your mind, haven't you, young lady." It was a statement, not a question.

"Sadie. My name's Sadie. And yes, I've a great deal on my mind."

In an effort to show his goodwill, his smile brightened like sunshine. "Ah, Sadie, is it love now? Has a love turned complicated for ya?"

"No, Father Mac," she smirked with the irony of the question, "love has actually left my life for the moment."

"Tsk, tsk, now," the priest said with an admonishing shake of his finger, "love never truly leaves a body's life. Love comes in many guises. Have you no family, then?"

She saw where he was going and felt chastised. "Well, yes," she conceded. "Yes, there is that love—the love of one's family members."

"Well, then. There you are, lass! Love is still truly with you now, isn't it?"

"Oh yes," she admitted, thinking of Savannah. "It surely is, Father." Then, not sure why she did it, she told him about her niece's problem.

He intently listened and, when the story was done, offered his opinion.

"Things like this cannot be forced. The child must be given all the time she needs to come 'round on her own. I've seen one or two cases like that. In the end, it's the child who discovers the key to unlocking the mystery."

Mystery. Why did he have to say that? "Yes, I suppose you're right, but . . ."

Father McElveney watched the woman's eyes cloud with doubt as her voice trailed off into a place where unspoken thoughts lived. He leaned forward to catch her attention.

She remained frozen in her own world. *Mystery. Mystery.* Now that the priest had said the word, she couldn't shake her mind clear of it.

"Sadie?" he gently asked, with a hint of concern.

Wistfully, her head inclined toward the man. She remained mute.

"Your niece will come out of it eventually. She's reacting to a terrible shock. Sometimes it takes something dramatic to reverse the state she's in. What I mean is, something the child interprets as being a great event, not necessarily another negative or traumatic event. Are you understandin' my meanin', lass?"

The woman's head began to imperceptibly move back and forth. "No. No, Father, I wasn't thinking of Savannah."

Puzzlement showed on the man's face. "Well, then, is there something else I can help you with? If nothing else," he smiled, "I've been told I'm a good listener."

"Mystery," she whispered.

"Mystery?" he echoed.

"Yes. You said the word 'mystery' when you were talking about my niece."

He paused to recall his words. "You're right, I did. Only the traumatized child—"

"No, Father. There's another mystery in my life. And I think it's driving me a little crazy because I can't seem to get away from it."

"Well," he sighed, "then perhaps you are not supposed to get away from it. Are you trying to run away from it?"

The question intrigued her. She thought on it before replying. "I'm not sure how to answer that. It just came into my life and keeps returning. She keeps getting in my face."

"She?"

The woman frowned. "Did I say 'she'?"

A curious brow rose. "D'ya wanna talk 'bout it, Sadie? 'Bout her?"

For several minutes, the woman made no reply. Stalling for time, she nervously fidgeted with her fingertips. She looked here and there about the church. Then, without looking up, she quietly asked, "Do you believe in miracles, Father?"

"Oh, now," he chuckled with a hint of mirth. "What kind of question is that to ask a man of the cloth?"

Her gaze remained locked on her hands. Her voice was low. "You didn't answer me, Father. I know you're supposed to believe in them because, after all, you're a priest. I know what the party line is." Her eyes rose to meet his. It was clear that her look was meant to garner the truth behind the man's personal belief. "But do *you* believe in miracles?"

Without hesitation, he replied, "I do, Sadie. I do believe in miracles. But then again," he chuckled with a twinkle sparking from his eye, "you're talkin' to a dyed-in-the-wool Irishman who was brought up on bedtime tales of the Little People and fairy queens throwin' parties for their subjects in the deep, green glen at gloamin' time."

The man suddenly reminded her of Josef. Visions of his garden gnomes flashed through her mind. Her shoulders slouched. "Then you're not being serious. Not really."

"Oh! But I surely am being serious!" His hand tenderly covered hers. "Sadie, lass, we humans, as a people, have chosen to shape our world with boundaries that we can understand through touch and sight. All those touchable fences, walls, partitions, levees, and surveyor's stakes we create—they all enclose something we define and believe in because we've given it shape. That shape validates everything existing inside it as having an accredited identity. That identity makes it a known, an accepted known. But, lass, what is the shape of a miracle? What shape is belief? What shape is air? Can we make a shape of air by putting it in a box or mold? What shape is a mystery?"

Sadie was fascinated by the way Father Mac had drawn her into the riddle. "They have no shape," she instinctively replied. "They just are, aren't they? They're any shape. Or," she speculated, "maybe no shape at all."

The priest winked then. "Aye. Nine and a half times out of ten, belief is determined by what folks put stock in. If stock is put in shapes and boundaries, then those people won't necessarily believe in anything without a recognizable form to identify it by. But for those who place stock in the *potential* of the unknown, those folks have open minds and withhold judgment."

"They withhold judgment until?" Sadie interjected. "They're on the fence waiting for proof?"

"No, lass, they've already jumped that fence of indecision. They stand in the sunny field called possibilities. Something inside them tells 'em that the world is full of unimagined possibilities—those many unknowns that are yet to be boxed in and named. They are the dreamers, the visionaries, the inventors, and the ones who ponder and aren't fearful to question the shape, the bounds, of the current knowns. They're the ones who aren't afraid to stand up and shout that the emperor has no clothes. They're the ones who make the discoveries for those who require the shapes and forms for their belief to kick in. They're the ones who go beyond the 'what is' to the 'what ifs.'"

Sadie grinned. "So you do believe in miracles."

Amused, he upturned one side of his mouth. "I said I did." Then he qualified that by wagging a cautioning finger. "I also believe that miracles are just mysteries we haven't put a shape to yet."

They had come full circle back to the mystery.

He wasn't finished. "Take rainbows, for instance. I'm sure rainbows were once a mystery to some folks. Maybe they thought they were magic or a sign from a higher power. But once science discovered that light had a color spectrum, rainbows had a shape, an identity, and the mystery aspect of the event dissipated. We're always learning more about our world, lass. We're still neophytes on this amazing planet. We're still babies who are stretching and reaching. We're still babies learning about the wonders of our reality."

His words prompted her to put it another way. "Mysteries are just puzzles that we don't have all the pieces for. Sometimes we need time to acquire them all before we can see the true reality, how everything fits together to make the greater, complete picture."

He reassuringly patted her hand. "Now you got it. So . . . do you want to talk about your mysterious lady?"

Sadie felt sheepish about the whole issue now. She was embarrassed that she'd made such a big hoopla over the frequent sighting of a little old lady. The priest had made her feel so much better that she felt foolish for blowing things out of proportion. Undecided about how to respond to the man's question, she averted her eyes to the front of the church. What she saw made the hair on her neck stand on end. Her hand shot over her mouth to muffle her outburst.

"Oh, my *God!*"

The priest felt the woman's other hand begin to shake. He snapped his head away from her shocked expression to scan the front of the church before looking back at her again. He hadn't seen anything amiss.

"What is it, lass? You're tremblin' like a leaf. Tell me what's frightened you so?"

Sadie leapt to her feet and frantically attempted to push past the seated man. His cassock was draped on the floor, compromising her footing.

"It's *her!*" she cried. "I've got to go! I told you I couldn't get away from her!"

Father Mac's spine tingled from the sudden display of panic. He gently blocked the hysterical woman's way by placing his hand on the back of the pew in front of them.

"Sadie, who? Tell me who is 'her.'"

She repeatedly jabbed her finger toward the front of the church. "That *woman* up there! Now let me through! I'm not staying here. I've got to leave!"

The priest peered past Sadie to the front of the church. Within a lazy sunbeam floating down through the high stained glass, he saw an old woman with long grey hair and an ankle-length skirt going about the business of dusting the altar. He saw no one else.

"But, lass," he calmly said, "I see no one up there but the Altar Society lady. Are you meanin' Mrs. O'Brien? Is it her who's suddenly got you riled?"

Sadie's eyes fluttered. *Mrs. O'Brien? The Altar Society lady?* She whipped her head around to again set eyes on the woman tidying up the altar area. The elderly lady wore no red hat, no army coat, and no carpetbag was to be seen. Sadie put her hand to her chest and crumpled like a rag doll into the pew beside the priest. "Oh God," she gasped. "Oh God, oh God. Oh, Jesus H., I'm losing it."

For a long while, neither spoke.

Sadie needed time to calm down.

The priest needed time to think. While he did so, his eyes kept being surreptitiously drawn back to the widow O'Brien.

It was Father McElveney who was first to break the silence with a softly whispered statement. "You thought Mrs. O'Brien was Ruby."

Sadie's skin crawled. Her mouth fell open as their eyes met. Her reaction confirmed the priest's suspicion.

"Ruby's your mystery," he said with a guarded smile. "Sadie, my dear, you can't run from Ruby. Why, that's like trying to run from your own shadow. The shadow disappears only when you surround yourself with the light. Only then will the impulse to run disappear."

The woman was incredulous. Her eyes narrowed. "A riddle? I can't believe this. You *know* about *Ruby* and you expect to soothe me with a riddle? A freaking *riddle?*"

"Oh now, I can assure you it's not a riddle," he said with confidence. "I understand your reaction though and, if you'll just give me a mite of a minute, I may be able to help you understand a little more of what you've been dealing with."

Outraged, half of Sadie wanted to storm out of the church. The other half—her curious half—won. She sighed and grumbled under her breath. "I can't believe this," she smoldered. "I just can't believe this."

"Maybe that's why it's all a mystery to you."

She flashed the priest a perturbed look. "Now what're you talking about? *What's* why it's all a mystery to me?"

"Belief."

"Belief?"

"Belief," he echoed. "Belief, Sadie. You see, when we don't *believe* something can happen, then most times we don't even believe it when we actually *see* it happening right before our eyes. We'd much rather doubt our senses and think our eyes are playing tricks on us. That sort of mental switcheroo is more comfortable to us. Instead of simply accepting an anomaly that enters our realm of what we like to term normalcy, we'd rather make it into a mystery. And when that same mystery keeps recurring in our lives, we want to hide so we can remain in denial. We want to hide and cover our eyes so we don't encounter it any more. Denial means safety. We believe that, by choosing blindness, the oddity no longer exists and we won't be forced to accept it by digging in our heels and squaring off with it—facing it head-on. Therefore . . . we run. We run and keep on running. We run like the screechin' banshee's after us because we fear what we don't fully understand."

The defensive bristles on Sadie's back softened with the man's explanation. "I understand what you're saying, but," she countered, "I'm not . . . well, I'm not officially fearful." Her head shook. "No. No, I wouldn't say I was officially fearful."

Father Mac looked down at her and arched a bushy brow. "Not 'officially' fearful?"

"I mean that I'm not *afraid* afraid of her. Know what I mean?"

A corner of his mouth curled. "You're admitting that you are afraid but . . . not really. That is a dichotomy if I ever heard one. It has to be one way or the other if you're talking about the same subject." Both brows rose. "Are we talking about just the one subject here or have we inadvertently mixed several together along the line?"

Now Sadie hid a tight-lipped grin beneath glinting eyes. "I suppose our problem is with the term we're using. I'd say that *afraid* isn't the right word for how I've been feeling about my encounters with Ruby." She thought a minute. "Maybe . . . *unsettled* fits the situation better. I'm unsettled over the things I've seen her do because I don't understand them."

He playfully bantered back. "Some folks don't understand why people want to hug trees, yet they don't go around being unsettled about not being able to understand that behavior. They don't try to run away from that behavior. They might shake their heads, maybe call the tree-huggers a few unflattering names, but they surely don't turn tail and run like the devil 'imself is after them. Lassie," he suggested, "I think you should admit that you are a bit more than unsettled over Ruby."

"Well, dammit!" she blurted, forgetting where she was. She cringed. "Oops, sorry, Father," she apologized, while covering her mouth with her hand and guiltily looking about.

No one in the church seemed to be paying them any attention. All heads were either bowed in fervent prayer or gazing transfixed at the life-size crucifix.

She lowered her voice. "So maybe I'm in between fearful and unsettled. It's just that I can't figure her. She does these, these amazing . . . things!" Her heart began to pound. "Savannah and I saw her heal a lame dog and also a bird that had a broken wing. She appears to magically transform her footwear and pulls objects out of her empty—"

"Wait, lass," he said, cutting her off. "Did you say that your niece also saw these things Ruby did?"

"Yes!"

The priest silently considered that information.

"Why?" Sadie asked. "Is that significant?"

"It could be. How did the child react to these events?"

"Well . . . well, I suppose she was just as puzzled as I was. She's not speaking so she never voiced her thoughts about them."

"But you're certain she witnessed them as well."

"Oh, absolutely."

"Have you spoken about these events to anyone else?"

"Only my best friend back in Maine. I call her every evening after I tuck my niece in bed for the night."

"If you don't think I'm being overly intrusive, may I ask what your friend thinks?"

Sadie rolled her eyes. "You don't want to know, Father. Believe me, you don't really want to know the answer to that."

"Oh, but I do."

"Well . . . she's not into established religions. She, ah . . . she believes in some of the ancient deities—the feminine type."

Without batting an eye or without showing the slightest hint of ridicule in his voice, the priest replied, "The old goddesses, you mean."

Taken aback by the man's ready acceptance, she hesitantly nodded.

In a matter-of-fact tone, he continued. "Those are within the realm of established religions. They are simply established religions of very old cultures."

"Then you're not shocked? You're not going to shake your head in pity and call her a pagan or anything?"

"Oh, lass," he sighed, "what do you take me for? All spiritual belief systems must be respected, even those which greatly vary from one's own. I've found that there are grains of truth to be found in each of them."

Sadie wasn't quite sure what the man was attempting to convey. She sought greater clarity. "Are you saying that you actually believe in the goddesses of the old religions of Rome, Asia, Greece, and the like?"

His hands upturned. "What I'm saying is that I believe there was something behind them. Something to the *spirit* of the beliefs. If God is omnipotent—if God is truly All—shouldn't God also be a balanced blend of both genders? Shouldn't God have a feminine side then? Shouldn't there be representative female images to reflect the divine feminine aspect to the rather one-sided concept of God? Shouldn't there be a God the Mother as the balance to God the Father? And why would it be sacrilegious or heretical to depict that Supreme Being in an either/or form? Even both? Depending. You know, a representation of the Mother or the Father aspect, so to speak."

Sadie mulled that over for a while before asking, "So, what happened to that idea? I mean, the specific Mother aspect of the God concept? It's certainly foreign to the Church's line on the subject."

The priest leaned closer to the woman's ear. His voice was purposely lowered. "Many very wise, ancient cultures attributed a feminine image to the *spirit* aspect of the Divine. The Church came along and did a thorough coverup by calling that aspect the Holy Ghost. Now," he chuckled under his breath, "I tend to think that the Church's founding fathers, taking the old staunch patriarchal hard line in order to rid the faithful of their former strong goddess beliefs, would no longer contribute toward perpetuating the idea of a female deity. They got together and decided to cut her out of the picture altogether by stripping the MotherGod of her title and renaming her aspect . . . Holy Ghost. The Holy Ghost, as we all know, was never given a gender."

In a secretive manner, she inclined her head toward the priest and whispered, "Father," she teased, "you sound like a rogue priest."

Mac's fair Celtic complexion couldn't conceal the flush that colored his cheeks.

He recovered quickly. "But, lass," he conspiratorially countered, "the Church line cannot keep a man, priest or no, from thinkin' for 'imself. I've done a good bit o' readin' in my time and there are certain recognizable threads runnin' through many belief systems that cannot be ignored. To the casual eye, the threads may be fine and fragile lookin', but they be strong as silk to stand the test of time without frayin' or showin' wear."

She grinned. "So what happened to all those goddesses then? I mean, in actuality, nothing happened to them, their beingness. It's the *belief* in them that suffered an alteration."

"Did you forget 'bout all I just said?"

"No, Father Mac, it just sank in." She gave it a name. "Christianity. Christianity was the culprit that erased the concept of MotherGod from all the pylons, papyri, and burial chambers."

"Excuse me?"

"It's an analogy. The Egyptians. When they wanted to get back at a deceased king or queen, the successor had his predecessor's name wiped from all records."

"Well, yes," he hedged. "I suppose that was very similar to the beginnin' of the end for those divine ladies. The Church literally wiped out her former existence. But the Church got so much flak from banning goddess worship that they were forced to provide a substitute in the way of the Holy Virgin. That's when her status was elevated some."

Sadie patiently waited for him to continue. He'd sounded as though he had more to add, but nothing was forthcoming. She peered over at him. "And?" she prodded.

"Well," he said with a shoulder shrug. "I suppose that's the end of it then, eh?"

She had the feeling he'd just tried to wheedle out of giving further information that he wasn't comfortable enough to discuss. He'd backpedaled to a comfort zone that she wasn't willing to let him hide in. In a nonchalant voice, she tried baiting him. "But the Holy Virgin wasn't a goddess."

The priest nervously toyed with the crucifix hanging against his chest. "Ahh, no. No, she was not a goddess."

A weighted silence fell over the two. It fell over them like a rain-soaked blanket. Sadie wasn't sure where the conversation had been leading. At one point she'd glimpsed a road sign the priest was heading toward, then he'd abruptly taken a detour. The name of the road dissipated from her mind like spindrift in a breeze. She couldn't hold onto it. Now she was adrift again without it. The cleric had been hedging toward making some kind of comparison between the goddesses of old and . . . and what? Who? She was frustrated now at having lost that all-important thread that had shed a momentary flash of light on her mystery. She was sure this man held the key, yet he wasn't prepared to take his rogue speculation that far, at least not publicly. He needed prompting. He had to be convinced that she desperately needed the one key he held so guardedly.

Flinging off the blanket of silence, she left off the subject of goddesses and brought them back to the homeless woman. "How do you know Ruby?" she softly began.

"Through the needy who come to our soup kitchen on Saturdays. The homeless folk talk about her among themselves. It's a type of counterculture, you know."

"Counterculture? You mean the homeless?"

"Yes. The general public doesn't realize it, but the homeless don't much like mixing with the rest of society. They're leery of people's motives. The street folk are part of a whole different level of our world—a level beneath the surface of the everyday living which the general populace is familiar with. It runs like an undercurrent beneath our surface world."

The woman had never viewed the homeless population in quite that way before. She wondered how many people like Ruby there were. Was she really without a home? What seemed so different about her? She blended in with the homeless yet didn't appear to shy away from public places either. The woman was just as comfortable in the dilapidated, gutted, warehouses of South Chicago as she was in the museum.

"Your Ruby's unique, though," came the statement as though the priest had read Sadie's wandering thoughts. "She's somewhat of an enigma. Unlike you, one being from the surface level of our world, those members of the homeless treat her as one of their own. She's a clever one, that one, always findin' ways to come up with new shoes for those in need."

"Yes!" Sadie cried. "Her shoes! Did I tell you that that's one of the mysterious things about her? She changes shoes without anyone seeing her do it!"

"Ahhh, I believe you did mention something about her shoes earlier on," he recalled, giving her a dubious look. "But, Sadie," he warned, lowering his voice, "hold on, lass. I have to tell you that I think you're letting your imagination carry you away here. It sounds like it's getting the better of you. If you think about it, I'm sure *someone* sees her change her shoes. You can't really say that nobody's seen her do it, can you now?"

It was an awkward moment. It was then that Sadie knew Father Mac wasn't going to reveal any more about the enigmatic bag lady. He was not going to discuss the old woman's unexplainable habits. She was disappointed that he'd resorted to trying to place doubt in her mind over what she'd seen. Why had he done that? Was he protecting the woman? And if so, from what?

"Well . . . well, sure," she said, forcing a chuckle. "I'm sure you're right about that. I'm sure *someone's* seen her do it. After all," she lied, "I couldn't keep my eye on her every single second." She didn't bother to remind him that a certain eight-year-old had also been watching the woman.

Father McElveney smiled wide. "There you go, lass. That's using a mite more logic. See now? Things are not quite so mysterious and complicated as you thought, are they?"

Sadie's gaze shifted to the front of the church. She was watching Mrs. O'Brien busy herself in the sacristy. "No, Father, they're not," she said in an effort to placate him. *Thanks to you, they're more so. What the hell are you hiding?*

The priest also gave his attention to the woman at the altar. "She does resemble Ruby a bit," he commented. "I suppose it's the long grey hair. You don't see that on many older ladies. I could see where you'd make that mistake."

"Father?"

"Yes?"

"What did you mean before when you said that I couldn't run from Ruby?"

His eyes narrowed as their gaze met. "You're not lookin' for somethin' sinister in that statement, I hope."

"Why would you think that? I can't very well make anything out of it if I don't know what you meant."

"All I meant was that she's a gadabout. She may or may not be truly homeless, but she does have a way of getting all over this big city of ours. She goes anywhere and everywhere. That's all I meant," he said with an innocent shrug. "Nothing more."

Sadie nodded, letting the man think she believed him. He wasn't actually dissembling, but was getting close to it. "So you don't know for sure if she's homeless?"

The man's shoulders hitched up. "My contact with her has been limited and those on the street aren't talkin' to outsiders 'bout her. If you want my opinion, I think they don't care one way or the other. She's been accepted as one of 'em and that seems to be all that matters to 'em." He paused before adding, "I have seen her begging, though."

"Begging!" An image of Ruby begging on the streets was a mental picture she couldn't pull into focus. The idea was unimaginable to her and she didn't know why.

"Why, yes," he said, after being surprised by Sadie's reaction. "Most homeless folks panhandle at one time or another. When out driving about town I've caught sight of her selling little trinkets on street corners. Sometimes she had her hand out without the trinkets. Why should that surprise you so?"

Because she has everything she needs in her satchel. "I . . . I don't know. It just did. For some reason, I can't picture her doing that. Or why."

"Well," he knowingly sighed, "none of us find that a very pretty picture, do we now? It's a sad, sad day when old women are livin' on the streets. And as for the why of it, she probably needed money."

She could pull the Denver Mint from that bag of hers. "But they don't have to, the women, I mean. They don't have to live on the streets. There are shelters. There are social programs. Wouldn't she have Social Security coming in?"

"I couldn't say about Social Security. Don't know if she ever worked. Maybe she never applied for benefits? And as far as the social programs and shelters, it's like I said, some homeless folks prefer to avoid 'em. Sadie, I don't have all the answers. Ruby is just one of our city's hundreds of unfortunates. She just happened to be the one who caught your eye."

Nice try. "I suppose so. I guess it was that long hair and red hat she always wears. It makes her stand out more than the others."

"Oh, indeed it does," he agreed. "You probably haven't even noticed all the others, have you?"

"I can't say that I have, at least not like I've noticed Ruby."

The man gave a merry laugh and quietly slapped both hands to his knees. "Mystery solved!"

"Pardon me?"

"Your Ruby mystery. Why you imagined seeing her everywhere. It's only because she stands out. She's so noticeable and hard to miss! It's that red hat! Mystery solved!"

Not likely. Sadie forced an agreeable grin. "Of course! I feel so silly now for blowing this out of proportion."

"Ah, lass, don't beat yourself up. We all get caught up in that kind of thing now and again. When it comes to confusin' times, there's nothin' better than talking things out. Sometimes a bit o' conversation can clarify everything."

As clear as clam chowder. Sadie managed to make her smile appear genuine. "I sure appreciate the time you've given me, Father. You've really helped. I knew there was a reason I stopped in here today." She got to her feet.

He followed her lead and stood. "You're quite welcome. God works in mysterious ways."

I could tell you a little about that. I tried.

With that, their eyes locked.

"You're bringing up the mystery word again. Was that a slip of the tongue?" she asked.

Making no direct reply, he sheepishly grinned. "Let me walk you out," he offered.

When they reached the vestibule, he played the gentleman and opened the door. Brilliant afternoon sunlight caused them to squint.

"Lovely day out there," he said, shading his eyes from the sudden glare.

Sadie was bathed in the warming autumn sunshine. "Father?"

"Yes?"

"About Ruby. Do you happen to know where she calls home?"

He pursed his lips. Sadie had the feeling he wanted her to go away. "As I said, lass, I've no proof as to whether or not she's truly a homeless person. I've no idea where she might call home."

"I'm not asking for a specific location, Father. I was only wondering where she could most likely be found . . . if someone was looking for her."

The priest thoughtfully rubbed his chin. "Some of the folks who know her come a ways." The man grinned. "Maybe the food we serve is worth it."

Sadie tilted her head. "Where exactly is a ways?"

"Oh, yes," he proudly said. "They manage to make it to our soup kitchen from the South Chicago area and—"

The woman was already down the steps.

Dread pounded through Father McElveney's veins when he'd realized he'd been had. "Miss! *Sadie!*" he called after her. "You can't *go* into that area!" His voice went unheard, for she had already disappeared into the crowd.

Sadie strode with renewed purpose toward her van. Her heart drummed with building excitement.

The people on the street warily stepped aside for the woman who was wildly gesturing with her hands. They suspiciously eyed the grinning lady who took no notice of them as she tossed her head while animatedly talking to herself.

"Well, that's that then! That's that, isn't it, Father Mac? You know a whole lot more than you're letting on. You thought I couldn't *see* behind all your hedging just because you're hiding behind that black *robe?"* With a self-satisfied huff, she chuckled. "Well! Ha! Let me tell *you* a thing or two, Father McBubba! I don't know *what* you've been trying to *hide*, but I sure as hell am going to find out! And you just told *this* lass where to start *looking!*"

The driver of the blue commercial van veered off the nubby cobble-stones of the estate's sweeping drive. As she rolled her vehicle to a stop beneath the arbor shading the kitchen delivery entrance, the windshield was dappled with late afternoon light shining through the twining clematis vines. Sadie, well satisfied with her decision to save her sleuthing for tomorrow when she could devote an entire day to it, exited the vehicle. With a new spring to her step, she returned a spirited wave from the gardener and made her way over to him. He was busy setting bulbs alongside the landscaped border of the reflecting pool.

"Is it that time already?" she cheerily asked the man bent to his task.

Josef, looking up beyond the edge of his straw hat's broad rim, replied, "I remember a time when a certain young whippersnapper used to have her calendar marked when it was time to help set the autumn bulbs. I recall a time when she'd race me to the potting shed to be first to gather up the tools."

Ms. Brennan smiled with the pleasing memories of those times. "And she'd throw them all into the wheelbarrow that she couldn't quite manage to push all by herself."

"Oh yes," he laughed, "that she did. That's when she would impatiently cross her arms and be forced to wait for me to catch up with her." Josef humorously shook his head. "You were so impetuous back then." An amused smile tipped the corners of his mouth. "Always so eager to start new projects, yet even more eager to see them finished out. Come spring you'd keep check three times a day to be the first to spy the new shoots from the bulbs." His head slowly swung from side to side. "I never did see a young'un so intent on seeing something through. No, I never did see a child with so much drive to see things come full circle, a closure to things. You'd fret over loose ends until they were all nicely tucked in where they belonged. You liked things nice an' tidy-like."

Sadie thought of Ruby. "I never got over that drive, Josef. It's still with me. I still do fret over loose ends. To this day, they can still drive me crazy."

The young woman hadn't told him anything he hadn't already known. The old man's eyes flickered with a glint of mischief. "You don't say. I suppose," he casually added, "some habits have a way of sticking with us through life."

Sadie knelt beside Josef and set a bulb into the hole the gardener had pulled a plug of soil from, ignoring his enlivened protestations. Her smile washed away his concerned frown. "This can't hurt these jeans any. Besides, wasn't it you who always reminded me that the good earth was clean dirt?"

He inclined his head to her. "You remember that?"

"Sure I do. I remember a lot of things about our times together. I was a good listener. I may have not given that impression at the time, but I took everything you said to heart."

That greatly pleased the man and he energetically twisted the bulb tool into another well-chosen spot.

Reaching for another bulb, she asked, "How's Savannah doing with that fever?"

Hearing the question, Josef momentarily became distracted. His smooth motion had been marred by a slightly telltale hitch.

Sadie noticed the hesitation. "Is she worse? Did she have to go to the doctor?"

Trying to recoup his metered rhythm, he casually said, "Oh no, no. She's just fine. It takes a lot to keep that one down."

Knowing the gardener was hedging, Sadie pushed. "Josef? What's up?"

"Nothing's up. Here," he said, handing her another bulb, "you're not keeping up with me. Set this down in there, will you? Gotta get this section done b'fore dinner."

She dutifully took the bulb and set it in the prepared hole. Gently covering it, she patted the soil, then reached for the man's garden tool. "My turn."

He grinned with relief and happily handed over the implement. The grin faded when she held it on her lap with the intent to halt their progress until he coughed up an answer. He pretended to miss her meaning. "Well?" he asked, "Are you rusty or what? Are you going to pull out a plug of soil or not?"

"Or not," came the quick reply. "I'm not rusty, but I'm also not moving a muscle until you come clean." Their eyes locked. "What's going on with Savannah? What aren't you telling me?"

The old gardener sighed. He knew that look. He'd seen it count-less times before. It was the look of unrelenting determination that had frequently come from a little girl no taller than June hollyhocks. It was a look he'd known meant a streak of iron stubbornness. He sighed. "You're not going to let this go, are you?"

"You, of all people, didn't need to ask that. You already know the answer. No," came the staunch response. "I am not."

His shoulders slumped in mild irritation. He ran a hand over the bib of his coveralls, fingers curled around the shoulder strap; a thumb absently began to rub the metal of the buckle. Looking off in the distance, he muttered in indecision. "I don't know . . . Ma's going to read me the riot act if she finds out I said anything. I don't know about—"

"Josef. Nobody's going to know you gave anything away. I prom-ise I won't give away anything. Just tell me what's going on with Savannah. Please."

The intensity of his eyes softened. "Oh now," he said, "it's not as bad as you're thinking. It's nothing so bad as I know you're imagin-ing. The child's fine," he reassured. "She's really just fine."

"Well then, what? If she's just fine, then what's the deal about Greta reading you the riot act if you say something about it? Say what, Josef?"

Releasing a long resigned sigh, Josef slowly removed his straw hat, then rested back on his heels. When their eyes finally met, he was sup-pressing a grin.

"Sadie, dear," he softly began. "When you were a wee girl, were you always ill when you had a morning fever?"

Her delicate brows knitted. *What was he getting at?* Her gaze shifted from the man to the grey stone exterior of the estate house. Looking through the autumn leaves that the light breeze lazily low-ered through the afternoon's golden rays, she fixed her gaze on the mansion's stonework and raised her eyes to the mullioned windows of her childhood bedroom. Staring through those windows now, she mentally saw the little girl of her past. The flowing white nightgown, the folds of the soft fabric covering the arm, the eyelet lace encircling the wrist of the hand, the hand reaching to touch the end of the ther-mometer to the hot bulb of the bedside table lamp.

The color rose in her cheeks as she turned back to face the gar-dener. Her eyes widened like twin harvest moons. "No," she whispered in amused disbelief. "She didn't pull my old thermometer trick. Not Savannah, too."

Josef's lips pursed while he nodded. "Did you think I'd been telling tales all this time when I'd say that she took after you?"

Sadie broke out in laughter. "Why, that little minx!"

Hearing Sadie's genuine mirth warmed the old man's heart. "Did you teach her that little trick of yours?" he asked.

"Did I teach . . . teach her that one?" She was laughing and shaking her head at the same time. "It never occurred to me to show her that one. Guess it's in the genes." She rose to her feet, brushing off the loose soil from her knees. "Does Greta know about the trick?" And as she supported the gardener's arm to help him rise, he shot her an incredulous look.

"Of course, she does. Why do you think I said I'd be in trouble with Ma if I said anything? No child can pull the wool over my Greta's eyes. Even you when you were that age. Poor Savannah never had a chance. Greta had already learned all the tricks from taking care of you."

Together they returned to the potting shed to wipe off the tools and put them away. As they strolled toward the manor house, Sadie couldn't get over the new revelation.

"So you and Greta were never fooled by my lightbulb ruse back then?"

He winked at her. "You didn't give us half a chance to be fooled. Guess you were too anxious to try your little game because you jumped the gun by making a false start right from the starting gate. You pulled your little trick before it was perfected. No, you never gave us an opportunity to be fooled, not after you ran the mercury up to 105 degrees the first time you tried it!"

Sadie burst out laughing again. "Oh no, I did? Nobody ever told me I did that. Nobody ever let on that they knew. I bet I got better at it, though."

"You sure did. That trial run of 105 degrees was what happens when impatience wins out over readiness."

In defense of her youth, she reiterated, "I improved, though."

"Oh, you got more than better at it," he agreed. "That you did, indeed."

"Well!" she exclaimed. "Savannah's going to have to get a better feel for it. She's going to have to learn the right touch if she plans on pulling that sort of thing."

The gardener raised a brow and eyed her. "Now I believe you've jumped the gun again." He cleared his throat before delivering the clincher. "Unlike her auntie, our little Miss Smarty Savannah has never run the mercury over 101 degrees."

Sadie was impressed that her niece had bettered her. A reason for it was quickly voiced. "Well then, I suppose that 'trickery gene' evolved then. It most likely became more sophisticated with the next generation."

Josef suppressed a grin. "I guess that could be the reason she's so good at things her aunt took a bit more practice to perfect. Yes," he half mused, "that must be it."

She teasingly swatted the man's arm. "Stop it. We're lying through our teeth. We both know that Savannah's brighter than I was at her age."

Respectfully, he upturned his palms. "Maybe. Maybe not. One thing I do know, though, is that she has inherited that obstinate drive of yours."

"Which one would that be?"

"The one that doesn't cotton to unanswered questions. The one that won't let loose ends be. The one that needs a rock-solid ending to things. You know, the drive that takes hold of your every waking hour and has your mind going like there's a bee in your bonnet."

There was only one bonnet consuming the thoughts of Sadie's waking hours right now. It was a red one with a big glass jewel that kept catching the light and blinking at her like a lighthouse beacon on a velvety, moonless night. And now, Josef's words made her wonder if her niece's eye had also been drawn to that same blinking light. Did she have the same bee in her bonnet? Was she secretly drawn in by the odd behavior of the mysterious woman?

"Sadie!" came the word accompanied by a gentle jab on the arm. She turned. "What?"

"I've been talking to you and you haven't heard a word."

She apologized. "Actually, I did hear you. And no. No, I won't let on that I know she really wasn't ill this morning."

"Greta, as well? You can't let her know either."

Sadie winked. "Nobody will know, Josef. We're okay."

The gardener released a sigh of relief as they passed through the kitchen doorway.

The air was heavy with the scent of garlic and fresh baked bread. Greta was lifting a pan of lasagna from the oven.

"You two always did time things right. Dinner will be on the table in five minutes." She flashed her husband a suspicious look.

He knew what her unvoiced question was and he quickly assuaged her concern. "I was just telling Sadie how much better Savannah feels."

"You don't say," she replied with a hint of uncertainty.

Sadie jumped in. "I was glad to hear that it was just one of those things kids get now and again. A fever in the morning and then nothing seems to come of it. I remember Mira having spells of that when she was young." She beamed a bright smile at the housekeeper. "I'm just glad she bounced back and it wasn't anything to be alarmed about." Looking around, she added, "Where is she?"

The three turned to the doorway leading into the formal dining room.

The child was standing there. She was holding the new trinket box out to her aunt.

"There she is!" Greta exclaimed while tending to her meal preparations.

While Josef went off to wash up, Sadie closed the distance between herself and the girl. "I was so glad to hear that you're not ill. When your mom and I were little, she'd get sick with everything that went through the school. I think you have better resistance than she did." She took the trinket box. "What've you got here? Did you already put something in it?"

The girl just stared at her aunt, then followed her to the kitchen table.

Sadie set it down. "May I open it?"

The answer came in the form of a nod.

Slowly the aunt unlatched the metal catch and lifted the lid. "Oh look," she said with a pleased smile, "your two tiny pumpkins fit perfectly in this."

Greta came over to have a look. "Those are some teeny pumpkins you have there." With a playful grin, she added, "Josef would call them pixie pumpkins. Is that what they are? Pumpkins grown by the little Wee Folk?"

Savannah's eyes went from Greta's to Sadie's. These were special pumpkins. They were not grown by the fairies and, most certainly, were not to be made light of. Stone-faced, she reached up and gently closed the lid of the brass box.

Greta took the cue and returned to her kitchen work. "We're eating in five minutes," she announced.

The girl set the box by her place at the table and went to get the place mats and silverware to help set the table.

After Sadie had taken care of getting the dishes, the four of them sat down to one of Greta's famous Italian meals.

"Mira's not home?" Sadie asked, while looking about the room and into the doorway.

The housekeeper sharply eyed her.

Sadie took the hint from the elder woman's frown and slight shake of the head. It was a subject the housekeeper didn't want to get into in front of the girl. Savannah's aunt clenched her teeth. "She's working, I suppose."

Greta nodded. "She had to fly to Boston. She needed to be present for a deposition. She'll be back sometime tomorrow afternoon."

Sadie was disgusted with her sister's frequent absence from the house. "Sounds like she prefers work over—"

"More bread?" Josef asked, shoving the basket beneath Sadie's nose.

Embarrassed by her lack of control, she took two slices, then passed the warm basket to the girl. "Here, honey, nobody bakes herb and garlic bread better than our own Greta."

Savannah couldn't have agreed more. She helped herself to a generous portion and immediately began swirling it around in the tomato sauce in her plate. While noticing how the adults' dinner conversation had switched from the taboo subject of her mother's absence to what sort of dancing classes she was attending tomorrow, she quietly wondered where her aunt had gone that day. And why wasn't her aunt sharing anything about her day? Had she gone to browse through secondhand shops? Did she visit some of her antique dealer friends? Did she go sit in the park? Did she see Ruby again? That idea gave her a sinking feeling because Savannah wanted to be included in all sightings of the old woman. She couldn't miss any new clues. And she surprised herself to realize that she'd become somewhat possessive of the old lady. She wanted to be with Sadie whenever she and the old one crossed paths.

The adults noticed the child's sullen mood. She'd been preoccupied. Her thoughts had tumbled far away from the dinner conversation. They saw her delicate eyebrows dip into a hard vee.

"So, what do you think, honey?" Sadie asked the girl as she touched her arm.

Pulled from her private thoughts, she jumped and looked up into her aunt's shining eyes.

"Will you show me your dancing shoes after dinner? I hear you take ballet and tap. I hear you're pretty good, too."

In turn, Savannah's gaze went from Greta to Josef and then settled on her aunt's sea-green eyes. She was glad her aunt was interested enough to want to see her dancing shoes. She nodded.

"Good!" Sadie exclaimed. "I bet you're the best dancer in every one of your classes!"

Following dinner, Savannah proudly showed her aunt the dancing shoes. They spent the evening watching a DVD movie in the girl's room and wrapping up the evening with three rounds of a favorite video game.

After Savannah was tucked into bed for the night she was disappointed that she didn't feel her usual anticipation towards her dancing classes tomorrow. She realized that it was because she preferred to be with her aunt instead—just in case she ran into Ruby again.

Sadie, cradled by the softness of her billowy comforter, stared at the moonlit ceiling of her room. Shadows wavered there as the night breeze shifted the branches of the old maple outside her window. She hadn't called Tina this evening. She hadn't called because she'd been afraid that her friend would wheedle her plans out of her. No one, she vowed, no one was going to know where she was headed in the morning. No one was going to know because she didn't want anyone trying to stop her from going into Chicago's most notoriously dreaded section of the city.

Eight

Saturday

It was a picture-perfect autumn morning. It was starting out to be the type of day when nature caught the sunlight and reflected back the vividness that camera buffs only dreamed of capturing in their amateur photographs. Shadows from the tree-lined boulevard chased one another across the van's broad windshield. The driver, though excited about what this day would reveal, thought back on the auspicious nature of the morning.

Josef was going to be busy instructing the crew of the new land-scaping company that Mira had hired. She was particular in how she wanted the grounds kept, yet not as demanding as the old gardener himself. Over breakfast, he'd winked while telling Sadie that he still ruled the yard. It was still his domain—his and the elfin ones. So, naturally, it was imperative that the estate's parklike grounds be groomed accordingly. He was going to make it quite clear that the vegetation surrounding the ponds and the reflecting pool were not the maintenance people's concern. He'd continue tending to those areas because, he'd most seriously declared, "the Little Folk don't take kindly to strangers trampling around and carelessly disturbing their territory."

The driver of the van caught herself smiling as the gardener's words replayed in her mind. He was a sweet and gentle man from the Old Country who'd firmly clung to the age-old tales. He never outgrew his belief in the likes of sprites and pixies, but then again, he still claimed to see them and carry on a conversation or two as well. Sadie shrugged. Hadn't she caught sight of a movement or two out of the corner of her eye while tending the gardens? Weren't there inexplicable feelings that had suddenly swept over her while culling the errant weeds from among the dense pondside flora? Oh yes, she thoughtfully considered, Josef was going to be a busy man today.

And Greta, she too had a busy day ahead of her. At breakfast, she'd been anxious to begin her day of canning. Before Sadie had even left, the housekeeper had the stove top full of steaming pots of empty jars. Today she was going to make jams and preserves from the bushel of farm-fresh peaches Josef had brought her. Later, Sadie knew, the wonderful fragrance of apples mixed with the spices of nutmeg and cinnamon would fill the house when Greta turned her attention to making applesauce. This thought pulled at her as memories of her youth washed over her like warm bath water, pleasantly soothing, bringing remembered moments of great contentment. She wished she could've been helping out in that busy kitchen today, yet a far more pressing issue held sway over that rare opportunity to recapture childhood experiences.

Thoughts then turned to Savannah. She'd been exuberant with the anticipation of getting to her dance classes. Her dancing case containing the shoes rested beside her chair at the breakfast table. Conversation among the adults over the Belgian waffle meal was spearheaded by Greta's glowing compliments over the child's developing gracefulness. The class had been hard at work learning routines for the school's *Nutcracker* production for the Christmas performance. Savannah was going to be a sugarplum fairy.

Sadie's vision of her niece on stage with the footlights shining full on her sparkling costume made her grin. The girl would look like a glittering star. Then the smile disappeared when another thought came on its heels. Would Mira even be around to see the grand performance her daughter had worked so hard to perfect? It appeared that her sister had left the raising of her daughter to maids who came and went, temporary tutors, and the elderly husband and wife team who had been a staple of the Brennan-Woodward household for so many years. At any rate, Sadie was glad that those she left behind this morning had a full day's activities planned. This, she realized, assuaged her guilt over needing to be away for the day. Alone.

When she spied an indigent man rummaging through a trash bin, she looked to his cohort dragging plastic bags of aluminum cans. The clatter was a sound that snapped her to attention. The racket pulled her back into the moment. She straightened. All former thoughts were chased away by a new attentiveness, for she'd entered the beginning of neighborhoods which were markedly frayed around the edges. Here and there, empty buildings in weed-choked yards were for sale. Further on, their plywood-covered windows gave way to gaping window frames which allowed vagrants an opportunity to claim squatter's rights.

Noticing that graffiti were now more prevalent than clean billboard ads, she slowed the vehicle to better take in the surroundings. As she did this, a rheumy-eyed panhandler appeared at the van window. A grimy hand was shoved beneath the driver's chin.

"Gotta dolla'?" He asked, filling the interior with the odor of cheap gin.

Quickly recovering from her sudden trepidation, she braked and reached into her purse to hand the man a five-dollar bill.

He would've snatched it out of her hands if she hadn't been firmly holding onto it. "This is for food," she sternly stipulated. "You go buy yourself something good to eat."

This time the vagrant made a lightning lunge for the money.

Again the bill shot out of range to temptingly dangle like a carrot before a bunny. "I'm serious," the dangler stressed in a more authoritative voice. Though the man's filthy trench coat exuded old urine stench, the driver ignored the offensive odor and held firm.

"I'll be glad to help you out if you're hungry, but not for more booze. Do you hear me? Promise me that you'll use this for food and nothing else?"

The man enthusiastically nodded. He was near salivating while never taking his eyes from the bill. "Yup. Yup, I sure do hear you,

ma'am. I haven't had a decent thing to eat in a long while. That there
money will git me a hot meal."

Her heart sank. *When had he eaten last?* She pulled a second five
from her purse and added it to the first. "Okay then. You promised."
This time she released her grip on the bills when the man swiped for
them. He grinned and raised his hand to an imaginary hat brim to
salute her. She watched him pocket the money and saunter away. She
watched him join his wino buddy who was staggering along the sidewalk swilling the last dregs from an upturned bottle in a paper bag.
"You poor old fool," she whispered, "you're off to buy more gin, aren't
you? What do you care about a promise? You'll never see me again."

As the van cruised down the street, the driver took in more details
of the neighborhood. Though she'd seen a couple of bridge people and
street-smart kids shouting the rap verses coming from their blaring
boomboxes, she noticed that this was not a hard-core residential section. It had an element of deeply caring folks who appeared to be
hanging onto their integrity by their fingernails. Signs of the desperation of trying to hold onto one's dignity were visible in the lingering
pride of a few single-family homeowners. Flower boxes and freshly
painted porch rails were a valiant effort to mask the dwellings' slow
decline into shabbiness. Yet, for every one of these that Sadie noted,
she saw three run-down places where brassy women slouched in
yawning doorways, places that had grown too volatile for the slum-
lords to tend.

Three blocks down from the single homes, a different type of
dwelling became the norm. These were run-down, hourly rate motels
tucked tightly amid the row houses where laundry hung in the narrow
space between the buildings. Here was where the pawn shops with
iron grills on windows and doors took up shop. Here was where the
tattoo parlors and soup kitchens shared a common building wall. This
section of town was for those people who had fallen through society's
cracks in the system; for them, life was a series of unforgiving bumps
and punches.

As the blue commercial van slowly passed broken-down cars and
pickups, Sadie's eyes were drawn across the street to see hunger-
driven urchins sifting through dumpsters in search of food, or perhaps
in search of something to salvage and sell.

Striding past the preoccupied children who were apparently
ignored, two men in long coats proudly high-stepped along the side-

walk, the heels of their new alligator shoes strutting out a call to all within hearing range. Sadie pulled over to watch rappers and idlers alike gravitate to the call of the shoes. She watched the two men open their coats, their linings drooping with clipped-on Rolex watches and diamond-studded bracelets—all stolen, she was sure. All could be had for pennies on the dollar for anyone to buy and, in turn, sell on the street.

A chilling fear rippled through her when she realized that she'd been seen. One of the hustlers was staring at her. In turn, the group of rappers followed his lead and looked her way. None of them wore welcoming smiles.

Sadie began to head down the street when three youths strode over to the van. Two blocked her progress by standing in front of the vehicle. The third sauntered up to the driver's side window. "Yo, lady! Hold up a sec."

Neck hairs stood on end. These were hoodlums, for God's sake. She had no idea how to defend herself because the boy was already resting his elbows on her door. She acted without thinking.

"Yo, yourself," she said, thinking that that was about the most idiotic thing to say.

The boy at her door, wearing a bandanna on his head, grinned. He looked her over—slowly. "You ain't no local ho, so youse must be lost. Are youse lost, nice lady?"

"L-lost? Well," she nervously sighed, trying to keep her voice from quaking, "I wouldn't say that I was exactly lost. I just, well you see—"

The boy turned to shout back at the two men. "Dis white lady's lost!"

The two on the sidewalk laughed. "Well, show her the way, man!"

As she realized the group was having a good time at her expense, all sense of fear fled. She sat up taller and looked the boy in the eye. "Young man. I am not lost. I'm looking for someone."

Again the boy relayed the message. "Says she be lookin' for somebody!" he shouted.

One of the men in front of the van suggestively rocked his hips. "Maybe she's looking for me!" He leered at the driver. "I got some-body to show you, lady!"

Now Sadie's ire had been roused. "Look. I'm looking for a little old bag lady who wears a red knit cap with a gaudy gemstone pin. She's supposed to be homeless, but everyone I talk to about her can't really tell me if she is or not. I need—"

The lure of mischief melted away from the boys' eyes. Their entire demeanor changed. The one beside the van softened. The incident was no longer treated as a means of having a little fun with a white woman lost on their turf.

"Watch it, Lady. Youse talkin' some heavy shit now. Youse talkin' 'bout our Ruby."

"Yes!" Sadie excitedly replied. "I'm so glad I found someone who knows her."

The boy flashed a mouthful of discolored teeth. "Youse wouldn't find anyone around here who don't know her. She like our mama. She like a mama to all of us." He inclined his head to the two hustlers. "Even to dem bad dudes over there. Ruby be like a mama to even dem."

"Well, can you tell me where to find her? I really need to talk to her."

The boy leaned back and cast an appraising eye over the upscale van. He gave it a good once-over. "Lady, youse don't look like nobody Ruby needs to rap wif. Know what I'm sayin'?"

"No. No, I don't. I was under the impression that she helped folks."

"Dat's true 'nuff. But not folks like youse."

Now Sadie became defensive. "And just what are folks like me?"

"Rich."

She opened her mouth to object.

"Lady, so maybe youse ain't 'xactly rich, but youse sure 'nough ain't one of us neither."

"That's true," she agreed. "I guess I was mistaken when I thought she would help anyone in need."

"Youse in need?" He leaned his head inside the window to scan the van's interior. "Youse don't look needy."

"Needs aren't always of a material nature," she advised. "I have a great need to talk with Ruby. We've been crossing each other's paths for days and—"

"And youse two keep missin' each other."

"Yes. How did you know that?"

"Dat's her way," he said before straightening up. He looked up and down the street, stalling while thinking things out. When he leaned back down, his eyes met the driver's.

"Youse a nice lady. I think youse better hightail it back home."
He scratched his head as though trying to come to the right decision,
the best advice. Sending this classy woman into the Combat Zone
wasn't his choice, yet he figured that her frequent sightings with
Ruby must be for a reason—Ruby's reason. But did Ruby really want
this country bumpkin going into the rough turf of South Chicago? He
doubted it.

The boy heaved a weighted sigh. He backed away from the van.
And without uttering a word, his arm lifted from his side. He pointed
up the road. He pointed toward the depths of the Combat Zone.

Sadie smiled. "Thank you so much. You've been very helpful." As
an afterthought, she held out a twenty-dollar bill. "Please," she called,
"please take this. I'm so grateful for your information."

The boy looked at the bill, then locked his eyes on her. Had he just
doomed a babe in the woods? No one of her caliber went in there
alone. Would she find Ruby? Would the old woman protect her? He
didn't know the answers to any of those questions. And because he
didn't know those answers, he just lowered his eyes and walked away
from the woman, her van, and the money.

What a curious young man. Sadie's head was full of such thoughts
as she watched the group of young men in her rearview mirror. As
they became smaller and smaller, she gave her attention to what was
ahead. After traveling ten more blocks, the van crept toward the sur-
real core of skid row. Beads of trepidation eased from the pores of her
brow. Apprehension gripped her soul in a last effort to dissuade her
from the determined destination. The dismal district was populated
by seedy characters that were most often referred to as the dregs of
society.

Ignoring the screeching alarm tripped by her psyche, she nervously eyed the ragged squatters sitting on the broken porch stoops of
abandoned homes. They watched her pass with disinterest, their emotionally barren expressions dull and frozen. Whether the deadpan eyes
were due to drugs or the result of a downward spiral into apathy, none
of the onlookers thought the fancy van worth commenting on. The
squalor, the driver noted, markedly deepened after entering the
decayed core of the Combat Zone.

Abandoned warehouses with broken or missing window panes
took blind note of her passing. Looking at the buildings' dark, vacant

eyes and yawning entry doors gave her the unsettling feeling that they were alive—alive and waiting. Waiting and watching. And as she stared back, the sound of a bottle breaking made her jump. Snapping her head around to the sharp report, she saw a mangy mongrel leading a pack of junkyard dogs on a routine prowl. The sound of her nervous laugh made her realize how tense she'd been. After heaving a long sigh, she watched the dogs wrangle through a chain-link fence that someone's bolt cutters had sliced like butter. The cut fence made a mockery of the razor wire strung along the top—the curling wire made a poor testimony to the property owner's idea of security. The businesses behind the fencing had been gutted long ago to make room for the chop shops that left nothing but abandoned steel cadavers behind to rest on rusted wheel rims.

"Ouch!" she exclaimed after hitting her chin on the steering wheel she'd been crouched over. Looking down at the road she saw that it was littered with potholes. She was about to swear at them until she realized that this region was definitely not a priority for the Department of Transportation to maintain. It was never going to be at the top of their work schedule. She shook her head. No maintenance crew was going to risk life and limb to repair these streets.

When she checked around to see if anyone had seen her bounce in and out of the pothole, her suspicions were confirmed. A clutch of hollow-eyed addicts, gaunt and paranoid, paced the littered street corner. Frantic, with darting eyes, they kept a restless vigil for their contact to arrive. They appeared to be so entrenched in the seedy lifestyle that there was nowhere to go but deeper. Their suspicious eyes twitched nervously at the sight of the van. The driver felt like an interloper intruding into the shifted reality of South Chicago's projects.

Not wanting to make the group any more paranoid than they were, she eased the van through the intersection without glancing in their direction. While making her way up the next block, she spied hookers in scanty outfits who ignored the October chill in order to maintain the required come-hither game face. The women's lackluster hair and pallid complexions indicated poor diets. Lanky. Too thin. Too little sleep, yet ready for anything with the aid of the "speed" that kept them hyped.

Nearing the next cross street, the driver of the van eased over to the curb and cut the engine. Just ahead, on the corner, people were gathered.

Laughter rang out above the metered beat of the boombox's megabass.

Women in heavy makeup, wearing short skirts and thigh-high boots with killer heels, were dancing with one another.

A man in a leopard coat and Panama hat waved his flashy bejeweled fingers like he was a symphony conductor. When he laughed, diamonds in his front teeth caught the light. Young gang members dressed in their colors jived about, clapping their hands and getting into their rap.

And in the center of the street-corner dance, an old woman in an army coat was trying to emulate the fancy Irish footwork of the Lord of the Dance. She cut a lively jig, the large gemstone bouncing around on the red cap. And when the cap was about to fall from her flying hair, she grabbed it, pretending it was a gypsy's tambourine. Around and around she went, spreading the gaiety to all who wished to be touched by it. To all who wanted to join in and forget their troubles for a span of time.

Sadie gawked at the amazing sight. Her mouth hung open on seemingly broken jaw hinges. She'd steeled herself to see a lot of unpleasant and pitiful sights today, but this, this joyous tableau was the last thing she was expecting. She was stupefied. *What on earth?* And as she watched the mesmerizing scene, she realized she was smiling. Not just smiling, she was grinning from ear to ear. The beat of the music and the sounds of the old one's tapping feet had a Pied Piper effect. She wanted to be a part of it. She wanted to clap and twirl and sing right along with the rest of them.

She couldn't resist the magnetic pull and put her hand on the door handle.

An arm reached in. A strong hand clamped down on her own.

Panicked, she knew she was in peril . . . until she looked into the man's eyes. They were soft with understanding. She looked back to the group on the corner. They were still having the time of their lives. Then she snapped her head around to the hand gripping her own.

"W-hho are you?" she stammered.

The voice that answered was deep. "Don't matter none who I be. Question is, who be you? You be in dangerous territory. You stupid or sometin'?" He eyed her. "No. No way you dat stupid."

"But listen," she began, while pointing to the scene beyond the windshield. "I came here to see that old woman who's dancing over there."

The man slowly removed his hand. "You didn't need to come down here to see her. You seen her 'nough already. Huh? You goin' to see her 'gain. You knows dat, too. You knows you goin' to see her 'gain. You shouldn't be down here. You knows dat, girl."

"But I, I, well . . . but I had to come to where she lives and—"

The man threw his hands in the air and impatiently shifted his weight from one foot to the other. "Who tol' you dat? Who tol' you dat she live here? Huh?" He didn't give her time to respond. "Oh, man. Don't you knows dat Ruby lives wherever she be at da time? How'd you not know dat? Ruby lives anywhere. Everywhere is where dat lady call home."

"But the priest! The priest said folks who live down here . . . the ones who go to the church's soup kitchen talk about her among themselves. Like they know her well. I thought I could find where she lives by coming down here."

"Listen to me. Folks everywhere knows her. Dat priest shouldn't have put dat idea in yo head. He wasn't real smart tellin' dat to a little lady like yo'self." Then he leaned closer. "You hightail it back to wherever you done come from and I promise you dat you gonna meet up with Ruby 'gain. Soon. Soon you gonna be face to face wif her."

The man struck her as being sincere.

The celebration on the corner drew her attention, then it shifted back to the man. He was smiling.

"Okay," she relented. "I believe you."

"Little lady, you can take what I said to da bank! Now," he asked, "where's home for you?"

When she told him, both of his brows rose. He was impressed. "Lady, you sure be a long ways from yo' home turf!" He rubbed his chin. "Don't go back da way you came." He pointed to his left. "You can catch da freeway four blocks dat way. Git on dat an' head fo' dem green an' shady lawns. Don't look right or left until you on da freeway. You gonna get dat chance to meet Ruby." He winked. "Ohhh, yea, you gonna get dat chance fo' sure!"

Sadie smiled. "I don't know why, but I believe you."

He let out a belly laugh. "You better believe me. Jist wait an' see. I wouldn't steer you wrong. Now git' goin', little lady befo' somebody takes dem fancy wheels off dat van so smooth you won't even know'd dey was gone."

She laughed. "Guess I'll be on my way then."

He bowed and swung out his arm to show the way.

As Sadie pulled away from the curb she gave him a grateful wave, but not before she first took a final look at the old woman who was twirling like a dervish—twirling with hair wildly flying and laughing with the voice of a child at play.

After she'd driven three blocks, the freeway was visible up ahead. The sound of the speeding traffic was a glorious one that came as overwhelming relief. One more block and she'd be riding the road to home. It was her ticket to safety, her escape from danger's clutch. Yet the mental picture of the dancing woman stuck in her head like a needle stuck in a scratch of an old vinyl record.

She eased up on the accelerator.

Her heart pounded with sudden indecision.

Her hands felt clammy.

And, before her courage faltered, she spun the steering wheel. The vehicle was no longer facing the way out. The U-turn pointed the van straight back into the heart of the most jaded and hardened part of the city.

Shaky with the shocking impulsiveness of the snap decision, she slowly veered the van to the right and slunk down the nearest side street. Her first goal was to avoid being spotted by the man she had just spoken to. He'd been kind enough, but her inner radar, her intuition, began beeping like a Fuzz Buster whenever she thought of him catching sight of her again. The idea of a repeat encounter was not a pleasing one.

The new plan was to cruise the area and try to glean more information about Ruby. Empowered by a stalwart determination, she fully intended to get that information before she again headed for the freeway. She'd ferret it out from those who knew Ruby best. She'd get it straight from the man on the street—the hookers, the young drug runners, the dealers, and the gangbangers. These were Ruby's friends in the hood. *I'll be okay. This is Ruby's hood.*

And although her rash decision to pursue this perilous adventure gave her a case of the jitters and set every nerve ending trembling, she forced herself to stay the course. Despite the alarms going off in her head to warn her away, she defiantly pulled their plugs to silence them. Wisdom and better judgment were tossed to the wind because there would never be a better place to get the true lowdown on Ruby than right here. The opportunity was in hand. And the time, the time was now.

Row houses, suffering from decades of ravaging weather and human apathy, hunkered shoulder to shoulder, each appearing to bravely prevent its weakening neighbor from slumping into final collapse. Here, the driver noted, the windows and doors had no steel security gates. She supposed the reason for this was as simple as futility, that any and all attempts to shield one's home from criminal infiltration proved to be nothing more than an act of folly. When you're already surrounded by decay, preventative measures geared toward preservation can do nothing but fail. In a no-win situation, no one wanted to waste the energy anymore.

There were toys in some of the grassless front yards. They were as desperately in need of care as the children playing with them. Thin mongrel dogs roamed idly about. All of them tagless, they spent their days being clever opportunists sniffing out morsels of food wherever they could be found, their greatest crime being hunger. Like their human counterparts, these animals acquired their own type of street smarts. For them, survival of the fittest was the only rule to live by, for every scrap of food brought fierce competition. The neighborhood pets not only competed with each other, they had to outsmart the rats which, because of their size, were often the first scavengers to find the best pickings.

When the blue van approached the cross street, it slowed. On the opposite corner was a busy tattoo parlor. Sadie brought the vehicle to a full stop and wondered what the place's draw was. There couldn't be that many people getting tattoos at once. The comings and goings of unsavory characters seemed to be endless. When she realized that she'd been noticed, there were few options for her. Should she gun the van away from the rough-looking group or drive straight for it?

She swallowed to wet her dry throat. *Here goes!* Then eased the van across the street. Pulling up behind a couple of motorcycles parked at the crumbling curb, she let the engine idle while deciding if it was wise to turn it off.

The newcomer drew frowns from the leather-clad onlookers. The woman was clearly out of her element.

The growing crowd gathering in the doorway of the tattoo shop stared at the occupant of the van. They glared.

Inside the vehicle, the driver stared back. She felt like a scared rabbit before snake eyes . . . frozen in place. *How crazy was this idea? Am I nuts? Should I just pull away and head for the freeway while I still have a chance?*

No one moved.

To Sadie, it seemed like an eternity passed before a movement made her blink. A man stepped from the group and sauntered toward her. She straightened in her seat as he came around to her window. "You gotta be lost."

Though she smiled, the man's body language wasn't reciprocal. Figuring it couldn't hurt, she kept the smile going anyway. "No. Actually, I'm not. I'm looking for someone."

The man leaned forward. Crouching with elbows on the door, he lowered his nose to hers. "You police?"

She thought the question was outrageous. "Do I look like a cop?"

His brows furrowed. Backing his head out, his eyes swept over the van's exterior. "Hard to tell these days. They come in all disguises, even drive phony business vans. This a phony business van you drive around for cover, cop? You didn't answer me. Are you a cop?"

"No. No, I am not a cop. I'm not a private investigator, either."

"An attorney?"

Sadie was already getting tired of the third degree. "Are you?"

Now it was the man's turn to blink. What moxie this lady had! "Am I what?"

"An attorney!"

He burst out laughing and turned to the crowd. "She wants to know if I'm an attorney!"

Everyone looked at one another and, as one, moved toward the vehicle to surround it. Curious faces peered inside.

Sadie didn't like being the butt of their amusement. "Look," she said impatiently, "I came down here because I had to. I had to look for an elderly woman who wears an army coat and a red cap with a gaudy pin on it. It probably wouldn't mean much to you if somebody was always crossing your path, but it sure does to me. I've got to find out more about her and I don't expect you to know who I'm—"

As a chorus, everyone whispered, "Ruubeee."

The driver's eyes widened in surprise. Not only did the crowd know who she was talking about, their threatening demeanor altered as well. "Yes!" she exclaimed. Now her smile was genuine. "You *do* know her!"

The man at her window was the first to recover. He had serious questions for anyone looking for the old woman. "What'd you say your name was?"

"I didn't, but it's Sadie . . . Sadie Brennan, not that it makes any difference one way or the other what my name is. The fact is, Ruby has come into my life and, well, she keeps entering my life. She's been entering my life so often that I can't get her out of my head. Everywhere I go I see her—in the cemetery, at the museum, at the Farmers' Market. I see her in my sleep! I can't get her out of my mind. She's become like a ghostly presence floating in and out of my daily life! For my own peace of mind I just need to know more about her." She tore her eyes from the man at her window and scanned the curious faces of the rough-looking crowd.

They were nodding to each other.

Sadie snapped her head back to the spokesman. "Well? What do you say? Can you help me out here, or what?"

Without answering, the man strode over to the parked bikes. One by one, the members of the group joined him. They conferred with each other, then sauntered back to the waiting woman.

"You shouldn't be down here," he said.

"I'm here because someone told me that this is where she's best known."

The man looked her over. Though she wore jeans, they were expensive ones. "Like I'm trying to say, you took a big chance coming down here. Someone of your caliber wouldn't do that unless they were plain stupid or mighty determined."

"Well, I'm not stupid."

He glanced down to read the signage on the side of the van. "I'm betting you're not the delivery person for this company."

"That'd be a good bet," she said.

"So if you own this business, you can't be stupid."

"That's what I said. I'm not stupid. I'm *determined.*"

The man thought on that for several seconds. After mentally performing some type of inner debate with himself, he finally said, "Buck. My name's Buck and we can help you out." He pointed a warning finger at her after he saw her pleased reaction. "Now, wait a minute. None of us here are going to spill our own personal stories about your little old lady. None of us would do that, but we can . . . well, I suppose we can watch out for you while you do your own looking around. We can point you in the right direction and make sure this fancy van don't get stripped out while you're driving it. Does any of that sound like what you're so friggin' determined to do down here?"

She was so surprised by her good luck that she could've kissed him. "You mean it? You really mean to help me out?"

He pointed to the passenger door. "Pop that lock open. If you don't mind me riding shotgun, you and me are going for a little ride."

As he made his way around the vehicle, she instinctively pressed the unlock lever. It wasn't until he'd actually opened the door that a new thought struck her. *Was that a huge mistake?*

He slid into the seat and ran his hand admiringly over the supple leather. "Sweet," he said. "Real sweet. I know a guy who runs a chop shop. He'd pay top dollar for seats like this."

Her heart skipped a couple of beats. *Oh, my God.*

"Well," the biker shrugged, "his loss." He pointed up the street. "Hang a right up here. Let's get going. I need to get you back on your way long before dark."

"What's up there?"

"You'll see. I figure the best way for you to get what you're after is to give you a little inside tour." He caught her eye. "That is, as long as you're not squeamish. Know what I mean?"

"Depends on what you mean by squeamish. I don't do well watching blood 'n' guts movies."

He grinned. "That's why you don't live in the hood."

She tilted her head toward her passenger. "That's *one* of the reasons I don't live in the hood . . . not *this* hood."

"You got a hood of your own?"

Sadie felt a surge of defensiveness rise in her. "Sure, I do. Doesn't everybody?"

"Where at?"

"Northwest of where Lake Shore Drive ends."

"You kiddin' me? That's not a hood. Just *one* of those monstrosity houses got its own private neighborhood walled inside its grounds. They got gardener's cottages, guest houses, the horse trainer, and groom's quarters back by the whitewashed stables. Oh, man!" he trailed on. "They got maids, cooks, decoratin' designers, personal trainers, and nannies! Aww man, don't tell me you come from one a them!"

She rolled her eyes. "Not from one quite that elaborate."

"Whew, that's a relief 'cuz them folks are real pointy-headed snobs. They think their private grounds *is* their neighborhood. Everything outside their walls is somewhere else! Know what I mean?"

She did know. He'd been describing her sister. She couldn't conceal the grin that curled the corners of her mouth.

"Yeah, Buck, I know exactly what you mean. Actually, that's just where I spent my childhood. When I grew up, I grew up in more ways than one. I moved away from that elitist society crap. Now I live on the coast of Maine above my shop."

He made a great show of shivering.

"What's the matter?" she asked.

"Maine, man. That place's colder than a witch's t . . . ahh, a witch's nose."

"I'm impressed. You're censoring your language for me. You don't have to do that, you know. I'm not one of those pointy-headed snobs."

"I know I don't have to watch my mouth, but I don't ever have reason to, either. I kinda like this reason. You're a nice lady. I'm going to show you where you can get some of your answers and keep you safe at the same time." He pointed down the block. "Pull over to them brownstones up ahead. My man up there will watch your wheels while I watch your back when you're doin' your thing."

"My thing?"

"Yeah, your thing. While you're doin' that askin' 'round thing."

"Let me get this straight. You and I are going to walk the streets while your . . . your *man* . . . watches my van?"

"You got it. That's the plan. Somebody's gotta watch over this fancy vehicle after you park it an' somebody's gotta watch over this fancy vehicle's *owner* when she out walkin' the hood. I'm jist *one* somebody. Gotta have *two* somebodies for the plan to work."

The out-of-place vehicle crept toward the middle of the block. It nosed over to the curb at the passenger's directive.

The second somebody came out of one of the brownstones and swaggered his way down the steps. Sunlight bounced off the facial metal piercings. A wide headband cut across his forehead to encircle the thick, black hair tied back at the nape of his neck. The grey cutoff sweatshirt exposed defined biceps. The man was into major bodywork. Black leather wristbands were studded. His eyes lit up when Buck got out of the van.

"Hey, man!" he laughed, noticing the unusual driver. "What kind of trouble you find already?"

"I was jist minding my own business and trouble pulled right up behind my bike. Believe me, this time, trouble came an' found me."

The two put distance between the van and themselves. Buck slung his arm around the man's shoulders. They strolled over to the steps and discussed the type of trouble that had found him. Buck's friend was seen to nod his head. Then, more energetically, he shook it. Several times he pointed to the vehicle. It was clear that the two didn't see eye to eye about Buck's plan. Finally they both strode back to the waiting vehicle.

"Raoul, this is Sadie Brennan. Sadie? Meet Raoul. He's been kind enough to volunteer his professional services. He is going to guard your van while we're gone."

A flicker of concern twitched her eye. *I'm actually leaving the van?*

Buck chuckled and jabbed an elbow in his friend's side. "Raoul will make sure that, when you return, nothing will be missing. Nothing will even be out of place. Right, Raoul?"

The tall Latino flashed a proud smile. "Nobody messes with Raoul. Your possessions will be safe with me. Have no worry. It will be right here waiting for you when you return."

"Let's get going," Buck said, while opening the driver's door. "We have some ground to cover."

Sadie reached for her purse.

"Leave that," Buck ordered.

Aghast at the idea, she turned to the man standing beside her. "You've got to be kidding. I'm not going to leave my purse with someone I don't even know. It's got my ID and credit cards, my checkbook and cash. What do you take me for?"

Buck rested his arm on the roof of the vehicle. He leaned in close to the woman.

"I don't take you for a very smart lady. A smart lady wouldn't be driving around down here all by herself. I also take you for someone who's been drawn into Ruby's world. It's not a friendly world, if you get my drift, but the residents here would rather cut off their own hand than to steal from anyone connected with her." He raised a brow. "Nobody but nobody messes with Ruby."

The man's serious tone sent a shiver through her. She tried to offset the unnerving effect with a stab at humor. "Why? She a mob boss or something?"

A greater level of intenseness deepened his unsmiling stare. "Or something. Let's leave it at that." He nodded toward the purse. "It'll be safer here with Raoul than with you. Nobody's going to mess with him either. C'mon, let's get going."

She thought better than to protest. She was on his turf and had to play by his rules if she was going to make any progress. Wondering at the wisdom of trusting this man, she threw caution to the wind and placed her van, purse, and life in his hands.

Together, she and Buck walked away from everything that could identify her as Sadie Brennan from Bayport, Maine. The thought occurred to her that now she would be classified as a Jane Doe if she ended up lifeless in some back alley.

"You're trembling," Buck said. "That's good."

"I . . . I am? That's good?"

He flashed her a big smile. "Hell, yes, that's good. Shows you're not as dumb as I thought. It shows you're more in touch with the reality of your situation. You have no idea how you've put yourself in jeopardy by coming here to learn about the old woman."

He'd been holding onto her elbow while they walked at a fast pace along the littered sidewalk. They'd gone two blocks before he pulled her around a corner.

She looked up the street and found that her feet suddenly refused to do her bidding. She froze in place. The sight before her looked like something out of a science fiction movie after an H-bomb went off. The street stretching before her seemed deserted. On both sides, old warehouses lined the way with dark, gaping doorways and broken windows. Litter, prodded by stray breezes, was the only thing that stirred.

"This isn't the way to Ruby," she said with a quiver in her voice. "I saw her over—"

"I know that," he said impatiently. "You said you needed to get to know more about her. That's what I'm doing. I'm taking you to people who can tell you what you think you want to know."

"What I 'think' I want to know? What does that mean?"

Without answering, the man yanked her through a dark, yawning doorway.

She began to protest when a sound distracted her.

Sunlight speared through the entryway, then faded to grey as she followed the source of the sound. It came from the back wall of the cavernous building. She looked to her guide.

He inclined his head. "Go on. Go start getting your answers."

Unsure of her footing, Sadie cautiously stepped around the debris. Her silent companion followed close behind.

When they'd crossed the expanse of cement flooring, they'd come to a makeshift cave made from cardboard boxes. Sadie looked back to her guide.

He inclined his head, urging her toward the boxes.

Hesitantly, she bent down and peered in. There was just enough light for her to see the whites of a man's eyes.

He blinked back at her. "You come to steal my shoes?" he gruffly asked.

Before she could find her voice, Buck lowered his head beside the woman's.

"Yo, Tommy. It's just me. How doin'? I brought you some fancy company today. Why don't you come out of your bedroom and talk a bit to this nice lady."

Tommy, untangling himself from the heap of discarded blankets, swung his legs off the cot. "Buck! You brung me female company? I woulda cleaned up this place if I'd known you was bringin' a lady by." The man squinted up at them, then eyed Buck. "What you doin' bringin' a real lady here? I kin tell she don't b'long here."

"Eh," Buck grunted, moving back to make way for the cave's owner. "She came down here all by herself and—"

Tommy, unshaven and dressed in fatigues, squinted up at the woman. "You stupid? You tryin' ta count how many lives you got? Why, you got to be the most brainless bit—"

"Tommy," Buck cut in. "She came to learn about Ruby."

The small man's eyes widened, then narrowed. "Well, then. That s'plains it, don't it, Buck. Still," he said, shaking a finger in Sadie's face, "you took a mighty big chance comin' down here. Good thing Buck was the first person you run into." The veteran turned to Buck and mumbled, "Her mojo musta rubbed off on her."

"Mojo?" Sadie repeated.

"Magic," Buck clarified.

"I don't have any magic," she said.

The man frowned. "I don't mean you. Even I can see you ain't got no magic. I meant the old woman's. That old gal's got more mojo packed in her bones than Houdini ever hoped to have!"

Before Sadie realized it, the man had pulled her into a conversation. "Well," she said defensively, "Houdini didn't really do magic, did he? I mean, he claimed he knew magic but they were just tricks . . . escape artist tricks."

"Tricks? Tricks you say?"

She caught Buck's eye before responding to the ragtag man. She noted that Buck seemed to be reaping some measure of amusement from the verbal exchange, and his pleasure pricked at the woman's pride. "Yes, tricks. Tricks like Ruby does."

She'd said the wrong thing. The conversation abruptly shut down.

The army vet searched about the floor for something. When he found it, he slid a three-legged low bench toward the woman.

"You can sit here if you park yourself on this corner." He then rummaged about the rubble for more seating. "Don't have much company anymore. I ain't set up to receive no guests," he grumbled, shooting Buck a sidelong look of disgust. Facing his unexpected guest, he growled, "Sorry I ain't got no tea 'n' crumpets. It's the cook's day off."

Buck grinned and upturned his palms. "Hey, man, she didn't exactly make an appointment with me, either."

"Whatever," Tommy griped, while using his boot to scoot an upended metal bookshelf toward the other two. Placing a board on top, he announced sarcastically, "There, a settee!"

Buck motioned to Sadie. "I'll take the bench, you sit on this. It's more sturdy."

That seating arrangement didn't suit Tommy. "No, dang it. I'll take the bench an' you two sit on the shelving. I wanna sit across from this little lady so I can be face to face with her."

After they'd shifted places, a couple uncomfortable minutes of silence fell on the shoulders of the trio sitting in the dusky light.

Finally Sadie broke the stillness with her soft voice. "Tommy," she began, "I want you to know that I didn't come here to intrude on you or pass judgment on your chosen way of life."

"First off," Tommy said, "I don't care none 'bout anyone's judgment." He narrowed his eyes and waved his arm over the warehouse. "An' what makes you so sure I *chose* this way of life?"

"I can't answer that. It's just a feeling. You did choose it, didn't you?"

"You bet I did." He wasn't about to elaborate.

She kept the momentum going. "I'm not here as a social worker. I'm not here to butt into anyone's life or—"

"Good," said the vet, "'cause none of us need do-gooders around here."

Sadie cleared her throat. "As I was saying, I'm not here to change anyone's life. I'm here to learn more about Ruby." She motioned to the young man sitting beside her. "He wouldn't have brought me to you if you couldn't help me with that. I'm pretty much in the dark about her and would greatly appreciate any light you could shed on the subject."

While the ex-soldier thought on her words, she noticed the name sewn on his uniform. Cozlewsky. It was faded and she wondered how many changes of clothes he had. Did he wear any clothing other than his military uniforms? Gauging his age, she decided he was probably a Vietnam vet. She'd heard that many of them shunned society, preferring to live solitary lives in the wilds of nature and the inner cities.

"Tell me what you already know," he said.

She thought that that was a reasonable request and started by recounting all of her encounters. She began with the initial sighting as she came upon the old woman on her way into the city, including the shiver that swept through her as Ruby stared after her passing vehicle.

Sadie grinned when she retold the part about Ruby's bold and explicit outburst in the museum gift shop, yet neither of the two listening men thought the incident was amusing. Subconsciously, she thought it odd that the woman's words didn't crack their sober expressions. After expressing how she couldn't account for Ruby's baffling changes of footwear, she detailed the cemetery encounter and what she and her niece had witnessed. The list of bizarre incidents concluded when she voiced her confoundment over the fact that Ruby seemed to speak fluent Thai at the Farmers' Market.

Silence followed her monologue.

"Well?" she asked, trying to break the ice. "That's all I know of her. I can't help but think our encounters mean more than just chance." She explained about her visit to the cathedral and what the priest had said. "I can't believe that the only reason I notice her is because of that red hat she wears." She shrugged. "That's what Father McElveney tried to make me believe. I'm not buying it. There's got to be a greater reason here. This woman is constantly on my mind. I can't sleep for thinking of her. When I do manage to sleep, she's in my dreams."

"Why?" Tommy asked.

"Why? Why, what?"

"Why can't you let go of her?"

"Well," she indignantly huffed, "that's why I'm here, isn't it? I can't figure her out. I can't rationalize the things I've witnessed her doing. She's become a mystery that's intruded into my life."

"Intruded?" repeated the vet as he pulled a cigarette from his pocket and lit it.

Sadie wondered how he managed to afford smokes. The thought didn't distract her from the subject at hand. Her shoulders apologetically slumped.

"That was a poor choice of wording. I didn't mean *intrude* intrude, I meant it in a far kinder way. When I said intrude, I didn't exactly mean that she was being intrusive, I meant something more like intermingling. Our paths are always crisscrossing, merging, intermingling."

Tommy considered the woman's attempts to clarify her meaning. "Crisscrossing, maybe," he said. "Influencing, yes, but not yet merging. Ruby's been known to touch many people's lives without them ever taking notice of her. They were never the wiser. But whether or not your paths will actually merge together for a time isn't for you to force by spying on her."

Sadie was offended. "I'm not spying on her." The memory of her earlier spying crept to the fore of her mind. "Well," she admitted, "I did happen to spot her this morning. She was having the time of her life dancing on a corner with . . . with hookers! And gangbangers with their boomboxes were supplying the music, egging them all on!"

This time, Buck's stone-faced expression crumbled into laughter.

"What?" she asked. "What's so all-fired funny? It was like watching Snow White prancing around with Blackbeard's pirates!"

The words came just after Tommy had taken a deep draw on his cigarette. He laughed and sputtered out smoke at the same time. He coughed, laughed, and choked until he was blue in the face.

Buck laughed until tears came to his eyes.

Sadie was indignant, yet kept her voice level. "I didn't risk life and limb coming down here to be laughed at."

Her statement had no effect. "Gentlemen," she persisted, "you could at least share the joke."

The vet was first to recover. "We're not laughing at you. It's what you said. You got the first part—the Snow White part—almost right."

"And the last part?" she asked.

"Is relative," Buck finished. "The last part is relative. It's only relative in regard to the types of people you can easily identify with— relate to. You could identify with an old woman but you can't feel any kinship with miscreants. They're the real bad guys."

"I told you, I'm not here to pass judgment."

"You already have," said the vet. "You compared the street people to evildoing pirates."

"You're being unfair. Everyone knows better than to come down here alone."

Buck raised a brow. "Everyone?"

"Look, dammit!" she said in frustration. "You know why I came down here. And yes, I knew it wasn't the smartest thing to do, but here I am and you said you'd help. Are you going to help me or criticize me?"

The two apologized, then qualified their apology by letting her know that what she'd said was actually quite hilarious, especially how she'd equated the old woman to Snow White.

Tommy leaned forward in a relaxed manner, elbows on his knees. All humor in his demeanor shifted to seriousness. "There's nobody like Ruby. Comparing her to Snow White doesn't even come close to this little woman. She's beyond Snow White."

"An angel, then," she interjected.

Tommy's head shook. He pointed to the man sitting beside her. "If you want to talk of angels you'd better look to the man next to you. He may not be a real angel, but he sure took on the job when you came into his life today. You wouldn't get ten feet in this part of town without somebody like him watchin' over you."

Embarrassed by her thoughtlessness, Sadie realized the truth to the vet's words. She thanked Buck for being her protector.

He was more than embarrassed. "Thank Ruby," he said. "If you weren't here because of her, things might've gone differently for you." He inclined his head to Tommy. "Just listen," he advised.

Tommy's words struck home. Sadie's life was being protected solely because of Ruby. The vet made it very clear that Sadie was being protected by the old woman. The old woman's name had been viewed by the street people as a kind of password that continued to keep her safe in this most hazardous part of the city. The respect given her by the city's criminal element was beyond belief. The realization sobered her. She dutifully shifted her gaze from Buck to Tommy and gave him her full attention.

"Now that you understand things better, we can get on with it," Tommy said with a smile meant to shave the edge off the woman's new tenseness. "Nothing's going to happen to you. Like I said before, Buck may not be an angel, but he'll keep you safe while he guides you to those you need to meet.

"You were right when you presumed that I chose this lifestyle. I don't trust folks on the outside. Whether people are ready to admit it to themselves or not, everyone of them has an agenda. I don't want to play their games. Social programs are tied up in miles of red tape that gets more tangled by the hour. Me, I don't need to get myself wrapped like a Christmas package. It don't get you anywhere anyway. So, here I am. Nobody bothers me an' I don't bother nobody. That's the way I like it. Folks down here have a kind of respect for one another that folks like you probably wouldn't understand. We're all siblings of one family—desperation. Desperation over one thing or another is common to all of us."

Honor among thieves?

Tommy's authoritative voice seemed incongruous coming from someone dressed in dingy fatigues. "It's not like honor among thieves," he said. "It goes much deeper than that. We're a different breed than those on the outside."

Goosebumps rose on her arms when he'd voiced her private thought. It served to keep her attention on his every word. Stay watchful.

"We manage differently than those on the outside. We have different ways of taking care of each other. Some don't want any help. Ruby makes sure they get it anyway."

"So she does live down here," she cut in.

"Didn't say that. Don't take things I say and run off in different directions with them. I never said she lives down here. As a matter of fact, she lives wherever she wants to."

That was the second time she'd heard that idea. "But if she helps people with their needs, then she's got to be getting those things from somewhere. She has to be hoarding them somewhere until someone needs them."

Tommy shook his head. Sighing, he tilted his head to Buck. "Didn't I just tell her not to run off with things I tell her?"

Sadie looked from one to the other.

Without comment, Buck's eyes rolled up to the metal girders of the high warehouse ceiling.

A hand shook in front of her eyes. She followed it back to Tommy. "Look at me, pretty lady." He pointed to his eyes. "Right here.

Look right here in my eyes. Ruby lives wherever she wants. Anywhere and everywhere is home to her. *Capisce? Comprende?"*

She smiled. "Just so I do *comprende*, you're saying that she has no permanent address. She has no one physical place where she keeps her stuff and calls home."

"She ain't got no stuff. That's the point."

"How can she have no stuff? You said she gives stuff to those in need."

"No. *You* said she *helps* those who need it."

Sadie was getting confused. "Okay, let's back up. Are you saying that she doesn't do this helping by giving stuff away?"

"No."

"No, what?"

"She *does* give stuff away."

Now Sadie rolled her eyes. "Well, you just said—"

"No," Tommy interrupted, "*we* were talking about her giving stuff away. *You* complicated matters by assuming she was *hoarding* things to give away, like she has a house full of goods or a warehouse someplace. She has no home base. There is no one place she goes to every night. No single house, room, structure, dwelling she calls home. Jesus," he sputtered, "I thought we got that straight already."

"Okay, then. What about *this* if she doesn't hoard things? I've never seen her in the same pair of shoes. She's always got a different pair of shoes on. I've even seen her wearing two *different* sets of shoes during *one* encounter with her! What about those? Where does she keep all those shoes?"

Buck cleared his throat. He was curious to see how Tommy was going to explain that one.

Tommy bought some thinking time by readjusting his backside on the broken bench. He fiddled around by searching his pockets for his lighter.

"You're stalling," she said.

Their eyes met again. "Ahh, no, I'm not stalling. I, ah . . . I was just looking for where I put my—"

"Your answer?" she finished.

He chuckled. "No, I know where that answer is. No question about that. She carries what she needs around in that old carpetbag of hers."

He thinks I'm an idiot. "Oh, sure! That wraps everything up nice and tidy, doesn't it," she sarcastically quipped. "That explains where the extra pair of shoes came from! And the trowel, grass clippers, and weeder tools she used in the cemetery. Of course!" she said, hitting her forehead with her palm. "Why didn't I think of that?"

Neither men realized she was being sarcastic until she added, "All that *stuff* came out of the *flat* satchel she was carrying!"

The men were no longer clueless about her attitude.

Buck jumped right in. "That's right. Everything she needs is in that flowered satchel."

"In the *empty* flowered satchel?"

"That's what I said. That's where she hoards the stuff. And the shoes, she gives 'em to folks who need 'em."

They're not leveling with me. "Look. I came here to get some answers, not be out and out lied to." She stood.

Surprised, they looked up at her. "Sadie," Tommy tried, "it's no lie. Everything's just like I told you."

"Uh-huh, and I'm the queen of freaking Sheba." She gave her attention to her protector. "Did you have someplace else to take me to or should we just head back to my van . . . *if* it's still sitting on rubber, that is."

Tommy Cozlewsky didn't care if the woman believed him. He shrugged and stood. "I'll walk you to the door. That's the least I can do."

"Oh, you needn't bother yourself. I've taken enough of your time."

"No bother," he grinned. "Gotta pick up my delivery."

Sadie had no idea what he was mumbling about until the trio reached the sunlit doorway. Two bags of stuff were just inside the opening. The contents, she could see, were mostly food items with a few hygiene products thrown in. A carton of Tommy's brand of cigarettes was angled on top.

She looked from one man to the other. "Where did these come from?" she asked. "They weren't here when we came in."

"You must've missed seeing them," Buck offered.

Hoping for a more plausible answer, she looked to Tommy.

He gave it with a poker face. "They came from her satchel. She came by while we was talkin'."

"Oh, for God's sake," she spouted, while striding out onto the sidewalk. "I'm outta here." She impatiently paced while the two men conferred in hushed voices.

When Buck joined her, she wasn't in the best frame of mind. "Honestly," she scolded, "how on earth do you expect me to get my answers when you bring me to crazy people?"

"Tommy's not crazy."

"Hell he isn't."

The woman's protector worked to keep up with her quickened stride. "Do you know where you're going?" he asked.

"No, and I don't care. I'll find someone else who'll tell me what I want to know. I'll find someone who'll tell me the truth!"

As it happened, she was walking in the same direction he was going to lead her. And without warning, when they came to his chosen destination, he yanked her kicking and screaming down a darkened stairwell. "You can holler and scream all you want. Nobody in this neighborhood will come running."

"Hey!" she yelled, beating at his arms. "What do you think you're doing?"

Reaching the doorless opening at the bottom, he faced her and put a finger to his lips. "Shhh, you need to see something." Gently, he loosened his grip on her. "You okay?"

Smoothing the fabric on the arms of her jacket, she nodded and lowered her head to give attention to her footing. She screamed again.

Buck got in her face. "I told you to be quiet!"

She pointed to the ground. "D-did you see that rat scuttle around the doorway? It was bigger than a wharf cat!"

He inclined his head to the mysterious blackness beyond the door frame. "There's more in there where that one came from. Control yourself. Show some respect for those who can't help themselves. You're going to be like a voyeur in there. I'd appreciate it if you kept your voice as low as possible so we don't disturb anyone."

Her eyes widened with his cryptic advice. She whispered. "What kinds of things will the people in there be able to tell me?"

"They can't *tell* you anything about Ruby. It's their actions, their body language that'll be their voice."

"Why is that? Are they deaf mutes? Are they too ill to speak?"

Suddenly, air rank with the stench of human waste and fouled with the underlying clamminess of years of mold buildup assailed her senses. She flinched, a hand covering her nose like a respirator mask. The offensive odor still made its way through her mouth. She grimaced with fading bravado.

Buck gingerly urged her forward into the sleazy dive. Makeshift beds took shape as their eyes adjusted to the bleakness of the room. Some people were prone on cots. Others crouched in corners on nests of soiled blankets.

As the newcomers quietly wove their way among the unaware people, Sadie winced when her eye caught that of another woman's. The listless one's gaze was unseeing. It focused on imaginary visions of her own heroine-induced reality. Dark circles made rings around the recessed eyes. Her complexion sallow, cheeks sunken.

In one of the corners, three young men huddled together. They were helping each other find veins that weren't collapsed.

Sadie scanned the repulsive scene. She whispered to her companion. "You brought me to a shooting gallery."

He nodded.

Inching closer to her protector, she kept her voice low. "I see why you said they couldn't tell me anything. They're not even aware of us. But I don't get it. How can these people's body language show me anything about Ruby?"

"Their drugged state is what I wanted you to see. Ruby helps these people."

"How on earth can anyone help them? They're all strung out."

Buck led his questing companion forward. They picked their way over prone bodies until they reached a low table. "Look in the bag."

Hesitantly, she did. Even in the dim light, she could see that it was full of packaged syringes.

Her instinctual outrage clouded reason. Her voice rose. "She supplies them with needles?"

"Shhhh," he reminded with a nod.

"Oh, mygod, how could she do such a horrible thing!"

Her raised voice roused a couple of people.

Buck jerked her back to the doorway and hauled her up the steps. It took all of his self-control to refrain from shaking her. "I told you to be quiet down there!"

She blinked in the bright sunlight. "But needles? C'mon! I thought Ruby went around doing *good* things for people. Jesus," she said, running her hands through her hair, "needles for drug addicts, of all things! I can't believe this!"

He grabbed her arm and pulled her away from the shooting gallery. They began walking. This time he took the lead.

"You can't believe it because you let your emotions override your sense of logic. You flew off the handle and left your mind behind."

"Oh, really," she said, staying close beside him. "I don't see how aiding and abetting addicts has any logic to it. Maybe you'd better enlighten me."

Though the man kept his head facing forward, his eyes slid sideways to momentarily look at the know-it-all striding beside him.

"You're acting like this is some kind of mysterious puzzle."

"Well? Isn't it? You tell me where the common logic lies in Ruby supplying syringes to those addicts."

His answer was swift. "The common logic is the prevention of serious health problems. Infection. Hepatitis. HIV. AIDS. I guess you think those are real esoteric."

She flushed with embarrassment. "I . . . I'm sorry. I forgot about those."

"That was obvious," he muttered beneath his breath.

"I heard that," she shot back. "But why does she encourage them to keep doing the drugs?"

As they quickly rounded another corner, Buck was about to explain more; instead, he let her ramble and ramble until she got herself caught up in the bramble bush of gnarled thinking.

"I mean, if she's such a good person, why doesn't she get them to the methadone clinics? Or to some of those free rehab centers? Now, doing something like that would surely be a hell of a lot more helpful than leaving bags of sterile syringes for them to keep injecting themselves with."

Her protector remained silent.

"I suppose you don't have an answer for those alternatives. It just seems to me that she's going about her humanitarian works in some very questionable ways. She should be—"

Buck raised a hand. "May I have a word?"

"Certainly," she acquiesced. "I wish you would."

"Hypothetically speaking," he began, "if you had a friend who accidentally cut her arm—severely—yet refused to call for medical assistance, wouldn't you at least come to her aid by applying a clean bandage and then routinely change the dressing?"

She smiled at the simplicity. "That'd be a given."

"A given," he thoughtfully repeated.

"Sure. If I couldn't force her to go to a hospital or see a doctor, I'd at least be there to make sure the wound was kept clean with fresh dressings. And I'd—"

A smile was creeping up his mouth. "And you'd what?"

"I'd do my best with the situation because I had no other choice if my friend refused the normal channels for obtaining medical assistance." She looked up at him. "This has been all about not forcing people into doing things they don't want to do, isn't it?"

"There's a simpler way to put it," he said. "The will. Ruby's big on that. She says that you can't mess around with people's wills. She's a stickler for that. That's something she'd never do. So, for people who are determined to use drugs, all she can do to help is to at least see to it that they use sterile syringes. It's her small way of helping folks who refuse to help themselves or change their ways."

His explanation was so obvious she was embarrassed. "I feel pretty stupid for going off like that. Why didn't I see that right away?"

"You didn't see it right away because you couldn't think past your outrage. You were incensed over something you should've been appreciative of. You thought you saw evil instead of something good. You misread what you saw. You weren't in the right frame of mind to see anything but what your first reaction caused."

"I don't know," she said, while looking around the decrepit district. "That wasn't like me. It must be this neighborhood. It's got me on edge."

"It should. You don't belong here."

"Does anybody? Really? I mean—"

Buck distracted her by pointing. He held her arm to stop her forward movement. She was eased back into the shadows against a building.

On the far corner, an ongoing procession of youths was meeting up with a man slouched against the recessed doorway of a vacant storefront. Money from the kids went into one deep pocket of his trench coat while he distributed something from the other. What gave the scene an element of otherworldliness was the woman standing beside him. Her hat, the only color in the world of drabness, stood out like a diamond among coals. When the children's business was finished with the man, none of them left without taking something from her as well. She'd been pulling things out of her carpetbag.

As Sadie watched in fascination, she saw that each child was handed something different.

She watched the scene unfold. *I'm not jumping to conclusions again.* She squinted and strained to make out what was being passed out to the young people. Some of them tarried longer than others. Some, she could tell, shyly accepted whatever was handed them and then ran off. She watched the old woman pat several on the head while their items were received. When one child came before her she squatted down to his level and, closing her eyes, held her hands over both of his ears.

Sadie startled when Buck bent to whisper in her ear. "That kid's got an ear infection," he informed. "He won't have it for long, though."

Sadie couldn't pull her eyes away. Mesmerized, she whispered back, "She heals, doesn't she."

"Her touch is what you might call . . . therapeutic."

"Uh-huh. So I've noticed a time or two. What's she handing out to all of them?"

"Different things. Whatever each needs at the time. Sometimes they'll get some kind of toy. Medicine mostly. That one there," he said, watching a boy wearing the backward baseball cap. "That one's brother has pneumonia. She probably gave him antibiotics."

"She's a pharmacy?"

"She's a whatever. Mostly she's everyone's surrogate mother. If you were down here enough, you'd hear people talk of Mother. That's what a lot of us call her."

Sadie recalled the cemetery incident when Ruby acted like every resident was her child. "Mother," she softly echoed, "I think it suits her."

"It more than suits her," he said.

Spellbound by the action on the corner, she added, "Like a Mother Teresa. A Mother Teresa of the Hood."

Buck snickered. "I like that. That was good. But that was still wrong. You're starting to get the message but you've still got one thing wrong."

"I do?"

"Yep."

"Well, tell me so I stay on the right track."

"This whole thing with Ruby is your quest, not mine." Then he noticed that the sunlight had lost its brilliance. Shadows were stretching. The beginnings of dusk wouldn't be far off. He eased her from their hidden vantage point and guided her back the way they'd come.

Though Sadie let herself be led away, she craned her neck to keep her eyes on the corner. When she had no choice but to turn back around, she asked, "C'mon, tell me what I have wrong."

He quickened their pace. "I gotta get you back so you can be outta here. The action's going to triple around here before long. You came at the right time. But now it's time to end your little foray into the armpit of Chicago and get back to your green lawns and stone turrets."

She took offense. "I told you, I live above a shop . . . on a wharf . . . in Maine."

"I remember. You're still going home to the Land of the Disadvantaged."

Her heels dug in as she brought herself to an abrupt stop. "I'll have you kno—"

He reached for her arm and yanked her forward. "Don't stop like that. We need to keep going. You want to see your belongings in one piece, don't you?"

She suspiciously eyed him. "You said they'd be safe!"

"I'm sure they are," he responded with a glance toward the sky. "If we're gone much longer Raoul's going to have to call in some of his friends to help do that. He's only one. Like I said, in about half an hour, there's going to be a lot more action on the street."

She didn't need further prompting to hurry along.

They passed the shooting gallery. Nervous people were entering.

Buck pulled Sadie closer to him. "Don't make eye contact. Just keep walking like you're doing. These people are suspicious of you. They'd roll you for those shoes you're wearing."

"These are not Gucci shoes, they're old."

"Not to them," he quipped back. "They're good enough to sell. You wouldn't believe the stuff they can sell to keep their habit going."

The woman's heart beat faster while she did as she was told. "How's this?" she whispered beneath her breath."

"Fine," he reassured, "you're doing just fine."

They were nearly jogging. "What do you sell?" she asked.

"Nothing. I'm not into that drug shit. I got me another line of work."

Something in his tone made her drop her line of questioning.

They quick-stepped past Tommy's warehouse. She didn't bother to look in as they passed. It sounded as though Sgt. Cozlewsky had company. She'd been lucky so far and didn't want to press her good fortune. The vet's friends might not be as sociable as he'd been.

When they rounded the corner, her van was in sight. Its shiny paint so sharply contrasted with its surroundings that it reminded Sadie of a lone palm tree sticking up out of a barren desert landscape. She breathed a silent sigh of relief. The sigh wasn't as silent as she'd thought.

"I told you it'd still be there," the voice beside her said.

"Yeah, I know," she replied sheepishly. "It's just good to have the reassurance."

As they neared the vehicle, she saw Raoul lounging on the stoop, his legs out before him, elbows as a support on the step behind him. Three of his friends were with him, one leaning up against each side door of the van, and one slouched against the back door.

Buck winked down at Sadie. "Good boy," he said, grinning, "he already brought reinforcements in. Snake and Julio were good choices." He nodded to the man at the back. "Him, too."

Three more to trust with my purse. She didn't voice that concern, of course. She thought it'd be terribly rude. It wouldn't show appreciation for four tires still holding the van off the pavement. No, no. A comment like that would ruffle feathers. She definitely did not want to ruffle any of these characters' feathers.

The street-side man saw them first. He straightened. "Hey, man," he exclaimed to Buck, "who's your class-e-e lad-e-e-e?"

"Hey, Snake! What's up?"

Sadie hung back. When Buck motioned her forward, she saw the partial cobra tattoo that peered from beneath the man's rolled-up black tee sleeve.

Snake nodded toward the woman and repeated his question.

"Nobody," Buck replied."

The tattooed man looked her over. "This ain't 'nobody,' man."

"Okay then," Buck said, catching Sadie's eye. "She's someone who's not staying long enough for introductions."

As Raoul sauntered over to join the group, Buck held the vehicle's door open. With a sweeping wave of the arm, he motioned her inside.

The first thing she saw was her purse. *Should I check the contents?* She lifted the keys that were on top and put them into the ignition.

Julio never spoke a word, but Snake brought his head close to the opened window. "Hey, classy lady, you ain't gonna check your wallet?" he sarcastically asked.

She forced a winning smile and nodded to Buck. "Why, do I need to? He said I could trust you."

Snake laughed. "And you believed him?"

"As a matter of fact, I do." She looked to Raoul. "Thanks for watching over my things."

He made a hat-tipping gesture. "My pleasure."

She turned the key.

Nothing happened. *Oh, God, the engine's gone.*

Trying again without success, she eyed Buck.

He flashed a disgusted look to the third member of the group. "Julio. Hey, man, did you mess with her distributor cap?"

The third man, hair pulled back in a ponytail like Raoul's minus the rolled bandana around the forehead, innocently crossed his heart before raising both hands.

Buck was only ninety percent convinced that Ponytail hadn't lifted the hood. "She still got the same engine? Your friends from the chop shop didn't make a visit, did they?"

"No, man. Raoul was hangin' here the whole time!"

The woman in the driver's seat took that to mean that nobody crossed Raoul. He was the one responsible for her vehicle staying in one piece. She tried the key a second time.

The engine turned over and purred like a cat curled up with catnip.

She blushed. "Sorry."

Third man shook his head. "Women drivers."

Ignoring the comment, Snake backed away from the vehicle.

The fourth man stepped away from the rear.

Buck tapped the driver's door. "You know your way to the freeway?"

She nodded. "Thanks for everything. You've been a big help."

"Yeah," was all he said. "Get going."

The blue commercial van angled away from the curb. Then stopped.

Buck went up to the driver's window. "Now what? You stop to check your purse before you got too far away?"

"No. I said I trusted you. Doing that wouldn't show a vote of confidence, would it?"

"Then what's the problem?"

"You never answered my question."

He rolled his eyes. "What question?"

"Well, actually two questions."

The man at her window glanced up and down the street. "Make it quick."

"I was about to ask you what you meant by me 'going home to the Land of the Disadvantaged.' What did you mean by that?"

"Nothing."

"No. Please, I want to know."

"Rich folks are disadvantaged because they never get their manicured hands dirty. They never—"

Her eyes subconsciously checked her fingernails. They were unpolished and chewed down to the quick.

He, too, glanced at her hands. "Not you," he grinned. "They never get to see the reality of their world. Their world's nice an' tidy. It's sterile. That's the way they like it. The way they like it ends up being a disadvantage, a handicap."

She'd never viewed the wealthy in quite that way before now. "I think you're right," she replied. "There's a lot to what you say."

Wanting to prompt her departure, he didn't expound on the concept. "You had a second question?"

"When I said Ruby was like the Mother Teresa of the Hood, you said that that idea was still wrong. I asked what I had wrong and you completely evaded my question by saying we had to get back. I still need to know how I was thinking wrong about her."

He sighed. "You compared her to Mother Teresa."

"So?"

"So think bigger."

Their eyes locked. And although she wasn't sure what his answer meant, his words had a powerful effect on her.

"Promise me something," he added. "Promise me just one thing."

"What?"

"That you'll never try to come down here again."

She smiled at him. "That won't even be necessary. I got what I came for. Thanks."

He slapped the driver's door. "Now, get going."

Out of habit, she checked for traffic in both directions before pulling away.

She saw the man shake his head.

There was no traffic.

When the van came up to the house and passed the opened garage,

Sadie noticed that the Lexus was parked in one of the bays. Mira was home. She'd thought her sister's business trip was going to take longer. Checking her watch, she was surprised to discover that it was already dinnertime. She also wondered what kind of mood Mira was in. With her, one never knew.

Savannah had been anxiously awaiting her aunt's return. She flew out the kitchen door to wrap her arms about the driver, who was just getting out of her vehicle.

"Hey, you!" Sadie greeted. "Miss me?"

The girl nodded, then gave the interior of the van a quick once-over.

"I didn't go antiquing today," Sadie said. Then, to avoid talking about where she'd been, she distracted the child's attention. "How's my little dancer?"

Again the little one's head bobbed.

They walked toward the open door. Mouthwatering smells drifted out. "I see your mom's home. Has she been home long?"

The question was answered with a slow shake of the head.

Greta turned to the two entering the kitchen. She was in a cheery mood. "Made your favorite," she said. "Pumpkin bread and a pie to match."

Sadie smacked her lips. "I'll just have pie for dinner, then."

"Oh," exclaimed the housekeeper, "I don't think you want to do that because then you'd be missing out on your favorite meal." Her smile drooped. "Mira's home."

"I saw the car when I pulled in. It must've been an exhausting day for her. She tired?" It was a roundabout way of inquiring about her sister's frame of mind.

"I'm sure she is," Greta replied, "but I think her deposition went her way. She acts like the trip was well worth it. She had that satisfied look of triumph."

Sadie knew that that meant a certain self-satisfied smugness her sister displayed so well to the world. She wasn't sure if that was good or bad. Either way, Mira could be difficult even when she was celebrating a legal victory. By nature, Mira had a touchy personality. Since David's death, it'd become volatile.

"Maybe I should go see her," Sadie suggested.

Greta shook her head. "She's on the phone. She's been on the phone since she got in the door. I suppose she wants to keep on top of today's office messages."

"On a Saturday? Since when does Caitlin work on Saturday, too?"

"Not too, *instead* of. She's off on Sundays and Tuesdays."

"Since when?"

"Since two years ago when a high-profile client read Mira the riot act for not being able to deliver signed papers to her office on a Saturday."

"Oh, I bet that bruised her ego."

Josef strolled into the room. "It did more than that," he added. "Everyone stayed well away from her for nearly a week."

Sadie turned to him. "Did you have a good day? Get the rest of the mums planted?"

"I did," he proudly said, while reaching for the dishes to set the table for five.

When all was ready, the friendly warmth of the room chilled twenty degrees when the mistress of the house entered. She brought an icy mood that served to freeze everyone's attempt at conversation. Her irascible disposition was about to ruin dinner.

It put Sadie on a slow burn. Family dinnertime should be gay and cheerful, filled with light chatter about everyone's day. That gaiety shouldn't be suppressed by one member's black mood.

"Greta tells me your deposition was a success," she said in a chipper attempt to point out a bright spot in her sister's testy attitude.

"It was," she snapped without looking up from her plate.

"And your flights? They went off without a hitch? You didn't have to wait too long with all of those new security measures they have now?"

Purposely averting her eyes from the questioner, Mira reluctantly responded. "Fine. Everything was fine."

It was clear that the mistress of the Woodward manor wasn't inclined to participate in congenial family conversation over dinner. The rest of the diners found enough things to talk and laugh about without needing Mira's input. And although she didn't take part, everyone could see her mood growing darker by the minute. Every time laughter broke out at the end of someone's story, it acted like a flammable accelerant thrown on her already smoldering emotional fire. Not wishing to wait until her fuming reached flashpoint level, Mira picked up her wineglass and stood.

"After all of you are finished with your little festivities," she said, turning to glare at her sister, "I'd like to see *you* in my study."

Irritated with the excessively authoritative tone, Sadie glared back. "I don't know what your problem is, but I'm not one of your paralegals who await your every utterance and jump to do your every menial bidding."

Ignoring the statement, Mira left the table. "I'll be waiting," she said before whisking from the room.

Greta whispered, "I don't get it. What's up with her? She was in an exceptionally good mood when she got back. I can't imagine what's got into her."

Josef shrugged. "She picked up a burr somewhere along the way. Maybe it had to do with the call to Caitlin."

Sadie disgustedly grunted. "Whatever it is, she shouldn't be bringing it to the table. She's around here little enough. She could at least not act like a despot when she's home." She glanced at Savannah, then back to the old couple. "For her," she said, inclining her head to the child. "Mira could at least be civil around her own daughter."

There wasn't much anyone could add to that sentiment. They all agreed. And while the four began to busy themselves with clearing the table, they heard Mira bellow.

"Sadie-e-e-e! I'm waiting!"

The unnerving sound caused Savannah to drop the armful of plates. They shattered on the ceramic tiled floor.

Sadie looked to Greta, who motioned for the younger woman to leave for the study.

Instead, the child's aunt bent to help with the cleanup. "It's okay," she cooed to her niece. "She made me jump, too, only not the way she expected me to."

Greta bent to help, but Sadie wouldn't have it. "No, Greta, you don't need more work due to Mira's temper. Savannah and I almost have it."

The housekeeper straightened her back and returned to the table to clear leftovers.

Josef sauntered toward the kitchen door. He addressed his wife. "If you won't be needing me for anything, I got me some tinkering to do in the garden shed."

Greta waved her husband away. "You go on and do your tinkering. At least one of us will be spared her ladyship's wrath." After she watched him walk out into the exterior security lights, she gave her attention to the child. "Savannah, dear, why don't you go up to your room and watch a movie or something."

The girl acted as though she hadn't heard the suggestion. She wanted to be with her aunt.

Greta shrugged. "Whatever you want to do is okay by me," she said, while wrapping up the leftovers. "I know you missed your auntie today. Maybe you two can do something together tomorrow. Perhaps you two can—"

"*Tomorrow* I am taking Savannah to the theater," came the voice from the doorway.

Savannah gave her aunt a desperately pleading look. She didn't want to go.

"And how on earth did those plates get broken?"

Sadie had been balancing the plate shards piled in her hands. After she ceremoniously dumped them into the trash container, she turned to squarely face her sister.

"Sudden bellowing does that sometimes," she calmly said. "People tend to get startled by hearing an unexpected bellow. It makes them drop things."

"I've been waiting for you," the attorney said.

"I had more pressing matters," the sister shot back.

"Savannah," said her mother, "go play in your room."

The girl stood rooted to the floor.

"All right, then," Mira summed up. She locked eyes with each one in turn. Bringing them back to lock on her sister, she said, "We can do this here as well as in my study. I was hoping to spare you the embarrassment of being brought up on the carpet, but well . . . since you had more *pressing matters* to handle, we may as well get it out in the open." In a well-practiced, controlled voice, she struck a pose of overconfidence. "You are not to take my daughter out anymore."

Greta froze in midstep.

Savannah's jaw dropped. She couldn't believe her ears. Her aunt had driven all the way out here to help her. How could her mother do something so mean?

Sadie maintained her reserve. "On what basis?"

"Oh, I think you know," came the smooth-as-silk reply.

Sadie's mind did a quick rewind of her day. Then unaided, it played forward. The slums. Tommy Cozlewsky's warehouse. The hookers. The shooting gallery. *But there's no way her sister could know about those things.* She remained mute.

Mira smirked. "Oh, come now. Don't play innocent and pretend

you're clueless. You know exactly what I'm talking about. If you want
to bend your neck and put your head into the jaws of the shark, that's
your choice, but you are *not* going to shove *Savannah's* in there as
well!" She cast her gaze over the puzzled onlookers while Sadie stood
speechless. "Our family *wanderer* here drove smack into the heart of
South Chicago today. She parked her vehicle and walked the streets
with a known *felon!*"

She can't know, but . . . she does! How does she know?

Mira began to pace before the accused. "Now, a reasonable question that you might be asking yourself right about now would be this:
How did I know that?" She glowered at Sadie. "I know that because
I have *connections.* I have connections all over this city. Now, what do
you have to say for yourself before I send you packing?"

Packing? Would she really throw me out?

The child rushed to her aunt's defense. Much to the chagrin of her
mother, Savannah threw her arms around the woman's waist.

Silence hung heavily in the room.

Her daughter's strong response took the mother off guard. "Well,"
she softened, "maybe not *packing*, exactly, but I never want you to
take—"

"I have no more need to go there again," Sadie said, without
sounding contrite. "I came here to help Savannah and that's *exactly*
what I'm going to try to do. That includes taking her places."

Mira's eyes lowered to meet those of her daughter's. She noted they
were moist, brimming.

The sight touched her. She softened. "Just don't make any plans
to take her anywhere tomorrow." She smiled at the child. "Tomorrow
Savannah and I are going to lunch at the club and then on to the theater. *The Lion King* is in town. You'll like that, won't you, Savannah?"

The little girl's only response was to hug her aunt tighter.

"Of course, you will," Mira patronized as she spun on her heels.
When the plush carpeting of the hallway silenced her retreating footfalls, she called back to no one in particular, "By the way, you need to
call Caitlin tonight. She said it was important."

Caitlin? What did Caitlin want?

Sadie knelt to embrace her niece. "Thanks for the vote of confidence," she said, using the sleeve of her blouse to dab at the girl's
teary eyes. "I think that's what made the verdict swing in our favor."
Seeing the wide eyes, green as emeralds, looking back at her made her

want to hug the girl as tightly as she could and never let go. She was a treasure. "It seems that your mom's already got tomorrow booked, huh?"

Savannah frowned and nodded.

"That's okay," Sadie reassured, while fluffing the girl's mass of natural curls. "It's good to do something with your mom. It's more than good, it's great! She loves you, you know. And it's really not her fault that she's not home much. She works hard to be one of the top attorneys in the city. It'll be fun going to the club and the theater. I heard *The Lion King* is a great play. The elaborate costumes make it an extravaganza. What do you say we make a date to spend all of Monday together?"

Savannah pointed to her aunt and then upturned her palms.

"You won't be with me tomorrow? Is that your concern?"

A nod confirmed the guess.

"Oh, honey, don't you worry about me being alone for another day. I have the feeling that when I call Caitlin back she's going to want to get together. We'd mentioned something about trying to do lunch while I was here. That's probably what she wants me to call her about. So you go and have a great time with your mom tomorrow. Okay?"

Savannah pressed her lips together and nodded just before skipping out of the room.

When Sadie stood and turned, Greta's hard gaze took her by surprise. "What? I know that look. Now what'd I do?"

"It's true, then? You went to South Chicago? You purposely went there? Alone?"

"Yes, I did. But—"

The housekeeper was stupefied. Her voice barely above a whisper. "Why, I can't hardly believe you'd do such a foolhardy thing."

"Greta," Sadie tried to explain, "I had to. There was something I had to do and that was the only place to do it. You see, Savannah and I have seen this mysterious woman—a bag lady, really—who does these extraordinary . . ."

"Savannah! A bag lady? Oh, Sadie!" Greta cried. "What have you two been up to? Whatever it is, it doesn't sound good if it led you into the Combat Zone. And . . . all by yourself? Well," she sighed with relief, "at least the child wasn't with you."

"Greta! I'd never put her at risk! Of course she wasn't with me." She took the woman's elbow and guided her to the long trestle table.

"Sit down. Let me tell you about this amazing woman that Savannah and I keep seeing."

The housekeeper listened intently to the unfolding story. As improbable as the bizarre tale sounded, she believed every word. She believed every word because her keen sense of observation couldn't discount the younger woman's growing excitement that exponentially built with the telling of each remarkable encounter. Sadie was never one to tell tall tales. And the excitement that clung to the tails of this one was not only contagious, it was downright electrifying.

Nine

Sunday

"Will there be anything else for you ladies?" the waiter asked after clearing their table.

The two patrons of the popular Tuscan Gardens restaurant both smiled politely. The woman with the cropped hair ordered a margarita. Her companion, a bloody mary. An uncomfortable silence hung between them until after their drinks arrived and they were alone again.

Caitlin leaned forward over her drink. "So," she began lightheartedly. "You've let me ramble nonstop during the drive over here and all through lunch. I've yakked about my family, my job, my latest shopping trip, and my love life. I'm all talked out." Wanting to ferret out the reason behind her companion's uncharacteristic quietness, she gave her friend a prompting look. "Your turn."

Sadie took a superficial sip of her drink. "They make the best bloody marys here," she said.

"I know. And every time we come here, you always say that. Tell me something I don't already know."

"Did I thank you for picking me up at the house?"

"Oh, for heaven's sake. Yes, you thanked me. You thanked me twice." Her eyes narrowed. "Now what's going on with you? You've been distracted and distant all through lunch. Is it Paul?"

Sadie's heart skipped a beat at the mention of the name. It skipped two beats when she realized that she hadn't thought of him in several days. The fact momentarily unnerved her. She didn't know if she should be remorseful or relieved.

Seeing the blood drain from her friend's face, Caitlin became alarmed. "What? You're as white as a ghost. Have you heard from him?"

"I . . . ahhh . . . no. No, I haven't." She took in a couple of halting breaths and leaned back into the receiving support of the leather booth.

A knowing smile tipped one corner of Caitlin's mouth. "I see," she murmured. "You haven't given him a thought because you've had your mind on other things."

Emerald eyes bored accusingly across the table. "As if that's a surprise to you."

"What's that look for? What did I do? This is about yesterday, isn't it? You think it was me? You think I narced on you."

"Well? You were the one who talked to her last night. Last night she was so mad that she was ready to send me packing after she talked to—"

"Nick." The secretary's initial hurt expression turned into a defensive position. Caitlin leaned far forward toward her friend. "*Nick,*" she repeated in a whisper. "Yesterday, I'd called to give Mira her messages *after* Nick had already spoken to her moments before." Trying for nonchalance, she surreptitiously scanned the room to see if any other diners were giving them attention. When she was satisfied nobody was observing them, she secretively lowered her voice even more. "Now, I realize that you probably don't know who Nick is, but he's an undercover informant working for the Chicago P.D."

Likely story. She's trying to wheedle out of it. "So?"

The secretary clenched her jaw. She made an urgent hand signal meant to beckon her dinner partner closer.

The dinner partner failed to respond as desired.

After a sigh of irritation, frustration took over. "Will you *pul-eeze* stop being so stubborn and listen to the rest of this? You need to hear this."

No response.

"Come on. Please?"

Sadie straightened. "This better be good," she warned, while shifting her weight forward, "because I've been fairly single-minded since you picked me up."

"That's not news, either." Again her critical gaze swept the crowded restaurant. "Do I have your attention?"

Eyes rolled to the ceiling.

"Don't patronize me."

Green eyes settled on the hazel pair. "I'm all ears."

"As I said, my call to Mira was right after she got an earful from the first caller. How do I know that? I know that because I got railed at *before* you did."

Sadie raised a brow.

"That's right. I got the third degree because I was suspected of having foreknowledge of your whereabouts yesterday. Mira automatically assumed I'd been privy to your planned activities and laid into me for not stopping you from pulling such a wildly asinine stunt. Those are her words, not mine. Although, if truth be told, I gotta say—"

"Don't," Sadie cut off. "I'm well aware of how asinine it was. I don't need to hear it coming from everyone around me."

"Okay. I'll give you that." Her expression turned quizzical. "How could I have spilled the beans when I didn't even know there were beans to be spilled?"

"I apologize for that," Sadie heartfeltly said. "I automatically tied your call into Mira's outrage after speaking with you. Of course you couldn't have known where I'd been."

Caitlin disagreed. "*Au contraire!*" she softly sang. "I knew *after* the fact—after Nick spilled the beans."

"Well, yes, I see that now. So, that leads me to the next question— who told this Nick character?"

Caitlin's eyes took a final sweep over the restaurant before giving her full attention to the woman sitting across from her.

The woman eyed her back. "Do I need to point out that you're overdramatizing the paranoia?"

"With due cause," came the reply. "With due cause. For your

information," she retorted in a hushed tone, *"nobody* had to tell Nick. Nobody *had* to tell him because he was *there* yesterday!"

The information was met with rounded eyes. "You're kidding. Where?"

"Do I look like I'm kidding? He was watching your van while you were traipsing around God knows where with Buck-the-felon!"

Sadie mentally called up the visual of the men around her van. Nick was the fourth man. "The man without a name," Sadie mumbled to herself.

A clueless shrug preceded the secretary's response. "The man without a name? All Mira said was that he guarded your vehicle and purse while you were gone." She had to bite her tongue to keep from asking how her friend justified leaving her purse with criminal types.

"It was trust them or the boys from the chop shop. I wasn't given long to think it over. And," she added, "I knew the question was on the tip of your tongue."

"I was being polite. How did you know?"

"You were biting your tongue. You've always done that whenever you're trying to stop yourself from verbally exacerbating something."

"I do?"

"You do," Sadie replied. "Anyway, as it turned out, my trust was well placed, wasn't it? I ended up putting my trust in one of the good guys, a cop."

"A cop who went through your purse to find out what the crazy lady's name was."

Sadie rephrased her friend's harsh statement in an effort to soften it. "A cop who wanted to keep the crooks from finding out who I was. Going through my stuff was probably inevitable and he didn't want it to be one of the bad guys doing the snooping." Her brows knitted together. "How did he connect me to Mira, though?

The question was met with a dumbfounded look. "Hello? Your sister's got private investigators and undercover operatives in the pockets of every designer suit she owns! Her closet's full of them."

"Including Nick," Sadie concluded.

"Not officially, it turns out, but they're not strangers, either."

Still puzzled, Sadie stressed her point. "That still doesn't explain how he connected me to her, though. We have different last names."

Caitlin held the key to that mystery as well. "Seems he didn't make the connection, not at first. He was curious about the identity of an obviously upscale professional woman who would voluntarily put herself at risk like you did. His curiosity deepened when he saw that the state of Maine was on your license plate, all of your ID cards. Then he hit pay dirt by coming across the one lead he needed."

"Lead?"

"Lead. He found Mira's business card in your wallet." Her tone turned supportive. "No one intentionally told on you, Sadie. The man had no idea who you were. He'd been just as surprised as Mira to find out that the woman in the Combat Zone was her sister." She noticed that the revelation had put her dinner partner into a pensive state. "What?" Caitlin asked. "Now what're you spinning your wheels over?"

A faraway look had glazed Sadie's eyes. "This Nick must know about Ruby," she muttered.

Caitlin waved her hand in front of the staring woman.

Sadie blinked. "What?"

"Welcome back! Who's Ruby?"

So much had happened since she'd come to town nearly a week ago, she forgot that the secretary was in the dark.

"Remember that first day I got here and mentioned how I was so deeply affected by that bag lady's stare—how intense it was?"

"Sure I remember. And I clearly recall how you were also affected by the mystique of Tina's runes. I've been anxious to find out if anything's developed regarding them." She tilted her head, then suspiciously squinted. "That was Monday. This is Sunday. What sort of soup have you jumped into in six days' time?"

"Soup? Clam chowder comes to mind," she grumbled, while motioning to attract their waiter's attention. "You and I are going to need another round."

When the server arrived at the table, Caitlin made a change to Sadie's order. "No more margaritas for me. I'm doing the driving. Black coffee will be fine."

The young man nodded before casting a questioning look at the other woman. He thought she might want to change her order as well.

She didn't. Instead, she handed the man her empty bar glass. "She's driving. I'm not. I'll have another one of these."

Forty-five minutes later, silence finally hung between the two women.

One was processing the new information she'd heard.

One was waiting for the first volley of questions from the barrage she anticipated being launched from across the table.

"What's Tina's take on all of this?" Caitlin asked.

It wasn't one of the anticipated questions. "She doesn't know about yesterday. My little foray into the dregs of Chicago followed by Mira's subsequent wrath took everything out of me. Now Tina's probably furious with me as well. I can't help it if she is. I was just too worn out last night to rehash my day."

Caitlin understood that. Her second question wasn't anticipated any more than the first. "What's your take on it? Who do *you* think Ruby is?"

"She's an old woman."

"That's a given, isn't it? I think we can move beyond the obvious."

"Well, other than that, I don't know what you mean by asking me *who* I think she is."

The response was received with a stone face that masked any indication of the listener's reaction. The eyes behind the mask furtively lowered to check the time on a watch.

Sadie noticed the gesture and made light of it. "I'm allowed to stay out after dark," she grinned. "Mira didn't put me under a curfew."

"That's because she knew it'd never stick," Caitlin said, tossing enough cash on the table to cover their bill plus a generous tip. Abruptly, she stood. Flashing her friend a conspiratorial look, she chided, "Forget about Mira. Let's go find some trouble to get into."

Sadie slid out of the booth. "Just as long as it's not a replay of yesterday."

Caitlin didn't reply until they were in the car and on their way. "No way I'd go roaming around South Chicago. I value my life too much for that." Quickly changing the subject, she inquired, "How's Savannah doing? Can you tell if she's any closer to talking?"

Once Sadie got on the subject of her niece, she paid little attention to where they were going. The passenger got on the subject of Halloween and expressed her excitement over taking the child trick-or-treating on Thursday. The extended holiday talk pulled her thoughts back to when she and Mira were youngsters at that time of year. And reminiscing about the pranks they'd pulled had the two women laughing so hard that the driver had to pull over to wipe her eyes and regain control of herself.

Sadie's uproarious laughter was silenced when, in her gaiety, she'd playfully tossed her head and her gaze swept past a storefront sign they'd randomly parked in front of. She did a double take. Then froze.

Marie Claire deRouge, Spiritualist.

Incredulous, she stared at the sign. *Readings by appointment only.* Like a spectral manifestation, an image of Caitlin in the restaurant—checking her watch—superimposed itself over the sign. In slow motion, Sadie's head rotated toward the driver. Narrowing her eyes, she whispered, "Tell me this is coincidental. Tell me this wasn't planned."

The driver cut the engine and dropped the keys into her bag. She smiled at her disgruntled passenger. "No, I'm not going to tell you that. Lighten up, Sadie."

"Lighten up? You tricked me! You offered to pick me up today so you'd have control over where we went. I told you I was *not* going to go to some voodoo person!"

"And you're not. Stop profiling. All Haitians are not voodoo practitioners. Not all of them come with trappings and theatrics. Marie Claire is a classy Haitian woman who happens to be remarkably gifted with extraordinary insight. I told you she could probably be the only one to shed some light on those runes. And now—"

"And now," Sadie cut in, "I still haven't changed my mind."

"And now," Caitlin continued, voicing the rest of her intended sentence, "from what you told me about your bag lady, I believe Marie Claire can shed even more light on things. If you really want to get to the bottom of these confusing events in your life, why on earth wouldn't you want to explore every possible lead? What could it hurt?"

Good question. Exasperated with the feeling of being trapped, and wrestling with indecision, Sadie shifted her gaze back to the storefront. The absence of the usual esoteric symbols for such an establishment struck her as being odd. It was odd that it was so atypical. There were no crystal balls, tarot cards, or even moon and stars represented in the signage. Looking beyond the windowpane, she could see a small reception area with a few comfortable chairs, tables with magazines, and plants. There was an abundance of plants. It looked like any generic waiting room. *Where were the display cases with dolls and stick pins for sale? Where were the racks with brightly colored ceremonial robes? Or book racks bursting with pamphlets on* How to Get

Revenge *or* Attracting the Love of Your Life? *Where were the gaudy beaded curtains?* The innocuous look of the place took the sharply defined edge off her vivid preconception.

Without taking her eyes off the place, Sadie spoke in a monotone voice that snapped the tension between the two. "What time is my appointment?"

"Five minutes ago."

The passenger reached for the door handle. "We're late. This better be good."

Yes! Caitlin thought, scrambling out of the car before her friend had a chance to change her mind again. Yes. Yes. Yes! And by the time she got to the sidewalk, Sadie was already through the door and impatiently tapping the counter's bell.

Elevator music meant to soothe the jittery nerves of anxious clients softly filled the room.

"Not exactly drums and chanting," Sadie said, while turning to give the place a closer inspection.

"If it's drumming and chanting you be after, you need to go three blocks down to Mama Jakeeta's place."

Sadie spun around at the sound of the clipped Haitian accent that was delivered in a velvety mellowed tone. It'd come from a petite woman with large dark eyes shining out from a warm cinnamon complexion. Elaborate dreadlocks were pulled back in a fashionable style, giving her a well-bred look. Dressed in a casual blazer over a silk blouse and designer jeans, she exuded an aura of professionalism.

Blushing at being overheard, Sadie attempted to recover. "I . . . well," she stuttered, extending her arm to the room. "This isn't what I was expecting."

"I can see that," the woman said, while politely raising a delicate hand toward the befuddled client. "Let me introduce myself. I am Marie Claire."

The client reached for it. *No jingly bangles.*

"Wearing jewelry can be distracting," the Haitian said with an understanding smile. "Especially bangle bracelets. They can be so noisy, don't you think?"

The blush on Sadie's face flushed deeper.

With professional savoir-faire, Marie Claire tactfully ignored her new client's flustered response. Her smile widened with genuine warmth. "And you must be Sadie Brennan from Maine, yes?"

The smile was returned. It was just as genuine.

"Do you wish to have your friend wait out here during your reading?"

For a split second, Sadie considered it the perfect way to get back at her friend—exclude her. A sly grin impishly tipped one corner of her mouth.

Sensing the mischievous hesitation, Caitlin's eyes rounded at the outrageous possibility. Her jaw dropped. "Absolutely not! No way you're leaving me out of this!"

Sadie, knowing she'd royally scared her friend, decided that that in itself had been enough payback. She gave her attention to the waiting woman. "Absolutely not. No way."

The spiritualist, understanding the mental duel that had just taken place, was pleased with her client's decision to avoid vindictiveness. She nodded, stepped back a pace, and silently motioned for the two women to enter the consultation room.

The calming ambiance of the area designated for the Haitian woman's readings immediately put the new client at ease. The remaining butterflies fluttering in her stomach settled down after she was struck by the room's lack of ethnically and spiritually related clutter. Again she'd realized that she'd had an expectation as to the appearance of the woman's setup. She was unprepared to walk into a place so strikingly different from that of her friend's back home. Here, there was no cloying scent of incense curling through the air like ghostly tendrils of a nebulous vine. Here, there were no statues of deities silently watching from every nook and cranny. Here was a place that held nothing to differentiate it from any other well-appointed psychotherapist's conference room. Softly muted hues of mauve and lavender drew her forward. The soothing blend of appealing colors and plush English country furnishings was clearly chosen for the tranquil effect it had on fretful clients who entered with apprehensive angst over the personal unknowns in their lives.

Relieved by what she saw, Sadie addressed the psychic. "Where do you want me to sit for this?"

Marie Claire swept her hand over the furniture that offered a choice of seating based on the client's sense of personal space, their comfort level.

The new client scanned her options and chose the matching pair of love seats that were separated by a low coffee table.

Caitlin parked herself beside her friend.

Marie Claire sat opposite.

A few butterflies made their presence known. They stirred. Wings quivered. *Oh, go away! I need a drink.*

"I can provide you with a beverage before we begin," the reader said, inclining her head toward the stylish armoire that concealed the beverages. "Green tea, coffee, soft drinks, or something more substantial, if you prefer. Whatever you like. Some clients want a little something to take the edge off, calm their jitters." Her smile was open and nonjudgmental.

Sadie decided right then and there that she really liked this woman. "Nothing for me," she replied.

Caitlin also declined.

Marie Claire and Caitlin comfortably settled themselves into their love seats.

Sadie remained teetering on the cushion's edge. "I'm not sure where to begin," she admitted. "This is the first time I've ever done this."

"Of course, I understand," the sensitive said. "I can save us some time by recapping what's transpired up to the time Caitlin apprised me of your situation." The statement was made to test the air. The woman wanted to begin on an even playing level. She wanted everything out in the open at the outset. As expected, her client's response indicated that everything hadn't been laid on the table.

Sadie was not only shocked that her friend had told her story, she was indignant that she'd kept it from her. She chose not to look at Caitlin. "No, I wasn't aware that you already knew some of the background." A smile was forced. "I won't bother rehashing those parts because a great deal has happened since then."

With her suspicions verified, Marie Claire wisely moved on. "We can narrow things down somewhat if you let me know which issue you would like to focus on most. Let's start with Paul. Are you clear with that aspect or do you have questions that I may be able to shed more light on?"

"I don't think I'll ever be clear on that aspect, but right now, he's not the immediate issue in my life."

The advisor continued. "How about your niece?" She checked her notes for the correct name. "Savannah, is it?"

Sadie nodded. "Yes, Savannah."

"And I understand she's suffering from sudden onset hysterical muteness caused by a traumatic event? A car accident?"

"Yes. Her mother—my sister—thought there was an outside chance that I might be able to help her if I came out here. I live in Maine."

"I assume all other methods of treatment were exhausted?"

"Yes."

"Why do you think your sister thought you'd make a difference when all other avenues failed to improve the child's condition?"

"Savannah and I, we're . . . well, close."

"By close, do you mean that you two seem to share a psychic sensitivity?"

The woman on the edge of the couch grimaced. "*Psychic* sensitivity?"

Marie Claire politely rephrased. "A *mental* connection much like identical twins might exhibit. Or perhaps there's an emotional rapport?"

Sadie allowed herself a smile. "Physically, I'm told she looks just like I did at her age. I'm also told that she has many of the same behaviors and mannerisms." She hesitated before continuing. "Yes. Yes, I'd say we have a strong emotional link."

"And because the mother reluctantly acknowledges that unique bond, she had reservations about calling you in until you became her daughter's last resort."

"It seems so."

Caitlin was quickly drawn in by the interesting exchange between both of her friends. Her head went from one to the other as they batted questions and responses back and forth. Even knowing her role in this consultation was to be an observer only and she shouldn't butt in, she couldn't suppress the urge to put her two cents in. "Savannah loves Sadie. She just adores her!"

Although the psychic never took her eyes from Sadie's, she commented, "Love has great strength. It moves mountains. Your niece will speak before the week's out."

In tandem, Sadie and Caitlin dropped their jaws and locked eyes. In tandem, they turned to the woman across from them.

Sadie was first to find her voice. "How can you say that? How can you be so sure?"

Marie Claire was accustomed to clients' shocked expressions and responses weighted with doubt. "That," she softly said, "I can't tell you. These things come as a knowing, a knowing I've come to trust over time."

"But to say that Savannah will speak this week is . . . unbelievable. Why, I can't believe that my presence carries that kind of power."

"And you're right. With you alone, I would anticipate it taking her several months to show a positive response. But add your presence to a new purpose in her life and you end up with a highly volatile combination."

"Wait a minute. Back up. What new purpose?"

The sensitive's shoulders hitched up and fell.

Sadie, thoroughly engrossed in the reading, leaned forward. "If you can't tell me *what* this purpose is then how do you know there even *is* a new purpose in her life?"

"Again," Marie Claire reinforced, "it comes back to strong feelings. Your niece definitely has some type of mental stimulation that's serving as a new motivation. It's as though a tempest has blown into her life and stirred things up. It's disturbed the shield she'd subconsciously pulled around herself. It sparked a unique type of revitalization within her. Whatever it is, it's given her a sense of purpose."

Sadie thought on that. "Could that sense of purpose be as simple as wanting to please me by finally speaking?"

Marie Claire's answer, though sympathetic, was unequivocal. "No. There's more to it than that. I see your presence as being a catalyst in this case. A catalyst serving as a coupler to something else. Something bigger."

Bigger. Where have I heard that before?

In an effort to mentally grasp the wispy thought, she let the word roll off her tongue. "Bigger. Bigger!" she said with more force behind it. "I've heard that before. Someone said that to me recently but I'm unable to place it in the right context."

"Don't force it," the psychic advised. "Let it be. Like a rainbow, it'll remain elusive if you have to chase it down. Let it come back around in its own time."

Sadie was pensive. "So, you're saying that my presence is a link to this bigger thing in my niece's life. And . . . and, I guess this is where I lose the thread."

"You've almost got it. I think you're doing yourself an injustice by demeaning your role here. You're not just a link to this other unknown, you're also the tandem element because of your inimitable affinity with the child. It's that affinity that makes you a key to her recovery."

Sadie pursed her lips. "Okay then, to simplify matters, there are two keys needed to release her from her self-imposed prison of silence."

"Yes," the spiritualist agreed. "You are one of them. And this unknown bigger element is the other. I believe that once the two keys come together they'll make a powerful impression on the girl."

The psychic's last words made Sadie envision an expanding mushroom cloud. She involuntarily shuddered. "This is supposed to happen sometime this coming week, then. You said she'd speak this week. Theoretically, that means that the two keys will be brought together and I'll find out what the other one is."

Marie Claire slowly shook her head. "There's nothing theoretic about it, Sadie. It's all going to happen this coming week."

"But, how can you be so confident about—"

Caitlin could no longer hold her tongue. "Sadie, quit! Enough of the skepticism! I brought you here because Marie Claire is the best in the city. Maybe she's the best in the whole country! If she says it's all going to happen this week then that's when it's going to happen!"

Sadie's response came as a long sigh. Her gaze fell on the woman sitting across from her. The woman had no arrogant airs. There was a genuine simplicity about her that brought Sadie closer to belief.

A sweet silence of growing acceptance hung between the trio. It hovered until the client was comfortable enough to move on. Her green eyes rose to meet the psychic's. The corners of Sadie's mouth curled. "Caitlin here is antsy to find out more about the unusual rune layouts that my friend back in Maine did for me just prior . . ."

Caitlin jumped in. "No! Tell her about Ruby first!"

Sadie glared back. "First things first. Let's not start reading from the back of the book."

"But Ruby's the one whose got your wheels spinning right—"

Marie Claire stepped into the verbal fray. "It'd be best if the issues were addressed in the sequence they occurred," she said.

Caitlin respectfully relented. She held the spiritual reader in high regard and left the proceedings up to her judgment.

Marie Claire artfully recapped what she'd been told about the rune incident. It was clear that Caitlin had relayed everything perfectly. She wanted to make sure. "Is that the way it happened?"

Sadie nodded.

"Is there anything that was left out? Perhaps something you'd like to add? Maybe include your reactions to the layouts? How they affected you?"

"There's nothing to add as far as the incident. At first I thought Tina was pulling my leg; you know, showing off a new trick or something. I mean, what were the odds of the same tokens showing up in the same placements?"

The psychic made no comment.

"Anyway, the more times it happened, the more creepy I felt."

"Creepy?"

"Yeah. You know, I broke out in a bad case of the heebie-jeebies. The hair on my arms stood up. Goosebumps. Every hair on my scalp snapped to attention. The whole nine yards."

"What was your first mental reaction?"

"Denial. No question. Then, after I couldn't discount what my eyes saw—after I couldn't explain it away with trickery or logic I accepted what I saw as unexplainable, yet real. That's when I pushed it out of my mind by shifting my focus to something unrelated; to the letter from my sister."

Marie Claire's delicate brows furrowed slightly. "Yes, the letter. But tell me, Sadie, I'm interested in knowing why you say that the two incidents are unrelated?"

Sadie felt her cheeks flush. *They're not!*

The psychic noticed the reaction. "No. They're not."

"But how—"

"Now we return to the runes. There is no question about what the Journey token meant because it correlates with the letter. The letter was the physical manifestation of the Journey token. Do you see that, Sadie?"

She did. "That's probably the most obvious one of the bunch. It's the others that remain murky."

"Some messages need time to clarify their meaning."

The client tilted her head in question. "Wealth? Why would a Wealth token keep showing up? I was surrounded by it growing up. I do all right for myself now. I don't see how it comes into play." She sniggered. "I don't want it."

Marie Claire smiled. "Life tends to drop unwanted things in our laps—things we think we don't want . . . or need."

"Things we *think* we don't want or need?"

"Yes. Time usually proves us wrong. Somewhere down the line something happens to change our minds. It's then that we realize how fortunate we were by being given the things we thought we didn't want."

Sadie's face scrunched. She wasn't following.

The psychic thought a minute. "Keeping it simple, let's say you had a favorite bracelet and then received an identical one as a gift. You didn't need it. Didn't really want another one just like it. So it went into your jewelry box, forgotten about until, after some months passed, the clasp on your favorite one broke while you were rinsing dishes. The mishap wasn't noticed until the garbage disposal jammed. So in the end, time proved out the need for the unwanted, unneeded gift."

Still dubious, Sadie asked, "But wealth? What, my business is suddenly going to take a dive? That's just not likely. If anything, it's going to improve with my expanding client base."

"You're confining your basis for wealth to a single source—money. The face of wealth has many expressions."

Tina's voice echoed in Sadie's mind. *There are other types of riches.* "Yes, of course, I realize that. My friend back in Maine reminded me of the same thing."

Marie Claire nodded. "Okay then, I think it'd be good if you could stay mindful regarding the Wealth token because that still remains to be seen."

"You can't foresee the meaning?"

The woman in the casual blazer was hoping her client wouldn't think to ask the question she'd voiced. Deciding not to conceal what she foresaw, she replied, "Both."

"Both? Both what?"

"In this instance, the Wealth token represents one source possessing a dual nature. It has both kinds of riches—material and spiritual. What you *do* with that gift will be a choice determining *how* you ultimately end up benefiting. More than that I can't say because the outcome is up to you."

Without warning, Sadie shifted gears. "Who is the Dove Woman?"

Without batting an eye, the psychic replied, "The same as the token of the primitive icon. They're reciprocal images."

"They're identical?"

"Not exactly." Marie Claire hoped she could explain the concept without further confusing her client. "Each of those two symbols carries its own meaning. It's when they both appear in the same layout that they represent a direct connection to one another. The most common interpretation for the Dove Woman is that of a real-time person of light. By that I mean someone in the *physical*. A touchable person of goodwill.

"The other image, the pregnant primitive, always refers to the primal woman in all women. The primal mother . . . the MotherGod, so to speak. Naturally, she carries a *spiritual* connotation. In your case, when they both continued to appear in every layout, the message is indicating that the Primal Mother is manifesting her influence through a physical person."

Caitlin was awestruck. "Oh, my God!" she blurted. "That's awesome!"

Sadie wasn't so quickly astounded. "Hold on," she cautioned, placing her hand on her friend's arm. "Aren't we *all* influenced by our spiritual beliefs . . . no matter who we worship as our idea of a Supreme Being? Isn't every spiritual woman a Dove Woman acting on how she's spiritually influenced by a Higher Power?"

Caitlin didn't want the mystery of the tokens to end up having such an unremarkable explanation. She didn't want her beautiful esoteric bubble to burst so quickly from a prick of commonality. She snapped her hopeful gaze to the psychic for an answer that would keep it high aloft.

Marie Claire strongly suspected that Ms. Brennan would walk out of the room if the concept were further refined to better clarify the reality of the issue. She knew her client wasn't ready to accept the staggering truth of the matter. The connection between the primitive icon and the Dove Woman would be too much for her to accept at this point. She wisely decided not to provide that clarification at this time. Instead, she smiled. "Of course."

The bubble burst. Caitlin's shoulders slumped with the weight of disappointment. "You mean to say that that's all there is to this cryptic stuff? That there's no big mystery person out there? No secret pal to identify? No enchanted forest . . . no summoning oracle to meet? No abracadabra?" she haltingly sputtered. "That's it?"

Not giving the Haitian woman time to respond to the questioning outburst, Sadie flashed an amused grin. "Can you tell that my friend is enamored by all things esoteric?"

The friend was indignant. "You're one to talk," she spouted back. "That bag lady's got you going in so many circles that you're spinning like a dust devil!"

Up to this point, Sadie had been undecided about whether to drag the details of Ruby into the consultation session. She wasn't pleased that her companion had jumped the gun. Her gaze slid to the psychic, whose eyes narrowed after hearing the revelation. "Cait!" Sadie warned, "that's enough!"

"I don't think so," the secretary replied, before turning her attention to the woman across from them. "She's so taken with a mysterious homeless person that she actually threw caution to the wind and risked her life by going down into the Combat Zone to look for her! Alone! Can you believe it?"

Indicating no sign of judgment, Marie Claire's head inclined toward her client. Without speaking, her questioning expression sought verification.

It came with the heightened flush of Sadie's cheeks.

"Well?" Caitlin prodded in defense of herself. "What about that? I'm not the only one hooked on enigmas. You're the one obsessing over your mystery lady. You're the one with the perilous case of fixation."

The words settled like a dense cloud lowering on the trio's shoulders. No one spoke. No one moved.

After a couple of minutes, the psychic's mellow voice speared a ray of sunlight into the mist. The fog evaporated when she locked eyes with her client and softly said, "Sometimes, a compelling compulsion can *mimic* an obsession that seemingly cannot be ignored. These unique compulsions come from an ember that ignites a fire in the soul."

Sadie felt her heart lunge. *Yes! A fire in the soul.*

The two women seated side by side listened with bated breath.

"The fire is fed by the external source. The fire is both fed and tempered by that source. It can be fed until it blazes and it can be tempered down to a gently warming glow. The tempered glow is the residual effect of experiencing the source. Yet the fire, once ignited, can never be extinguished. Forever after, it burns eternal in the heart of the soul."

Experiencing the source. Encounters with Ruby.

Marie Claire stood. "Our time is up."

With her quest now galvanized, the client sprang to her feet.

Caitlin was upset that the session had sped by so quickly. She reluctantly rose from her seat. "But we never talked about the main issue, the mysterious bag lady! She was never discussed!" Wide-eyed with the letdown, she pointedly addressed the psychic. "You were supposed to tell her something about this Ruby person. You were supposed to guide her in the right direction! Help her deal—"

Sadie rested a calming hand on her friend's arm. "Cait," she whispered, "she did."

Caitlin blinked. "She did? No, she didn't."

"Believe me. She did. She told me all I need to know."

As the two women walked out into the autumn sunlight, perceptions of what had just transpired with the spiritual reader were polarized.

One, at long last, was finally at ease with her direction.

The other, unable to connect the poignant dots of information the psychic gave, remained clueless.

The evening at the Woodward estate was a pleasant one. Mira held court over the dinner table while she regaled her captive audience by detailing the rich elements of the musical she and her daughter had attended.

Afterward, Sadie lost nine out of the twelve video games she and Savannah played in the girl's room. And when the bedside table clock caught her attention, she couldn't believe how much time had passed.

"It's past your bedtime," she whispered to her niece. "Your mom's going to have my hide for keeping you up so late."

The girl silently objected, pleading for one more game.

Sadie put her finger to her lips. "Shhh. I'll be right back."

Savannah curiously watched her aunt tiptoe from the room and wondered what she was up to. A few minutes later, her smile turned into a mute giggle of conspiracy when she saw Sadie return with a plate of pumpkin pie in each hand. A mound of Greta's homemade whipped cream was piled on top of the generous slices.

Sadie handed her niece one of the plates, then plopped herself cross-legged in the middle of the bed. After she scooped the first forkful into her mouth, she grinned, winked, then mumbled through the pie.

"Your mom's down in her office . . . buried in a mountain of paperwork. She never even knew I'd been in the kitchen."

Savannah thought her aunt was the coolest and secretly wished her mom could be more like her. Together they rolled their eyes and smacked their lips in exaggerated pleasure over the scrumptious snack they'd purloined from the larder.

While they worked on making the desserts disappear, Sadie talked about the day they'd spend together tomorrow. "You and I are going to have an adventure tomorrow. We're going to get into my van and go wherever we're led. Sound weird?"

The girl shook her head.

"No? Huh, that's good. I'm glad you don't think it's an odd thing to do. Sometimes people have to stop chasing their tails and let the dust settle. Sometimes they . . . you have no idea what I'm talking about, do you?"

Though Savannah had a suspicion, she didn't let on. She again shook her head.

"Well, that's okay. All I meant was that some things can't be forced. As much as we want something to happen, we can't make it happen just because we want it so bad. We need to pull back and take the time to smell the roses. You know, sit back and experience the moment. That kind of thing."

The girl understood that kind of thing. She smiled.

When they finished the treats, Sadie tucked her niece under the covers. And just before turning out the light, she picked up the plates. "I'll take these to my room" she whispered, "so there's no telltale signs left in here for your mom to see."

After Savannah heard the door to her aunt's room close, she threw back the covers. Her bare feet made silent footfalls over the thick hallway carpet.

Once in her own room, Sadie set the plates down on the bedside table and stared at the phone. If she didn't place a call to Tina now, it'd be two nights in a row that she blew it off. Before she lost her nerve, she dialed the familiar number. Instead of the expected greeting, she was met with a question.

"I know you're all right," Tina blurted, "but what the hell did you do yesterday? Every time I thought about you I was so agitated and worried that I did a dozen layouts for you. They kept giving the same bottom line. They kept telling me that you flirted with danger and were protected! I'm all ears, my friend. And, please, do both of us a favor by starting from the beginning. I'm not interested in hearing just the sketchy highlights, I want you to fill me in on everything."

"Hello to you, too!" Sadie chirped.

"Hello. Now, out with it."

Sadie had expected this. Tina was too good a psychic not to pick up on something out of the ordinary transpiring with a close friend, even though that friend was hundreds of miles away.

"Do you remember me telling you how Father McElveney inadvertently gave away the location of Ruby's hangout?"

"Of course I remember . . . oh, shit! You went there, didn't you? You did! You went down to the friggin' projects! That's the danger you were flirting with! Omigod. Oh . . . my . . . God."

Sadie began pacing about the room with the phone. "Do you need to go pop a Xanax or something before I get to the story?"

"No! No, I'm fine. Honest, I really am." Then she listened. Without interrupting with her questions, she listened to how her friend first saw the bag lady dancing with hookers on the street corner. She heard how Sadie had decided to double back to end up meeting Buck and his unsavory cohorts. The extraordinary story continued with the homeless vet, the visit into the shadowy shooting gallery, the kids collecting dope from the dealer, and Ruby there to supply the young ones with whatever their personal needs were. Tina heard about Mira's fury over where Sadie had been, how Mira had discovered the misadventure through one of her undercover contacts. And without skipping a beat, she heard how, the following day, Caitlin had hoodwinked Sadie into keeping a prescheduled appointment with the Haitian seeress.

"Haven't you been the busy little bee," Tina sang when the voice on the other end of the line finally fell silent.

"That's an understatement. But, Tina," Sadie said with growing excitement trembling in her voice, "don't you see? Marie Claire gave me the answer! She knew! I think she knew! She said that the 'fire in my soul will be tempered by experiencing the source'!"

"And the source, of course, is your Ruby."

"Yes! It means that this drive I have to know more about her will be satisfied by *experiencing* her through a personal, one-on-one encounter! Isn't that your take on this?"

"It is. That's exactly how I interpret things. Now, can I give you another little something that struck me while you were talking?"

"Of course. I want to hear all your impressions."

"The psychic was right about the Dove Woman's relationship to the Primal Woman. Sadie, you need to take things very seriously here because this is really big!"

Big. Bigger. Think bigger. Big!

"Ahh," Sadie said, "not to sound ungrateful for all the hints, but I think I'm getting the message of a 'bigger' picture involved here. I've heard this idea from too many different sources to discount it. It's beginning to sink in."

Tina wasn't convinced. "I believe you've accepted the idea of Ruby being special, but you're not truly *there* yet."

"What makes you say that?"

"Because . . . because I know you. In this case, you're reluctant to think outside the box . . . think big *enough*."

"Well, how big is big, for heaven's sake?"

Silence.

"Tina?"

"You said 'for heaven's sake'? Yeah, Sadie, for *heaven's* sake. *That's* how big *this* big is."

Now it was Tina's turn to hear silence on the line. She kept talking despite the lack of response. "Listen, the Primal Woman token symbolizes the supreme feminine deity. Supreme, as in the Mother of all female deities. The MotherGod. And that concept's associated with the Dove Woman . . . your homeless bag lady."

Sadie's skin crawled, then she guffawed. "You can't be serious."

"I wouldn't joke about something as monumental as this."

"You're loony! Are you suggesting that I should actually believe that Ruby's some kind of . . . some kind of *god?*"

"No. *Goddess*, to be precise."

"Were you doing a little nipping at the bottle before I called?"

"Oh, stop! Quit being the smartass and think about this. Who did Jesus keep company with? Beggars. Trollops. Those with addictions and afflictions. The outcasts and the unclean. Jesus danced with prostitutes! Why wouldn't a female deity do the same? Why is that so far out there that it's too extreme to even consider? Why does it seem impossible for a deity to walk among us in the guise of a beggarwoman? Wouldn't that guise be most useful to help the downtrodden? You know, appear as one of them."

"You actually think Ruby is this MotherGod come in the form of a bag lady? Tina? Is that what you're telling me?"

Tina sighed. "What about when you were in the cemetery and heard her talking to the dead as though they were all her children? What about that?"

"Any crazy lady can talk like that."

"You think Ruby is a crazy lady?"

Sadie hesitated. "I didn't say that."

"What about her healing animals? What about her fluent Thai? Her knowledge of ancient temple dances? The damn *shoes* you keep going on about? Sadie, if God came here once before, who's to prove He or She *hasn't* been here again? Or lots of times. Or right now for that matter? Taking the persona public one time and going incognito the next. A deity can do whatever She or He wants . . . come in whatever form suits the purpose best."

Sadie's pacing took her past the bedroom door. "But to imply that Ruby is this MotherGod is . . . well, Tina, it's so far-fetched. To compare her to Jesus walking among the downtrodden seems so—"

"Sadie," Tina cut in, "belaboring this anymore tonight isn't going to be productive. Go to bed. Get some sleep. See how you think about it in the morning. Speaking of morning, what're you doing tomorrow?"

"I haven't planned anything definite. I thought it'd be a good idea for Savannah and me to just play it by ear. Let the moment dictate what we do."

"Sounds good. Are you okay?"

"Yeah, I'm okay. You're right about not talking about this anymore tonight. I think I need to let some of this soak in a little at a time. It's not that I doubt your intuitiveness on this. Or that I totally discount the idea. You gotta admit that it's no small thing that you're asking me to put my faith in."

"Sadie?"

"Mmmm?"

"Believe. Like everyone's been trying to tell you . . . think bigger. Big, Sadie, big. *Huge.*"

Down the hall, little feet left the plush carpeting and were slipped beneath the downy coverlet. The child had previously heard of the concept of the Trinity—of God the Father, God the Son, and God the Holy Spirit—and it had always been a source of great puzzlement regarding where God the Mother was. If there was a God the Father and a God the Son, there had to be a Mother somewhere because it took a father *and* a mother to make a child. Everyone knew that. There just couldn't be a son without a mother being in the picture. Now her small heart raced. *I knew it! I knew she had to be there, too!*

Her eyes slowly scanned the frilly pink room. They came to rest on the marionette hanging from its stand. The clown's smile was illumined by the soft glow of the night-light.

Wanna hear a secret, Mister Jangles? Ruby's just like Jesus! Ruby is the MotherGod! Sadie even said so. Know what else, Mister Jangles? I think we're going to see her tomorrow.

*T*en

Monday

They had been aimlessly driving around for a little under two hours. The young passenger patiently listened to her aunt haltingly tell humorous tales of her youth while distractedly scanning the pedestrians they were passing.

She's looking for her, the girl thought as she recalled Sadie's words. *She's not "letting the moment dictate what we do" today.* Savannah could feel the increasing atmosphere of tension build in the van. Her aunt's anxiety—her heightened excitement over the day's high expectations—filled the vehicle with electricity. She desperately wanted to suggest that it'd probably be the other way around. *They* wouldn't have to go searching for Ruby. *She'd* find *them.* If it was meant to be, she'd find them wherever they happened to end up today. The girl longed to convey this important idea, but instead, felt only frustration at not being able get the words out. She wanted to say it so bad that she felt like jumping out of her skin. Though she made several attempts, she just couldn't find her voice.

"What's the matter, honey?" Sadie asked, noticing her niece's distressed expression.

Not knowing how to respond, the girl pointed at something outside.

The driver looked. "The park? Do you want to stop here?"

The child's head eagerly bobbed up and down.

The van slowed. They'd been skirting a commercial section of an upscale subdivision. Boutique shops ringed the parklike square in which a white gazebo was centered. Oaks and maples, brilliant with seasonal color, rimmed a duck pond. Park benches were occupied by resting shoppers and mothers watching their children in the play area.

Frantically sweeping her green eyes back and forth over the unremarkable scene, she could not spot a red hat. Fearful of wasting precious time, she managed to hide her irritation.

"This isn't really a *park* park, if you know what I mean. Are you sure you want to stop here?"

Savannah was already removing her seatbelt.

"Hold on. Let me find a place to park before you do that." And while the van was rolling to a complete stop, the girl was off and running toward the swing set.

Again, Sadie gave the area a quick once-over before heading toward the play area.

Her niece wasn't among the laughing children on the swings. In a moment of heart-thumping panic, she spun back to reinspect the crowd; this time her quest was not for a red hat, it was for a small girl dressed in a Stewart hunting green plaid fall jacket. As she squinted through the glaring autumn light, her attention was drawn by the sparkle of auburn tresses touched by the sun.

The frantic woman's heart lunged. Savannah was by the pond's edge and she wasn't alone. A man was bent down to her. She was about to take something from the stranger's open palm.

"Savannah!" Sadie screamed as she broke into a run. "Savannah! No!"

Both man and child turned to the distraught sound.

The man looked startled.

The girl's smile widened to see her aunt.

Sadie rushed to her niece's side and was about to yank her from harm's way when Savannah purposely held up her hand to show what she'd taken.

"Bread," the man meekly said. "Only morsels of bread . . . for the ducks out on the pond. I apologize if I worried you, ma'am. I'm truly sorry. I meant no harm."

The alarming situation diffused itself when Sadie saw that the man leaned into a cane, a half-filled bread bag dangling from between arthritic fingers clutching the supportive staff.

"The child was watching me feed the ducks," he explained. "Though she never came right out and asked, I could tell she was wanting to feed them, as well."

"She didn't ask because she can't . . ." Sadie realized that the man didn't need to know about her niece's temporary affliction. "She knows better than to talk to strangers."

The elderly gentleman warmly looked down at the child. "That's a good little girl." Then he offered the bag to her. "My time to dally is over," he said, inclining his head to the building across the common. "I have to mosey over there to a doctor appointment. Here," he said, extending the bag that shook with an involuntary hand tremor. "You may have the rest of this if you like."

Savannah looked up at her aunt for permission to accept the bag.

"That's very kind of you, sir. I'm sure my niece would love to take over the feeding for you. Thank you."

The bag changed ownership. "You're quite welcome, ma'am," he said, raising a hand to respectfully tip a nonexistent hat before ambling away.

When the octogenarian was well out of earshot, Sadie tilted her head and scowled down at the girl.

Savannah, feeling guilty, scrunched her face in expectation of a scolding.

"Don't ever do that again!" the aunt warned with a wagging finger for emphasis. "Do you know how scared I was when I didn't see you at the swings?"

The headful of auburn ringlets tumbled in front of the girl's face when she shamefully looked down and toyed with the bread wrapper.

A hand gently lifted her chin. "Oh, sweetie, I love you so much. You just gave me a really bad scare. I was ready to fly at that guy and tackle him to the ground when I saw you with him." She knelt on one knee and tenderly brushed the girl's errant tendrils from her freckled face. "I . . . I couldn't live with myself if—"

With a featherlike touch, a small hand molded itself to Sadie's cheek.

Moved by the young one's affection, she covered the little hand with her own, then kissed it. "I love you, Savannah. I love you so much."

Short arms were flung around her neck.

Sadie wrapped her arms about the small waist. "Hey, you!" she suddenly exclaimed, surprised to feel the bulkiness of the girl's jacket pocket. Slowly easing her back to arm's length, she asked, "What've you got there?"

Embarrassed, Savannah pulled back. She impishly put a finger to her lips.

"It's a secret?" asked her aunt.

Curls bounced with the nod.

"Oh-kaaay then. Let's go feed those ducks."

Savannah looked about and spied a set of back-to-back park benches. At their base, pigeons were rooting around for people's lunch scraps left in the grass. She gave her aunt's blazer a hard yank.

Sadie cast her gaze at the empty bench. A middle-aged woman engrossed in a book was seated on the bench backing the empty one. Sadie eyed her niece.

"I take it you're feeling sorry for the pigeons," she grinned. And while allowing herself be led to the wooden seat, she couldn't keep herself from scanning the park for any sign of a red hat.

She's still looking, the girl quietly sighed as they settled themselves and each dipped her hand in the bag.

Seven pigeons suddenly became twelve. Eighteen. Then over thirty were gathered around the duo on the bench.

"Where'd they all come from?"

Savannah's shoulders rose and fell. She didn't know where they all came from, but thought it a lot of fun feeding them.

Sadie had her own thoughts. She wished their dialogues could be two-sided. The sound of her niece's voice was deeply missed. The missing caused a yearning for the sweet sound to fill her ears as it used to whenever she visited the family. She had no doubt that she'd hear it again. Right now, even hearing two or three words would be a joy-ful sound. In the meantime, she'd have to be satisfied by filling the silence between them with her own voice.

She turned to give a cursory glance at the woman seated behind them. The book seemed engrossing enough to hold the lady's focused attention. She was in her own world and wouldn't be eavesdropping on anything spoken behind her back.

Sadie cast her gaze up into the bright sunlight streaming down through the thinning trees. She inhaled the undeniably heady aroma of the season. A light breeze showered the park with a colorful veil of falling leaves. Children's laughter rang out as they reveled in playfully shuffling through the accumulated piles of the crisp leaves.

"You've been lucky so far this year," Sadie said, while randomly tossing bread bits to the gaggle of birds at their feet. "It's stayed fairly mild for the last week of October. It'd be nice if it held through Halloween."

The girl smiled without taking her eyes off the birds.

"Anyway," Sadie continued, "I always felt sorry for the trick-or-treaters when the weather was bad. There's only so much room to layer up beneath a costume, and nobody wants to hide a costume beneath a bulky winter coat. Speaking of costumes, I haven't heard what yours is going to be. You're still planning on me taking you around on Thursday, aren't you?"

A nod came.

"I know you don't want to reveal what your costume is . . . I just hope it's the kind you can wear a coat with in case the weather turns."

Lacking a reply from her niece, Sadie thought a while before taking the one-sided conversation in another direction. Watching the girl's body language, she tested the waters to see if the intended subject matter sparked any response from the child.

"I had lunch with Caitlin yesterday," she nonchalantly said. "We went to a fortuneteller."

No sign of piqued interest showed.

Sadie figured it was an issue the girl didn't care about and found herself beginning to ramble. "If it'd been up to me, I wouldn't have gone to the psychic. Caitlin had an appointment already set for me. She went ahead and did it even though I'd already made it clear that I wasn't the least bit interested in going to see this Haitian voodoo person. Well," she huffed, "to be fair to Marie Claire—that's the woman's name—she didn't turn out to be a real voodoo practitioner. You know, the kind with the drums, trance dancing, stick pins, and all."

Behind them, the woman with the book was joined by a friend. They conversed in French.

The listeners subliminally took note of the foreign language being spoken, but didn't give the women attention.

Sadie's rambling never broke its meter. "Actually, she was a very down-to-earth lady. To pass her on the street, you'd never know she made a living from giving readings. I'd been so upset when Caitlin first brought the subject up because I'd envisioned all the typical trappings associated with Haitian voodoo. After all," she chuckled, "the first thing someone thinks of is zombies and dolls looking like pin cushions.

"Anyway, Caitlin got the harebrained idea after I'd told her about some rune layouts Tina had done for me. To make a long story short, the layouts ended up being very odd. Cait was sure her psychic friend could shed some light on what they meant."

I know all of this. Savannah was prepared to hear the details of the rune layouts and what Marie Claire had to say about them. Instead, her aunt switched to the subject of relationships—men, in particular.

"Who can figure them? Men are always going on and on about how hard women are to figure out, but their own thought processes are even harder to follow." Sadie shook a cautionary finger in the air. "You've got some time yet. It'll be a while before you have to deal with boys. Enjoy the peace and quiet while you can because, believe me, there will come a day when boys will make you want to pull your hair out. When I was a few years older than you, there was this boy who I had the worst crush on. Gads," she spewed, getting deeper into her reminiscing, "I thought he was the most—"

I don't even like boys yet, Savannah thought as German words drifted past her ears. When she realized that the women behind them were no longer speaking French, attention on her aunt momentarily wavered. *When did the book lady and her friend leave?*

"—so right then I decided that I didn't need boys in my life and swore them off forever. Forever, however, was a wildly fanciful idea that turned out to be a big disappointment. Forever didn't last nearly as long as I'd planned because, two months later—"

Savannah noticed the two German women walk away. She and her aunt were truly alone now.

"—this new boy transferred into my class from another school. Well," she sighed with an exaggerated roll of her eyes, "let me tell you, all the girls went absolutely gaga over him. Not that I didn't, mind you. I had to make double sure he noticed me. I had to go one step further and . . . ." The story abruptly came to a standstill when Sadie noticed that the birds had disappeared without cleaning up their scattered bread pieces. "How odd," she curiously exclaimed. "Where did all the birds go?"

Sounds of soft cooing and fluttering wings came from behind them.

When they craned their necks around, Savannah's jaw dropped.

The deafening crack of a thunderbolt ripped through Sadie's cerebral canyons. Its rolling resonance shot through her every cell and left her heart pounding with a jolting surge of blood that reddened her cheeks. The hair on the nape of her neck stood on end. She snapped her head forward.

The missing birds were not only rooting around the feet of the woman seated directly behind them, they were happily roosting on Ruby's lap, her shoulders.

Oh, shit. Shit! Now that the long-awaited time had finally arrived, Sadie was caught in a state of flustered paralysis. Every nerve ending was tingling, spiking. She was shaken, thoughts were jumbled, and panic was furiously banging on the door.

Oh, God, I don't think I'm really ready for this! Ohhhh, God. Oh God, what should I do? What the hell should I do? But before she could receive divine inspiration or pull a clear plan of action from those tangled thoughts, the little girl sitting beside her hopped off her seat and skipped around to the backside of the bench.

"No, Savannah! No!" *Shit!*

Visibly trembling with indecision, Sadie fretted over the sudden attack of stomach-churning trepidation. *She's right there! We're back to back! Oh, God, what do I do?* Her whirling thoughts froze when she heard the woman speak. The voice quality gave the impression of liquid gold, fluid with a rich sheen of staid genteelness gilded by more than a glint of sagacious sophistication. Beneath it all flowed an overwhelming undercurrent of quietude which swept away Sadie's faltering courage.

Suddenly, feeling emboldened by a new resolve, she stood.

The movement brought a rush of pigeons taking flight toward the near skeletal tree limbs.

Confidently rounding the end of the double benches, she felt her smile twitch with an involuntary quiver. Noticing the unexpected hitch in her newfound bravado, she willed herself not to falter.

"Hello," she politely greeted. "Beautiful day for a sit in the park, isn't it?" And before the seated woman could reply, Sadie had swiftly observed the physical facets of her quest. Like a black hole devouring matter, her mind instantly ingested each visible detail.

The bulky outerwear was the same drab military issue Sadie had always seen on the woman. After closer inspection, she noted that the edges of the cuffs were frayed. Two buttons were missing from the front.

But the biggest surprise was the glaring incongruity between the cumbersome overcoat and what lay beneath. The heavy cloth of the calf-length army coat hung open to frame vintage Victorian clothing. The delicate blouse, complete with the traditional cameo brooch at the high, lacy neck, was primly tucked into a chocolate brown full skirt. The soft folds sent a cascade of fabric over small feet trimly encased in footwear from the same bygone era. The black leather of the laced-up granny shoes was supple from wear. And propped against one shoe's scuffed toe, the infamous carpetbag was bent over itself—flat as folded paper. Empty.

Gnarled fingers were loosely entwined together as they demurely rested on the homespun fabric of her lap. There were no rings. No bracelets nor watch.

Eyes, leaving observers to hotly dispute whether they were of an inviting sky blue or cool gunmetal grey, sparkled from a time-worn face. It was a face that glowed with a youthful radiance despite the deceiving crevices and freckling age spots.

And the hat—the eye-catching bright red hat—was made of nubby Berber fleece material. The narrow, turned-up rim encircled the thatch of silver hair like a halo. The garish pin caught the light like a jewel in a crown.

"Ohhh, indeed!" the elder cheerily agreed. "It surely is a fine, *fine* day for a park-sit!"

The younger woman's head inclined toward the child, whose eyes were ready to pop with suppressed excitement.

"I hope my niece hasn't bothered you. We were over on the opposite bench feeding the pigeons and they disappeared on us. You must come here often. They seem to be familiar with you."

Instead of revealing the fact that today was her first visit to this particular parklike commons—that the aunt and niece were the only reason she'd come here—she smile wider.

"Oh, my no! This sweet child has been no bother. No, no, none at all." She winked at the girl. "I rather enjoy having the young ones around. Keeps this old mind of mine off my age." Patting the empty place beside her, she leaned her shoulder toward the small listener. "You be a dear and make room for your auntie," she quietly suggested. "There's plenty of room for the three of us here."

The child needed no coercion. She scooted close enough for their clothing to touch. Savannah shot her aunt a questionable look. Urgency speared from her eyes. *This is what you've been wanting, isn't it? This is the big moment! What are you waiting for?*

"Are . . . are you sure?" Sadie asked. "You looked as though you were really enjoying the birds."

Catching the sunlight, the elder's mass of unruly hair turned to quicksilver when her gaze drifted to the treetops, then back again.

"It appears that the birds flew the coop. They always come back home to roost, though. Then we'll continue our little tête-à-tête." Now the eyes had a definite bluish cast as they settled on the watchful sea-green ones. "Please," she softly urged. "This glorious day won't last long. Won't you join us and we'll sit a while?"

The duo on the bench became a trio.

The woman's words hadn't been lost on Sadie. "According to the TV weather person, this glorious weather is supposed to be with us all week. You know, a late Indian summer."

The elder pursed her lips. "A cold wind is going to blow. Maybe bring flurries with it. I can feel these things in my bones."

Feeling it disrespectful to dispute what the old one's bones told her, Sadie moved away from the issue. "My name's Sadie. This is my niece, Savannah." As soon as the words left her lips, she had the feeling that she wasn't telling the woman anything new.

The red hat nodded. "Yesss. Pleased to meet you both. I'm Ruby."

"Ruby . . ."

"Oh, just Ruby. Last names are such a bother, don't you think? Since I can never remember them I assume people don't remember mine, either. Being on a first-name basis seems so much friendlier." Lowering her gaze to the child, she added, "And you, my dear, have a very beautiful name. Do you know what it means?"

The child shook her head.

Ruby's arm extended out to sweep the horizon. "It means a tree-less plain."

Savannah made a sour face. *Yuck!*

"Now that's not a yucky thing, mind you," she replied. "That's nothing to look so glum over. Oh no, not at all."

The girl's eyes rounded. *She read my mind. She's psychic!*

"In fact," the woman continued, "a treeless plain can be a very beautiful thing, indeed! It makes an unobstructed view of the horizon. Perhaps you've never seen a full moon rise over a treeless plain. It's truly a wonder to see. You can watch its light spread over the ground, as though an angel had tipped over a pail of silver paint.

"Oh, yes, dear, only a savannah can give us the feel of awesome expansiveness. Only the grandness of a savannah can give us a panoramic sense of perspective—of life and where we fit in. Sometimes," she grinned, "folks can get a bit uppity about them-selves. The savannah has a way of trimming that attitude some. It keeps them from becoming overly full of themselves.

"By their very nature, those vast, open plains can inspire creativ-ity. They remind folks that some barriers are only in their minds. They pique the idea that people don't have as many things in their way as they believed—they can go further, reach higher, attain goals once thought to be too littered with obstacles to surmount. Oh yes, by their very nature, those vast plains can push folks beyond their imaginary limitations!"

Wow!

Amused by how easily the woman put an appealing spin on the boring image of a treeless plain, Sadie chuckled. "I think you've changed my niece's mind about the meaning of her name."

The elder's eyes twinkled like a wishing star as she patted the girl's knee. "I do, too. I think maybe her yuck became a wow."

The girl stiffened. *How could she know that? She* must *be God!* And Savannah's former curiosity about the bag lady quickly turned to awe. She was hooked, enamored. She was so enthralled she wished she could tell her aunt that their mystery friend had just read her mind. Twice! She slipped her hand in her jacket pocket. Small fingers wrapped securely around the hidden object. She was glad she'd brought it along. It was a symbol verifying her own precognition about today. Smoothing her fingertips back and forth over the object's surface, she became lost in thought before the sound of her aunt's voice pulled her back. There would be plenty of time later to think on things. Now was the time to remain alert and attentive, just like Nancy Drew would. Not wanting to miss a single word that passed over the old one's lips, she eagerly looked up, eyes riveted on the woman's face.

Ruby's eyes were twinkling when they locked on the girl's. "I believe I've seen you two somewhere before," she commented, while appearing to recall the time and place. "Let me see now . . ."

Savannah shot a guilty glance at her aunt. *Does the old woman know we've been spying on her? She'd know about that if she were really God, wouldn't she? Are we in big trouble?*

Sadie caught the girl's anxious look. She narrowed her eyes as a silent signal of caution, then smiled over at the elder.

"It's possible we've been in the same places at the same time. This is a big city, but not so big that folks' paths can't cross once in a while."

The toe of a scuffed granny shoe began tapping the grass as though the metered movement would help jar her memory.

Savannah stiffened with the fearful expectation of being caught at stalking. The idea gripped her like an icy hand about to clutch her neck.

Sparkling grey eyes flared to blue. "I know!" the woman suddenly exclaimed, making the other two startle. "I believe I saw you two in the museum last Tuesday!"

Two auburn heads bobbed in unison.

"Oh my," Ruby huffed with a hint of concern, "you were in the gift shop, weren't you?" Without waiting for an answer, she began to explain herself. "Yes, you were there. I remember passing you when I was so rudely escorted out." The silver hair, glistening in the sunlight, seemed to dance about whenever the woman moved her head. "I don't often fly off the handle like that, but every once in a while people's ignorance becomes more than one can bear. God can tolerate only so much abuse, you know." She released a long, exhausted sigh of dismay. "When it comes to God, people can't think past maleness. It doesn't even cross their minds that God may be a woman with a soft voice, tender heart, and a vagina to go along with those other things."

Coming from the mouth of an elder lady, the unexpected words were shocking. They were met by questioning frowns.

"I can see you probably think me an old, senile woman and—"

Both listeners immediately denied the idea.

"Well," Ruby sighed, "fact is, I see God getting a raw deal a lot of the time. Folks have so many cockamamie ideas about who God is. God gets pretty beaten up with blame, what with everybody making God into their personal, handy-dandy scapegoat every time something goes awry in their lives. They don't even know *what* God is." Her eyes rounded. "Why, they'd as soon cut out their tongues as to even utter the possibility that God could be anything other than a *he*." Ruby looked down at her hands to study her nails. A corner of her lip slyly tipped up. "Wouldn't they just fall over dead to know that the very first time God broke a nail was when She used her finger to carve those blasted Ten Commandments that nobody bothers with anymore! What a waste that was!"

Savannah gulped.

Sadie's cheeks flushed in reaction to the startling statement. *She's a crackpot. She's certifiably nuts.* Quickly recovering, she posited a theory. "Maybe She should appear and make herself known to people. You know, set everything straight . . . once and for all."

Ruby broke out in uproarious laughter. The girl and her aunt were taken aback by the woman's unexpected response. She laughed so hard she kept slapping her knees, then had to wipe her eyes.

Smiling from the infectious effect of the old one's merry reaction, Sadie grinned down at her niece, who was smiling without knowing why. "Was the idea that funny?"

"Funny!" Ruby repeated. "It was hilarious! Ohhh, my," she sighed, making an effort to regain control. "You have no idea how funny that was."

Leaning forward, Sadie hesitantly asked, "But why?"

"Because it never works! Can you imagine? God making the all-important Second Coming as a woman? Why, unless She came down in the *expected* manner on a flaming chariot complete with trumpeting angels announcing Her arrival, everyone would meet Her claim with outrage. They'd call Her a crackpot! Slap a straitjacket on Her. They'd say She was certifiably nuts! Ohhh," she bemoaned, "can't you just see it?"

A chill rippled through Sadie when she heard the woman repeat her own former thoughts. *Crackpot. Certifiably nuts.* She made an effort to forge forward. "But if She performed miracles then the people would have to believe . . . wouldn't they?"

"Miracles! Miracles, you say? What is a miracle, Sadie? Fire was a miracle to the people living in caves in dinosaur times. An airplane would be called a miracle in the time of Guinevere. The television remote, microwave ovens, cell phones, and computers would be a miracle marvel to those in the time of Mary Queen of Scots. Today, you'd think they'd grown a bit wiser about things. Today they still flock to light candles and prostrate themselves before a reflection on a skyscraper! If you're going to talk to me of miracles, talk to me after people stop seeing them in every odd-shaped tree trunk."

Sadie's shoulders slumped with the realization that Ruby was right. Her tone mirrored the disappointment. "So, if God were a woman, She wouldn't make Herself known. She'd probably stay low-key, maybe strive to go about incognito."

"Wouldn't you?" Ruby replied.

A nervous chuckle preceded the younger woman's answer. "It's not the type of thing I've ever thought about. I mean, well . . ."

"Well, what? Is it too outlandish to think that the office building cleaning lady or the woman sitting beside you on a city bus could be God in street clothing?"

Though the question did sound outlandish when verbalized, the concept itself no longer had that wildly provocative feel to it.

"It's just too scandalous," Ruby added. "God coming as a *woman* is too ludicrous a thought, much less the *idea* of God actually *being* a woman. It's totally unthinkable to people because it's a breach of their religious protocol it undermines the very foundational premise of their belief systems."

Intrigued, Sadie suddenly found herself taking a cavalier stance. She began sounding like Tina. "But there have been lots of female deities throughout time . . . in lots of different cultures around the world."

"Yes, this is so. Besides the familiar Greek and Roman goddesses, there were hosts of others. Minoan frescoes depict womanly images of the Life Giver. In Ireland and Scotland, she is the Triple Brigit. Dating back to the fifth and sixth millennia B.C.E., artifacts of the Goddess of Fertility—the Divine Great Mother figure—have been discovered in tombs in Europe and the British Isles. More archaic evidence has been unearthed in Romania, Bulgaria, Asia, and Scandinavia.

"But remember now," Ruby carefully reminded, "those goddesses were a solid spiritual element of cultures that were thousands of years old . . . thousands of years *before* Christianity became the newborn in the family of religious belief systems. Now, now you're talking about beliefs in today's world, a world that's, in the main, based on a Judeo-Christian belief system. And the Christian aspect comes from a male Christ. Sadie," the old one sadly said with a slow shake of her head, "the misogynistic founding fathers made sure there was no room left for a God-the-*Mother* to fit into their well-defined Trinity."

Captivated by the old one's voice, Savannah had been switching her gaze back and forth between the two women as they talked. Hearing Ruby's last words made her think of what she'd heard the woman shout in the museum. Now the elder didn't seem like the crazy homeless person she appeared to be to the crowd in the gift shop. Now the things she'd said made much more sense to her. Trying to convince people that God could be a woman was an impossible job. The girl felt sorry for Ruby. And when she looked up at the weathered face, grey eyes were locked on her own.

"What is this long face for, child? I hope you don't feel sorry for God. I think She can handle people's disbelief. Do you think She needs their belief to validate Her own beingness? To thrive? Oh no, She goes about Her work despite their disbelief. She does just fine."

The thought crossed Sadie's mind that perhaps the old woman was thinking the child rude by not talking. She thought it prudent to explain why her niece wasn't telling this herself. She began to mention the child's silence. "Savannah isn't being rude by not speaking. She's had a traum—"

The old one's eyes twinkled with understanding. "Oh, I know the child's not being rude. I've seen rude and know what it looks like. Rudeness has a smell, as well. Did you know that?"

Two heads shook.

"Well, it does. It has a bad smell. Stinks like eggs left to rot in the August sun." Ruby's left hand rose to her face. She pinched her nose. "Awful!" she said with a nasal-sounding exclamation.

Sadie laughed at the woman's dramatized antics.

Savannah's hand went to her mouth to cover her silent mirth.

Ruby's right hand immediately lowered the child's hand. "Uncover that pretty smile," she gently ordered. "You're far too pretty to be hiding behind that hand."

Like a moon in full eclipse, a shadow of question moved across the girl's mind.

"And wipe that frown off, as well," the elder added. "You know exactly what I'm talking about, don't you."

The curly auburn tendrils bounced neither up and down nor sideways. As in a wig on a mannequin, not a single strand stirred for fear the woman was going to address the taboo subject.

She did. "That's okay," the bag lady assured, "I'm going to tell you a little story. It's about feelings. It's about having good and bad feelings.

"There was a young lady I once knew. Her name was Margaret. Margaret was about sixteen at the time of our acquaintance. She was very sad all of the time. She was so sad because one day, while she was walking to school with her best friend, Kathy, a car ran the stop sign and hit the friend. Kathy later died in the hospital. Well, Margaret, you see, blamed herself for her friend's death. She felt guilty because she was still alive and Kathy wasn't. Do you think she was right to blame herself like that?"

Savannah made a slight nod.

"I see. So then you must also believe that she should feel guilty."

Again the nod came.

Chills rippled down Sadie's spine. *How does she know the traumatic cause of Savannah's silence?* Not wishing the discourse between the two to be interrupted, she remained silent and listened for where it was going to lead.

"Okay," Ruby said thoughtfully. "If you won a dance contest—"

Savannah's heart lunged. *She knows I take dance lessons.*

"—would you feel guilty because the others didn't win?"

Savannah shook her head.

"No? You wouldn't blame yourself because you won and they didn't?"

Again, the auburn curls swayed from side to side.

"Oh, I see. But you'd feel guilty for winning a spelling bee."

The curls vigorously shook back and forth.

"No? But all those other dancers in the contest and all those other children participating in the spelling bee felt really bad that they didn't win. You wouldn't blame yourself for their feelings of disappointment? You wouldn't feel guilty over their sad feelings?"

Though some glimmer of connectedness between the woman's simple examples and her own past situation pricked her logic, the girl's answer remained unchanged.

"Good girl," Ruby said. "You'd be right not to feel guilty or blame yourself over such things because winning and losing are just parts of life. Sometimes we win and other times we lose. Life comes with ups and downs." She winked. "It also comes with everything in between those highs and lows. Life is life, child. Things happen without anyone causing them."

She pointed to the trees. "Those falling leaves aren't causing those oak and maple trees to die. Oh sure, they may look dead, but we know better, don't we. We know that, although the deciduous trees are bare for a time, they're still very much alive. All the signs of their living essence are hidden from us for a while. Do the trees blame the leaves for going away? Do the leaves feel guilty for leaving the tree? Do the leaves blame the breeze for breaking their connection to the tree?" Ruby raised a cautionary finger. "Does one leaf feel guilt when the one beside it falls? Does that remaining leaf blame itself for the sudden absence of its neighbor?"

The child's head barely moved back and forth. She was deep in thought.

Ruby continued in an expressively singsong manner. "Of *course* that leaf doesn't blame itself nor feel guilt because it *knows* that it and *all* its kind are joyfully *participating* in the *natural* course of *nature!* Of *life!* Of the ever-circling cycle of *life!*

"And," she quietly added, "*people* participate in that beautiful cycle, as well. Oh yes, indeed! We're all riding the tide of life, child. Everyone breathes life's air and dances to life's rhythm. Some folks prefer the slow dance while others jump about with a sprightly jig. How they step to their dance depends on how they each hear the music. But, mind you, not a one is given a free pass. Oh, no. Not a one is exempt from participation. And, for each, the day comes when the music is heard no more. That's the day the dancing stops for them, and the resting time begins." At this point, Ruby looked off in the distance and released a long, pleasurable sigh. "Ohhh, that resting time. How *wonderful* it is!"

Both of her listeners startled when the woman suddenly straightened her back and shot out of her reverie. "But!" she exclaimed, eyes round with the appearance of revealing a secret. "Let me remind you that *no* other dancer blames *herself* for the participant who no longer hears the music! That's because each one is aware of life's rules. Those rules are sandwiched between the beginning and the end. Life and

death. The music is heard at one's first breath, at birth. And the dancing begins shortly afterward. When one's rest time is at hand, the
music grows fainter and fainter until it becomes a most peaceful chorus of angels quietly chanting. That's when the dancing stops. That's
when the dancer becomes mesmerized by the holy singers and is
drawn toward the sound which surrounds her and carries her to that
wonderful resting place."

The analogy was not lost on the young woman nor her niece.

Sadie was about to thank Ruby, when the woman bent to retrieve
her satchel.

"Now where'd I put that?" she mumbled, while rummaging her
hand around in the flat carpetbag.

Savannah curiously looked to her aunt.

"Here we are!" came the mirthful cry.

The other two stared at the small knit tam in the woman's hand.
It had a tartan plaid pattern with a fluffy tassel on the top.

"Here, child," she said, looking at Savannah's bare head. "You're
going to need this. It's going to snow."

Hesitantly, Savannah accepted the head covering and held it in her
lap.

"No, child, put it *on*."

Sadie secretly nudged her niece as a signal to oblige the woman.
*Need. Need. The homeless vet said something about Ruby supplying
whatever folks need.*

When Ruby saw the tam perched on the girl's head, she pursed her
lips. Silver brows made a sharp vee above the sparkling eyes. "Tsk,
tsk, child. You look like a Nairobi woman balancing a vessel of water
on your head! Have you never worn a tam? You need to set it firmly,
with a saucy tilt like a beret," she instructed, while making the adjust-
ment herself. "Like so."

Savannah almost giggled. As her smile began to grow, it stopped
midway.

A shower of red and orange leaves rained over the trio.

A curtain of angry clouds moved over the sun.

Park goers glanced skyward, pulling up the collars of their jackets.

Eerily, the girl recalled the woman's comment. *A cold wind is
going to blow.*

Slowly, the old one stood. "Time to be on my way now. It's been
lovely chatting with the both of you."

Savannah jumped to her feet and shot her aunt an urgent look.

Standing, Sadie put her hand on the woman's arm. Fingertips tingled at the touch. "Thank you so much for the tam, Ruby. Ahh . . . ah, can we drop you off anywhere? My van's just over—"

"Oh, my, how very considerate of you. But no, thank you, Sadie Brennan. I'm meeting with someone else in a few minutes."

Had I told her my last name? She couldn't remember. "Well," she said, looking up at the sky. "You're a far better weather person than the one on TV."

A wry smile curled the woman's lips. "They don't think outside the box."

"How did you know our balmy day was going to turn so fast?"

She winked. "Like I said, I can feel it in my bones."

An uncomfortable moment hung between the trio. Two of them were reluctant to turn their backs.

Ruby politely checked her watch.

Sadie could've sworn Ruby hadn't been wearing a watch. Now she resigned herself to take Savannah's hand and take a couple of backpedaling steps. "Maybe we'll meet again," she tested.

"Oh, I'd surely like that. Yes, one never knows, does one. Goodbye, now," she said, clomping away in snow boots two sizes too big for her.

The klutzy sound pulled two sets of green eyes to the woman's feet. Minds numb with disbelief, the two slowly turned and began walking away.

The girl slipped her hands in her pockets to warm them. Touching the object inside was enough to jar her mind from the shocked state. She spun around and raced back toward the retreating woman.

"Wha . . . ? Savannah!" Sadie called as she spun back around. "What are you doing?"

As she ran, the girl held up her index finger to indicate that she'd be right back.

Sadie watched her niece catch up with Ruby. She watched the woman bend to the child. She watched as Savannah pulled out one of the miniature pumpkins from her pocket and placed it in the elder's upturned palm.

It was golden moments like this when Sadie remembered why she loved her niece so much. Only Savannah would've had the bag lady in mind the day they'd gone to the pumpkin farm. And, while thinking on these things, she saw the old woman rest her hand on the girl's head and say something to her before tucking the tiny pumpkin into an inside pocket of her coat—next to her heart. She saw her niece nod her head in response to a question the woman had put to her. She saw all of this through a sprinkling of white. Words echoed in her mind. *A cold wind is going to blow. Maybe bring flurries with it.*

That evening, instead of calling Tina, Sadie lounged with Savannah on the girl's billowy pink quilt. Savannah pulled her aunt's arm tightly around herself and snuggled into the comfort she felt from their shared experience. To anyone passing by the hallway door leading into the flowery Laura Ashley bedroom, it looked as though the two occupants were deep into the DVD movie. Little would anyone suspect that their eyes were blind to the screen, that they were mentally watching a visual replay of their day. Little would anyone suspect that their ears were deaf to the harsh, mechanical audio while sharply attuned to an old woman's gentle tale of the music and the dancing to life's natural cycles—that of trees and people, even for a little girl's daddy.

Eleven

Tuesday

Shortly after dawn on Tuesday morning, the Woodward kitchen was bustling with activity. While Greta and Josef were eating a light breakfast, Savannah came down early. She literally skipped into the room.

"Well, aren't you the chipper one," Greta exclaimed through a mouthful of orange marmalade toast.

Mira entered. As always, she was dressed to the nines. "Morning, everyone," she greeted to the tune of her high heels clicking across the tile on her way to the refrigerator. Then, balancing bagels and cream cheese while pouring herself a cup of coffee, she addressed her daughter, "Are you and your auntie going out today?"

The girl happily nodded while watching her mother daintily spread cream cheese on the heated bagel.

Greta got up from the table and quickly got Savannah a glass of orange juice. "You're up pretty early this morning, missy," she said, handing over the glass. "Work on this until I get the sausages cooked." And as the links began to sizzle, the cook snuck furtive side glances at the little one who kept pacing the floor. The housekeeper knew her moods like the back of her hand. The girl was bursting at the seams with pent-up excitement.

Not wanting to take the time to sit down, Mira stayed by the toaster. With the bagel in one hand and the coffee cup in the other, she leaned her tweed Versace suit against the counter. "So, honey, I suppose you and your auntie have plans for—" She stopped after watching her daughter restlessly circling the trestle table. "Savannah, whatever has gotten into you? You're making me dizzy. Please, sit down."

The girl dutifully plopped herself down in the nearest chair, but still needed a way to dissipate the energy. Her legs began to swing like twin clock pendulums that swung increasingly faster as the girl strove in desperation to give herself encouragement. *I can do this! I can! I can! I can tell Mama about Ruby. I can!* While she privately strove to bolster her resolve, she heard her mother ask where Sadie was.

The room filled with the scent of cooking sausage. Greta began mixing hotcake batter. "She's not up yet. Didn't sleep well," she commented. "I heard her get up a couple of times during the night."

Mira raised a well-shaped eyebrow. "That woman's got some real problems, personal issues. I'm not sure my letter was timed well. Caitlin let it slip that Sadie's love life fell to pieces right before she left. She's probably better off without that loser, but knowing her, she most likely doesn't see it. I wish she'd get her life together. She's getting too old to be wasting time with deadbeats who can't . . ."

Savannah didn't like her mother talking about her aunt that way. She didn't want to listen to it.

"I mean, Sadie's a big girl," the voice rambled on. "She deserves better. Her business is beginning to take off and that fisherman was beneath her. Sadie needs to associate with a higher class of people, find one of her own kind to get romantically involved with. Honestly," she sighed, "I never could see what she saw in that guy. He was one of those dreamers who is forever straining to reach the brass ring but never—"

Savannah wanted to silence the haughty voice. *I can do this. I can!*

"—manages to grab hold of it. She has to realize that the success or failure of her business could depend on the social standing of those she surrounds herself with. She needs to move in better circles to elevate her image. Of course, that may be difficult living in that little fishing village. Quaint or not, it's still little more than a hamlet. She had so much going for her here. I never understood why she willingly threw it all away to follow that—"

Greta noticed that Savannah was scowling. She knew how much the girl loved her aunt and realized that Mira's vilifying comments were greatly upsetting her. "Well, Mira," she said in a placating tone. "Love happens, you know. It strikes between the most unlikely people and takes them by surprise. Love is blind to class distinctions. Nothing can stir the pot more than love."

Mira poured herself a fresh cup of coffee. "That pot can't be stirred unless one purposely mixes with those outside their own class, purposely contaminates the brew by sprinkling it with substandard ingredients. Sadie shunned the status she was born into and defiantly dove beneath the cream at the top. So now she has to deal with—"

Stop it! Stop it, Mama! The incessant drone of her mother's condescending tone was more than she could bear. It was enough to propel the girl's courage through the hairline crack that had been slowly etching itself across the soft inner layer of her shell. The courage exploded like a cannon shot. "I SAW GOD!"

The sound of the cannon was deafening.

Everyone froze.

Time stood still.

The sound of a fragile china cup shattering on the kitchen tiles pulled the numb minds back to the moment.

Mira's gaze hypnotically lowered to her splattered Ferragamo shoes. Coffee stains were darkening the grey suede. Her shocked expression locked onto that of Greta's, then Josef's.

Inch by inch, the miraculous import of the event sank into everyone's mind.

"Oh, dear God," Mira whispered.

Greta's hand went to her mouth. Eyes were round as twin hunter's moons. "She talked!" came the choked-up whisper. "Savannah talked!"

Instantly, three adults rushed to the child. Mira knelt beside the chair and, taking the small hands in hers, asked, "Did you say something, honey?"

Savannah nodded apprehensively while looking from one tense face to the other. Her jade-green eyes settled on her mother's anxious umber ones. When she spoke again, the words were delivered in a quivering murmur. "I saw God."

The adults exchanged dubious glances of concern.

Mira's mind automatically went on lawyerly autopilot. "G-God? You saw God?"

The girl nodded. *She doesn't believe me. Why did I say it?*

"When did you see God, honey?"

"With Aunt Sadie."

Greta and Josef eyed one another as Mira continued to coax more information from her daughter.

"Where? Where did you two see God?"

Silence.

"Honey?" Mira patiently pushed. "Where did you two see God?"

"Lots of places." *I blew it. I shouldn't have said anything.*

"What's burning?" Sadie asked, entering the kitchen.

"Ohhh!" Greta cried, racing to the smoking griddle. "The pancakes!"

The newcomer had seen the adults clustered around the girl before Greta ran to the stove to handle the emergency. "What's going on? Is Savannah sick or something?"

The elderly couple spoke at once.

"Far from it," Josef beamed, while attending to the broken china.

Greta couldn't contain her joy. "Savannah talked! She said something!"

Nearing her niece, Sadie noticed her sister's narrowing eyes and she couldn't understand why she wasn't showing elation. "Is that true?" she asked Mira. "What did she say?"

Mira stood. Venom dripped from her poisonous expression. "She *said* she saw *God!* That's a curious thing to say, don't you think? You, of course, wouldn't know anything about that, would you?"

Sadie tried to swallow, but found her throat too dry.

The child guiltily hunkered beneath the weight of shameful embarrassment. She'd let their secret out of the bag. She'd betrayed two people. Not only had she told on Ruby, she'd gotten her aunt in big trouble. Like a snake silently side-winding toward its unsuspecting prey, mortification slithered through the marrow of her bones. Now, with every fiber of her being, she wished she could take it all back. Since she knew that that was impossible, maybe she could just vanish instead. And when that didn't look like it was going to happen, she scrambled out of her chair and took a defensive stance in front of her aunt.

Mira flashed her daughter an indignant look. "Trying to protect your aunt, are you? Well," she huffed sarcastically, "I can see whose side you're on. Move aside, Savannah."

Little feet were frozen to the floor.

The mother's eyes widened. "Savannah, did you hear me? I asked you to move aside. I don't want you in the middle of something that's between your aunt and me."

The girl stood her ground. Her arms reached back and wrapped around Sadie's jean-clad legs.

"Savannah. Are you defying me? If you do not obey me right this minute—"

Sadie bent to extricate herself from the child's clinging arms. Her voice was gentle, forgiving. "Your mother's right. Neither of us wants you in the middle of this."

The girl shot a glowering look at her mother before racing from the room. *I'm never going to talk again! Never, ever!*

"Savannah!" Sadie called, worried over the girl's reaction.

"Leave her be," Mira coldly advised. "You've done quite enough already. If there's any comforting to be done, I'll do it. After she's settled down."

"Mira—"

"I've got the floor," Mira broke in. "And I'll probably have it for a while."

Josef grabbed his jacket off the peg by the door. Snugging a cap over his ears, he rolled his eyes at his wife before turning and disappearing out the kitchen door.

Greta sighed while wrapping up the cooked sausage. There wasn't going to be any hot breakfast this morning. Her head shook in exasperation. The two siblings were going to go at it tooth and nail again. As usual, the altercation was spawned by Mira's sense of superiority since she was the elder of the two by four years. Even when young, she tended to play the mother role to her "baby" sister. Now she again threw down the gauntlet in challenge. And, as was the case when the two were growing up, Greta attempted to stave off the verbal duel. "Mira," she softly began, "you've missed the whole point of this wonderf—"

Mira spun around to lock flaring eyes on the housekeeper. "No, Greta! Not this time. Things have gone way too far. It's obviously time for me to stop looking the other way."

Greta sighed and returned to her cleanup chores. She hated the fact that the two women couldn't ever be on the same page, or even reading the same book. She didn't know what Mira had meant, but had no doubt that everyone was about to be enlightened.

The attorney began speaking while crossing the floor to the cupboards above the coffeepot. She extracted a fresh cup and filled it. "All of you thought you were so slick, so damned clever. You thought you'd pulled the wool over my eyes with your sneaky little game of Hide the Tutor, but—"

Greta turned just long enough to snag Sadie's attention. Both of their eyes rolled to the ceiling. They had believed their antics had been smoothly managed behind Mira's back; evidently she'd had eyes in the back of her head. In the end, it was they who'd been duped.

"That's right," the elder sister smugly announced. "I *know* about your little ruse to give the tutor time off. In fact, while the four of you were snickering with your deception, I was privately reveling in the fact that I was the one who was *allowing* it to take place. How's that for dropping an evidentiary bomb on the courtroom floor?"

"It wasn't that we purposely tried to—"

"Objection! Objection sustained!" Mira cut in. "Don't!" she warned. "Don't even go anywhere near insulting my intelligence. I knew from day one that the tutor wasn't coming here. I let it slide because I was ready to overlook anything if it brought Savannah's voice back. I was ready to ignore her preference for you over me." A wry smile tipped one corner of her mouth. "Oh yes, don't think I was in the dark about her love for you. Why do you think you were the last resort? Why I turned to you after all else failed?"

"That's not fair. Savannah ador—"

"Oh, cut the crap, Sadie. It's bad enough for you to try to wriggle out of your deceit by trying to put a palatable spin on it, but don't try to do it to evidence that's long been tagged and sitting in plain sight on the prosecutor's table."

The younger sister bristled with rising ire. "Well, maybe if you were *home* more things would be different! My God, Mira, you're always off somewhere. Everything's more important than her. You're gone whole days at a time. When's the last time you took a day off to just hang out with her in her room? When's the last time you were wearing something other than Chanel or Versace clothing that you felt free to get dirty? Huh? When?"

"My preference in clothing isn't on trial here."

"Oh, and I am?"

"Your questionable behavior is. You're behaving irrationally. Even for you, your recent behavior is over the top. You should've given Savannah and me more respect. You should've declined my invitation to come here knowing you were reeling from being jilted. What's-his-name left you in an emotional—"

"Paul. His name is Paul."

"Whatever. *Paul* left you in an emotional tailspin, yet you came anyway."

"I came because I was asked to help my niece."

"How in God's name could you entertain thoughts of aiding her when you're the one needing the help!"

"Bait and switch."

Mira's meticulously plucked brow arched. "What? What are you talking about? What kind of thing is that to say?"

"Bait and switch," Sadie repeated. "You baited me about my emotional stability for the purpose of switching the issue away from your own absence."

"Oh, for God's sake." Then her demeanor shifted from guilty to accusatory. Her defensive position turned to offense. Her tone was acrimonious.

"Speaking of God, what sort of delirium are you dragging my child through? God? She saw *God?* I'm incredulous that you've somehow made her think such an outrageous thing. I'll not have you turning her into someone as delusional as you. Whatever your problem is, *fix* it! Do you hear me? *Fix* it! Because until you do, I forbid Savannah to go anywhere with you. Do you hear me, Sadie? She is not to go anywhere with you!"

Sadie started to plead her case. "You're not being fair. You don't understand what's been going on. Savannah's been deeply affected by—"

"You!" Mira finished. "She's been deeply affected by you and your preposterous presence in this house!" Mira set her cup down, then studied her stained shoes. "I've got to change my shoes," she said, striding to the doorway. Before passing through, she turned and wagged a warning finger. "Remember, if you go out, you go alone!"

Even the walls sighed in relief when the barrister's flaring aura left the room.

Sadie ran to the archway in time to see her sister ascending the wide stairway. She called to the retreating figure. "You should've listened to Greta! You still missed the whole point. Don't you care? Your daughter *talked!*"

Without comment, the woman stubbornly kept climbing the stairs.

Sadie reentered the kitchen with hunched shoulders. She crossed to the table and slumped in a chair. Elbows on the table, she crossed her arms and bent her head into them. Auburn hair spilled over the arms.

A featherlike touch massaged her back. Greta, ever the comforter, was sitting beside her. "I can't believe she made a bigger deal about what Savannah *said* than the fact that she'd finally *found* her voice. I just can't believe it. After so long, who cares what the child actually said?"

Sadie raised her head. "Mira cares. She cares because she's the one in the shell. Mira doesn't see it, but she's made her own shell to hide in. She cowers behind the Chanels, the Anne Kleins, the Versaces, they're the barriers that keep her true persona safe from exposure, from injury."

"While that may be true," Greta commented, "I think she would rather stay in denial over the fact that it was you who spurred the child's speech."

The idea pained Sadie. "Oh no, Greta," she moaned. "Why, that would mean that Mira despises me so much that she'd rather ignore the fact that Savannah spoke. Oh, no. I can't believe that she hates me that much."

"I'm not talking about hate, Sadie. I'm talking about resentment."

"Why would she resent me? She's got everything a successful career woman could possibly want."

"Does she? Is that a fact?"

"What're you getting at?"

Both women's attention was drawn to the kitchen door. Josef peeked in. "All clear?" he meekly asked.

"You're safe," Sadie said. "I've been officially branded as off-limits to Savannah. A restraining order's been issued. She can't go out with me anymore."

The gardener made a long face. "What? She can't do that. Not when the girl has just started to talk! That makes no sense. What's got into her?"

They all jumped when the explosive sound of the front door slamming blasted through the house like detonated dynamite. Seconds later, they heard the screech of tires on the cobblestone drive.

Josef shook his head. "Her hackles are still up. Probably mad as hell over those fancy ruined shoes."

"I don't think so," his wife replied. "I think that, for once, something else took precedence over her clothing. Call me crazy," she said, "but I feel there's been a shift in the way the wind blows."

"Meaning?" Sadie asked.

Greta wasn't sure. "Just a feeling. But something. There's more to her reaction. If you ask me, the jolt of the child talking rumbled a lot deeper beneath the surface than any of us realized. Mira included. Especially Mira. She didn't know how to handle it so she resorted to doing what she does best—making accusations."

"Shifting the issue, you mean," Sadie clarified.

"One and the same, as it turns out. She's the litigation expert. Shifting the issue or introducing a new one by sneaking up behind it is her forte. This time, I think, it was a tried-and-true maneuver that she fell back on. It was used to shove away something she wasn't ready to look at. In the end, her ploy backfired. She hadn't counted on feeling something that surprised the hell out of her."

Josef scratched his hairline. "She came face to face with it, didn't she, lovey."

Greta blushed at the use of his private endearment for her.

Sadie curiously looked back and forth between the two elders. "Came face to face with what? You two are doing that spooky, wordless communication again. C'mon, share the wealth. What did Mira see that sent her running for cover?"

"Herself. She saw herself," Greta replied.

The answer didn't clear the murky waters. "I don't get it. She sees herself every day in the mirror."

Josef, elbows on the table, leaned forward. "The mirror shows her a reflection of someone impeccably dressed in designer clothing. The mirror bounces back the image of a perfectly coiffed, successful career woman wearing flawless makeup. Today Mira saw her true self. The one she's kept locked up ever since David passed."

The housekeeper refined the issue. "Sadie," she softly said, "we believe that, today, your sister looked straight into the face of her heart and saw the well of love staring back at her. She's kept the core of her emotions in a chest bound with chains and under lock and key for two and a half years."

The words sent a shiver through Sadie. "Then Savannah's is not the only shell that's showing signs of weakening."

"No, we don't think so," Josef offered. Then he leaned back in his chair. "I don't know which shell will prove to be the thickest."

Sadie thought his comment didn't match the current situation. "Savannah's shell already broke open. She talked, remember?"

A dubious expression washed over his face. "It's not likely any of us will forget what we witnessed this morning, but the event may have been only a glimmer of hope—a flash of what's to come, what's possible. We'll see about the girl. This morning was a start. A good start. It's her mother I'm not so sure about. If it's the way we think it is," he said, inclining his head to Greta, "we may all be in for some rough seas ahead."

Rough seas. Odd choice of words, Sadie thought. She was well acquainted with rough seas. She'd ridden out more than her share and wasn't looking forward to sinking down into the deep watery troughs and then being propelled up to the dizzying heights of the curling crests. Sinking troughs, teetering crests.

Up and down at a furious pace.

The lashing winds.

The roar of the waves crashing over stern and bow. King Neptune's sick idea of a killer roller coaster ride. Sadie could hear him now. *Ahoy up there, me maties! Look smart, now! Down ya go from yardarm and crow's nest! Batten down the hatches! I be taking ya for a bit of a riiide!*

"Dear?" Greta called from somewhere far away.

Sadie blinked. "Sorry. I was thinking about those rough seas. Seems that's all I've been riding lately. The stillness of the doldrums looks pretty inviting right about now."

Josef chuckled. "Oh, now. You don't really mean that, do you? The doldrums are a stuck place to be. Nobody gets anywhere on a sea of glass day after day. Why, it's like being stuck in a painted seascape."

A wisp of a smile broke the woman's dark mood. "You always did know the right thing to say, Josef. Yeah, being stuck in a painting would be pretty hard to endure. Still," she snuck in, "it'd sure be a welcomed respite for a while. Just long enough to catch my breath and relax my grip on the storm holds. It'd be nice to stand in the pilot house and be a helmswoman who has the wheel respond to my touch instead of me always straining to keep it from whipping my arms about. I'm weary of being at the mercy of a ship that steers itself."

"Ahhh, now, Sadie," Josef began to soothe before he caught sight of Savannah slowly rounding the kitchen doorway.

Sadie straightened when she saw the man lock his gaze on something behind her. She turned. "There she is!" she exclaimed, while waving the girl over to them. "There's our shining star!"

Savannah stood next to her aunt's chair and leaned into her. The girl's body language reminded Sadie of a recently disciplined dog that attempts to make things right again.

Greta also noticed. "Today's a wonderful day, Savannah. You spoke for the first time in months! You've made us all so happy. You should be, too! How about we begin celebrating by having a big, hot breakfast?"

The soundless response was barely perceptible. It came by way of a minute shake of the head.

Sadie wrapped her arm about the little one standing beside her. She smiled while fluffing the girl's bouncy auburn curls. "There's nothing to feel bad about, honey. None of us here are upset by what you said. You shouldn't let your mom's reaction make you feel guilty or lessen the joy of your breakthrough. She still hasn't come to terms with things and you need to cut her some slack. Know what I think? I think you wanted to share Ruby with the most important person in your world. I think you wanted to tell your mom all about her. Am I right?"

The girl distractedly picked at a hangnail. The idea took her off guard. Was that right? Was that why she had blurted out those particular words?

"What do you think?" Josef pointedly asked the child.

A shrug was given as a response.

The adults eyed one another. Where was the girl's voice? Was it only a glimmer of hope as Josef had cryptically suggested earlier? Even if it was, it was a beginning that indicated bricks were falling away from the wall she had solidly built around herself.

The housekeeper wondered if bad news would spur another outburst. Her eyes fixed on the girl's. "I suppose there's no purpose in putting off saying this . . . your mom's forbidden you to go out with your aunt anymore."

Small eyes widened in panic. The mouth formed an O with the silent scream. *No!* Her mom couldn't take Ruby away. She couldn't. Not now. Not after contact had been made and there was the possibility of meeting her again.

Sadie's voice was meant to be sympathetic. "I'm sorry, honey. But we've got to respect your mother's wishes in this."

Red tendrils wildly shook back and forth.

"Honey, please don't blame her. She just doesn't understand about Ruby. Maybe, if I talk to her I can make her see how instrumental Ruby was in helping you find your voice and then . . ."

It's all my fault! I shouldn't have opened my big mouth about her! Mother won't ever understand about Ruby!

In a blur of movement, the girl was gone from the room. Upstairs, the trio sitting at the kitchen table heard her bedroom door slam with finality.

The young woman shifted her gaze to the elders. "Well? Are we back to square one with her? Has Mira's reaction set everything back?"

Greta sighed. "Possibly. Who knows anything anymore? Only time will tell for sure. One thing's clear, though. That child is full of anger and frustration right now."

"So is her mother," the gardener added. Then his gaze slid to the young woman. "Seems to me that this household has *three* members in turmoil beneath its roof."

Mira's caustic words about Paul echoed in Sadie's mind. "You're right, Josef. I've got buried issues that I need to dig up and deal with, as well. But there's a time and a place for that. The miracle of Savannah's speech takes precedence." She stood and pushed her chair in. "Just the fact that she finally spoke overrides the possibility that Mira's reaction may have caused a setback. We don't know if it actually did. The bottom line is that her voice was heard in this house. I just wish I could've heard it."

"Perhaps with some coaxing, you will. Are you going up to talk to her?"

"I'm going to try."

The closed door sealed the girl off from the rest of the world. It acted like a tightly shut shell protecting the softness of the clam hiding inside.

"Savannah? Savannah, honey? May I come in?"

The request was met with silence.

Sadie put her ear to the door. "Honey? It might help if you'll let me talk to you about all of this. Don't be mad at your mom. She's just worried about you. It may not seem like it now, but it'll all work out." Gently, she tried to turn the door handle. It met with resistance. It was locked.

"I hope you're not upset with me, honey. Savannah? Did I do something to upset you? Won't you let me come in? I promise we don't even have to talk about anything if you don't want to. We can just hang together and be company for one another."

Silence.

After a few more fruitless attempts, Sadie gave up and went to her own room. She picked up the phone. It was time to bring Tina up to speed on the ongoing intrigue permeating the walls of Woodward manor.

That evening, Savannah made a brief appearance at dinnertime. She listened to Greta inform the group that Mira had called to say that a couple of attorneys were going to be joining her for cocktails at the house at seven to review tactics for an early morning court date. Their case was first on tomorrow's crowded docket. She listened to Josef recount humorous escapades of his youth. She listened to her aunt's account of a particularly tricky antique deal she had negotiated for a nationally famous client.

Savannah hadn't cared about her mother's expected company. She herself was never expected to make an appearance.

Josef's funny tales brought her no mirth. Though she suspected they were intended to make her laugh, no smile threatened to crack her solemn mood.

And Aunt Sadie's intricate story about getting her client a "steal of a deal" for the 1840 Shaker blanket chest didn't impress her. Who ever heard of forty-eight thousand dollars being a steal for anything?

Later in the evening, Savannah returned to her room without ever uttering so much as a mouse squeak. Once again, her locked door kept all well-intended intruders at bay. It was only after Savannah was sure everyone in the house was in bed for the night that she tiptoed across the plush pile of the bedroom carpet. Kneeling by the window, the small, penitent form was awash in silvery light. Moonbeams fell upon the tousled auburn curls, anointing them with liquid starshine. Small palms were pressed together in an attitude of prayer. And spurred by a heart beating with unswerving belief, her searching eyes were full of wonder as they scanned the vast, twinkling expanse above.

"I hope you can hear me, God," she whispered to the divine Chatelaine of the Heavens. "I don't know if you're a girl or a boy. I've been doing a lot of thinking today about what Ruby said. You know, about God being a lady and having a you-know-what instead of that other you-know-what. I'd like to think she's right because I kinda like the idea of you being everybody's mother.

"My mom is having a hard time right now. I was hoping that maybe you could help her. I know she loves me. I know she loves my Aunt Sadie, too. But ever since my daddy died, she's been . . . well, like she's afraid of something. I don't know. It's like she has to keep herself so busy that she doesn't have any spare time . . . you know, to *think* about certain things. And she keeps herself in a grumpy mood so she doesn't *feel* certain things.

"God? Holy Mother Ruby? Is that really you up there? If you're not God then you're an angel or something because I saw you do things nobody else can do. I saw what I saw. Aunt Sadie saw, too. I heard Aunt Sadie tell Tina about your shoes, that you give them away to people who need them. You know what kind of shoes people need so you make them appear on your own feet first. We saw you do that. We saw it.

"Anyway, Holy Mother, I just wanted to ask if you had the time to help my mom. I guess that's about everything I wanted to say. Bye now. Amen."

Before Savannah rose from her knees, she looked over at the marionette. Moonlight illumined his forever-open eyes and painted laugh.

"Shhh, Mister Jangles," she whispered with a finger to her lips. "I'm not supposed to be talking, so this is just between you and me."

Twelve

Wednesday

The Harbor Heirlooms commercial van crept at a snail's pace around the wind-blown commons. For the third time, it circled the parklike grounds like a sleepy turtle searching for the perfect place to nap.

Oaks, sycamores, and maples quaked in the light breeze as more of their scarlet and orange garments momentarily drifted aloft before gently landing to enrich the new cloak covering the ground.

Laughing children chased one another through the colorful carpet of leaves. Others took delight in the shushing sound their feet made while shuffling a trail through the crispness.

Mothers chatted while keeping one eye on their children at play.

Surrounded by the semiprivacy of the gazebo's white lattice, heads cozily nestled together, an old man and woman held hands like young lovers.

On a bench beside a landscaped knoll of brilliant yellow and rust chrysanthemums, a young college student filled the air with the clackety-clack of fingers flying over a laptop keyboard.

Soaking up the autumn sun, a couple of elderly men challenged one other with a game of chess. They paid no mind to the gleeful shouts and screams of the boisterous children running about.

Two shoppers sitting at a picnic bench with packages piled at their feet shared a takeout lunch and exclamations over the latest soap opera cliffhanger.

And by the time the blue van had cruised its fourth circle, the driver was drawing curious looks from the park goers. Disappointed, she eased back onto the tertiary road of the bucolic residential neighborhood.

With thoughts caught fast in a logjam of indecision, her eyes scanned the neat middle-class homes trimmed with signs of the season.

Autumn flower sprays hung on entry doors.

Jack-o-lanterns, with an array of both laughing and fearsome expressions, perched on porches and doorsteps.

Stalks of tied corn were secured to gas lamp poles beside narrow front walks.

The various images of hooked-nose, green-faced witches peered from windows along with ghastly monsters and all manner of ghosts.

A life-sized scarecrow sat on a porch rocker at one house. At another, a stuffed Frankenstein chummed with Count Dracula.

All these incoming images speared into the driver's mind to spark thoughts of the upcoming Halloween night. What was Savannah going to dress up as? Did she still want to go out? For that matter, would Mira balk at the two of them going out together?

Sadie's mind drifted to this morning when she'd walked by the girl's bedroom door and found it still locked. No amount of cajoling, pleading, or bribing could entice the young one to unlock the door or respond by speaking. When Sadie had walked into the kitchen, she'd learned from Greta that Mira had left early and Savannah had been down shortly after her mother left. The girl had unceremoniously taken breakfast back to her room. She'd done this with eyes lowered, without uttering a sound to either Greta or Josef.

Feeling empathy for her niece, Sadie had had little stomach for anything more than an English muffin. While eating, she and the housekeeper had discussed how they'd all suffered Mira's wrath the day before. How they were all expected to do penance for the words the girl had spoken. Granted, the child had chosen shocking words to break her long period of silence, but still, the more amazing thing about the whole event was the fact that she'd finally spoken.

The blue van randomly turned down another side street. The driver, deep in thought, gave scant notice to the trim, turn-of-the-century homes gaily decked out for All Hallow's Eve.

Though the driver's eyes scanned all the decorations, her mind was elsewhere. Thoughts of Caitlin revealing Paul's sudden departure made her recoil from the smarting twinge of betrayal that pricked at her like a thistle burr. She'd thought Caitlin had understood that the broken relationship had been information shared in confidence. How was it Caitlin thought it her business to blab it to her boss? If Sadie had wanted Mira to know about it she would've told her herself. Wasn't anything sacred anymore? Was there any such thing as a secret? Where had the idea of trust fled to?

An infestation of black spiders crept along wispy webs spookily stretching across window frames and door lintels.

Bats, wings spread wide, alighted on fence posts.

Twin crows, ebony orbs darkly glistening, looked out from their perches atop a witch's rounded shoulder and crooked-handled broomstick.

A blood-red tear squeezed from the corner of Dracula's eye as he longingly eyed all who passed his opened, front-yard coffin.

A distant sparkle of light from someone's camera flash.

Tombstones, scribbled with R.I.P., dotted leaf-strewn lawns.

But still, the hauntingly macabre scene could not draw the driver's attention away from her thoughts.

And where did Mira get off saying that Paul left me an emotional basket case? She's one to talk! She's in such an emotional mess that she's in denial! She'd rather be in denial than face her grief. How does she know what I'm feeling? Or what sort of state Paul's leaving left me in? Who the hell does she think she is?

Frankenstein had his arm swung casually around a bug-eyed zombie, and the two lounged like old buddies on a porch swing.

Bright orange trash bags, made to look like smiling Jack-o-lanterns, were fat with leaves and set out by the street.

A ray of blinding sunlight sparked off the windshield causing the driver to suddenly squint in reaction.

Children's drawings and cutouts of ghosts and goblins obscured the view of front windows.

Chains made of black and orange construction paper draped over doorways and wound around step railings.

Mira's the one who needs to snap out of it! For cryin' out loud, she's got a daughter to think of! She's got a lot more at stake here than I do. She can't just fly away to her own little world of courtrooms and torts! She's got to pull herself together and get with the program, for God's sake! The driver smirked. *Aren't* you *the kettle calling the skillet black. Look to your* own *house, you blind woman. Open up your eyes and look around you! You don't need me. You never did.* "All she ever needed was you," she whispered. "Just you back in her life."

The commercial van passed a spewing cauldron of dry ice. Vapors billowed into the air and tumbled in cascading waves over its rim.

Another brighter spear of light glanced off the windshield. The driver responded with another quick recoil.

Standing guard at the top step of a covered porch, the small but powerful figure of Yoda watched for the approach of inept intruders.

Again the driver was forced to squint in response to the reflections that were catching the windshield. The flashes were becoming brighter and more frequent as the vehicle inched its way toward their source. Once believing them to be brilliant pinpoints of light from someone's flash camera, she had dramatically changed that opinion. The intermittent flashes were emitting from none other than a cheap chunk of red glass. Like a lighthouse beacon it blinked from atop an old woman's hat.

Slowing to a stop in the middle of the road, Sadie pressed herself over the steering wheel to peer down the street. "Ohhh, my God," she murmured.

Closing the distance between them and acting as though she were out for a sunny Sunday stroll, Ruby aimlessly ambled up the sidewalk. The skinny carpetbag, keeping time to a silent tune, happily swung at the woman's side. She looked as though she hadn't a care in the world. The familiar overcoat hung open, revealing a fisherman's sweater and a beige calico skirt, its hemline flounced about ankles covered by black stockings. New hiking shoes with crepe soles hushed the lively stride.

Sadie's head spun to check for traffic behind her, then focused on the approaching woman. "Oh, God," she hastily sputtered. Then, without wasting precious time in debate with herself, she eased down on the accelerator until she was abreast of the elderly pedestrian.

"Hello, again!" she called through the lowered passenger window.

The senior citizen stopped humming. "Why, hello there! Beauty of a day!"

"Yes, it is. Can I drop you off somewhere?" Sadie nervously asked, without knowing why. All she knew was that she had to say something. Anything. Anything to have another encounter with the curious woman.

Ruby shook her head in irritation. She shook it like she was trying to rid herself of a pesky mosquito. Then she crossed a driveway apron to approach the van. Peering inside, she apologized. "I'm sorry. I didn't hear what you said."

"I was wondering if I could drop you off anywhere? Can I give you a lift?"

Shocked, Sadie watched the lady open the door and climb inside.

"As a matter of fact, you may," she said, while settling herself in the bucket seat. "I just came from a home visit. You know, doing a little of that visiting-the-sick thing. I'd been sitting with Ida all night long and," she admitted with a playful smile, "I'm not quite up to par without my full eight hours of beauty sleep. Poor dear has folks from Hospice staying with her." She frowned. "Not the same as having friends close by. No. Not the same a'tall."

"That's very kind of you to sit with a sick friend. And you said you were there all night long?"

"Oh yes, but it's not such a chore for someone who's alone like I am. I can come and go as I please. Staying with Ida is a good way to spend a night or two."

She is *homeless.*

"Oh, it's not like I don't enjoy being in my own place, mind you," the woman added. "No, ma'am! There's no place like home, now, is there?"

The driver's head shook in reply. *She's* not *homeless.*

Their attention was pulled to a passing vehicle. The driver sat on the horn and angrily glared while having to veer around the angled van.

"You're obstructing traffic," Ruby announced. "Let's be on our way."

"To where?"

Replying as though the answer were as plain as the nose on the driver's face, Ruby said, "To wherever you were going when you spied me."

"But I wasn't going any—"

"Nonsense," the elder sputtered. "Everyone's going *some*where!"

"It's not important where I was going. Now I have a new place to go. And you have to tell me where that is."

Silver brows knitted. "I do?"

This is a crackpot conversation. "Well, yes. I can't drop you off somewhere if you don't tell me where it is that you want to go," the driver explained, while easing back onto the main thoroughfare.

The old woman was studying her. Recognition suddenly dawned and her countenance beamed. "Now I recall where we've met. The Commons! The little park in the Commons!"

"Yes," Sadie grinned. "I'm Sa—"

"You're Sadie Brennan and little Savannah."

I still don't recall ever giving her my last name. "Yes. However, today it's just Sadie because—"

"Hi again, Sadie!" Ruby chirped.

The driver's smile widened with the woman's bubbly attitude. "Hi again, Ruby!"

"Hi again, Savannah, dear!" the woman added.

"Ahh, she's not with—"

"Hi again, Savannah, dear!" Ruby repeated.

"Hi," came the tiny voice from the back of the van.

Sadie's eyes shot to the rearview mirror. They were met by a smaller pair of green orbs. *"Sa-vannnn-ah!!!"*

The steering wheel jerked to the right with the driver's shocked reaction. Before she could correct, the sound of metal on metal was chilling. In slow motion, she watched the back quarter panel of the parked car buckle. Her stomach churned at the sight.

Panic-stricken, Sadie froze.

Ruby nimbly slid from the passenger seat and was at the impact site in seconds.

Spurred by the elder's quick reaction and expecting the car's owner to come flying from the residence, Sadie came to her senses and got out. *Oh God, I don't need this. I really don't need this. Not now!* As she tried to prepare herself for the sight of the damage she'd inflicted, her eyes slowly lowered to the parked vehicle.

Ruby's hand was moving back and forth over the exterior finish. It was flawless.

"That's some paint job!" Ruby exclaimed. "In the old days—"

Incredulous, Sadie bent to examine the impact site. No dent was in evidence. Not even a scratch in the paint. Awestruck, her eyes drifted to the right bumper of her van. A good three inches of space separated the two vehicles. No scratch on her bumper. No telltale red paint transference from the other vehicle. Mesmerized by the mystery, she gave the old woman a baffled look.

Ruby's shoulders nonchalantly hitched up, then dropped. "What? You gonna question a lucky day? Come on, count your blessings and be done with it. Let's get going. Drive me back to the Commons park. I need to rest a bit."

Dazed, Sadie made her way back behind the wheel. The shock of discovering she'd had a stowaway was nothing compared with what had just happened.

No one spoke during the time the van took to cover three blocks.

Finally, the old one broke the silence. "Isn't it amazing how an accident can jumble the mind? Everything happens so fast that everyone involved, even bystanders, can have different versions of what occurred."

The driver kept her eyes on the road ahead. "My mind wasn't that jumbled. I know what I heard, saw, and felt. I hit that car. I felt the impact. I heard the crunch. I saw the quarter panel dent."

"There you go," Ruby chuckled, "that's what I mean. Everyone thinks they saw something different. Not one witness will give the same details. That's because emotions run high during accidents and the like. The old adrenaline cuts loose and changes how folks see things."

Sadie pulled her eyes from the road just long enough to give the woman a suspicious side glance. "Adrenaline. You think it's the adrenaline."

"Sure, it is! What else?"

What else, indeed, dear woman? It wouldn't be right to call it what it was, would it? It wouldn't be right to call it a miracle. A miracle you created with a swipe of your hand!

When Sadie didn't immediately respond, Ruby inclined her head toward the space between herself and the driver where the stowaway had wedged herself. "I'm pleased you're here, Savannah, dear, but you really shouldn't disobey your mother."

The driver shot back a lightning response. "How did you know that?"

"Know what?"

"Know she wasn't supposed to be here."

"You—"

"No. No, no. I never said that. I never said anything of a kind."

"You didn't have to. May I finish what I was about to say?"

Sigh.

"Thank you. I was about to say that you had a strong reaction of surprise to hear your niece greet me. One didn't have to be God to recognize how taken aback you were. You obviously hadn't realized she'd been in the van with you. I was about to say that your reaction said it all."

"Maybe it showed my surprise, but it didn't also show that her mother forbade her to come with me. Where'd that little tidbit come from?"

Silence.

Sadie pushed for an answer. "Well? Where'd it come from?"

The woman's grey eyes twinkled to blue. They twinkled like all the stars gathered in one place. Like a million Christmas lights they twinkled with an impish mirth.

"Must'a been a good guess. I'm a good guesser."

No, you're a good B-esser.

"I've been known to be called a lot of things," she added. "Mostly a very good guesser."

How about mind reader?

A tired sigh escaped the woman's lips. She absently gazed out the window. "Oh, yes, a lot of things I've been called in my time."

The driver could tell that it was time to change the subject. If this wily old woman was anywhere near to being who Tina thought she might be, Sadie figured the women had had her fill of names. "So, Ruby. Where do you hail from? Are you a native of Chicago?"

"Oh, my, no. Not from Chicago. Why, I've been so many places over time I feel like every one of them is home to me. Every one of them has a special place in my heart."

"I'm sure it must seem like that, but where do you originally hail from? Where were you born?"

"Oh! Look there!" the old one exclaimed, while pointing to something beyond the windshield. "We're here already! We were closer than I thought!" She gave the young girl a beaming smile. "We're at the park already, child. And look here," she said, raising the fat carpetbag. "I've brought bread for the ducks!"

Savannah's eyes grew to the size of dinner plates. She sucked in her breath at the sight of the magic satchel's fullness and gave her aunt an awed smile.

The surprises were sprouting faster than dandelions after a spring rain. Before Sadie could dig up the answer to one curiosity, another popped up right beside it. If she tried to keep pace, she'd be bone weary by lunchtime. Instead of reminding the old one that her bag had been empty when she'd gotten into the van, the driver let it pass with a sigh and swung into a parking spot. "Let's go feed the ducks!" *And maybe the pigeons will come* home *to roost on your shoulder again.*

As the three passed the play area, Ruby addressed the child. "There's a swing open, do you want to grab it before someone else does?"

Fighting an urge to slip her hand in the woman's, Savannah shyly shook her head. "No, thank you. I'd rather feed the birds."

Ruby's mouth dropped. "Well, I'll be!" she chirped. "That's the most I've ever heard you say!"

A nervous giggle came as a response.

"The bench beside the pond's empty," Sadie pointed out as the trio veered toward it. "We're in luck. We'll have the ducks all to ourselves."

"Let's be on our way then," Ruby commented. "Yes, we're all on our way, aren't we." Cutting across the grass, the three headed toward the quacking ducks.

Hearing the woman's words, Sadie had the distinct impression that they held far more meaning than them being on their way to just the pond. Did she mean that Savannah was on her way toward emotional healing because she'd finally spoken? Did she mean that Sadie herself was on her way because they'd met up again today? Or was she being presumptuous by thinking that everything the woman said was going to hold greater meaning than intended? Was she going into this chance encounter today with a head full of assumptions and overblown expectations? Was she already playing the role of a fool by not going into this with an open mind instead of being so tense and watchful? She needed to relax and take each moment as it came.

"This is a relaxing place," Ruby said.

"What? What did you say?"

As the woman settled herself onto the park bench, her eyes were on Sadie's clenched fists. "I said that this is a relaxing place, don't you think?" She patted the empty place beside her and, lowering her lashes, tilted her face to the sun. After inhaling a deep breath, she held it a bit before slowly letting it out through her mouth. "Wonderful," she sighed. "Isn't life wonderful? Precious?"

Sadie realized that she hadn't held the same opinion. When she didn't immediately respond, the woman nonchalantly shrugged.

"Ah, well. Perhaps you don't feel it, but don't despair, you will. You will," she repeated over the sound of crinkling bread wrapper. She pulled two loaves out of the satchel and handed one to the girl patiently waiting in front of her. "There you go, dear. We can begin with this one. Maybe divide the loaves between the ducks and pigeons. They'll all be little pigs if we let them."

Savannah scanned the park, then the trees.

Ruby smiled. "You're looking for the pigeons. What do you bet they're winging their way here right now?"

A wry grin brightened the girl's face. She wasn't about to make a bet with MotherGod. If the old one said that the birds were winging their way here, then . . .

The whooshing sound of wing beats attracted the trio's attention. One. Three. Six incoming flights quickly became a flock as the grey birds alighted four and five at a time.

Starry-eyed, Savannah beamed at the woman before her focus was drawn by the riot of quacking at her back. She turned.

Ruby laughed. "You're officially in charge of the ducks. Your auntie and I can handle these other feathered characters."

Watching the girl skip away, Sadie felt a welling of love begin to press against the inside of her rib cage. Her feelings for the girl ran deep. And she was convinced that the little lady seated beside her was the sole cause of Savannah's recovery. The woman's presence in their lives had been like a powerful magnet pulling the child from her shell. It had teased and tenderly tugged the girl's will with the spark of a mystery to solve. Sadie warmly smiled with the thought of how her niece loved nothing more than the promise of a good mystery. Ruby had ignited the Nancy Drew in her.

The aunt's thoughts were abruptly cut short when a stack of bread slices was dropped in her lap.

"I can see how much you love that child," came the perceptive comment that accompanied the cooing from the gaggle at their feet.

Tearing bits from the slices and tossing them past her knees, Sadie smiled wanly. "I suppose it must be pretty obvious. She's a sweet girl. Smart for her age, too. I don't see her as much as I'd like. I live up in—"

"Maine's a ways off," the woman acknowledged.

Sadie was bound and determined to catch one of Ruby's slippery statements by the tail. "I never told you I was from Maine."

Ruby looked off in the distance. "Well, dear, you hardly had to, did you now?"

The younger woman followed the woman's gaze. She followed it to her parked vehicle where the sunlight winked back the boldly advertised name and address of her business. Cheeks blushed with embarrassment. "No. I sure didn't have to. I'm sorry for coming back at you like that. It's not like me. I . . . I just . . ." At the touch of the woman's hand covering her own, suppressed emotion surged and her eyes filled with moisture.

The aged hand softly patted the younger one. Both pairs of eyes were drawn to the girl's joyful giggles over the clutch of ducks that were excitedly gathered at her feet.

"Love," Ruby said, "when it's truly felt, has a way of taking us on a merry roller coaster ride. It shoots us up to dizzying heights where the thin air of ecstasy threatens to take our breath away, then, without a smidgen of warning, plunges us down into the lowest of lows where only pain dares to dwell."

Cresting the curve of the smooth cheek, a tear landed with a silent splash on the old one's hand. Sadie noticed and apologetically wiped it away.

"I'm sorry. I don't know what's come over me. I'm blubbering all over someone I hardly know."

"Oh, but you do!" the elder crooned.

Sadie self-consciously swiped at her eyes. "No, I don't. Not really. I mean, we've only just recently met."

"Well, what *I* meant was the fact that we're all sisters and brothers on this planet we call Earth. We're all members of the *human* family. At the most primitive level we share a basic relatedness. We share the rights to the same basic needs. We feel the same emotions. We are, at heart, innately empathic beings who are moved by another's show of joy or pain."

She squeezed the youthful hand and inclined her head forward to peer into the blurred green eyes. "Have you never stopped to help a stranger? Has a stranger ever stopped to help you? Sadie, dear, have you never walked through a cemetery and been moved to tidy up an overgrown grave site for the poor soul who'd been forgotten and neg-lected? Or have you never felt the pull to drop coins into a Salvation Army's Christmas kettle as you passed; perhaps suffered the twinge of guilt if you didn't follow through?"

The younger woman's head tilted to one side as a sign of admis-sion.

"You see?" Ruby smiled while tapping her chest. "We all, in here, feel a relatedness to one another. We generally don't think of it as a relatedness, but it is. It surely is. We can be brought to tears by another's suffering or we can experience elation by the joys of another. And these caused by someone we don't even know. Someone we may think of as a stranger. This is because of one reason only, Sadie. It's because we *love*."

When their eyes met, the younger woman was taken aback by the electric blueness of the elder's. Nearly struck speechless, the sight dis-turbed her train of thought.

"I . . . I, ahhh, I . . . well, you're right, of course. I suppose it is love that plucks at our heartstrings and causes us to be affected by the joys and sorrows of others. Yes," she admitted, "I can see how we're all connected on a very basic level." Again, she raised her eyes to meet those of the old woman's. This time she was more prepared and had braced herself before locking onto their intensity. But they'd softened to baby blues. The mellowness was calming. "I apologize for saying I barely knew you and treating you like a stranger. I mean, especially when you so clearly see people as relations—like family members you're meeting for the first time."

The corners of Ruby's eyes crinkled. "Oh, not quite," she chuck-led, "but close enough. You got the idea." Her arm extended and swept the Commons. "Out of all these people walking around, not one is truly a stranger. To *you*, they're much like you said, just family members you haven't met yet and—"

"What are they to you?"

"Eh?"

Got her. "You said how those people looked to *me*, as though my perspective differed from your own. What are they to you? How do *you* see all those people?"

"I'll admit that my perspective does differ from yours. I'm looking at them through different eyes, older eyes. I'm an old woman now. I'm older than anyone you see walking around here. I tend to think like an old woman, as well. Being old, I naturally tend to see everyone as—"

"As your children."

"Ahh, call me an old fool, but yes," she guiltily replied.

Then she doesn't really *believe she's everyone's mother. Not literally.* Now that one element of the enigma had been solved, Sadie relaxed even more.

"You're hurting, aren't you, dear? You've recently experienced that plunge of love we mentioned, haven't you." It was more of a statement of fact than a question.

The words came as a shock. Her relaxed mood was short-lived. She felt her spine tense as though preparing to spring in self-defense.

"Excuse me?"

Ruby was busying herself with the pigeons. "Settle down, now," she told them. "There's enough for all of you. No need for all of that pushing and shoving. Let's not be rude to one another."

"Did you hear what I said?" Sadie asked.

"Oh, I did, indeed. May I ask why you became defensive?"

"Because . . . well, because . . ." Her shoulders slumped. "Because you're right. I have had a recent fender bender in that area. A major one. Love's been totaled."

The old one patiently listened to the details of the young antique dealer's shattered relationship. When the tale had ended, she offered an opinion. "I'm no expert in this department, mind you, but I've the feeling all is not lost. I think things are not as final as you believe them to be."

The opinion was met with a smirk. "Moving to Alaska is about as final as you can get," she replied. "Selling one's boat and hightailing it out of town sounds pretty final to me."

"Well, of course it does. Of course it sounds that way. At the time things are happening, they always feel set in stone. They always leave one with that sinking, sick feeling of finality. They leave one reeling with such nauseating dizziness that it's nearly impossible to unravel a single tangled thought."

"Yes! That's exactly how I felt! It's over, though. Finished."

The blue eyes drifted toward the pond's edge. She pointed to the girl who was having a grand time shuffling through the leaves, a line of ducks trailing from her heels. "She's playing mother duck," Ruby said with amusement.

Sadie had to admit that the sight served to be an uplifting pause in their serious conversation. "She loves animals. More than anything, she wants a puppy."

"So get her one."

"Her mother won't allow it. Says they ruin her precious carpets."

"And you're resentful."

"No. Not really resentful. I'm more disappointed that my sister makes her home a bigger priority than her daughter."

Silence.

Sadie thought it just as well that they not tamper with the lid of another Pandora's box by getting on the subject of Mira.

Ruby didn't dismiss it so easily. "She, too, is stuck down in that painful place at the bottom of the downward plunge. She treats her agony with a not so effective balm of denial."

Green eyes widened to stare into the blues. "Are you a psychiatrist, as well?"

"As what?"

Sadie's brows knit together. "What, as what? I don't follow."

"You asked me if I was a psychiatrist, as well. And I'm asking you, as well as what?"

As well as God! The very thought of voicing that ridiculous-sounding idea curled the corners of her lips. She chose another reply. "As well as someone who's willing to listen to a newly met relative's woes."

The woman's hands gleefully clapped together. "Oh, you are a *charm*, Sadie Brennan! I think I like you very much! You remember things I say!" The mass of silvery hair bent to touch the young woman's red tresses. The momentary touching of heads was the elder's way of saluting her park bench companion. "There's not been many I can say that about. My opinions and suggestions usually fall on deaf ears. It is refreshing to hear them taken to heart."

Sadie's smile widened. "What, are you in the habit of going around handing out advice? Are you known as the park bench analyst?"

Ruby feigned emotional injury and hung her head. "Now you're making fun of me. I've had some of that, as well."

"You can't be serious! I mean, you can't seriously believe I'm actually making fun of you. I was joking, Ruby. I was only joking. Surely, you must know that."

Ruby's sudden smile was met by a gentle jab to the arm.

"You were faking! You were pulling my leg! *You* were joking with *me!* You're good! You're *damn* good!"

"I better be. I've had a long time to perfect my style. Oh, granted, it took me a while, but I've learned a thing or two in my time. Folks get back what they give. They want jokes . . . jokes they get." And without missing a beat, she abruptly left the subject of herself and brought it back to Mira.

"Your sister was madly in love with her husband. She's hurting so bad that she's blind with the pain of it. The loss of the love of her life has made her turn from the face of love. Sadie, your sister's afraid to step back into love's aura. She's run off to hide herself behind a protective shield."

"But is that fair to Savannah? Is it fair to withhold her love like that? Run to such lengths as to sink every last ounce of her energy into her work and ignore her own blood? To not feel love for her daughter? Empathy for her?"

"She's not ignoring her daughter."

"Yes, she is," Sadie insisted. "I've seen it."

"You've seen peripherally. You've not seen *into* her heart. If you had, you couldn't bear the sight. She loves her daughter so much she can't stand it. She's afraid of losing her like she lost David. She's terrified of being forced to endure the pain that a second loss would surely bring. She's—"

Goosebumps covered the surface of Sadie's arms. Hair stood on end. "David?" she cut in after finding her voice. "Did I mention the name of Savannah's dad?"

The reply that wasn't an answer came like a bolt of lightning. "Well, I had to have heard it somewhere now, hadn't I? And whether or not you realize it, you're veering from the core of the issue. Stay focused, Sadie Brennan. Stay focused without thoughts that'll steal away your chance to reap some much-needed deeper understanding.

"Now, listen to me. You're very much like your sister. You, like her, have sunk all of your energies into your niece's problem instead of giving thought to your personal relationship and what happened to it."

"I haven't had time," came the quick defense.

One of Ruby's brows spoke for her. It arched high and poised without quiver at the apex.

"I honestly haven't," the younger woman reiterated with added emphasis. "My full attention needed to be with Savannah. If there was any way that I could help her I wanted to find it. She was so far into her shell that she even included me in her silent treatment."

"And you were hurt by that?"

"A little, at first. Then I realized that she had to include me in order for her to carry it off. You know, make it believable." Sadie, frustrated with her poor choice of words, tossed both handfuls of bread to the birds. "Ruby," she said, trying to begin again. "What I just said didn't come out right. Scratch all that. I didn't mean to imply that Savannah was faking the silent bit. I know it was real and that she had no control over it. What I meant to convey is that, well, if the truth of it be told, I was hoping that she'd respond better to me, that my presence would soften the shell she'd been emotionally crouching in. I came out here prepared to crouch inside with her if it would've been beneficial. God, I love her so much!" Her hands involuntarily made separate fists, nails cut into the palm's soft tissue. "I was ready to try anything!"

Ruby understood the younger's sense of frustration. "Those suffering from traumatically generated muteness aren't gifted with the pleasure of picking and choosing. A choice isn't offered to them. Therefore, no choice exists. The muteness, when it comes, is complete. Their muteness comes from a plunging fall into a bubbling pool of despair that sears one senseless. And when the hand of self-preservation gently drapes the cooling veil over their blistering wounds, the soul retreats to a place of tranquility to heal itself while immersing its savagely ravaged soul in meditation's cool, healing waters."

"You make it sound so grim," Sadie whispered.

"Not any more than it is. But it's that cooling veil that brings on the muteness, that lingering state of silence. After the healing, it's the veil that remains as a therapeutic shield from the world's harsh reality. And for these ones, the veil is perceived as being an essential part of life forever after because it's associated with the soul's defense against further injury. For these mute ones, it becomes a magical burka, if you will. It becomes imbued with magically protective powers. Only for these poor souls, there are no allowances for the eye openings. It's the way they prefer it. They can't see out, but more importantly, others can't see in."

"But it's not, is it? It's not really a forever-after essential."

"Perhaps not because, eventually, as the veil slips (and it always does) the mute ones discover—quite to their wonderment—that they can again dare to touch the world, to utter a weak, tentative sound, without experiencing the searing pain that was so cruelly burned into the memory."

Thinking. Thinking.

Waiting. Listening.

More thinking.

More listening.

The younger woman was first to break their shared silence. "I see what you mean about Mira and myself being so alike in this instance. In fact," she acknowledged, "all three of us are in the same place, wearing the concealing burkas."

Ruby slowly closed her eyes. The woman was focused. The sound of quacking pulled her away. When she opened them again, they twinkled to see the girl approaching the park bench. Pigeons scattered and took flight; some merely scrambled for ground safety. They looked like a sea of grey parting to make way for the child. Her miniature entourage, noisily bleating behind her, waddled this way and that while keeping their single file line in reasonable formation. The overall scene was an amusing sight.

"Look, Ruby," Savannah said, proudly holding up the empty bread wrapper. "The ducks ate it all, just like you said. They acted like hungry little piglets, too." She set her palms on the elder's lap and leaned in. "Do you know everything, Ruby? I think you do. Do you know absolutely everything about everything? Do ya? Huh, do ya?"

"Savannah," the aunt softly reminded, "where are your manners? It's impolite to get in someone's face like that. You were taught better than that. You're forgetting to respect the distance of another person's social comfort zone."

The light reprimand had no effect.

Without turning to look at her aunt or give her the courtesy of acknowledging her question, Savannah remained steadfast and sharply focused, just like she'd overheard Ruby say. After all, now was definitely not the time to care about the proper etiquette of those hoity-toity social graces. They were *way* stupid and tiring. This was definitely one of those exceptions her mother had taught her about.

"Well, Miss Ruby? *Do* ya know everything?"

The old one reached out to touch the child's hair. She made an unsuccessful attempt to tame a wild tress away from the sweet face. "Not being very cooperative, is it," she groaned.

"But, Miss Ruby . . ."

"Yes, dearie?"

"Aren't you going to answer my question? Are you going to ignore it like the grown-ups usually do?"

"Savannah!" Sadie warned.

"Oh my, child," Ruby finally said. "Every question is important, even important enough to deserve an answer. Of course I'm not going to ignore your question." But when she opened her mouth to respond, nothing came out.

"Miss Ruby?"

The old woman's entire face cracked into crinkles. So many wrinkles lined the face that it looked like a dried apple. A finger went to the front of her chin. She absently tapped at it.

"Oh my!" she muttered. "I'm so embarrassed. I truly am because I seem to have inadvertently misplaced the question! If it's not too much of a bother for one as bright as yourself, would you be so kind as to refresh this old memory?"

Without demonstrating a single sign of childish impatience, Savannah dutifully repeated her question. "Do you know everything about everything?"

The arthritic finger moved up to her lips. The voice was lowered. "If you lean in a tad closer, I'll tell you a secret."

A secret! That brought on the famous Nancy Drew adrenaline rush. She loved being invited into the inner circle of secrets. Expectantly, she leaned far forward.

The old one lowered her head to whisper in her ear. When she rested back against the bench, she winked.

Glowing with the revelation, Savannah conspiratorially winked back.

"Now," Ruby said, placing the last of the bread in the girl's hands, "you take this and see if you can't find some hungry little mouths to feed. I bet if you go park yourself under those trees over there, you'll have some takers before you can count to ten."

Savannah skipped off toward the trees while the two women watched. Soon they heard the count begin. At number eight, the pigeons began to greedily gather and the child scolded their rude push-and-shove behavior.

"It's so wonderful to hear her voice again," Sadie said. "It's like a miracle."

"Sometimes the power of love can make its effects seem like miracles. They're not, though. They're just love in action." She made a futile attempt to smooth down the long wisps of silver hair that burst from beneath the knitted hat like a flood of moonlight. "Some day I'm gonna chop this wild bushiness off," she complained. "Isn't it funny how we women have a love-hate relationship with our hair? One day we love how it looks, and the next morning we hate it and fall into a black mood for being caught in a bad hair day. I've come so close to lopping it off, I went as far as picking up the shears."

The woman beside her touched the elder's hair. "Oh, no, you don't want to do that. I think it's just beautiful. It's so striking. You don't see many women with hair that long, even younger ones. And the color is so . . . well, it's so unusual."

Ruby actually blushed. "Oh now, no need to go that far. No need to try to flatter an old lady. Grey is grey, Sadie Brennan. Grey is grey."

"Grey may be grey, Ruby, but silver is silver. Yours is definitely silver and it has a very attractive way of catching the light and making it glow like an aura. It's very eye-catching. I know you didn't ask my opinion, but I'm giving it just the same. Don't ever chop it off, no matter how tempted you are to be rid of it."

The blush deepened to rouge. "Oh, go on. Now you're making me downright embarrassed. We should get back to our discussion. You've had an epiphany, you know."

"I did?"

Ruby's eyes sparkled. "Oh, yes, ma'am. You realized that all three of you were wearing that worm veil. Arriving at that was a huge accomplishment and—"

"Wait a minute," Sadie said, shaking her head in puzzlement. "Worm veil?"

"Yes, that burkalike garment we were talking about. It's so strong and protective, it shields so completely, it's like being woven with silkworm threads." A brow arched. "You do know about silkworm threads, don't you?"

"Of course."

"So what I want to tell you, what I want you to also realize, is that those veils are slowly sliding off all of your heads. All three of you are allowing the veils to part. Each one of you is testing the waters of reality and gaining the courage to cautiously peek out from behind your barriers. And that, Sadie Brennan, is caused by love. That is one of those miracles of love."

The younger woman was confused by the elder's words. "If you're saying that Mira's going to change—soften—I'm not sure I'd be willing to take that to the bank. I just haven't seen any indications of that happening."

Ruby's eyes narrowed. "Ohhh," she sang, "the softening has to first begin in the mind, in the thought process, in here, as well," she emphasized by touching the cable knit sweater at her chest. "This is where it all begins, you see. And that's not always evident to others."

"She hates me," came the blurted statement. "Mira hates my intrusion into her perfectly ordered life. I disrupt her routine. Because of something Savannah said, she thinks I've brought discord and mayhem into her household."

The old one's veined hand reached over to alight on the younger's. "I reckon you've got things a bit twisted up in that regard. Love and hatred for the same person can't dwell in one heart. Your sister, deep down inside, loves you. And since she loves you, it's impossible for her to hate you, as well."

"No. No, I don't have things twisted. She really does hate me. She barely tolerates me in her house."

Ruby's eyes flared. "Yes! You've nailed it!"

Sadie recoiled with a frown. She had no clue as to why the woman had suddenly brightened like a power surge. "Nailed what? What did I say?"

"There's your answer! You said that your sister barely tolerates you in her house. Sadie, you've confused the emotion of hate with intolerance! Your sister loves you, yet sometimes finds you intolerable! Don't you see? They're two entirely different attitudes."

Silence. Sadie's gaze drifted over to the trees where her niece was carefully doling out small bits of bread to her eager audience. She was thinking on Ruby's words.

Meanwhile, the elder blew on the idea's ember to keep it going. "There's no denying that the world's full of hatred, Sadie. And a good deal of it has been born of intolerance, but they're still not the same.

Intolerance is associated with those things we believe we cannot bear, while hatred is the act of despising. Intolerance is grey. Hatred, as black as the bowels of a coal mine. Grey has a chance. Black turns its back on the very idea of that chance to change. It arbitrarily rejects it. It rejects it because it likes being black.

"Sadie, dear, your sister's merely in a stage which projects the sense of an emotional hardness. A phase of affected intolerance for anything and anyone who may have the slightest potential for cracking her protective shell—of tugging on that veil. Don't you see, it's simply an attempt to insulate herself from further pain. Oh no, she surely does not feel hatred for you. If anything she's outwardly showing intolerance because she's afraid of you. Afraid of what damage your presence in the house may do to her shield. When someone is that defensive, they don't want to be near anyone who could rekindle their suppressed emotional sensitivity. And nothing does that more than the feelings of love."

Every word carried the ring of truth. The ring was an uplifting sound, clear and true. "You make it all seem so simple."

"That's because it is. It's not me who's doing that. The situation itself is simple. Your sister's intolerance will fade as her willingness to feel love again gains its strength. And you, Sadie Brennan, the same goes for you when you find the courage—and will—to look at your other situation."

"My other situation?"

The woman's eyes closed, then slowly opened. "Your young man. Like I said before, all is not lost in that regard. Hope's heart still has a beat. Though it's beating slowly, it means that there's still hope for you two."

She's feeling sorry for me. She's trying to give me encouragement. "I don't want to go there. I appreciate your concern, but there's nothing to be gained by discussing the situation. You don't need to feel sorry for me because I've already resigned myself to the fact that it's over."

"That's not a fact," Ruby slipped in, "however, it's never wise to lock a door that's been closed. Perhaps you could find a way to slide the bolt back? Just in case?"

No response came.

"We cross bridges as we come to them. In the same vein, we shouldn't ever put a torch to them after our passing. We might unexpectedly need to travel back over them at some point. Mark my words, Sadie Brennan, you can close all the doors you want, but remember that one day you may want to leave them ajar. Leave those locks alone."

At that point, Savannah came running up to the two women. "Bread's all gone. I'm hungry. Are we going to go have lunch somewhere?" She turned to the old one. "Are you hungry too, Miss Ruby? Have you ever been to a country club? We could take you there. They have really good food. Wanna come with us?"

The child's exuberance tickled the woman. She laughed. "Savannah, dear, do I look like someone who frequents country clubs?" Her hands went up, then slapped her lap. "Do these frumpy clothes look like they have those spiffy, high-couture labels on them? Why, if I came traipsing in there with you everyone would be aghast. Their jaws would drop to the floor. I'm afraid I'd be a terrible embarrassment to you." Her eyes lowered to indicate her eccentric clothing. "I'm not exactly high society caliber."

No indeed, Sadie thought, *you're miles* above *those prudes who look down their noses at everyone beneath their imaginary pedestals.*

The girl's pleading expression shot to her aunt. "We don't care, do we, Aunt Sadie. Ruby wouldn't embarrass us, would she. She's just fine . . . just the way she is." Then, with eyes squeezed tight with the effort of coercion, she turned her head to the elder and pulled on her hand. "Please, Ruby. Pul-eeeze come with us?"

More and more, Sadie was liking the picture Ruby had painted. The idea was an attractive one. She could imagine the stir they'd cause walking in with the old one in her army coat and hiking boots. With her long, wild silver hair topped by the gaudy, dime-store pin in her hat, Ruby would cause more than a stir. It'd be a full-blown earthquake that rumbled through the club with aftershocks lasting till doomsday. What a deliciously novel idea. Oh yes, she was liking the image very much, indeed.

"We'd be honored to have you as our guest for lunch," Sadie smiled.

A side glance came from the old woman. Twin sparkles flared from the depths of her deep blues. She knew what game Sadie was offering to play with her sister's ta-ta crowd. She knew because she also liked to make waves once in a while. She liked to "accidentally" tip over a pail of milk on occasion. She liked to dip her hands in a bit of mischievousness and shake things up. It kept life so much more interesting, refreshing. So, feeling rather devilish, Ruby responded with an impish grin.

"Well, then, what are we all waiting for? Let's go!"

By the time the two rabble-rousers walked through the kitchen door, Greta was beside herself. She immediately got in Sadie's face. "You've both done it now," she said, voicing her worry. "That phone's been ringing off the wall since three o'clock! People have been looking for Mira. They're hotter than angry hornets!" Shaking her head and wringing her hands, she sighed. "Sadie? You're lucky Mira's not going to be home until ten in the morning because that's when all hell's going to break loose around here."

The housekeeper then lowered her head to address the shorter of the two culprits.

"And you, little missy. I was not thrilled to read that note you left on your pillow! You snuck out while your aunt and I were talking over breakfast. You willfully disobeyed your mother. You can expect to get a good tongue-lashing in the morning just like your auntie here. There's no way around it. If you two hadn't picked the club to make your little statement of rebellion in, I could've hidden the fact that you'd gone out with her. But no, you had to go someplace where everyone knows you're Mira's daughter. You did it now, missy. Oh my, how you've done it now!"

Sadie felt sorry for the flustered woman. "It'll be okay, Greta," she said in an attempt to soothe the harried housekeeper. "Nothing's going to happen tonight. And we'll handle tomorrow when it comes. Who knows," she added, "maybe Mira won't even care."

"She'll care about her image until hell freezes over," Greta huffed. "You're reaching for a slice of that pie in the sky if you think there's a ghost of a chance she won't care."

"Well, whatever," she said, with a wink down at the girl. "We'll face the music in the morning, won't we, honey?"

Savannah dramatized one big nod as if to add an exclamation point to her aunt's words. Then, feeling full of a new sense of accomplishment, she skipped from the room. "Gonna play computer games," she called back from the hallway.

Sadie looked to Greta and raised a brow. "See? All's well."

The housekeeper was already moving toward the sink to finish washing vegetables. She quietly mumbled while shaking her head.

The soft touch of arms about her didn't do much to pare away any of her anxiety.

"It'll be okay, Greta. It really will. Have I told you today that I love you?"

"Oh, Sadie . . ." the woman tiredly sighed.

"I love you, Greta. I love you and Josef so much. Sometimes things have to get worse before they get better. That's how some things have to work. Sometimes good comes from intolerance. What do you want to bet that something good comes for Mira after her tirade in the morning?"

"Dreamer," Greta said beneath her breath.

"I heard that. Maybe so. But I've left the door ajar just in case."

The lightning speed motion of the vegetable peeler paused. "Door ajar? What door ajar? What intolerance? Where? God above, I haven't the foggiest notion as to what you're talking about. How many cocktails did you say you and your guest had at the club?"

Laughter broke out. "That's the beauty of it. None!" she said, planting a kiss on the woman's cheek. "I'm going up and call Tina. She's probably tripled her meditation Oms and doubled the incense trying to maintain her patience."

Within three minutes, she'd covered the hallway stairs two at a time and had made her connection to Maine.

"You're breathless," said Tina. "Is anything wrong?"

"Far from it. I'm out of breath because I just scaled the stairs in record time."

"Hope Mira didn't see you do that. Isn't that one of her big bugaboos? Not socially acceptable?"

Sadie had so much to say, her heart was pounding. She began to pace. "She left early this morning and won't be back until mid-morning tomorrow when the shit hits the fan."

"Oh, sweet Goddess Above, spare me."

"Well, okay. What've *you* been up—"

"No! No, I didn't mean that. Back up, girlfriend! Fill me in!" And in an effort to concentrate as hard as she could on everything Sadie had to say, she kept her interruptions down to a minimum. At certain points during the narrative, she had chills ripple up her spine. Certain incidents in the story brought a sudden flush to her cheeks, a sure sign that she'd just heard something bearing monumental proportions.

"Well?" Sadie concluded. "What's your first impression of every-thing? What's your insightful analysis?"

Silence.

Waiting.

Thinking. Processing.

"Helloooo. Anybody there?"

"Shhhh!" Tina said, indicating that she wasn't quite done.

The waiting woman flung off her shoes and padded over to the window. Drawing aside the damask drapery, she looked down into the garden and watched Josef putter among the chrysanthemums. The man had the greenest thumb she'd ever seen. He was born with the knack.

"Okay," came the voice on the other end of the line. "I could take each incident individually or just give you an overall summation. Your call."

"Let's go with the bottom line. I don't want to be at this all night."

"Okay, then. It's everything I thought it was. For whatever reason, you got yourself the real McCoy. Or maybe I should say that for what-ever reason, the real McCoy's got you. Doesn't really matter which way you want to see it. Either way I only have one piece of advice."

"And that is . . ."

"Big breakthroughs are waiting around the corner. For everyone involved. Keep some Dramamine handy, girlfriend. Hold onto your hat because you're all about to have the ride of your lives."

"Around the corner? As in tomorrow?"

Tina blew out a sigh of exasperation. "Get a clue. You've all been drawn to this ride already. You're all together in the coaster car and it's making its slow climb up the track to the highest peak. If you were more psychically open, you'd be hearing the clicking of the wheels on the track. Click. Click. Click. Anyway, I believe that it's going to crest and make the long plunge tomorrow. That'll be the breaker that comes down like a hammer and shatters the—"

"Wait a minute. Hold on. What breaker? Hammer?"

"The *breaker!* The breaker for intolerance. The breaker of hard shells. Sadie," the voice reminded, "nothing can be rebuilt unless the former structure has been first broken down and carted away. Rebuilding can only be done on a clear plot."

Sadie noticed Savannah peer around the doorway. "Right," she said. "Look, I have to go. A certain little girl just came into my room.

I think she's looking for a video game partner to beat. We'll talk, okay?"

"Sure. Just remember to take my suggestion seriously."

"Your suggestion?"

"Yeah. Keep the Dramamine handy. You might forget about the hat, though. Yeah, scrap the hat altogether. Give my love to the little one. See ya."

When Sadie hung up the phone, Savannah moved further into the room. "Aunt Sadie?"

"Hi, sugar. You come to lure me to your computer again?"

The girl's mass of auburn hair went from side to side. "No. Not unless you want to come and play for a while. I came to tell you something."

Sadie knelt before the girl. "What is it, honey?"

Their eyes locked. "You really *did* hit that car today."

Thirteen

Halloween

The aroma of potatoes O'Brien and country gravy snaked up the hallway stairs. Halfway down, Sadie and Savannah simultaneously caught the tempting scent. Stomachs growling, they looked at one another.

"Race you to the table," Sadie challenged.

The girl thumped the rest of the way down the stairs, leaving her aunt in the dust. "I won! I won!" the aunt heard her niece announce from below.

Once in the kitchen, Sadie went over to the stove and peered over Greta's shoulder. "Smells great," she said, watching the housekeeper flip the Western omelets. "I'm going to be ten pounds heavier by the time I head back home."

The housekeeper snickered. "You could use ten pounds. Do you good."

"I'm hungry," came the small voice. "I could eat three omelets!"

Sadie caught the elder's eye. In a low voice that was meant to be masked by the sizzle of bacon, she asked, "Have we heard from the lady of the house yet?"

Attending to food preparations while carrying on a conversation was one of Greta's skills. She picked up the long-handled wooden spoon and stirred the gravy. "I don't know what's going on. She returned earlier than expected, then asked me to turn the ringer off of every phone except the one in your bedroom. That one's different, you have your own private number. Anyway, she said all the calls were tiring."

"That's it? No ranting tirade?" Surprised, Sadie raised her eyebrows. "No stamping of the feet? Nothing smashed?"

Greta's head shook. "Like I said, I don't know what's going on. After she took the first few angry calls, she announced that she didn't want to be bothered with any more of them. That's when she asked me to shut off every one. It's not like her to cut herself off from business access like that. Don't believe she's ever done that before."

Sadie took over the stirring while the housekeeper turned the bacon. "It's not only not like her, it's almost scary for her to react so calmly. She didn't blow a gasket when she found out about our little club caper?"

"Didn't even raise an eyebrow. Handled the calls with no more emotion than if she'd been making a nail salon appointment. Oddest thing I've ever seen."

"Good morning, everyone!" came the chipper voice from the doorway. And before anyone could answer, Mira strode over to her daughter, who was seated at the table. "Ready for the big night?" she asked.

The girl blessed her mother with a big smile and nodded. "Oh, yes! Do you want to come with us?"

Fighting to hold back tears of joy over hearing her daughter's voice again, Mira forced a laugh. "I think your auntie's really looking forward to taking you trick-or-treating. It's not like she's here every year to do that, you know. What are you going as?"

"It's a secret, Mama. Greta and Josef helped me with it. It's so cool! You'll have to wait until tonight!"

"All right, honey. I should be home for dinner." Then she looked to Greta. "Then again, I suppose you'll be having an early dinner so she can be out the door as soon as it's dark."

Sliding the omelets onto plates and handing them to Sadie, Greta agreed that an early meal was in order for tonight.

"Well," Mira said to the girl, "I'll try to get away early so I can at least see you two off." She poured coffee for the adults and a tall glass of orange juice for her daughter.

Five steaming plates were set before the five people seated at the Thursday morning breakfast table. For once it appeared as though a normal breakfast gathering was actually going to take place. And while the mother found assorted subject matters to talk about, the other three adults wondered when the other shoe was going to drop. Even while Josef talked about his latest woodworking project and Greta detailed her new streusel recipe, they eyed one another with a shared sense of puzzlement. Why hadn't Mira addressed the club incident? Why was she ignoring the matter?

When the meal concluded and the busyness of cleanup was about finished, Sadie excused herself to run upstairs for her wallet. As she left, she heard Savannah excitedly begin to tell her mother about the day she and her aunt had spent at the museum. As Sadie hit the steps, the child's voice was a nonstop narration critiquing the famous paintings. A smile broke out to brighten her face to think of all the things Savannah had to share now that they were no longer locked up behind her silence. She was out of earshot when the girl, in her eagerness to expound on her museum visit, decided to share everything.

"And guess what else, Mama?"

"What, honey bun?"

"God has a vagina!"

Time stood still.

"SADE-EEEEEE!"

The chilling scream froze her in midstep at the landing. Racing back down the stairs, she reached the kitchen to set eyes on a still-life tableau.

Greta and Josef were standing immobile at the sink, their expressions locked in that familiar here-it-comes mask.

Savannah, hunched down in her seat, had the paralyzing look of guilt etched on her face.

Mira, looming like the Hulk with arms stiff at her sides and hands clenching and unclenching, glared death rays at the newcomer.

"What? What's the matter?" Sadie breathlessly asked.

The Hulk shifted her eyes to the child. "Go to your room."

The tone of her mother's voice left no room for argument. It'd crackled like winter pond ice on a frigid morning. And as Savannah neared the doorway, she gave her aunt an apologetic look. "I'm sorry," she whispered, as she hung her head and inched past the woman.

Sadie moved into the room. "What's going on? What's this all about?"

Temples throbbing, Mira stared at her sister. "Leave us," she hissed at the housekeeper and her husband.

Alone now, Sadie was met by blazing eyes meant to scorch.

When the mouth beneath the fiery orbs moved, sound came out in a controlled whisper. "Do you have any idea what my daughter just said to me?"

"How am I supposed to know that when I was halfway up the stairs?"

"Then I'll tell you. She said that God has a vagina. A *vagina*. Would you have any—"

Sadie burst out laughing.

Aghast at the unexpected reaction, Mira recoiled. "You obviously think that's hilarious. Well, it's not."

Mira's seriousness pushed her sister further into hilarity. For whatever reason, seeing the shocked look on her sister's face struck her as being so funny she reacted as though she were being tickled. Maybe it was the sudden release of pent-up tension, but she couldn't seem to curb the laughter.

"Stop it! Listen to you! You sound like an idiot laughing at something that's not even funny! Pull yourself together!"

Sadie slowed long enough to catch her breath. She wiped the tears from her eyes and looked at her sister. The confusion wrinkling Mira's countenance brought on another round of guffaws.

"Stop! Stop it! Get a grip!" Mira shouted.

Her sister's hilarity began to wind down. "Ohhh, God," Sadie groaned, sinking into a chair. "I don't know when something struck me so funny."

Mira towered over her. "Funny! What in the Sam Hill's got into you that you think what Savannah said was funny? It's blasphemous! It's downright heretical!"

The younger sister flopped her hand in the air. "Oh, settle down. It is not."

The standing sister was outraged. "You think the same thing?

How dare you put such crazy ideas in my daughter's head? How *dare* you fill her head with a bunch of—"

Sadie mumbled something.

"What? What did you say?"

"If you'd stop ranting for a second you could hear what I'm trying to say. I said, Savannah didn't hear that from me."

"Well, then, who did she hear it from?"

They'd come to a point where Sadie could end the confrontation by simply saying that Savannah had heard it from a bag lady on the street, a bag lady who was nuttier than a holiday fruitcake. But that answer didn't set well. It left a twinge of guilt, of maligning. Instead of diffusing the explosive situation by blaming a loony bag lady, the look on Mira's face had the opposite effect: it tweaked her sense of integrity, spurring her to side with the greater truth. She shifted to a defensive position. Her answer, when it came, was the only one she couldn't resist giving. "She got it straight from the horse's mouth."

Mira flung her arms in the air. "Oh, that's rich, Sadie. That's real cute. Now you're trying to make me believe that she got it from God, that God Himself told her."

"Herself," Sadie corrected. "God *Her*self."

The woman in the Chanel suit was so outraged her face went red. Her jaw clenched. "You know what, Sadie? You're insane. You've finally gone around the bend, haven't you.

"When I got up this morning I vowed to ignore your little prank at the club. For Savannah's sake, I fully intended to let it ride and not even acknowledge it. But thanks to your continued questionable behavior, your poor judgment, I can no longer do that.

"Too many issues are piling up, Sadie. Not only did you blatantly disregard my wishes yesterday about Savannah never going out with you again, you've recklessly dragged her through God knows what sort of unhealthy situations where she's picking up outrageous ideas and, obviously, hobnobbing with unsavory elements."

That last went too far. "Since when does clothing define one's character?"

Mira smirked with smugness. "Anyone with an ounce of pride wouldn't show their face at a country club wearing an army coat!"

"That lady doesn't have one."

"Are you trying to tell me she didn't strut into the club wearing a ragged army coat?"

"No. I'm trying to tell you that Ruby doesn't have an ounce of *pride*."

"Well! That's rather obvious, isn't it? Ruby? Should I assume that that's supposed to be her name?"

The seated woman nodded.

"Ruby what? What's the rest of it?"

"Just Ruby."

"How perfectly theatrical. How completely bourgeois. No, it rings of something less than that, doesn't it? Ruby. Ru-beee," she sarcastically repeated, letting the distasteful word roll off her tongue. "Sounds like a name a stripper would call herself."

Sadie abruptly stood. "I've heard enough. You couldn't hold a cand—"

"You haven't begun to hear enough of what I've got to say, little sister."

A visual of a roller coaster making its death-plunge flashed on the screen of Sadie's mind. *This is all part of it. This is part of the ride we're all on. I can't bail out. I'm in it until the ride's over.* She was determined to hold on. She sat. With a hand gesture, she invited her sibling to do the same.

The sibling declined.

A second image insinuated itself. Mira standing before the witness stand while cleverly cross-examining a trembling witness. Mira standing in front of the judge's bench. Mira standing, hands gripping the rail of the jury box, delivering her dramatic closing statements. Mira had to remain standing now. It was how she carried the floor, how she did her best thinking. The stance was in her blood. It was essential for bolstering her sense of control.

"Sadie," she began, "ever since you arrived, your behavior here has been nothing short of reprehensible. There's no other word to describe it. Aside from the obvious fact that you were the inspiration for the break in Savannah's long-held silence, I'd be remiss not to—"

"Ruby was."

"Excuse me? I wasn't finished. Are you going to keep interrupting me?"

"I realize you weren't finished. As long as you're determined to detail my crimes, you probably should stick with the facts. You're a stickler for sticking with the facts, aren't you? So you need to know that it was *Ruby* who inspired Savannah to speak. That and the fact that your daughter *loved* you so much that she courageously overcame her fear of speaking so she could *share* Ruby with you. I had nothing to do with it. It was Ruby's presence and Savannah's love that broke her silence. The glory's all theirs."

"Oh, you see glory in any of this?"

"You don't?"

Mira spewed out a mocking chuckle. "Hardly."

"Your daughter's love isn't a glorious thing to behold?"

"Let's leave my daughter's love out of this, shall we? It has no bearing on anything."

Sadie looked off toward an imaginary judge. "Permission to prove relevance, Your Honor! Permission granted!" Then her green eyes locked on her sister's mahogany ones. "Savannah's love is exhibit number one on the evidence table. Without that love for you she never would've felt the compulsion to tell you about Ruby. Your courtroom tricks are slipping. Your suave cleverness has failed you if you ignore that critical piece of evidence; if you don't look at it, touch it, recognize all that it represents. Without that, you've no case. Without that, a prime element remains elusive to you."

Again, the attorney sarcastically cackled. "No case? Don't be ridiculous."

Sadie addressed the spectral judge. "Your Honor, if it please the court, may I approach the bench? Granted? Why, thank you, Your Honor. I move to dismiss this case on the grounds of incompetence. The prosecutor refuses to acknowledge the most essential piece of evidence. Without it there is no case."

Mira rolled her eyes. "Incompetence? Maybe a mistrial. Maybe a need to replace the trying attorney, but certainly not incompetence. You need to take Law 101. It's that or you've been watching far too many of those absurd courtroom dramatic series. They're so fatuous they're beyond laughable. They're about as inane as you can get." Her mouth twisted into a smirk, then she scoffed, "Oh, God, how pathetic."

"Your courtroom behavior's what's pathetic. Perhaps it's you who needs the refresher course because you're in denial over the most basic ingredient of any criminal trial."

"Pray tell."

"Motive. Savannah's love for you was the singular motive behind her breakthrough. You can't continue with your mock trial without looking at it, without touching it."

"The motivation was her love for *you*. Not me."

"Sorry, but the facts don't support that. Why didn't she speak to me first? Why, out of everyone in this house, did she choose you to speak to?"

Mira's brow shot up. "If memory serves, Greta and Josef were there as well."

"But it was *your* presence that brought it about. *You* were the one she was reaching out to. You were the target of her love, her motive."

Mira, recognizing the signs of losing control over the situation, felt the beginnings of panic trying to take hold. This was a subject she wasn't ready to get near. Clawing for a way out, she spun to face the sink. When she turned back, she swerved the focus of the conversation off course with a diversionary tactic. Her mistake was attempting to conclude the former discussion by stating that they were wasting time on an issue that wasn't germane. As soon as the statement was made, she knew that her own words lacked conviction. Without acknowledging the misstep, she quickly introduced the replacement issue.

"What's on trial here is your behavior, dear sister. So let's dispense with extraneous issues and not get sidetracked. As a matter of fact, this isn't even a trial. As it turns out, it is a competency hearing. Yours. And the growing evidence against you is piling up faster than a bachelor's dirty dishes.

"First it was your foolhardy trip into South Chicago. That was rich, Sadie. That, I believe, was the most mindless and reckless thing you've ever done. That alone would cause anyone to question your sanity. Then, out of the blue, my daughter speaks for the first time in months. And what does she say? She says she saw *God!* She's going around whispering, 'I saw God!' It makes me cringe every time I hear her say that. Sadie, it's wrong. It's sick! And it's got to stop!

"Oh," Mira arrogantly huffed on, "but that's just the tip of the garbage heap. My daughter then chooses to blatantly disobey me so she can be with you. She's always been a good kid. She's always been the model child . . . until you arrived and poisoned her mind with these delirious God ideas!

"And, as if that's not damning enough, you walk into the club bold as you please, with . . . with someone who looks like a scruffy bag lady off the street! Have you any idea how humiliating that was for me? Well, yes," she smirked, "you probably have a very good idea, don't you. And now, to top it all off, now my daughter's somehow got the cockamamie impression that God's a woman, that she has a . . . Sadie! What in the hell are you doing to my child?"

"I'm not doing anything. She heard those things from Ruby. When we were—"

"Then keep her the hell *away* from that flea-bitten miscreant! Do you hear me? Keep her the *hell* away from her!"

Desperately trying to keep the situation from flaring up into an out-of-control blaze, Sadie spoke softly. Deliberately.

"Ruby's not anything like you think. You're assuming that her clothing reflects what's inside. I thought attorneys never made assumptions. She may look like a bag lady, but she's not. She's highly intelligent, extremely learned. We've seen—Savannah and I have seen her do things we can't explain. Savannah's quite taken with her. We seem to run into her wherever we go and have observed her do some amaz—"

"Enough! I can't stand hearing you talk nonsense! It's gibberish! Do you hear me? Gibberish! You need some help, Sadie! Never mind keeping Savannah away from that bedraggled vagrant, *you* stay the hell away from my daughter until I see some proof that you've gotten serious professional help! You either do that or go pack your bags right now and head back to Maine! That's your choice. You've been driven to distraction from your breakup with Paul. You're delirious and delusional. You need to—"

The sound of the chair scraping over the floor was the only response the younger sister had made. She also had had enough. Mira had crossed the line. She'd gone too far. If she was determined to remain in denial over the real situation with her daughter, keeping the conversation going was nothing more than an effort wasted on futility. It was too much to hope for.

The kitchen door slammed.

The stunned prosecutor was left standing in a courtroom of one. By the time she'd made it to the door, the van's engine revved. "Do you hear me, Sadie?" Mira shouted over the squealing tires. "Get some help or go home!"

As the van pulled away, Mira's eyes rounded with shock to see a small face peer out at her from the vehicle's back window. She made an effort to holler her daughter's name, but her stunned state was unable to produce anything more than a feeble whisper. "Savannah!"

Returning to the kitchen, she closed the door and leaned against it. "Oh, Savannah, what's happening to all of us?"

The slow-cruising commercial van drew curious glances from the residents of the middle-class neighborhood. Mothers paused their lawn raking chore to eye the passing vehicle, then quickly double-checked on the whereabouts of their toddlers.

The driver was unaware she was drawing attention to herself. She saw the world through a blur of tears. She blinked, then swiped at her eyes to clear them. The initial search of the Commons park came up empty. Not knowing where else to go, she returned to the neighborhood where she'd picked up Ruby yesterday. The van continued to draw suspicion as it prowled past the well-kept homes.

Suddenly Sadie hit the brakes. A man was standing between the parked cars and waving his arms. He was motioning her to pull over.

She did.

"Excuse me, miss, but my wife noticed that this is the third time you've gone by the house. Are you looking for a particular address?"

"I, ahhhh. I . . . no. I was looking for someone. I, ahhh . . ."

He noticed that she'd been crying. "Is there anything I can do for you?"

"No, thank you. I think maybe I need to go have a cup of coffee and do some thinking. I appreciate your concern."

"You sure you're okay, ma'am?"

"I will be. Please tell your wife I apologize if I caused her concern. I never meant to alarm anyone, but I understand. These days you can't be too careful, especially when you have small children."

The man was understanding. "We all have those bad days that drive us from home, wanting nothing more than to just randomly cruise around while we try to sort things out." He winked. "I've been there myself a time or two. Say," he added as an afterthought, "if you're serious about getting that cup of coffee, there's a family-owned café up that way." He pointed straight ahead. "You keep going on this street until you come to Hemlock Lane, where you'll want to make a right. Go down four blocks to Mulholland Drive. You can't miss it. It's right on the corner. Folks around here make it their gathering place. It's mighty popular."

"Thank you very much. That sounds like what I need right about now."

He tapped her door. "Hope things will be looking up for you soon. These phases don't normally hang on for long."

After following the simple directions, Sadie drove past the café a couple of times before finding a place to park. Walking to the back of the vehicle, she cracked open one of the cargo doors. "I'm getting something to drink, wanna come?"

"You knew."

"Let's just say that, to begin with, the probability for it was fairly high. Don't go thinking I'm psychic. It was one of those no-brainers. On top of that, your mom also knows. Looking out the back window when I pulled away wasn't the best move you've ever made."

The child sheepishly crawled out. "Are you mad at me?"

"Not in the least. How could I be after that fiasco in the kitchen? I've no doubt that you were eavesdropping and heard every word." Without waiting for confirmation from the girl, the woman turned on her heels and headed for the small restaurant.

As they entered, the rich aroma of freshly ground beans held soothing promise. The two wove their way around the crowded tables. They headed straight to the counter, where they placed an order for hot cocoa with marshmallows and an espresso in a regular cup.

While they waited, Savannah tentatively nudged her aunt. "I got us in a mess of trouble, didn't I?"

The aunt looked down. Lips pursed, then settled into a wry smile. "Nope. We already were, sweetie. Seems to me that once you fall in a mud puddle the damage has already been done. Might as well play in it."

Hot drinks in hand, the child and her aunt looked about for an empty table.

"Sadie! Sadie Brennan and Savannah! Over here!"

"Who on earth . . . ?" she whispered, turning to the outburst. Face flushed when her sights fell on the sparkle off the red hat.

Savannah beamed.

"Ruby!" Sadie acknowledged with a nod. "We'll be right over!" *How coincidental is this?* And after they'd again wound their way through the crowd, they slid into the vacant chairs at Ruby's table. "How nice to see you here," Sadie exclaimed. "I truly mean it. Do you come here often?"

"Do you?"

"No, it's my first time."

Childlike, Ruby clapped her hands in an unabashed show of delight. "Mine, as well! I'd spent the night at Ida's again. A nice neighborhood man gave me directions when I told him I was looking for a place to sit with a relaxing cup of coffee."

"That man didn't happen to be wearing a Chicago Bears jacket, did he?"

The grey eyes sparked to blue. "Why, yes! Do you know him?"

"Not really, but . . . well, to keep it short, he pointed me in this direction. Small world, isn't it?"

"Oh, my dear, you've no idea how small this little world is." Her finger jabbed the air. "Merely a pinpoint in the cosmos. A tiny dot. A hiccup, if you will. Just a hiccup." Elfin eyes shifted to the girl. The twinkling orbs playfully narrowed with mischief. "The world's no more than a wee fledgling with its downy feathers barely dry," she whispered.

The child giggled. "Nahhh, no way. Everyone knows a fledgling can't be billions of years old."

The old one glanced about the room, then conspiratorially leaned closer. "Oh, but it can!" she whispered. "It can, indeed! It can when it's compared to its elders that are *trillions* of years old. *Older*, even."

The girl's eyes widened in wonder as they fixed on her aunt's.

The aunt grinned. "Hard to comprehend, huh?"

Savannah nodded.

Sadie switched her attention to the elder. "The concept's too massive in scope. It's one of those brainteasers that drive people nuts trying to think about it. It's like trying to think about the idea that God always existed. You know, one of those things that gets people's thoughts tied in knots. It's too esoteric for my little brain to sort out." She chuckled. "I have a hard enough time keeping events in my own life from becoming hopelessly tangled. This morning certainly didn't help matters, either."

Silver eyebrows knit in question as the elder gave the child a quick look before returning to settle on the aunt. "This morning?"

"Ohhh, it's my sister," Sadie sighed, not sure she should be getting into the issue. "She and I had a terrible row at breakfast. We don't ever seem to see eye-to-eye on anything anymore."

"Is it an act of betrayal for a priest to believe in reincarnation?"

Taken aback by the woman's seemingly unrelated question, Sadie's back stiffened. "What? Where'd that come from?"

"Is that your answer? Are two questions your answer?"

"No. Of course not." Then she gave greater thought to the woman's question. She spent several minutes thinking about it. Finally, "Is this one of those trick questions?"

"They're a waste of precious time. I don't cotton to those. No need for trick questions, they just cause unnecessary confusion."

"Okayyyy. So no trick question," she confirmed, preparing to slip on her thinking cap. "Before I answer I have another question . . . for clarification."

"Shoot."

"Do you specifically mean 'betrayal' or would 'heretical' be better suited? I'm having a bit of difficulty with the betrayal word. It doesn't seem to me that it accurately fits in with the rest of the issue."

"It fits. Betrayal can better be associated with a broader scope of societal aspects. I'm assuming you want to replace it with heresy?"

"Yes."

The mass of silver hair shook. "No, no. Heresy generally confines itself to the spiritual realm only. You're a bright woman. You do see the difference, don't you?"

"I do," Sadie admitted before taking a couple sips of her dark brew. And while she did her thinking, her eyes involuntarily scanned Ruby's clothing.

Today was a flannel shirt day. It was a day for two flannel shirts of clashing plaid patterns, a blue and yellow dress Campbell topped by a bright red buffalo plaid. Beneath the opened army coat, the tails of the shirts hung free over the waist of a long woolen skirt that brushed the tops of white Nike running shoes.

Off to one side of the table, the flat flowered satchel was neatly folded over on itself. Seeing it close up, Sadie noted that the wooden handle was marred by years of use; scratches and wear patches had damaged the varnish that was still visible on the ends. It needed refinishing. The fabric itself looked brand new.

Finally her answer was ready to deliver. It came in the form of a question. Just one, this time.

"Is there a mountain separating the dove and the eagle? The peacemaker and the activist?"

Ruby squealed with joy and again clapped her hands. "I love it! Oh, I love it! That was absolutely exquisite! So, your answer is no."

Sadie couldn't help but beam over the elder's spontaneous reaction. "Right, it's no. It's not a betrayal. And there's no mountain, either. Only narrow-band opinion and single-dimensional perspectives see betrayal and the mountain."

"And why is that, do you think?" the old one eagerly shot back.

Head turning back and forth like someone watching a tennis match, Savannah tried to keep up with the baffling conversation. "Huh?" she muttered to no one in particular.

Her aunt slowed down the pace when she gave the woman across from her a sideways grin. "Something to do with one's right to think for herself. Maybe one's right to think outside the box, explore new ideas, and wrap her mind around innovative concepts." The grin widened. "You'll have to take it from there."

The senior's face lit up as she bent over the table to quietly deliver her answer. "You're right, but there's more. It's because we tend to shape our absolutes in lopsided configurations—always asymmetrical! They've got no balance! They've got no life! How can they when the basic *potential* for possibilities is *imprisoned* by preconceived notions of such rigid and unyielding *limitations?*"

Savannah's face crinkled in puzzlement. *Huh? What'd you say?*

The old one's nimble mind both fascinated and amused her adult listener. Sadie's mind replayed the meaningful statement. *The potential for possibilities imprisoned by preconceived notions of rigid limitations.* Yes, she thought, just like Mira's rigid thinking. Just like her refusal to be open to uncommon possibilities. How utterly refreshing it was to have an intelligent conversation that wasn't cluttered with emotional entanglements or psychological roadblocks. No games. Just straightforward discussion. Sadie rested her forearms on the table and released a long sigh. As she looked her coffee partner in the eye, the widening smile deepened her dimples.

"It's so refreshing to talk to you. Do you know that you're easy to talk to? That you seem to talk about all the right things, the things one needs to hear?"

Ruby pursed her lips. "It's a knack, is all. Comes naturally. When folks reach my age, the eyes begin to go; the hearing, as well. But the mind takes up the slack that the weakening physical senses leave drooping in wrinkled folds about one's head. Then it's the *mind* that sees and hears as it instinctively begins to pick up on life's little innuendos—life's seldom-noticed subtleties." Her shoulders rose and fell. "It's nothing more than an acquired knack some of us old folks happen to be blessed with.

"Anyways," she added with a second shrug, "now that we've established that it's not a betrayal of one's principled beliefs to entertain radical ideas, that they're not *crazy* to expand their reach of possibilities beyond the realm of the accepted simple norms, we may have made some progress here. Huh?"

When the old one voiced the word crazy, her eyes had suddenly shimmered like pools of liquid sapphire. The noticeable flash of radiance caused Sadie's aura to flare with a thrilling rush. It crackled with excitement. Ruby had targeted the issue of belief. She had zeroed in on Sadie's own inner conflict about the elder's true identity. She had addressed the single focus of Mira's rage—that of the question of Sadie's competency.

Realizing that the woman had indirectly encouraged her to put faith in her feelings—her reach beyond the norm—Sadie's pulse quickened. Temples throbbed as blood coursed to keep pace with her racing thoughts. Ruby was telling her that it was okay to scratch at the paint covering the glass box of popular belief in order to peer at what lies outside its false blind. It was okay to push one's finger into the yielding barrier of conceptual thought until it stretches beyond endurance and pokes a hole, revealing a world of awesome realities on the other side—realities which were generally thought to be comprised of the insubstantial stardust of dreamers, the improbable fantasies of the visionary, the "crazy" ideas of those brave souls who dared to step off the beaten path.

Thoughtfully, the green eyes narrowed at the lustrous blues that welcomed the intense gaze. "But," the younger woman expanded, "the one who takes on the role of both eagle and dove—the one who holds both common and esoteric beliefs—draws suspicion. That one is looked upon with disfavor and perceived as making the leap beyond eccentricity into lunacy."

The blues mellowed to soft, pearly grey. "So? Do you think the eccentric cares? Do you think the eccentric cares what *perception* others have? The true eccentric has a deeper well of wisdom than her finger-pointing accusers. The true eccentric has acceptance in her heart. She *tolerates* their intolerance. She is serene in the knowledge that everyone needs to seek their own comfort level. Like water filling in the shallows and depths of a lake bottom, people are at varying levels as well. What brings them together in a common goal of tolerance is acceptance. Acceptance is the key, Sadie Brennan. Acceptance is that magical, golden key for tolerating each other's differences."

The sound of slurping drew two sets of eyes to the child.

"May I have another hot cocoa?"

Her aunt, acting as though the child's voice had pulled her out of a trance, blinked and looked about the café. None of the diners had the face of familiarity. None of them were the same ones she'd passed while weaving her way to the counter. The former aromas of bacon and country sausage sizzling on the grill were replaced with those of burgers and fries overlying the spicy soup of the day as it sent up curling steam from the stainless kettle. It was lunchtime.

She quickly checked her watch, then flushed with embarrassment. "I don't know where the time went," she said, shifting her gaze to the woman sitting across the table. "You must be hungry. Will you join us for lunch? My treat."

Expecting a polite decline of her offer, Sadie beamed with the blush of relief when the woman spoke.

"Why, thank you, Sadie Brennan. That soup does smell good."

Savannah wasn't altogether certain about everything the two women had been talking about. Their conversation was difficult for an eight-year-old to follow, even for an extraordinarily smart eight-year-old. One thing she did know was that she liked being with Ruby. She liked it a lot. It was like having a grandma. So when grandma agreed to stay for lunch, the girl's insides literally quivered with joy. Her eyes had the sparkle of pixie dust. She grinned like a Cheshire cat high on catnip.

During their meal, Sadie tried muddling through their earlier conversation and how it related to her current situation. "Mira and I need to show greater tolerance for each other's position," she said between bites of the mounded chef salad. "Even though my behavior seems a bit off the wall to her, she needs to loosen up and respect where I'm at, respect my beliefs."

Slowly passing the spoon back and forth through the steaming cream of mushroom soup, Ruby raised a brow. "And you, Sadie Brennan. What do you need to do?"

"Ride the wave, I guess. See where it takes us."

"I hope that means that you also have acceptance for where she's at. Patience is what you need to focus on right now. Patience for your sister's plunge into emotional turmoil."

"I'm there, as well. Remember? I was right beside her in that roller coaster car."

"I remember. I'm not senile, you know. That ride is taking you both on ups and downs. It's jerking you around sharply angled turns. It's twisting this way and that." Grey eyes narrowed. "I believe that you're heading up to the final summit point . . . then," she emphasized, using her spoon as a pointer, "then it's all downhill from there. And by downhill I mean smooth sailing."

"My friend Tina would say that means that I'm about to be teetering on the cusp of change."

The old woman pursed her lips while considering the idea. "Mmmm, more like *marinating* on the cusp of change. You two are entering a phase where issues can no longer be ignored or denied. It's a time of turning inward and facing reality. Time for exhuming those buried issues. It's a mental marinating time for you both." Ruby's eyes momentarily shifted toward the child, who was preoccupied with dipping her French fries in just the right amount of ketchup. "It's a mental marinating time for *all* of you," she added, sliding the empty soup bowl aside.

Before a reply could be made, the waitress came to remove the elder's used dinnerware. She recited the dessert menu, intentionally sprinkling the narrative with mouthwatering adjectives designed to tease the sweet tooth.

Ruby's eyes fluttered when she heard they offered homemade blackberry pie—warm and topped with a generous dollop of real whipped cream.

The young woman seated across from her noticed. "Don't worry about waiting for us to finish, Ruby. We're slow eaters. You go ahead and get some of that pie. We'll probably be too full for dessert anyway."

The elder demurred.

Sadie winked at the waitress. "She'll have the blackberry pie."

When the generous slice was set before the waiting woman, the thought crossed Sadie's mind that Ruby could probably pull such desserts out of that satchel of hers whenever she had the inclination. That thought made her realize that she'd lost her former curiosity about the mysterious carpetbag. She no longer focused on the baffling phenomenon. Instead, she had been drawn into the core of the matter, that of the old woman herself. An old woman who had the aura of a seasoned sojourner through life, an old woman whose depth of wisdom softly radiated from a cloak of genteel bearing interwoven with threads of regal spun gold.

During the pause in conversation while Ruby began to savor her favored dessert, Sadie also realized that her growing acquaintance with the woman had diminished her former sense of awe. That blazing awe had settled into a soft glowing ember of respect and she attributed that to the fact that she'd gained a simple acceptance of the woman. No longer speculating as to whether she was truly some manifested form of a MotherGod, she had, instead, become comfortable with the feeling of Ruby being just a wise mentor, an elderly friend. That was the effect the old one had on her. They'd become friends.

The younger woman's eyes fell on the satchel. The brilliance of Ruby's humble intellect far outshone any little luster cast by her bizarre bag. Sadie privately smiled, finally understanding that the infamous bag of tricks had become inconsequential to her, that it had been relegated to a readily accepted aspect that no longer caused any more amazement than pulling change from one's pocket. *You could pull a circus elephant out of that bag and it wouldn't be any big deal to me.*

As though the old woman responded to the younger's thoughts, Ruby nonchalantly slid the satchel to the edge of the table and unceremoniously flopped it onto her lap. "Wonderful pie," she mumbled, raising the dessert plate. "Would you like to have a taste?"

Sadie patted her midsection. Groaning, she pushed the oversized salad bowl away. "Thank you, but I couldn't eat another thing."

The dessert plate was then offered to the child.

She puffed her cheeks out. "Me, neither," she moaned as her eyes fell on the copious overflow of blackberries spilling from the flaky crust. "That was the biggest cheeseburger I ever ate! That sure does look good, though. I'll get some of that the next time we're here."

"Oh," the elder said, setting the plate back down in front of her, "are you going to be coming back here, then?"

Savannah didn't know how to respond. She shot her aunt a pleading look that was half question, half hope.

"I don't see why we can't come here again," Sadie cheerfully said. "Who knows? Maybe we'll run into each other again and share a round of that pie."

A disconcerting shadow fleetingly skimmed the old one's eyes. She recovered with a warm smile.

"Destiny has a peculiar way of bringing folks together. Even by way of a blackberry pie." The grey eyes glinted with twinkling specks of blue before she lowered them to her plate. The fork sank through the thick filling. "I'd like to think of us gathered here sharing warm blackberry pie on a chilly November day." The end of the tines found their mark. Ruby closed her eyes, savoring the flavor. When they half opened, sweet pleasure lazily swirled over the bright irises. "Yes," she crooned, "I believe destiny will use this place to bring us together again."

The child giggled. "And we'll all have pie!"

Over two more cups of coffee and one hot chocolate, the conversation between Ruby and Sadie stayed on the subject of destiny and how it related to one's purpose in life. "Oh," the elder assured, "that purpose doesn't have to be an earth-shattering event to be important. Oh no, indeed! It can be as simple as one kind word delivered at just the right time to the right person! That one act has the potential of creating monumental effects!" She explained that destiny could pull several people together at the same time so multiple purposes could be fulfilled. Or their multiple purposes could culminate in a single shared event. She laughed. "Like having one big birthday party to celebrate everyone's!"

Sadie read more into the concept. It sounded like the idea of a birthday party was used as a metaphor for that cusp of change they'd discussed earlier. A delicate eyebrow arched. "When will this big birthday party happen?"

Ruby closed her eyes. They opened slowly. "It's hypothetical, of course."

"Well, hypothetically, then. When would this hypothetical party happen?"

"Ohhh," she hedged. "I'd give it some time."

"How much time? Hypothetically, of course."

The last of the fruit filling disappeared from the plate. "Anywhere from a few days to a few weeks."

"That's a fairly generalized prediction, don't you think? C'mon, Ruby, give me a break and help me out here."

"Okay," she piped back. Her eyes danced like the twinkle of midday sunlight on mica. "Couple-a days."

The evening meal at the Woodward manor was held earlier than usual. In expectation of Savannah's annual rush to be out the door at dusk on this last day of October, Greta had been simmering a pot of her homemade chili. Chili was her traditional meal on this date every year because, she claimed, all the little ghosts and goblins had to be fortified with a good stick-to-your-ribs meal before they haunted the cold Chicago neighborhoods.

So dinner was a routinely casual affair on All Hallow's Eve. Each household member was expected to help themselves. It was a catch-as-catch-can kind of meal. What made this year different was the fact that each of the household's five members converged in the kitchen at the same time. And what made this mealtime so remarkably different from those preceding it was Mira's uncharacteristically congenial mood.

The dinner talk was lighthearted, almost to the point of being lively. Savannah fidgeted in her chair, antsy to get into her costume and on her way. Mostly, she was impatient to show her costume to her Aunt Sadie. It was a rare treat to have her aunt here on Halloween and Savannah had wanted to make it extra special.

Mira left the adults half stunned by telling jokes. Mira never told jokes. No one knew why that was, but thought perhaps it was because she felt it undignified, beneath her. Tonight they flew out of her faster than bats from a cave at twilight. There was no mention of the angry altercation between the sisters that morning. No reference or slightest innuendo made toward the matter of Sadie's suspected incompetence. No hint of chastisement given to a disobeying daughter.

As for the other three adults at the table, they exchanged baffled looks while putting on a good show of chuckling amusement. Although the trio were dumbfounded by Mira's peculiar behavior, no one wanted to do anything to send it flying off in another, more characteristic direction.

"Oh! Before I forget," Mira said, putting the mirth on pause for a minute, "I had a wonderful idea." She focused her attention on her daughter. "I'm taking you shopping tomorrow for school clothes!"

The girl glanced over to her aunt before settling dancing eyes on her mother's. "School? I'm going back to school? You mean it?"

"Of course, I mean it. Oh, not tomorrow or next week, but soon. Don't you want to get back to your friends?"

Torn between the idea of accompanying her aunt to be with Ruby or spending her days with a bunch of silly classmates who didn't have the least idea who God was, Savannah smartly chose to placate her mother. She knew that doing otherwise might provoke another argument. This night, she had decided, was for her and her Aunt Sadie. Nothing was going to spoil that. Without further hesitation, she flashed her mother an exuberant smile. "Yes! I can't wait to see them again!"

With a satisfied grin, the joke-telling resumed. It continued for ten minutes after Savannah had finished her meal and raced from the room. Believing they'd all given her enough time to don her surprise costume, the four of them gathered at the bottom of the stairs. Greta, holding the empty trick-or-treat bag for its owner, excitedly waited with the others for the grand entry. "Wait until you see her," she chuckled. "It's gonna knock your socks off. She had Josef running all over town for her outfit. Had to be just right, you know. I've been sewing my fingers to the bone making it fit to her satisfaction."

In response, the gardener chuckled. "I brought back the wrong thing. Twice! She sure was particular."

"That's my little girl," Mira proudly beamed. "Only the best for her! Only the right one will do! And," she added, "only perfect tailoring!"

Already bundled up for the cold that always came on this date, Sadie held the child's coat at the ready. "She's not going to like having to cover her costume. I bet she's going as one of Josef's garden fairies."

"Nope. And she won't be needing that coat, either," the housekeeper cryptically shot back.

Mira eyed the coat in her sister's hand. She had loftier ideas. "She probably doesn't need her little coat because she's going as a princess draped in fur!"

"Nope. Not a princess in fur, either," Josef said.

"But it's cold out there," Sadie cut in. "She's got to have—"

"Ta-daaa!" sang the proud voice from the top of the stairs.

Everyone looked up to see Savannah standing with her arms poised out to her sides; chin tilted just so, like a model's.

Layers of sweaters topped layers of ankle-length skirts that brushed the scuffed tops of snow boots.

The tailored military overcoat hung exactly an inch off the floor.

Red hair, brushed until it gleamed, frizzed out wildly from beneath the red knit hat that tilted at a cockeyed angle of sassy impertinence.

In one of the outstretched hands, fingers curled around the wooden handle of a tapestry knitting bag.

The light from the landing chandelier reflected off the facets of the big red pin. Sparkles shot from her head like rays of a halo.

Sadie's heart skipped a beat. The child looked absolutely celestial.

Mira's jaw dropped. "A bum? Is that what all this high secrecy was about? You're going trick-or-treating dressed as a tramp?"

"No, silly," Savannah squealed in delight. "I'm going as God!"

Three people froze in anticipation of Mira's exploding repercussion.

The arms in the Chanel suit flew into the air. "Well, of course!" She hit her forehead with her hand. "How silly of me! Anyone can see you're . . ." That's where she stopped and rolled her eyes. "Whatever. That's real nice, honey. You and your auntie have a good time tonight." Twirling on her heels, she strode toward her office and called over her shoulder. "Don't forget. Tomorrow we go shopping."

When Mira's fuse fizzled out before detonation, the three left standing at the bottom of the stairs eyed one another with dazed expressions. Each puzzled countenance mirrored a single unspoken question. *What was that all about?* Their combined relief was released in a joint sigh. Then, as one, their heads were drawn to a clamor on the landing.

Encumbered by layers of flouncing skirts, God was noisily clopping down the stairs.

Fourteen

Friday

The Harbor Heirlooms van pulled away from the loading dock and eased along the alleyway until it came to the cross street. Turning into traffic, Sadie was pleased with how things had turned out for today. Having the unexpected time alone, she'd decided to visit one of her business contacts in the city and now, thanks to destiny's perfect timing, she'd been given a prospective buyer's name for the rosewood sideboard she had in her shop. As an extra bonus, she'd come away from Vandemere, Worth, and Bothwell's with the Sheraton tea table one of her own clients had been looking for.

This first day of November had proven to be a productive start for the month. A smile tipped the corners of the driver's mouth as she envisioned how thrilled her client was going to be when she called her about the table. The business had its ups and downs, but there was nothing like the special feeling that came with locating a much-desired piece for one's client. Not only locating it, but actually procuring it at a respectable dealer's price.

The trip to Chicago had not only been a success in regard to Savannah, but the recent transaction had made the trip a financially profitable one, as well. Her client wouldn't blink at shelling out more than the piece would bring at auction. The table in the back, well bound with padding, represented a sizeable chunk of security and Sadie was glad she'd taken the time to set her feet on the solid ground of the real world. It'd been good seeing a couple of her business friends again. Chantel Vandemere had stepped into her father's shoes when he handed her the senior partnership keys upon retiring. She was as savvy as old Harold Worth and twice as knowledgeable as young Kurt Bothwell, who'd inherited his share of the concern from his mother, the renowned Kristina Bothwell. Sadie and Chantel were only a year apart in age and had known one another since their socialite mothers first began taking their toddlers to the same country club for tadpole swimming lessons.

Now Ms. Brennan was on her way to a second antique dealer that had been established in the heart of Chicago since World War I. It'd been started by the great-grandfather of a college friend of hers and Tina's. The friend, Josh Whitmore, had practically been raised amid the well-appointed display rooms of Whitmore Antiques and Appraisals. And, on any given day, Josh could be found in his plush, walnut-paneled office. He'd be leaning back in the thick leather chair while using the speaker phone to masterfully conduct private auctions between high-powered Fortune 500 bidders.

Weaving her way through a maze of secondary streets that supported family-run bodegas, independent bookstores, mom and pop restaurants, and the occasional pawnshop, she noticed that this old neighborhood was experiencing the growing pains of redevelopment. Decorative lampposts had replaced the outdated style of light poles.

Between the curb and the recently renovated storefronts, landscaping islands with a variety of young trees and low-growth shrubs had been added.

The overall effect was pleasing to the eye and Sadie was heartened to see that this once-tired section of town had become so successfully revitalized.

Impressed with the results of the area's shot in the arm, she scanned the signs on the storefronts. She noticed that a few upscale stores had given the area their vote of confidence. Specialty clothing shops rubbed shoulders with art galleries.

A Yankee Candle Company was nestled between a bodega and a Godiva chocolate shop.

When she spied the Starbucks sign, she slowed the vehicle and circled the block. The angled street parking was at a premium, but she found an empty slot at the end of the block. Not minding the walk, she pulled in. The walk, she figured, would give her a chance to peer into the interesting windows of the different boutiques.

It was the eclectic display of an import shop that drew her attention. Peering through the plate glass at a bisque statuette of an East Indian goddess, Sadie thought of Tina. The image was an unusual rendition and she was tempted to purchase it for her friend.

"Beautiful, isn't it?" said the disembodied voice.

Sadie raised her gaze from the statue to the image reflected on the windowpane.

Ruby was standing beside her.

In genuine surprise, the window-shopper turned to face the woman who was bundled in multiple sweaters beneath the usual overcoat. "Hi, Ruby! What brings you to this neighborhood?"

"Oh, this 'n' that," she said evasively. "I get all over this town." Pointing to the statue, she asked, "That interest you?"

"Actually, it did catch my eye. My friend, Tina, has a similar one and I was just debating whether I should get it for her. She's keeping an eye on my shop while I'm here. I need to bring her back something besides the sausage I picked up at the Farmers' Market."

The elder raised a hand to her brow and peeked through the window. A brittle nail tapped the glass. "Don't usually see Parvati done in bisque. Usually the Hindu figures are brass or glazed ceramic. The ceramic ones are usually painted. This is an unusual piece. Gonna buy it?"

"Maybe. You know who the statue is?"

Corners of the grey eyes crinkled like an elf's. "Sure, I do. That's the Hindu goddess Parvati. She's the wife of Shiva and considered to be the Earth Mother. She's generally perceived as the Mother Goddess."

Sadie twitched. *MotherGod.*

Ruby noticed. "You okay? You cold?"

"No. No, I . . . maybe I will get that for Tina," she muttered, inching toward the door.

The ragtag woman did a side shuffle that kept her close beside the younger one.

Sadie looked at her.

Ruby, giving an impatient look back, asked, "You goin' inside, or what?"

"Yes. Are you coming too?"

"You betcha!"

While Sadie waited for the proprietor to fetch the statuette from the window display and wrap it, Ruby moseyed about the cluttered shop. She picked up this and that and mumbled unintelligible opinions.

The shopkeeper divided his attention between attending to the sale at hand and watching the bizarre little woman clopping around his fragile wares in a pair of men's camouflage hunting boots. He eyed her handy satchel, making sure it didn't develop a sudden bulge.

Without turning to the man at the counter, Ruby's voice rang clear as carillon bells. "Mister Mahmoud, shoplifting's no different than those two sets of books you keep. If you wish to spy a thief I suggest you look into that mirror you have in the back room."

The little man froze. His ebony eyes locked on his customer's green ones. "Whaa . . . what did your friend say?"

Sadie spun around to see Ruby's back. The woman was hunched over an urn on the glass shelf. She was preoccupied with trying to decipher the imprint on the underside of the base.

Concern wrinkled Sadie's brow when she returned her attention to the man. "I don't think she said anything. Well," she corrected, "I think she was sort of talking to herself earlier, but she hasn't said anything directly to us."

Mr. Mahmoud pulled out a handkerchief and nervously dabbed at his face. His eyes turned shifty as they darted back and forth between the two women. "Will there be anything else?"

Ruby sidled up to the counter. She glowered at the man, slowly turned her head to the back room, then eyed him a second time before shuffling out the door.

He handed over the package. Jerking his head toward the entryway, he asked, "She your grandmother?"

"No, we're not related. She's a friend."

Mr. Mahmoud gave a nervous chuckle. "Very odd, that one."

Sadie leaned into the counter. "No, not really," she whispered.

"You need to get out more, Mister . . ." she advised, glancing down for the man's name printed on the stack of business cards beside the register. ". . . Mister Mahmoud. You need to get outside that box you've packed all your perspectives in." The wrapped statuette was ceremoniously secured under her arm. "Good day, Mister Mahmoud." And as Sadie turned on her heels, she felt like she could fly. The good feeling that had washed through her almost swept her off her feet. Defending Ruby had brought a buoyant sense of rightness that swelled her heart with a fullness of goodness. By the time she met up with the old one on the sidewalk, she was literally beaming with satisfaction.

"What's the silly grin for?" Ruby inquired. Not leaving time for a reply, she asked another. "You in a hurry to get somewhere?"

"Are you?"

"Asked you first."

"I had to cut through this section of town to get to . . . an old friend of mine is an antique dealer. I was on my way there and . . . this whole neighborhood's been so revitalized that it sort of drew me in. I spied the Starbucks down the way and decided to stop. I'm parked back by the corner—"

"You in a hurry or not?"

"Well, I . . . ahh, no."

The little woman's arm flew in front of Sadie. The empty carpetbag, used as a pointer, flipped up with a flick of her wrist. "Best coffee for miles around is across the street. There," she said.

Trying to pinpoint where "there" was, Sadie narrowed her eyes and scanned the block on the opposite side of the street. Her eyes glanced past a fire station, a card shop, a florist, and a Levi outlet store. Her gaze skipped over the construction equipment used to renovate the vacant building that abutted a little used bookstore and skimmed the rest of the storefront signage of Crabtree & Evelyn, Vandervan's Jewelers, Victoria's Secret, and Annabelle's Stained Glass. She failed to locate a coffee shop or even a small generic café. "Where?"

"There! Right in front of us! C'mon," Ruby urged with a yank on the other's coat sleeve. "Let's go have some good coffee. My treat this time."

Sadie hesitated, giving the famous coffeehouse up the block a last look.

Ruby impatiently shook her head. "Never mind about up that way.

I'm not talking about that overpriced, curlicue, cookie-cutter kind of coffee. We're going for the real stuff!"

Sadie allowed herself to be led across the street and the old woman pulled her through the narrow doorway of the used bookstore. As soon as the door closed behind them, Ruby spun around to peer up at her friend.

Sadie could've sworn the grey eyes glowed with delight.

"Smell that?" Ruby chirped. "Now, that's coffee!"

The aroma of freshly ground dark beans lazily wafted between the narrow aisles of shelving fronted with books of every description. The tempting fragrance, like warmed honey, dripped its caress over the leather-bound spines of beloved classics. Its allure tantalized one into following it past the stacks of steamy romance novels. Silently, it lured newcomers away from the door, drawing them beyond the rows of chilling true crime. Like the lingering perfume left by a passing ghost, it beckoned from behind the volumes of bone-tingling tales of the supernatural.

Wondering where all the people were, and feeling much like a young Jedi following Yoda through the tangled swamp, Sadie stayed on the heels of the camouflage boots as they noisily flapped on the worn wooden flooring of the narrow aisles. Deeper and deeper they went toward the furthest recess of the seemingly obscure bookshop. From up ahead, Sadie thought she could hear voices whispering, chanting.

The two women walked beneath an arched alcove and veered to the right. They walked into a brightly lit refreshment area where a young man was about to grind more beans. Leading away from the coffee room, a long hallway stretched out before them, three doorless rooms to either side.

The man's face lit up when he saw Ruby walk in. "Hi, there! Haven't seen you in a while. Everything been okay?"

"Oh, yes. I'd like you to meet my friend, Sadie Brennan. She's an antique dealer. Has a shop of her own way up in Maine."

"Maine!" he exclaimed with an animated shiver. "Good lord, you're a long ways from home. It's cold up there. Anyway, it's nice to meet you. I'm Chris, the owner of this little getaway from the world. I'm also in charge of making sure nobody runs out of coffee in this place." He handed each of them a steaming cup of black brew and, looking to Sadie, nodded to the wide assortment of sugar, cream, and flavorful additives.

She politely declined. Like Ruby, she preferred hers strong and black.

The low singing coming from one of the rooms beyond the kitchen area momentarily distracted Sadie until she heard Ruby's voice. It wasn't the voice so much as what she said to the young man.

"Chris," she huffed, while having trouble hefting her weighty satchel. "I brought you some new ones."

The young man rushed to take the heavy bag. "You're a jewel, Ruby. Let's see what you found for me." He lifted out one volume at a time, and his eyes widened with delight as each book was gently removed from the bulging fabric and carefully stacked on the counter. He handled them like a true book lover while inspecting each one in turn.

"These are all current bestsellers. First editions! This is fabulous!" He gave her a warm hug of appreciation, then turned to Ruby's friend. "This little lady is really something. She's one in a million. Always comes bearing gifts. You just never know what goodies she's got hidden away in that little satchel of hers."

The old one waved off the glowing accolades. "Oh, go on with you," came the playful gripe. "I'm not doing anything more than bartering for the coffee I bum off you." She faced her friend and nodded toward the hallway. "Let's go find us a place to kick back."

Chris offered a suggestion. "You might try the far one, on the left."

Sadie stepped back a pace to indicate that she intended to let Ruby take the lead. "After you," she said.

Again, she found herself following the elder into the unknown. Mimicking her leader, she likewise peeked into each room as they zigzagged back and forth along the hallway searching for their own little niche in the place.

They checked out the first two rooms. The one on the right held three women who were quietly singing along to used CDs they were trying out. Sadie berated herself for thinking she was hearing ominous chanting. The room on the left revealed four young men gathered around a study table taking notes from reference books they'd borrowed off the shelf.

Low murmuring came from both of the center rooms. In one, five people were quietly debating the merits of a book they'd jointly read. In the other, three individuals, with voices lowered, were having a private discussion which didn't seem to involve any literary focus.

Three people comfortably lounged in the overstuffed chairs in the back room on the right. Each was deeply engrossed in reading material. None looked up when the two women peeked through the doorway.

Sadie caught Ruby's eye. "Seems to be a popular place," she whispered.

The old one winked in agreement before clomping off to the last room on the left. "Here we are," she piped, leading the way inside. "Lucky us. We have one to ourselves. Make yourself at home."

Ruby removed her overcoat and tossed it on the wooden study table. Perching herself on the edge of a well-worn chaise, she politely removed the cumbersome hunting boots and primly set them side by side on the floor. Sliding herself into the welcoming space between the armrests and stretching out her legs, she wriggled her toes. White athletic socks were worn over argyle knee socks over thickly woven black support hose. She released a satisfied sigh. "Nothing like getting out of one's shoes and putting one's feet up." The flowered carpetbag was given a home on the floor. The fabric, tired from carting so much book weight, folded over on itself.

It wasn't hard for Sadie to imagine hearing it sigh. And after pulling off her jacket, she chose the upholstered chair beside her friend.

Ruby's gaze lowered to Sadie's hiking boots. "It's okay. Go ahead. You can free your toes from those heavy shoes."

Sadie grinned. "They're really not as heavy as they look. Actually, they're fairly comfortable. I'm okay."

"I hope you're not acting so proper on my account," Ruby added. "No need to be shy around me—especially here. This place is for doing that kicking back thing. Christopher wanted it to be a place where folks could come whenever they needed a little quiet corner away from the hectic hubbub of the noisy world."

"It's a nice idea. What's it called, anyway? I don't recall seeing a sign out front."

"That's because there isn't any. Chris can't decide what to call it. Browse 'n' Brew, The Booklover's Corner of the World, or Hideaway from the World with a Good Book never rang as a catchy name. He couldn't come up with a short name to describe the place. He's still working on it. I've no doubt he'll come up with just the right name one of these days. Meanwhile, he's not so desperate as to give himself an aneurism brainstorming over it. Figures it'll come to him out of the blue. He's waiting for an epiphany."

Sadie sipped the hot drink. It was dark and full-bodied. "You were right," she confirmed. "It is just as good as up the block. Maybe better."

"You bet it is. I told Chris he should start a chain of The Brewing Plot, but he likes things as they are."

"The brewing plot?"

Shoulders hitched up, then fell. "Eh, just a silly way to refer to what he's got going here. Instead of a brewing pot, I threw in plot. You know, a story plot."

"Sure, I got it right away. Why doesn't he use that?"

"Guess it has to come as that big lightning strike epiphany he's waiting for. Maybe thinks it's going to come as divine inspiration or something."

Chris really missed the boat on that one. And it wasn't some little rowboat he missed, it was the Titanic! Sadie, realizing how ridiculously ironic the whole thing was, couldn't keep herself from pushing it further. "Doesn't he first need to know how to recognize this divine inspiration when it comes?"

"That's the trouble with folks, isn't it? Can't see the forest for the trees. They got that limited set of perspectives we talked about before. They can't think outside the box. And when they *think* they're thinking outside the box, they're waiting for inspiration to come stuffed in the preformed shapes they're expecting to see. They're so hooked on their preconceived notions that they end up putting a face to illusions, expect them to have a certain voice, act a certain way, while the real reality walks right past them and goes unnoticed. Some folks believe in illusions, others stick to what they can touch and explain away. Most don't even know what's real. Eh, go figure."

Illusions. Was that what all the baffling things she and Savannah had seen were? What was real?

Sadie looked down into her cup, then up at the lounging woman with three different kinds of hosiery on.

"Ruby, this morning when I set off to visit an old friend of mine, it felt good. When we'd made a business transaction, it felt good. When I thought about hooking up with another friend of mine who's in the antique business, it felt good. All these things felt good because I had the sense that I was back in the real world again. My feet felt like they were back on solid ground."

Grey eyebrows furrowed. "Back from where, Sadie Brennan? Where had your feet been before then?"

"I don't know. Up in the air, caught in some esoteric web of illusions and unexplainable events."

"Are unexplainable events illusions, then?"

"Well, no. Not necessarily. But having my mind on old friends and business felt like I was back in the real world again."

"Unexplainable events happen in the real world, Sadie. There's only one world. There's only one *real* world. What makes you feel that there's more is a tendency to prioritize the varying aspects of that one real world—which elements of that one real world that you most want to relate to, derive the most comfort and security from. Those chosen elements are what you're picking out to define as your *personal* real world. Do you see?

"Your friends, business, shopping, and dining are those elements of the world that you want to call real. Other elements that you cannot readily explain—the spiritual or esoteric aspects of that one real world—you want to discount because they're not black and white. They're not soft or firm. They wear a stranger's face. They scratch at your preconceived notions and nitpick your mind with urgings to come away from the box, to push reason and logic into the realm of real possibilities—real possibilities that coexist right alongside all other aspects in that one real world. Sadie," the old one quietly advised, "one cannot live a full life by accepting only *half* or a specified *portion* of what the real world has to offer. It's like choosing to see out of only one eye, hear out of one ear, touch with only one hand. You can't push aside everything you can't explain. You can't push it all into a box labeled *Not Reality* or *Another World*. It's all—all of it—part of the *one* real world.

"Is that barefoot aborigine walking with his spear over the rocky ground of the Australian outback in another world? Is his world a different world from that of your antique shops, your five-star hotels or restaurants? Of course not. His world is the same as yours, you just both have differing elements of that same world. So too are those unexplained aspects of that world."

Her voice lowered. "Sometimes people don't want to include unexplainable aspects in their idea of the real world because their faith is lacking. Sometimes it comes down to belief. But, Sadie, the fact remains, skepticism can't make the unexplainable aspects vanish as though they never existed. Efforts spent on denial of those things that befuddle the mind cannot make them go away. They remain just the same. They remain in spite of disbelief or denial. Sadie, they remain as solid elements of that real world, just as solid as your friends, business, the mall you shop in, the restaurant you dine in."

Belief. Is my lack of belief what made this morning feel as though I was back in the real world? "But Ruby," Sadie tried to explain, "some very odd things have happened in my life recently. I've seen some truly bewildering things. Truly bizarre things that leave me so perplexed that I get dizzy from my spinning mind. I try to find rationale, but the mind just spins like a top."

A blue hue flared through the grey eyes. "Truly? I've also had a little experience with bizarre things. Perhaps I can help. What kind of things?"

Should I tell her? Should I tell her that she's *the bizarre perplexity in my life?* She stalled by taking a drink. Then another. She stalled until the last drop was gone.

"I don't mean to pry," the old one said.

Chris popped his head around the doorway. A full carafe was held high. "Anyone about ready for refills? A warm-up?"

The timing couldn't have been better for the young woman. "Sure. Don't tell me you're also a waiter."

"No," he said, as the steaming brew poured from the pot. "I'm not going to tell you any such thing. Ruby's the only one I personally take care of here. Everyone else is on their own. There's always a couple of pots ready for whomever. No set charge. The empty cup by the sugar's for donations . . . whatever people want to contribute."

"That's pretty generous of you."

Chris was refilling Ruby's cup. "It comes back. Folks always leave plenty. They're generous in return. They like having a calm port in the storm, a quiet place to chill. That's what it's all about. Well, I'll be off. Sorry if I interrupted anything."

Ms. Brennan fought the urge to ask him to stay and chat. Anything to avoid getting back to their conversation.

Ruby's voice preempted all thoughts of avoidance. "As I was saying, before we were so kindly interrupted. I don't mean to pry into your life, but since you've shared some of it already—the problems between you and your sister, Mira, and little Savannah's difficulties—I thought that perhaps I could be of help with other issues, as well. I'm a good listener and, although I have some rather strong opinions, I don't ever judge others."

"Never? You don't ever judge people?"

"Why are you so surprised at that? I don't need to judge anyone. They do that themselves. Oh yes," she smiled, "they always end up doing their own judging."

"Well," Sadie hedged, "I suppose I need to begin by saying that I have a confession to make."

The old one humorously lowered her head and peered up at her companion. "Do you see a priest's collar on me? I don't hear confessions."

"So maybe it's not really a bona fide confession, then. Maybe it's just something I have to get off my chest."

"That's different, isn't it? If you're sure you want to unburden yourself to me, I'm all ears. Go ahead, I'm listening."

"I . . . that is, Savannah and I . . . . Well, that day in the museum . . . and at the Commons . . . weren't the first times we'd seen you."

Ruby's eyes narrowed. "So? That's not the first time I'd seen you two, either."

Sadie wasn't expecting that. "You'd seen us before then?"

"Isn't that what I just said? Saw you both at the Farmers' Market a week ago. It was a week from yesterday to be exact."

"But my niece wasn't with me when I saw you. She was waiting for me back in the vehicle. She was in the van with Greta, the housekeeper."

"Is that what you think?"

"That's what I know. She was with Greta when I returned to the market for something I forgot to pick up. That's when I saw you with the Thai children."

The elder mulled the situation over. "The market's a big place; perhaps I saw you two together earlier in the day, then. Yes," she decided, "that must've been it."

"That's entirely possible." More coffee was used as a security blanket. The younger woman put the cup to her lips and took her time drinking. Then, "We also saw you in the museum gift shop."

"Well I already knew that. I recall seeing you there."

"And the cemetery. A week from last Wednesday, to be exact."

Ruby frowned. "Let me think a minute." When the eyes lit up, she said, "Yes! You two were coming out of a mausoleum, if I remember correctly."

Sadie hadn't realized they'd been noticed. "And the park on Lake Shore Drive. We saw you sitting on a bench beneath a tree there."

"My goodness, Sadie Brennan, Chicago's a mighty big place. People run into one another all the time. It's not like you've been spying on me or anything. Aren't you making much to-do about nothing? Simple coincidences?"

"What if they weren't simple coincidences? What if I said that we were spying on you?"

"Have you followed me around?"

"Not exactly, but—"

"Well, there you are, then. I'm afraid you've burdened yourself with some false guilt by believing that all our chance encounters have somehow been your doing." The mass of silver hair swished from side to side. "Tsk, tsk," she cautioned, "mustn't beat yourself up like that. Sometimes folks cross paths for a reason. Other times, there's no particular reason. Life happens, Sadie."

The younger woman wasn't so easily put off. "Ruby, from the very first day I pulled into this city, I saw you. And you saw me. You actually stared at me while I passed."

"Where was this?"

"The south end. You were walking with a street woman at the time. She was pushing a shopping cart full of her belongings. I don't mean to offend, but back then, I thought you were a street person."

Ignoring that last, Ruby offered an explanation. "I'd say it'd be a good bet that the sign on the side of your van caught my eye. I was probably reading it. Now that you mention it, I do seem to recall seeing that sign before we met in the Commons."

Realizing that they'd drifted a bit from the issue of Ruby's bizarre behavior of performing inexplicable feats, Sadie was relieved. She didn't really want to put the woman on the spot by pushing her to explain the seemingly magical satchel. Or the apparent instantaneous healing of the dog and bird. Or the issue of the ever-changing new shoes that the homeless veteran said she gave away to those needing them. Glancing down at the rubber hunting boots so neatly set on the floor, she wondered who was destined to receive them? Another homeless vet? And were they so large for Ruby because they were meant to fit a man whose feet were two or three sizes larger? Did she know everyone's size, as well?

Who was this enigmatic little woman who so freely walked both the fashionable and derelict sections of Chicago without fear of either ridicule from the affluent or violence from the criminal element? Who was this wisp of a lady beneath the worn army coat who had the temerity to openly challenge the correctness of Michelangelo's most famous painting? Simply put, she was Ruby. Just Ruby. Ruby, who spoke the Thai language without a hint of American accent and taught young Thai girls the intricacies of traditional temple dances. Ruby, who spoke eloquently about destiny and the finer points of perspective and belief. Ruby, who knew my last name without being told, who seemed to know what you were going to say before a word was ever uttered. She was the person who knew the cause of Savannah's silence and spoke of death being natural, without guilt, who spoke of the time when everyone stops hearing the music of life.

Suddenly Sadie was hit by another thought. Ruby had said that it was false guilt to think that Sadie had intentionally caused all of their encounters. But what if they were caused by someone else? What if Ruby herself had been the one to be placing herself in Sadie's path? Wasn't Ruby the one who had appeared outside the import window this morning? Appeared as though she'd manifested herself on the spot?

The walls of the bookstore couldn't shut out all of the noise from the construction site next door. It sounded as though a large trash container had been dropped in and the crew was using machinery to rid the area of their gutting debris. The racket suspended Sadie's thoughts. A testing side glance went in the old one's direction.

Ruby was patiently eyeing her. "Are you back? You drifted away for a while."

A sheepish grin followed. "That was rude. I'm sorry. I'm back now."

"No, not rude. There are times when we need to think things out during conversations. I suspect you were doing some of that. It's not rude to do that. I didn't feel ignored. So. Shall we continue?"

Sadie nodded.

"Okay. Now that the mystery of why I stared at your van is solved, that takes us back to the idea of not making those mysteries out of everyday events."

Your idea of everyday events is far different from mine. Yours ends up putting my mind in a spin. And it was that fact that nailed down Ruby's words about how personal perspectives play a role in determining how one looks at life—how one mistakenly separates out differing life elements into a belief in a solid, touchable real world from those more obscure aspects belonging to a reality they perceive as a questionable one.

"Yes. Everyday events are just that, aren't they," Sadie said. "Everyday events are really everyday events to everyone. I mean, in *reality*, they're everyday events in and of themselves, without people's different perspectives entering to alter them in any way." Her shoulders slumped after hearing her own words. "Jeez, that sounded pretty lame, didn't it."

"Not at all. You see, reality exists all by itself. Some of those elements of reality may seem mysterious to you, but nothing out of the ordinary to your neighbor. It all comes down to how reality is viewed through each person's perception. But what you just said means that people's differing perceptions have no effect on reality because reality is as reality does. Right?"

"Yeah, that's what I was trying to say."

"And you said it very well, indeed." The old one leaned forward. Her countenance was soft, full of an unnamed emotion, perhaps compassion. "Sadie," she whispered, "our everyday realities are the same. There is no veil dividing the one reality into two."

Emerald eyes met the pearlescent greys. "I'm beginning to believe that, Ruby. I'm beginning to understand that reality's baffling aspects don't need explanations to give them validation. That acceptance of what one sees with her own eyes is more than enough for belief to be strong. The need to discover the whys and the hows of those things wanes; it falls by the wayside because belief makes that need unnecessary. Gaining the proof is no longer a quest because one is left satiated by the knowing alone."

Greatly comforted by the younger woman's words, the old one closed her eyes, then slowly opened them. "You've come a long way, Sadie Brennan. You've been marinating."

Sadie responded with soft laughter. "That sounds as silly now as when you first said that. Difference is, now I know what you mean. Marinating. Ideas, the concepts of potentialities and possibilities, destiny and purpose, all marinating in the mind, mulling over the wisdom of reaching outside the box toward discovery." One side of her mouth tipped up. "Now I get it."

The elfin eyes twinkled. "I can see that. And once you get it, acceptance automatically gains a greater hold. Have you also noticed that?"

Her recent decline in the drive to know how Ruby did the things she did came to mind. If that strong impulse waned, it must have been due to acceptance gaining in strength and taking hold. "Yes, I've noticed. It was quite dramatic, actually. I'm not even sure when it happened."

"Ahhh, that's the way of it, you see," she quietly said, daintily walking her fingers across her lap. "Acceptance enters on little cat toes, advancing in a sure-footed and silent manner."

Ruby lifted her cup and drained the contents.

"Would you care for a refill? I can go get you one," Sadie offered.

The elder quickly waved away the idea. "Two's plenty for me. Any more than that and, sure as shootin', I'll be caught on the street with no place to pee." A hearty cackle erupted. "Whoever designed these bodies of ours never studied *interior* design! Now if it had been up to me, I would've made a closed system like others have . . . where there was no waste to constantly get rid of. It's such a bother." Her head shook. The red hat humorously slumped to one side. "Just imagine how clean the water would stay without the need for waste treatment plants!" Her hand shot up in the air. "Had a couple-a other great suggestions, too. But, oh no, nobody listens to my ideas. They might involve a little more planning, a little more *work*, you know!"

"Ruby?" Sadie cut in. "What other suggestions?"

"What?"

"What other suggestions did you have?"

"Doesn't matter now," she begrudgingly griped, "damage's already been done. The mistake was so obvious, I didn't even have to say I told you so."

"To who?"

Silence. Stewing.

Waiting.

The old one glanced at her coffee companion. "Eh, it's all water under the bridge now, isn't it? Never makes sense bemoaning what can't be undone. What's done is done. Where were we?"

"I'm not sure." She gazed down into her cup. "Oh yeah, we were talking about that marinating thing, remember."

"Sure, I remember. Just wanted to see if you did."

Sadie wasn't sure if that was really the case, but smiled just the same.

Ruby took a moment to rearrange herself on the chaise. "Marinating about potential and those possibilities. That's where we were. And, if truth be told, it's those possibilities that can get you every time."

"Get you?"

"Yes! Why, don't you know? Possibilities are the stuff of What's To Come, aren't they? The future, Sadie Brennan, the future!"

"Well, I suppose, but . . ."

"What but? No buts about it. When folks start talking about possibilities, destiny, potentialities, and acceptance, they can't leave out the future because they're all rolled into one big ball of wax."

Ball of wax?

"Figuratively speaking, of course," the old one clarified. "Just figuratively."

Without disturbing the meter of the conversation, Sadie's eyes narrowed. She blurted, "You know things, don't you. To use a friend's favorite word, you're fey."

"You talking about your friend Tina again?"

"No, my friend Josef. He's—"

"Oh, Josef! He's the gardener. How's he doing?"

"I didn't tell you about Josef."

"Yes, you did."

"No, I have to respectfully disagree about that. I don't believe I did. See what I mean? You know things."

In a roundabout way, the old one tried to downplay her "knowing."

"Oh, for heaven's sake. Everyone knows things. The plumber knows about the pipes under the kitchen sink. The beautician knows how to wreck your hair. The lawyer knows how to get himself a BMW. A policeman knows how to meet his ticket quota. The politician knows how to double-talk. Those who really listen well know how to read the double-talk. And you know about antiques. Everyone has a specialty. Even me. It's that simple. So don't go making me out as one who sees what's happening in her scrying mirror. The future is just something I know about. Do you want to hear about those possibilities or not?"

It seemed to Sadie that the old one's hackles had quivered. It sounded as though a defensiveness had crept into her voice.

"Ruby, I didn't mean to upset you. Believe me, I never meant to sound accusatory when I said you knew things. I know that everybody has some type of specialty knowledge and nobody knows everything about everything." A second after she'd said it, she knew it'd been a lie. She knew it was an untruth because it felt so much like one. *Except for you.*

Ruby sighed. "Ohh, I know you didn't mean anything by that. I'm getting on, you know. I'm tired. I'm so tired. This old body's about worn out. And the older it gets, the more I find myself getting testy over the silliest things. I never used to let things rile me. I suppose I ought to give some thought to moving . . . well," she smiled warmly, after reconsidering the need to introduce the issue of her mortality, "enough about dreary thoughts. Let's talk about those possibilities, shall we?"

Christopher had politely announced his arrival with an unobtrusive rapping on the door frame. "Time for a break, ladies," he beamed, holding up a tray of bakery sweets. As he dramatically swept the platter beneath each woman's nose, the mouth-watering aroma swirled about the room. "Fresh from the oven. Get them while they're still warm," he said while temptingly holding the goodies over the old one's lap.

Ruby rolled her eyes at the young man who was delighting in hovering the sweets in front of her. "You're a naughty boy to tempt an old woman like this."

He grinned and picked three napkins off the tray. Neatly spreading them over her lap, he turned to Sadie. "She can't resist these luscious goodies," he said. "They come from the bakery across the street." He winked. "This is really the only reason Ruby comes to see me." Then he winced in anticipation of the playful slap that tapped his arm.

"That's not so and you know it. Shame on you," she scolded while daintily choosing a raspberry filled Bismark from the assortment.

"Anyway," he explained, "every day at about this time I get a variety of these fresh-from-the-oven goodies for my people here. The baker's not only the owner, he's a bookaholic. It's his way of bartering for books." He set the tray in front of Sadie. "What's your pleasure? We're laid back here so don't be shy about taking more than one. There's plenty for everyone. I've two more platters back in the coffee room."

Sadie took a couple of napkins and chose a chocolate-covered custard long John.

He suspiciously eyed her choice. Then waited.

"What?" she asked. "That's it. Everything looks wonderful. One's enough for me."

The host released an exaggerated sigh. "Oh, honey, don't tell me you're dieting." He looked her over. "Just don't *tell* me you're dieting," he repeated.

"I won't. I'm not. I promise I'll go help myself to more if one doesn't do it."

He flashed her a dubious look before returning to Ruby and setting a second raspberry Bismark in her lap. "I know you'll eat another."

Her eyes lit up. "Naughty boy."

Shifting his weight in exasperation, he indignantly pouted. "If that's how you feel . . ." he said, making a move to retrieve the Bismark in her lap.

With lightning speed, she slapped the back of his hand.

"Uh-huh," he said. "That's what I thought. You can call me naughty all you want, but you love it, don't you?"

"Oh, go on," she said with a flutter of her hand. "Don't you have some books to dust or something?"

"Or something," he replied, turning on his heels and disappearing into the hallway. Playfully, he peeked his head back in. "Enjoy, ladies!"

Ruby had been opening her mouth to receive the first bite of her favorite sweet. At the unexpected sound of his voice, she startled. The doughnut went rolling across the floor like an errant golf ball. "Christopher!" she cried out. "Now look what you've done! You scared the doughnut right out of my hand! I'm too old for childish pranks like that!"

Visibly trying to suppress his amusement, the young man returned to the room. "Not to worry," he soothed, handing her a replacement from the tray.

Ruby scoffed. "I don't want another. I want the one I had."

Three sets of eyes shifted to the forlorn doughnut in the middle of the floor.

Christopher was aghast. "You can't be serious."

The grey eyes flared. "Young man, do I look like I'm joking? There's absolutely nothing wrong with that one. It's perfectly good. Don't you even think about wasting good food. You have no idea how many people would fight each other over that doughnut. Tsk, tsk," she reprimanded, "don't be wasteful, Christopher."

Visions of the homeless street people filled Sadie's mind.

The man's hand shot to his hip. "Ruby, I am not a wasteful person, but I am not giving that doughnut to you. I promise it won't go to waste. Hercules will love it."

Her mouth dropped open. "Your dog? You're going to give perfectly good food to the dog? You hand that to me this instant!"

Chris ignored her demand as he bent to retrieve the contaminated sweet. His singsong mantra could be heard all the way back to the coffee room. "I can't hear you . . . I can't hear you . . . I can't . . ."

Ruby caught Sadie's eye. "See what I mean?" she bitterly complained. "I get no respect. Nobody listens to me." Irritated, she bit down hard on her doughnut. A dollop of raspberry jelly oozed out and dropped onto the front of the buffalo plaid shirt. Without hesitation or embarrassment, she lifted the loose fabric to her lips and made the spill disappear. While wiping the spot with the napkin, she grumbled, "Insolent young man. Imagine, giving that good doughnut to the dog!"

After watching the drama unfold, Sadie thought it was time to come to the young man's defense. "Ruby," she tentatively began, "in all fairness, I would've done the same thing. Christopher *was* showing you respect by giving you a fresh one. He didn't want you to eat something that had picked up dirt from the floor. It was contaminated. He—"

The cool grey eyes squinted. "I'll tell you what was contaminated. Respect! Respect for my wish—my simple request—was contaminated by subjective opinion!"

Sadie had to think about that one. "Well, although that seems to be the case . . ."

"Seems? Sadie, dear," the old one softened, "a few specks of dirt never hurt anyone. Toddlers eat things off the floor all the time. The poor scavenging souls who try to beat the rats by sifting through trash bins in dark alleyways behind restaurants don't normally get sick from eating what they manage to salvage. Believe me, I know something about this kind of thing."

The words stabbed like a dagger into the heart and brought Sadie a sense of deep mortification. Of course the old one knew about such things. She knew about the street people's race to get the best scraps before the sewer rats did. She knew about frugality and the value of every morsel of food. She knew about people's most basic needs. She knew about the daily hardscrabble living of the truly destitute. If nothing else, she was their friend, their angel of mercy.

"I'm sorry, Ruby. I mean that sincerely. For people like Christopher and me who live in such a disposable society, our perspective of value becomes selective. True value gets lost somehow. It borders on shameful wastefulness."

Not wishing to let her cherished doughnut grow stale, Ruby munched on another generous bite. Through a mouthful of jelly and dough, she moaned. "Oh now, don't go wearing sackcloth over it. We all get our priorities jumbled once in a while. But," she mysteriously added with a sparkle glinting from her eye, "that's all going to change."

Missing the point, Sadie replied, "That'll be good."

Ruby's head tilted. "Will it?"

"Well, sure."

A silver eyebrow arched in question.

The response was hard to miss. "You're acting as though that's not such a good thing. What do you mean by that? I don't follow."

Finishing the last of the first doughnut, the old one unceremoniously licked the powdered sugar from her fingertips. After daintily wiping her hands, she picked up the second sweet. "It'd be good if change came willingly. You know, from inside. Voluntarily, by way of one's own free will. Through choice."

Sadie finished her long John and drained the last of her coffee. "Well, are you saying that people won't have a choice, then? That they'll somehow be forced to change their perspectives on things?"

"Yep. That's the 'not good' part. The opportunity to make that choice on their own will be gone by then. There won't be any choice left to make because life will have made the determination for them."

"But why? How so?"

The second doughnut was bitten into. The old one dreamily savored the flavor. "Mmm," she whispered, "a fine and fitting last supper."

"Excuse me?" the young woman said. She leaned forward. "I'm sorry, I didn't get what you just said."

The flannel-cuffed wrist flicked the doughnut back and forth. "Oh, nothing. Just an old woman rambling to herself. You didn't miss anything."

Sadie felt that she did. A shadow of concern whisked through her mind.

Ruby noticed. She smiled. "Wipe that frown off your forehead. You're too young to frown so hard. You'll get worry wrinkles if you don't watch that."

"Why did that just give me the sensation that you're trying to make light of something that's . . . well, I don't know . . . something that's *not* light?"

Ruby innocently shrugged. "All I know for sure is that things are going to do some changing around here."

"In the neighborhood?"

"In all neighborhoods. Everywhere. All over."

Sadie watched her elderly friend's doughnut vanish while she gave thought to the woman's words. Was she talking about world changes? "Do you mean changes all over the world?"

The mass of grey hair bobbed. A hand went up to catch the slipping hat. Fingers came in contact with the gaudy pin. "Say!" the old one exclaimed. "That reminds me, I have something for you!"

"For me?"

The hat was yanked off her head. "Why, yes. And little Savannah, as well. I've a little gift for each of you."

"Gifts? Whatever for?"

A mix of bafflement and disappointment washed over Ruby's face. "Must I have one? I didn't know I needed one."

"One what?"

"A reason. Do I need a reason to give a gift?"

"Of course not. But I haven't done anything to deserve a gift."

An electric blue wave surged across the steel grey irises. "How do you know that? How do you know, Sadie Brennan? People spend their days going through life without having the slightest hint of how they've affected others along the way." Although the eyes narrowed in response to some private pleasure felt, a second brilliant wave of blue illumined the glassy surfaces. "And is it also necessary to know the reason for a gift given?"

"I don't know. I . . . I suppose not." This whole idea was foreign, but it felt right.

"Okay, then," Ruby said, while running her fingers over the nubby fabric of her hat. "Perhaps a gift is given out of appreciation, maybe an appreciation of friendship. Or an appreciation of the joy that's been felt just knowing someone." She peered over at the young woman sitting beside her. "You think that's possible, Sadie Brennan?"

"To be honest, it never occurred to me. But sure, of course it's possible."

"Or perhaps a gift is given for other reasons." Her mouth thinned to form a crooked, impish grin. "Maybe a gift is given because somebody is tired of a possession and just wants to be rid of it. Do you think that's also possible?"

Sadie grinned back. "Are you tired of your hat, Ruby?"

The elder longingly looked down at the object in her fingers. "Oh, no. I've become rather fond of this old hat. No, I'm afraid I'll never tire of this hat."

Sadie watched the woman's fingers begin to work the jewelry clasp. *It's the pin. She's going to give me the pin.*

"I've had this pin for as long as I can remember. I believe I've had it as long as I've had the hat." She shrugged. "Folks started naming me after this pin. The name stuck."

Then what was her real name? "What did they call you before you put the pin in your hat?"

"They called me whatever they wanted."

"Where did the pin come from?" Sadie inquired.

Ruby glanced down at the floor. "Found it in the bottom of that old carpetbag. I took it out and pinned it to my hat," she said proudly. "It'd look pretty silly on an army coat, don't you think?"

"Oh, I don't know, Ruby. I think that pin belongs anywhere you want to put it."

"Really . . ."

Sadie knew she'd been had. She'd walked right over the spider's silken web threads. "And you think it belongs to me now," she smirked.

"Smart girl."

"Not so smart that I could see where you were going with all of this. Ruby, I'd be most honored to accept your gift." She hesitated, then took a deep breath. "And to be honest, without questioning the why of it, I feel humbled by it."

The old one reached over to set the pin in Sadie's hand.

A perceptible current passed between them. Gentle, yet powerful. Like dandelions popping up after a spring rain, goosebumps rose on the younger's arms. She felt the same sensation on her legs. The hair at the back of her neck stiffened. Scalp quivered. It reminded her of the time when she was six and had gotten an electric shock from trying to see what was in the slots of a wall plug.

The object felt heavy in her hand. Most tenderly, she curled her fingers over the pin, cradling it like a newborn baby in the soft bedding of her hand. And though she knew it was but a piece of dimestore costume jewelry, her instinct was to treat it like a crown jewel. To her, this piece of colored glass had more precious value than the Hope diamond. She closed her eyes to better feel its natural essence. Heat radiated from the cut glass. "It's warm," she whispered.

"It's been on my head," came the logical reply. "This mop of hair generates a lot of heat. Cover it with the hat which intensifies that heat, and you end up with a pretty warm piece of jewelry. Now it's your own body heat that's holding the heat, probably making it even warmer."

That was possible, thought Sadie, but it didn't feel probable. This felt like a different kind of heat, one more associated with an unnamed power than simple body heat. It was too much to think about now. Nor was it the time. She let it go. "Thank you, Ruby. I'll cherish it. Always."

"Oh, you don't have to say such gracious things. It's only a pin, after all. I just wanted to give you a little something to remember our . . . and Savannah!" she piped up with new exuberance meant to shift direction. "I have something for her, as well!"

Sadie watched as Ruby bent to excitedly lift the satchel from the floor. Thinking the owner was about to extract something from within, she waited.

Instead of opening the carpetbag as expected, she gently spread it across her lap. "I've had this for years and years," she informed with a warmly reminiscent tone, while lovingly smoothing her fingertips over the soft fabric. "We've been through a lot together. We've seen a lot, traveled from one end of this country to the other. This old bag has lugged an untold amount of needful things around for me." Fingertips lightly patted the bag. "Over the years it's probably carried more items than the hold of a merchant ship." She chuckled and corrected herself. "I suppose you call them freighters nowadays. Anyway, you must know what I mean."

The young woman nodded. "Sure, I do. I probably couldn't make an accurate list of everything I've seen you pull from that bag of yours.

The style is deceiving because it's amazing how much it actually holds.

"That first day in the Commons park, you pulled out a tam for Savannah to wear. The second visit to the Commons the satchel was bursting with bread bags for the ducks and pigeons. Candy for the Thai children. Medicine for the street kids' sick mothers and siblings." Sadie's wide smile gleamed. "Even various gardening tools." The smile faded when she saw the old one's curious expression.

"Medicine for the street kids' sick mothers? You say you saw that?"

Uh-ohhhh. Gulp. "Ruby, I told you I had a confession to make." Instead of lowering her eyes in contrition, she locked them on the intense greys. "Savannah and I really were spying on you."

Silence.

"I, ahhh . . . I saw you at the Farmers' Market when you were teaching the temple dances to the little Thai girls. I saw you pull candy out of your satchel just after I'd noticed how flat—empty—it'd been."

Mercurial eyes swirled with silver lights. "Oh yes! That's when I told you I'd also seen Savannah with you."

"No, no. Remember, I said she'd gone back to the car at that time. When I saw you at the Thai tent, I was alone."

The old one's eyes twinkled. "Sometimes we just think we're alone. Your niece was right behind you. It looked to me like she'd been try- ing to keep her distance so *she* could spy on *you*. If I'm not mistaken, I believe they call that tailing."

My nosey little Nancy Drew. "Then she also saw you dancing."

"That's probably so." And before Sadie could reply, Ruby had more to say. Her finger tapped her chin. "Now you say you saw me pull gardening tools from my bag. You did say that, didn't you?"

A nod came as a response.

"So . . . may I ask when that was?"

Sadie had to think back. "A week from last Wednesday. Savannah and I were in the cemetery visiting my parents' mausoleum. Afterward we strolled around reading some of the headstones. It was Savannah who spotted you. And then—"

"And you watched me clean up the forgotten graves."

Hit with guilt, Sadie lowered her head. "Yes," she admitted.

"Why? Why did you watch me do that?"

"I suppose because we'd seen you in so many other places around town, we never expected to see you in the cemetery as well. You surprised us." Sadie sighed. "To tell you the truth, Ruby, we were taken by the compassion you were showing. It's not something you see every day, even in a cemetery. We were anxious to know more about this remarkable woman we kept seeing. So, naturally, when we came across the groundskeeper, we asked about you."

Ruby's hands went up in the air. "Well, for crying out loud, why on earth did you put yourselves through so much trouble? Why not come straight to me with your questions? You could've helped me tidy up those sites. I could've introduced you to some of them."

"Them? Who's *them?*"

"The sleepers. The vagrants. The homeless ones."

"Homeless people roam cemeteries?"

"Well," she chortled, "only those who belong there. You know, the ones who have their names over their beds."

It didn't take long for the import of Ruby's words to sink in. "Ghosts? You're talking about ghosts?"

"They're really nothing more than confused spirits, Sadie, dear. Ghost is such a . . . well, a maudlin type of term with connotations of spookiness and frightful hauntings. Wouldn't you agree?" She raised her hands again. "Those poor confused spirits don't go flitting about saying 'wooo-wooo!' to everyone, you know. The poor folks have been given a bad rap by the living's Halloween tomfoolery—all a scant attempt to scare the pants off themselves. The poor souls out there just need a few kind words—a bit of a firm push—to get them headed in the right direction. Nothing spooky or hair-raising about that." She uncrossed her stretched-out legs. "I really wish you two would've joined me that day. It's so rewarding to help those souls along, let them know someone cares. You would've enjoyed it, I'm sure."

"Perhaps we can join you next time."

Ruby's lips pursed. She was thoughtful. "Perhaps our paths will cross the next time you two find yourselves in the cemetery. Destiny can work in the most unpredictable way. Mysterious ways. Loving ways."

The words seemed a bit more than curious to Sadie. She wasn't sure what the old one meant. "So, if it's meant to be, it'll happen."

"That's the way it works." Then she pointed a finger at her companion. "But . . ."

"But what, Ruby?"

"But I'm still curious as to when you saw me give medicine to the street kids. I can't imagine when that was? Are you sure?"

Sadie had the distinct feeling that the woman was asking leading questions. Fishing. "Maybe I was mistaken about that one. You've got to realize that I've seen you in so many unexpected places, I could have things a little mixed up."

Silence.

"I could've just assumed that that was what you were doing. It's not always clear what someone's doing when seen from a distance."

Silence.

"I saw you hand out toys once. That's probably what's got me confused."

Silence.

"Maybe I never saw you do that medicine thing after all. Yeah, come to think of it, it was the toys in the park I saw you hand out."

A silver eyebrow rose. It arched like a question mark above the intense stare of two pearly eyes. "If you don't watch it, you're going to break through to China pretty soon."

"What?"

"If you keep digging yourself deeper and deeper in that hole of yours, you're going to have to speak Chinese to the next people you see down there." Ruby released a long extended sigh. "How about I offer you a hand and pull you back up. How does last Saturday sound to you? Does that sound about right?"

The guilt-ridden reply came in a half whispered voice. "Yes."

"Now, would you be interested in knowing how I know it was last Saturday?"

"I'm not sure, but I've the feeling that you're going to tell me anyway, aren't you."

"Indeed I am. I know it was last Saturday because I saw you."

The blood drained from the young woman's face. Her throat went as dry as the watering hole of a desert mirage. Her gulp caught midway in her throat. "I . . . I—"

"It's okay, dear, don't be embarrassed. There's really nothing to be ashamed over." Ruby shyly lowered her head. "Actually, you've made me feel like quite the celebrity. I'm not used to that. In my line of work I've endeavored to remain in the background so that I can go about doing what I do without drawing attention to myself. Some folks can't understand that, you know."

Ruby had put Sadie at ease. She was comfortable enough to ask a question. "Folks can't understand what, Ruby?"

"The desire for anonymity. It blows their little minds. I'm talking about one's wish to stay in the background and out of the public eye. The need to avoid recognition and the natural fawning that follows."

"That's not hard to understand. It sounds like humility to me. Or maybe a case of shyness taken to the power of ten."

The old one gave each of those suggestions consideration. "Maybe it's fragments of them both. But mostly, it's the desire to work without extraneous distractions." A faraway look veiled the grey eyes.

"One works best without the hampering element of notoriety. That just gets in the way and makes the work more difficult, especially when it's the work that's more important than the one performing it." She gave her companion a wan, Mona Lisa smile. "When I'm with my own kind, nobody makes a big to-do about what I pull from my satchel. Nobody burns candles before my image or bends a knee in reverential posturing. No worshipers. No new religious sect begun in my name." She chuckled at the absurdity. "Can you imagine? The Church of Ruby? No, no. No, thank you. None of that for me. How it is . . . is exactly how it's supposed to be this time around." She shrugged. "If someone should happen to see an injured bird fly away from my hands, so be it. They may just smile and be on their way. If anybody notices that a mongrel dog romps away from me after limping up to me, it's no earth-shattering event that gets airtime the next day on all the television news channels. I don't get mobbed by reporters shoving microphones in my face. And that's just the way I want it. That's just the way I planned it. This time, I did it my way."

This time? "Ruby? Those nights you spent with Ida, were you healing her?"

"Ahh, Ida, now there was a sweet lady."

"Was?"

"Oh, yes. I sat with her. Held her hand and eased her out of her pain-wracked body. Helped guide her into the Light." She sighed with the glorious memory. "She was ready. She went so easily. Like slipping one's hand out of a soft, Italian leather glove."

"So . . . so you're not upset with me for wanting to discover why our paths kept crossing all the time?"

The grey eyes lowered to slits. "You going to burn candles?"

"No, Ruby. I'm not going to burn candles. I just feel incredibly blessed to have known you."

"And I as well, Sadie Brennan."

Sadie frowned.

"Oh yes, I feel blessed because you took my words to heart. Blessed for having your curiosity turn into a warm friendship rather than a type of adoration. You can't know how much that means to me unless you were in my shoes." At that point both women glanced down at the large hunting boots. Ruby snickered. "I have a lot of shoes."

Sadie grinned back. "So I've noticed. I've been told that you wear only brand new ones because you give them to the needy."

"You've been inquiring around about me? Besides the cemetery caretaker?"

"Father McElveney at the cathedral, for one, but it was the vet in the abandoned warehouse who clued me in about the oddity of your many shoes. Everyone's very protective of you, Ruby. A lot of good people love you. You do know that, don't you?"

"Love comes from doing for others without ever asking for or expecting anything in return. Love comes from unconditional giving. Love comes from accepting love at its face value, never suspiciously peeking around to see what's hidden behind it. Love comes from loving like you'll never get hurt. In love, time and time again, Sadie Brennan, love ends up causing deeply painful heartaches, but always keep going. Don't abandon it. Don't run or hide from it. Despite whatever former heartaches it caused, keep on loving like you'll never get hurt," she repeated, "because only then can a love be true. Remember that."

"That was beautiful, Ruby. But you do know that a lot of people love you, don't you?"

The old one absently fiddled with her hat. "Oh, sure. Yes, I do. Their love is what supports their perseverance when it begins to falter. Their love keeps them strong."

You really are God.

A sacred silence enveloped the room. The aroma drifting down the hall from Christopher's coffee room had suddenly transformed into a heady incense. In the first room on the right, the women quietly singing to the CDs became a choir of cloistered nuns chanting in an abbey, their angelic voices rising past the stained glass windows to swirl about the high vaulted ceiling. And the diffused afternoon light rays slanting down from the reading room's windows backlit the mass of silver hair with a glowing halo, its brightness spilling over her shoulders like a shining mantle.

Sadie didn't know if she'd ever felt so blessed as being in this room with an old woman in multiple flannel shirts, layered skirts and stockings, and an old military coat. She was overcome with the sacredness that flowed through every fiber of her being. She was weak with it. It filled her with such a sense of awe, tears formed in her eyes.

"Don't go there, Sadie Brennan," came the gently spoken advice.

A tear crested the lower eyelid when she looked up. She didn't bother to wipe it away. Like dew from the tip of a morning blossom, the tear fell onto her lap.

"I don't know who you are, Ruby. I used to care about discovering your identity after seeing you do so many curious and unexplainable things. I used to care so much that it became a driving obsession. But that's gone now. For the last couple of days I've been feeling that obsession falling away from me. I no longer care who you are, where you're from, or why you're here. I suppose you'd call that acceptance—the belief that fills the void left when the need for verification leaves.

"Now I don't care if you're some angelic being, a Goddess, or a kindly bag lady going around helping whomever she sees in need." She looked deep into the depths of Ruby's blue eyes. "It no longer matters because . . . because I believe I've come to love you. And I don't question that love because it's that love that makes me feel so incredibly blessed." She slid her chair closer to the chaise. Her knees were touching the sides. Leaning down and taking the woman's hands in her own, she whispered, "I hope you're around for a long, long time because the world's going to lose a great woman when you're gone. Although the world isn't aware of it, it needs you. It so desperately needs you."

When their eyes met again, a lone tear fell from the old one's eye. A second began coursing along the crevices of her cheek. It too fell without notice. "But there comes the time for each of us when we no longer hear the music. It can't be avoided."

"I don't think it's quite the same for you, though. You're different."

"Is that what you think? No, I'm no different." She looked down at herself. "I'm in one of these bodies just like everyone else is. They age. They get tired. The music will stop for me one day, as well."

That thought brought a rush of sadness. "Well, you're still spry of body and nimble of mind. You've got good years left in you." Sadie's hand patted the satchel on the woman's lap. "You've got many more needful things to pull out of your satchel."

Ruby straightened up. "That reminds me," she said, gently folding the beloved bag over on itself and then, with a feather-light touch, lowering it onto Sadie's lap. "My gift for Savannah."

Sadie's cheeks flushed. Hands frozen poised above the satchel, she was suddenly fearful that touching the sacred object would somehow be a sacrilege. Green eyes fixed on the elder's. "You can't be serious."

"Oh, but I am."

"But you need this. It's part of who you are."

"Nonsense. No object is ever a part of who someone is. No object defines one's identity. In a general manner of speaking, a particular object can be loosely associated with an individual, but to say that it actually defines them is going too far."

This was all too much. Sadie's head was spinning. She felt numb. And through that numbing haze, she reached for examples to prove her case.

"I disagree. For instance, Charlie Chaplin wouldn't have been Charlie Chaplin without his cane. George Burns wouldn't have been George Burns without his cigar. The same with Groucho Marx." Not wanting to break her momentum, she frantically scrambled for more ammunition. "Is Little Red Riding Hood recognizable without her red cape? What about Cinderella and her glass slipper? And—"

"Sadie."

"Cher's and Parton's wigs. Mickey Mouse's white gloves and—"

"Sadie." Ruby gave up trying to dam up the young woman's surging torrent of poor examples. Patiently waiting until it ran itself down to a trickle was the wiser course to take.

"—and there's Elton John's glasses, nuns' habits . . . ah, a witch's pointed hat and broomstick."

Silence.

"Marley's chains?"

Silence.

"King Neptune's forked staff?"

Silence.

The stream had gone dry.

"Sadie," the old one softly began, "when George Burns set his cigar stub down on the night stand ashtray and retired for the night, who was he?"

"George Burns," came the reluctant reply.

"And when Little Red Riding Hood hung up her cape on the wooden peg in her cottage, who was she?"

"Little Red Riding Hood."

"And is a nun not still a nun when she's in her nightie? Is Cher not still Cher when the wig returns to its stand at bedtime or when she's washing her own hair? Besides," she added, "I'm planning on getting a new satchel. You hardly gave me time to mention that I was going to replace it."

"The same kind of bag? A carpetbag?"

The elder nodded. "I've grown rather partial to them."

"Oh. Well, that's different."

"It is?"

"Sure, you'll still have your signature bag."

"You still aren't getting the point. A signature anything doesn't make the person, Sadie, who they are inside. Inside they're the same with or without any signature object that folks generally associate them with."

The whole issue had become irrelevant to Sadie now. The old one was still going to be carrying a carpetbag and that's all that mattered. She bent her head to study the satchel on her lap. Finally, she rested both hands on the fabric.

"Savannah will be thrilled," she said. "If I know her, she'll either carry it wherever she goes or swaddle it like a baby and hide it in the most protected place she can find. It'll mean the world to her. It'll be her most treasured possession."

That seemed to greatly please Ruby. "I knew I chose the right person to gift it to."

"She'll cherish it like something sacred. She'll treat it like the Philosopher's Stone, like Jack's magic beans, like the Lady of the Lake's returned sword."

The old one's bright look of pleasure fell to one of concern. "It's just an old ragtag bag," she reminded. "It's not wise to attribute magical properties to such a thing . . . to any *thing*. I have to caution you that it's never the object itself that holds the power. The object itself is nothing more than the *physical* vehicle through which one's faith can sometimes be manifested. This is very important, Sadie. Do you understand what I'm saying?"

The young woman's palms respectfully caressed the soft material. "Yes, I understand; it's Savannah who might have trouble grasping it."

Ruby leaned over and rested her hand over the younger's. Their eyes met. "I want you to give Savannah a message from me . . . the secret of the bag."

"The secret of it?"

The mass of silver hair bobbed. "Yes," she whispered. "Tell her that the satchel is never empty."

Green eyes lowered to the bag.

"Tell her that nothing is ever as empty as it appears." She tapped the carpetbag with her nail. "Tell her that this bag, even though it may *look* flat and empty, is always bursting with *possibilities!* Potential is what it holds, Sadie Brennan. Potential and possibilities. That's the big secret about this bag. Will you promise to tell her that for me?"

Why not tell her yourself? "Ruby, I know Savannah. I know that it'd mean the world to her if you could hold onto this until you could present it to her yourself. We don't have anything in particular planned for tomorrow. Depending on your schedule, maybe the three of us could meet somewhere. Receiving it directly from your hands would be the highlight of her life. Please say yes."

The old one's shoulders seemed to slump as though a great weight had been placed on them. "I'm afraid that won't be possible. I've a full day tomorrow."

That news didn't deter the young woman. "Another day, then. Nobody said it had to be tomorrow. We can arrange a date when you think you can fit us in."

Ruby patted the woman's hand. "Oh, Sadie, dear, it's not that I can't fit you two in. Oh, no, it's not that at all. My time with the two of you has been a blessed time for me. Truly blessed. It's been a respite from my work. My time with you and little Savannah has been uplifting. It's been like a sunny day breaking through winter's dreary greyness. You're both a joy to be around."

"Well, then?" Sadie brightened. "Let's set a date for the three of us to meet up. I won't let on that you have a gift for her. We'll keep it a secret, like a surprise party. Maybe we could even go back to—"

"Sadie."

"—that little family café in Ida's neighborhood and—"

"Sadie."

"—eat blackberry pie until we're blue in the face. Then, if you felt up to it, it might be fun to go over to . . ." Finally the excited woman realized that her exuberance wasn't mirrored in the old one's face. "What?"

"This is the only time I have to give you my gifts because I'm taking a bit of a hiatus, going to visit some of my longtime associates."

Associates? "Oh." Believing Ruby's associates were really none of her business and not wanting to intrude into her private affairs, she offered what she considered to be a viable alternate plan. "Well, when you return, then. Surely it can wait until you return?"

"I'm afraid not," came the unexpected reply. "I'm going to be picking up my new satchel and I'd rather not carry around two of them. It'd be rather cumbersome doing that. Unnecessary, as well."

Realizing that it'd be disrespectful to push it, Sadie let the issue go. "I see. In that case, I'd be honored to give this one to Savannah for you."

"Thank you, dear. Thank you so much." Her finger waved. "And you won't forget to tell her the secret of the bag, will you?"

"Potential and possibilities," Sadie said, smiling. "I won't forget."

"Now," the old one sighed, "if you'll be so kind as to take my cup up to the front, I'd like a refill. Get yourself one, as well. We got sidetracked, didn't we?"

Sadie set the pin inside the satchel. She rose and placed the bag on the reading table beside the sack from the import shop. "Sidetracked?" she asked, taking the woman's cup.

"We were going to talk some about the future, remember? I suppose you could say it was my fault for changing the order of things. I wanted to make sure I didn't forget to do my little gift-giving before we parted ways today." Her hands fluttered. "You go get us some of that fresh coffee. I heard Christopher grinding the beans a few moments ago." She winked. "Maybe see if there's anymore of those raspberry Bismarks left while you're at it."

"But, Ruby," Sadie teased, "what about not being able to find a place to pee when you're back on the street?"

"I'll be okay today."

"Are you sure?"

"Positive."

When Sadie left the reading room and headed up the hall toward the growing aroma of freshly brewed coffee, she puzzled over the woman's about-face regarding her prior worry. Surely finding an appropriate public restroom could be a problem for a street person such as Ruby. Although her appearance led one to initially perceive her as a typical homeless person, on the inside, she was a real lady.

While filling the cups, Sadie turned to the clopping sound that passed behind her. She grinned. "You come to check out the dough-nut trays for yourself?"

Without stopping, Ruby called over her shoulder. "Nope. You're going to do that. I'm on a mission to go see a girl about a cat. Wouldn't want to make a mess in the street, not that *I'd* care, mind you."

The woman standing at the refreshment counter heard the rest-room door slam shut. A frown furrowed her brow. She found nothing unusual about the first part of the woman's statement. It was the sec-ond part that sounded so off-key that it sent a shiver up her spine. It was like hearing a teacher's nails screech across a chalkboard. *Make a mess on the street? She wouldn't care? What an odd thing to say.*

Ruby, back in the chaise with her feet up, boots neatly turned out on the floor, was refreshed and ready to go another round. After tak-ing a healthy bite out of her doughnut, she took more time than was necessary to savor the flavor. "Okay," she finally said, after she washed it down, "let's not let ourselves get sidetracked again. This time we'll stay on track." She paused for a heartbeat to organize her thoughts. "Let's begin with you."

"Me?"

"Sure. Why not?"

Her face scrunched with a mixture of uncertainty and distaste. "Do we have to?"

"What, you don't want to know a few probabilities that line your future's path?"

The auburn head tilted. "Only if it's lined with flowerbeds leading to a rose-covered cottage with a white picket fence . . . on a hillside overlooking a sunlit harbor."

Ruby's eyes widened. "Maybe!" she cried, clapping her hands. "Do you have a crystal ball at home?"

Sadie's eyes grew big. "Serious? You're serious? That's what you see for me?"

The old one's gleeful grin dropped from her face like a cannonball landing in a lake. "No, I said maybe. We're talking probabilities here, not laser-carved sureties."

Sadie's mouth dropped when her balloon was so abruptly punctured. "You know what? I've changed my mind. I don't think I want to talk about my future after all. If it's all right with you, let's just skip that part."

Grey eyes narrowed as an extra tidbit was dangled. "Paul's going to come back with his—"

The younger woman's cheeks flushed. "Ohhh," she moaned. Then she grew indignant. "Oh!" she huffed. "Well, that's just hunky-dory! Am I supposed to be thrilled over that? Now I *know* I don't want to talk about my future. He can go to blazes for all I care. He can just take a flying—"

"—hat in hand."

"Ruby?" she began, trying to untangle the words that wanted to spill out in a knot of emotional clutter. "That man can hand me his beating *heart* for all I care. Hat or heart, it's not going to do him a damn bit of good. He threw away my love. He just treated it like an empty candy wrapper and dropped it into the nearest trash can!"

"Shall we move on . . . to a different aspect of the future?" Ruby wisely asked.

The suggestion had a cooling effect. It lowered the woman's boiling reaction to a simmer. "I'm sorry, Ruby," she apologized. "I just can't go there yet. I can't think about that situation right now." She shuddered. "It's still too raw."

"I understand. However," the elder hesitantly added, "that was the bright part of the future."

Green eyes rolled up to the ceiling. When they lowered to lock onto the pair swirling with pearly iridescence, Sadie sighed. "Spare me."

"Truly? You really don't want to hear about what's to be?"

"I thought you were going to speak of possibilities, how things *might* be."

"That's true, but there are a few specifics that have extremely high probabilities for showing up in that future."

The young woman accepted that answer. "Okay, so how about we skip the specifics and jump to the bottom line. Assuming there is a bottom line, that is."

After taking a moment to do a quick mental calculation, Ruby took another bite of the sweet, then replied, "All the particulars can be reduced to a generalized bottom line summation. Is that where you wish to jump to?"

Sadie looked to the window. The light had changed. She checked her watch, surprised at how quickly the afternoon had fled. "That's where I wish to jump to. You can fill in the details another time."

Ruby's expression held a hint of doubt. Without offering comment about the possibility of her detailing the specifics at a later date, she circumvented the issue. She pursed her lips over the idea, then raised the doughnut to her lips. Like a mime imitating the bliss of a gourmand, Ruby nearly moaned with the pleasure of licking out the last of the raspberry jelly. "A fine, fine specimen," she praised, after popping the last of the sweet into her mouth. Daintily, she dabbed at her lips. "Going to miss these marvelous little wonders."

Sadie understood the love of good food, of one's favorites. "That bakery across the street will still be here when you get back. I'm sure Chris knows which kind your sweet tooth craves. They'll be ready and waiting for you . . . fresh from the oven as always."

"He's a nice young man. Has a heart of gold, that one."

"It's easy to see that he thinks the same of you, Ruby. And although I've just met him, I can tell he's a very sensitive individual. Caring. Attentive and considerate."

The old one looked askance. "He's not for you, Sadie Brennan. You do know he's not for you, don't you? You two are equals playing in different leagues, if you know what I mean."

Sadie smirked. "I'm aware of that, Ruby. I'm a big girl. You don't need to explain the birds and the bees to me."

"And you like him just the same?"

"Of course!" she said, just before playfully displaying a false pout. "I'm a little offended that you didn't already know that."

"Oh, wipe that silly pout off your face. Who do you think you're kidding? I did already know that. I was just . . . well, testing the waters. I was thinking that you and he would make great friends."

"But I'm just visiting here. I live in Maine, remember?"

"I remember. Since when does distance interfere with friendship? Have you stopped being friends with Tina while you're here?"

"Of course not."

"There you go. Maybe you and Christopher will have a common interest to cement a long-term friendship."

"Is this something you see in my future?"

The old one's eyes narrowed. "Thought you didn't want to discuss your future."

"I don't, but I'll keep Chris in mind. Besides, now that you brought up the issue of the future, we seem to have gotten sidetracked again. You were going to tell me what the bottom line is."

"That's right. Before I get to the summation, I need to explain something first. The bottom line won't mean anything unless you're aware of the name of each part of the formula used to get us there."

Sadie didn't have a problem with that. "Sounds reasonable enough."

"Ready?"

"Ready."

"Okay then." Ruby took a deep breath. After exhaling, she paused just long enough to be sure her listener was paying attention. "The names of the formula parts are the following: a declining economy, dirty politics, cataclysmic geologic events, widespread civil unrest, increasing white collar crime, skyrocketing foreclosures and personal bankruptcies due to employer downsizing and offshoring—"

"Good grief." Sadie sighed.

"—unbearable personal stress, outbreaks of new diseases, warring nations, global weather changes, melting glaciers, a people's revolt, erosion of private citizens' civil liberties through the government's invasiveness under the blanket of national security, medical care collapse, escalating intolerance, intensified—"

Sadie upturned her palms. "That's enough. I get the picture. All of those elements will contribute to the bottom line which . . . is?"

"A pandemic of two very different diseases."

"New ones?"

Ruby sadly shook her head. "No. These two have been around for ages and ages. One afflicts the dispassionate wealthy, the other ravages the wretched disadvantaged."

"But how can that be? I've never heard of such heinous cells that have the discriminating ability to differentiate between target organisms. Germs and viral cells can't recognize whether or not someone is rich or poor. What kind of vile sicknesses are you talking about?"

Cerulean eddies whirled through the old one's opaline irises. "Oh, yes, they're insidious things to be sure, but, Sadie," the old one cautioned with a raised finger, "watch yourself. You've *assumed* that the noxious diseases themselves make the choices regarding whom to infect. Not so. I never said that."

"Then how—"

"It's the *people* who draw it to *themselves*. The wealthy bring it on by their arrogance, their heartless insensitivity to the suffering of others, their indifference. The disadvantaged contract it through the erosion of their perseverance, their loss of hope."

"The names, Ruby. What are the names of these two diabolical diseases?"

Their names," she whispered, "are Apathy and Despair."

A heavy cloak of silence settled over the two women sitting in the room. Neither wished to speak, for there was nothing more to say.

The younger one could feel the suffocating weight of the elder's great empathy. And although she desperately searched her mind for some type of effective comfort to offer the old one, nothing came to mind. She had the feeling that even if she continued sitting there searching her mind for just one uplifting thing to say, she'd still be there until her auburn hair turned to silver. There was just nothing good to say about apathy and despair.

Sadie reached over and took the old one's hands in her own. She gently squeezed them, then repeatedly ran her hand over the deeply veined surface. "No matter what may come," she said in a velvety voice, "one still has to live one day at a time, one hour, one minute at a time. And if one lives those days, hours, and minutes to the fullest— the best they can—then life is still worth living. It's still worth trying to salvage. Hope still has a strong heartbeat.

"Ruby, you've taught me more in the short time I've known you than all the years I spent in college. I've come to accept my sister's escapist behavior due to her choice to remain in denial. Through you, little Savannah found a reason to speak. It was you who became her inspiration. It was you who eased her from her shell. And it was you who made me realize a hundred things, not the least being a correction made in my perspective of value and priority. I've come to truly understand that the whys of things aren't important. Neither are the whos. What's ultimately most important is one's basic beingness, one's goodness."

Both women took note of a perceptible alteration in the room's light. The walls were awash in a warm, pink glow. It was Ruby who acknowledged it. She slowly withdrew her hands and patted her companion's. "The end of the day is drawing nigh," she said. "Time to be on our way." She swung her feet to the floor and padded to her overcoat. Reaching down into each pocket of it, she extracted two old tennis shoes and held them up. Without comment, she crouched to pull them on her feet.

Curious, Sadie pointed to the pair of hunting boots on the floor. "What about those?"

"Those go to Old Chet. I'll leave them outside by Christopher's door. Old Chet will be coming by in a few minutes and find them."

Sadie didn't quite understand how this shoe thing worked, but took the woman's word for it. She helped Ruby on with her coat, then donned her own. Picking up the carpetbag and the sack containing the statue, she turned to see the old one securing her hat down over the wild hair. Sadie grinned. "Doesn't look quite the same without that pin."

"It is the same, though. And I'm the same without that satchel. In a couple-a days I'll have the new one."

With nothing for her to carry now, Ruby picked up the cumbersome boots. "I'll take these. I know where to leave them."

Together they returned their cups to the coffee room.

"Should we wash these?" Sadie asked.

"Nah, gives Christopher something to do. Keeps him busy. Besides, he's fairly finicky about how they're washed."

After they said their goodbyes to the young man, they stood outside the door while Ruby looked about. "Here," she said, setting the pair of boots below the display window. "Old Chet will find them here."

"Aren't you afraid someone else will come by and take them before Old Chet gets here?"

"Nope."

They stood in the middle of the sidewalk for a few minutes, neither of them wanting to be the first to walk away from the other.

"Can I drop you off somewhere?" Sadie asked, hoping to prolong their departure.

"Oh no," Ruby said, pointing down the way. "I'm only going a short ways. Walking is such good exercise, you know. Keeps the old joints oiled."

Sadie smiled. "Are you sure?"

"Sure I'm sure. Don't you go worrying about me, I'll be gone lickety-split."

The noise from the construction site got louder when a worker started an auger. The women, even though they were standing shoulder to shoulder, had to raise their voices to be heard.

"No use us standing here hollering at one another," Ruby shouted.

"You're right. Well . . . guess I'll be off, then. Have a good evening." She raised the carpetbag. "Thank you, Ruby. We're honored."

"You're welcome. Tell Savannah I'll be thinking of her."

"I will. Bye, now. See you when you get back."

Ruby nodded and both women turned their backs to one another.

"Sadie! Oh, Sadie!" Ruby called after the retreating woman. "Sadie!"

But the young woman carrying the old carpetbag never heard her.

Ruby sighed and hung her head. "Probably just as well," she mumbled, stepping off the curb. "Who can hear anything with all this racket going on?"

"Hey! Lady!" a worker frantically shouted, wildly waving his arms. "Hey, lady! Watch OUT!"

Another laborer began to run toward the street. "Stop! STOP!"

Ruby wondered if those men ever developed hearing problems working around so much loud machinery. Shouting all day like they do, they must go home at night with hoarse throats. She shook her head as she turned for one last glance at Sadie. Above the worker's voices, Ruby heard the beeping of a heavy equipment vehicle backing up. It was the last thing she heard.

Sadie, crossing to her van, looked up to see a woman standing on the sidewalk. The lady's hand shot up to her mouth and, eyes wide in utter disbelief, a shocked expression froze on her face. Pointing to the opposite side of the street, she began to scream.

Sadie spun around. From all directions, bystanders were rushing toward a construction vehicle to join others gathering around someone on the ground by its back wheel. Sadie recognized Christopher. He was on his knees, bent over the downed person. "Oh, my God," she said. It was then that her eyes were drawn to the legs of the fallen victim. Multiple socks covered one foot. An old white tennis shoe had been flung against the curb.

"RU-BE-E-E-E!"

Racing to the scene, Sadie was deaf to the squeal of an approaching fire rescue siren. She pushed through the crowd gathered around the fallen woman.

"Move aside! Move aside!" she screamed, while shoving people this way and that. When she reached Ruby, she fell to her knees beside the young man who was checking for a pulse. Brushing aside the old one's mass of hair, she laid her hand on the creviced cheek.

Christopher had begun CPR.

"Ohh, my God!" she cried. "Ohh, no, Ruby! Ruby, no-o-o-o!" She heard Christopher count to three with his compressions when her jacket was suddenly tugged from behind.

"Move aside, miss. We need to get in here."

She looked up at a policewoman clearing the way for the EMS crew. "But I . . . I—"

"Step back, ma'am," said the officer. "Let them do their job."

Mentally numb with shock, she let the uniformed woman ease her back from the scene.

Christopher stood and joined her. He wrapped his arm around Ruby's friend.

Trembling with anxiety, her breaths tried to keep pace with her thundering heart as she watched the emergency crew charge up the paddles.

The old one's body jerked violently in response.

Again the paddles were charged.

A delicate rosy glow fell over the scene. *She's gone. She's gone to meet up with her associates. She knew all along this was going to happen.* Sadie's blurry eyes lifted to the sky. A blood-red veil of clouds silently trailed in front of the lowering sun. It reminded her of a queen's royal robe, its long train gracefully sweeping over an azure marble floor. *Goodbye, Ruby. Goodbye, sweet Queen of Heaven.*

Crushing the satchel to her chest, she lowered her gaze. A paramedic checked her watch, then called the time. Sadie's disbelief slowed all motion. Dazed, she watched the crew gently place Ruby onto a stretcher.

As if in a dream, she heard the double doors of the ambulance close. No siren sounded as it pulled away.

Christopher led her to the curb. Neither could find their voice. Neither knew what to say.

Behind them, two bystanders were shaking their heads. "Did you see how she was dressed?"

"Yeah," the other grunted, "heard they couldn't find any ID. They made her for a street person. What's a street person doing around here?"

"Panhandling, probably. Eh, who the hell knows. Go figure. At least that's one more homeless person off the street. Yep. One more bum for Potter's Field."

Overhearing their crude comments, Sadie's tightened her grip like a vise around the statue she'd been holding. She felt the urge to haul off and swing it at the insensitive men.

Christopher turned and glared at them.

They noticed. One raised his chin in challenge. "You got a problem, buddy?"

"You a bum lover?" the other asked, taking a step closer.

Sadie felt Christopher's arm tense. "Don't," she whispered, "they're not worth it. Let it go . . . for Ruby."

Christopher ignored the bullies and guided Sadie over to the door of his shop.

"Weenie!" one of the men called as they joined the disbursing crowd.

"Come inside," Chris offered. "I've got a bottle of Bailey's in the cupboard. It might help to settle you a bit."

"No, ahh . . . no, thank you. I . . ."

"I don't think you should get in your car right now." He put his hands on her shoulders and gently ran them down to her elbows. "You're shaking like a leaf. Come inside for a few minutes."

She didn't know what to do. "Somebody should be with her. You know, claim the body. She didn't have family, did she? Who's going to see she gets a decent burial? I . . ." Her words trailed off when she spied a man approaching. A soiled, beige trench coat hung from shoulders bent under the yoke of a lifetime of stress. Food particles were caught in the ragged beard growing over sunken cheeks. Dark, hollow eyes, shaded by a ridge of heavy brows, shifted from side to side as they swept the sidewalk for some unknown object. Intent on his quest, he ignored the two standing in the bookshop doorway.

The two watched his shuffle quicken when he passed them.

Eyeing something, he did a quick-step toward it.

The pair heard the man make a grunt of pleasure as he bent to claim his prize. Their eyes met in shared understanding when they saw the man clutch the hunting boots to his chest and hightail it down the street.

"Old Chet," Sadie murmured.

"Who?"

"Old Chet. Ruby left those boots there. Said they were for Old Chet."

And it was seeing Old Chet fulfill Ruby's last mission of compassion that seemed to calm the two better than any hot cup of Bailey's could.

Sadie sighed. She looked up into Christopher's eyes. "I'm a little better now."

"Me, too," he said, squeezing her arm. "But the offer still stands."

"I know, but I'll be okay. I'm going to go home and try to find out where they took her. She's not going to end up in Potter's Field. She's given me so much. She's given so much of herself. That's the least I can do for her."

He pulled a business card from his pocket. "Will you call me and let me know what you find out? I'd like to help. In fact," he added, "I know a lot of people who would be mortified if they couldn't also help. Ruby touched so many lives. They'd love to do a little something in return."

She promised she'd call.

The drive home wasn't as direct as planned. Sadie found herself circling the Commons where the three of them had first met. In the twilight, she sat on the park bench and stared into the cold waters of the pond. Fragments of their different conversations replayed in her mind. Snapshots of the old one's various facial expressions flipped past like the pages of a family photo album.

When Sadie eventually arrived home, the first thing she did was call the ambulance company to track down where Ruby had been taken. Her second call was to a hospital. The third, to the medical examiner's. The last number she dialed was Christopher's, but she hung up before it had a chance to ring. After three fretful starts and stops, she found the courage to hang on until he answered.

"Chris, it's Sadie. Are you sitting down?"

His voice was shaky. "Oh, God, why do I need to sit down?"

"There's . . . it seems there's no body to claim."

"What!"

"The M.E. says there's no record of a Jane Doe coming in. They said it'd been four days since they had a couple homeless people. Both were men. Chris," she whispered, "Ruby's vanished."

Later, Savannah sat on the edge of her bed, body slumped into the cradling arms of her aunt. Held close to the child's heart was the old tapestry carpetbag. The two had spent hours hugging and crying, sharing each other's deep sorrow. When the child's red and burning eyes began to get heavy with grief's weariness, Sadie pulled the covers back and tucked her in. Savannah, having no strength or will to resist, snuggled the satchel beneath her chin. After the light was turned out, the child called to her aunt. "Aunt Sadie?"

Returning to the girl's side, she smoothed back the coppery red tendrils. "What, sweetie?"

"I have a question. Will you answer me truly?"

"All right, truly."

"If this satchel is full of possibilities like Ruby said, and since nobody knows where she is, you know . . . um, her body . . . could she still be alive somewhere?"

Sadie thought she was all cried out until the innocence of the child's question brought renewed stinging. Trying to be strong, she blinked the tears back.

"Oh, honey, no. The dead can't come back to life. That's just not possible. And since it's not a possible thing, it can't be one of the possibilities in that bag. I'm sorry. I'm so sorry."

The child was persistent. "But the dead can come back to life, Aunt Sadie. What about Lazarus? And Jesus. Jesus came back to life."

"Well, yes, but Jesus was the Son of God."

"That's what I mean. Ruby wasn't the son or daughter of God. She was bigger. Ruby *was* God."

The logic left Sadie speechless. In her sudden quandary, she stuttered, "I . . . I—"

The delicate little eyebrows arched. "What's the matter, Aunt Sadie? Don't you believe in Ruby?"

"Sure I do, honey. We just can't say for sure if she was really God."

"I believe she was, don't you?"

Do I? "Savannah," she confessed, "I just don't know. Maybe she was. And if she really was, I think she needed to move on to attend to other work. Someplace else. If she was God, she knew that the accident was going to happen. And," she added, "that's probably the real reason why she gave her pin and satchel away. She wasn't going to need them anymore. The accident happened for a reason, honey. We have to accept that."

"Okay. Do you have anything planned for tomorrow?"

A shadow of concern crossed Sadie's face over the child's lightning switch to another matter. "No, honey. Why?"

"Can we go back to the cemetery?"

Considering what had just happened, Sadie thought the child's request was odd. "Sure, if that's what you want. Why do you want to go there?"

"I want to tell my daddy something."

The girl's answer was unexpected. It showed that a lot of healing had occurred . . . healing that could've only come from one person. Ruby.

"Sure we can go do that. I think it's a wonderful idea." Sadie bent to kiss her niece once more. "Goodnight, sugar. If you wake up later and want to talk or just be close to someone, there's lots of room in with me. Okay?"

Savannah's eyes fluttered with heaviness. She sleepily nodded.

And after Sadie returned to her own room, she headed straight for the phone. "Tina? I know it's late but . . . can we talk?"

Fifteen

Saturday

Before the girl came down for breakfast, her aunt had called the dance school to cancel the two lessons. Now she sat with Greta and Josef while the kitchen filled with the tantalizing aroma of blueberry muffins. The couple were brought up to date on everything there was to tell about Ruby.

"What do you think?" Sadie asked the two elders. "Could it have been possible?"

Josef puffed on a pipe. Smoke curled up from the glowing ember on top of the squat, well-used bowl. Normally, he wouldn't have been smoking in the house because Mira claimed it made every-thing stink. But she'd left early. Although nobody knew for sure where she'd gone, it was naturally assumed by all that another business conference was the reason for her absence. The rising fra-grant smoke of his cherry blend tobacco was his only reply. Deep in rumination, he reserved his reply until the idea had been fully thought out.

The young woman waited for someone to answer.

The housekeeper stared into the dark liquid in her cup. When her eyes finally rose to meet the emerald pair, her manner was solemn.

"Strange things have happened in this world of ours. Josef has seen the Little People in all of his gardens. Most folks scoff at the very idea of their existence. Yet, once you've seen something with your own eyes, no amount of skeptical scoffing or ridicule can change your mind because you've seen what you've seen. People's disbelief can't make it not so, can't undo reality. Same with UFOs.

"As to the idea of God actually walking among us, who knows, Sadie? It's not up to us to question the ways of Providence." She shrugged. "The way I see it, a Divine Being wouldn't be bound to make an appearance in a form humans have devised. It seems to me that God would come however She or He deemed best. Whether that form is a bearded man riding a blazing golden chariot trailing fire through the sky from its flaming wheels or in the form of a beggar woman walking the streets doing quiet miracles isn't really germane. I think the *form* is what's got you stuck."

"I think you have a point," the younger woman admitted. "So you're saying that you think Ruby was the real thing?"

"No, I'm not saying that. I'm saying that I don't discount it out of hand. I don't disbelieve in the *possibility* of it."

Sadie glanced over to Josef. "You ready to give us your opinion, yet?"

He smiled through a full load of smoke in his mouth. Taking his time, he slowly released it as perfectly formed smoke rings.

"I believe in the possibility of it, as well. And if it's a possibility, why should we think it impossible for it to be Ruby?"

"So you do believe Ruby was real."

His head shook. "Don't put words in my mouth. I said I believe in the *possibility* of Ruby being divine."

Possibility. Possibilities. She'd heard a great deal about that concept recently. "So what you're both saying is that Ruby *could've* been . . ." She cringed. ". . . God."

"You can't speak it, can you?" Josef asked. "Reticence to voice something shouldn't go hand in hand with a strong belief in it unless one fears ridicule. You'll get none of that from us," he said, indicating himself and his wife. "So what are you afraid of?"

Sadie looked from one elder to the other. "Being wrong? I don't know."

Greta felt empathy rise within her. "I don't envy your situation, Sadie. However, you're the one who spent time with the old one. I would think that your verification, one way or the other, wouldn't come from mental analysis. I would think that it'd come from how you *felt* . . . in here," she said, pointing to her heart. "If you want my opinion, I think your mind is having one hell of a tug-of-war with your heart."

Greta was more than observant, Sadie thought, she was downright fey. "So which do I turn off and ignore?"

The cooking timer went off. Greta rose and replied while heading toward the oven. "Nobody can tell you the answer to that one. That's something you will have decide all by yourself." She slipped on an oven mitt and pulled out the golden muffins. "Don't forget, though, you can mentally beat at something until it's unrecognizable. The heart won't do that. The heart's more connected to the psyche, the soul. When folks let feelings be their guide, they're rarely wrong. It's that 'thinking things to death' that can scramble what's real and turn one around like a train car in a roundhouse. You know, shift them off onto another track, usually the wrong one."

"But people have to think things out."

Josef cut in. "Of course, they do. We're not saying they shouldn't think things out. Certainly, logic has to be applied in order to reason things out. But, Sadie," he reminded, "it's a fact that logic only goes so far—such a short way. Our rules of logic only fit elements of reality that are crammed into the box. What about the other ninety percent of reality that surrounds that box? Can logic accurately be applied to undiscovered or unproven aspects?"

"Well, no," she said, "because we haven't identified all of their behavioral characteristics. We can only use logic when we know the form of something, its composition, how it predictably behaves under every condition. I'm dealing with a formless abstract. I'm dealing with something that . . . well, who knows how God's mind works? We think we know, but we really don't, do we? We think we have the pattern of God's mind figured out, mapped out in the finest detailing. That it always goes for the good and right ways of doing things. But that's really *our* concept of God's behavior. In reality, God may think and behave in completely different ways altogether. So . . . to say that God *couldn't* come here in the form of Ruby and dressed as a bag lady would be a completely arrogant statement. It'd be arrogant because it makes the assumption that we know how God will behave, that we can second-guess how God intends to carry out a plan or purpose."

Josef and Greta respectfully let the young woman reach the only conclusion possible.

"So . . . it'd be more logical for us to not make such assumptions. It'd be more logical—and respectful—to say that God *could* come as a Ruby."

"Ruby? Did they find Ruby?" a little voice asked from the doorway.

"No, honey," Sadie said. "We were just doing some big person thinking."

The fuzzy satchel was carefully laid on the table beside the child's usual place setting. A small lump between the double layer of fabric gave evidence of something inside. She plopped in her chair, then licked her lips. "I smell fresh blueberry muffins." Without breaking meter, she added, "Why is saying that God could come as a Ruby big person thinking? I think that and I'm not a big person."

Greta was whipping eggs for omelets. "We were doing big person thinking about why it was *possible* for God to come as a Ruby," she explained.

Savannah's eyes slid to the carpetbag. "I know about possibilities," she proudly announced. "Ruby told us all about them."

"I know," Greta replied with an understanding smile. "Ruby was pretty smart, wasn't she?"

"She was the smartest person ever. That's because she's God."

Everyone noticed that the girl didn't use the past tense when speaking about Ruby.

Concerned, her aunt tried to make a clarification. "And we know that she's gone now, don't we? Right?"

"Right."

With relief, Sadie smiled.

"She's gone on a little trip somewhere," Savannah added.

Sadie's eyes shifted to Josef's. His expression reflected possibility. She gave her attention back to her niece. Reaching for her hand, she patted it. "You okay this morning?"

"Sure. Like I said, Ruby's just gone on a little trip." The small eyes twinkled like a starry sky. "What do you wanna bet we see each other again?"

Sadie's smile widened like a Cheshire cat's. "Everything I have, honey. I'd bet every last thing I had."

The ride to the cemetery was uneventful. Despite their destination, Savannah's incessant chatter reminded her aunt of a squirrel scolding a bird for discovering its secret stash of pinecone nuts. The girl talked about the school clothes she got when she went shopping with her mother. She excitedly talked about seeing her school friends again and then went into which girls were stuck up and which were the best athletes on the field, in the pool, and on the gymnasium floor. After the driver had heard all the gossip about school, she listened to a critical analysis of each dance school classmate's talent and its prognosis with respect to going professional one day. Savannah was a thinker. She had strong opinions about everything.

The girl's nonstop jabbering made Sadie smile. Compared to the silence that had greeted her when she first arrived, the sound of the running little voice was music to her ears.

"Haven't you been listening to me?" the passenger stopped to ask.

"Of course I have. We're the only ones in the car, who else am I going to listen to?"

"But you keep smiling like something's funny and I haven't said anything funny."

The driver winked at the girl. "People smile for all kinds of reasons. I've been doing it because the sound of your voice brings me a warm, fuzzy feeling."

The inquisitive face lit up. "Really?"

"Really. All the talking you've been doing reminded me of how far you've come since I first arrived. Then, you weren't letting out a peep, not even a whisper. I missed the sound of your voice. I wanted more than anything for you to speak. Even if it was just one little word. I remember worrying over whether or not I could help you. But it's been like a miracle. It's been a miracle from Ruby."

"No, Aunt Sadie, it wasn't Ruby. It was you. If it wasn't for you I never would've met her. She started appearing to you first."

Appearing to me. God appearing to me. She shook the unbelievable thought from her mind as she flipped down the turn signal. "Here we are. Let's see if I can remember where to go without having to drive all over."

"I remember," the little one piped up. "I can show you." She extended her arm and rested her wrist on the dash. "Here," she pointed, "turn left here."

After veering off on several different curving ribbons of blacktop, the van eased over to the side and stopped. The two got out. All signs of autumn had disappeared from the big old-growth trees. Their skeletal frames etched ragged silhouettes against the pewter backdrop of the pale November sky. The grounds held scant signs of fallen leaves. Grass gone yellow and prickly crunched beneath their feet.

Suddenly Savannah sucked in her breath. She let out a feeble sound, then raced forward, legs pumping, satchel bouncing in her hand.

Sadie, taken off guard by the girl's unexpected behavior, hurried after her. Up ahead, she saw her bend to reach for a brightly colored object perched on the center of a headstone.

"Look!" Savannah squealed, holding the object up in the air. Jumping up and down with excitement, she was impatient to show what she had. "Hurry, Aunt Sadie! Look! She did it! She really, really did it!"

Not wanting to shout, Sadie waited until she was near the grave site. "Who did it? Did what?"

Holding the object in both hands and extending it to her aunt, Savannah shook it. "Ruby! She left it *here!*"

Sadie nervously scanned the grounds before giving her full attention to the tiny pumpkin. "I don't understand," she admitted. "That looks like one of the little ones you picked out at the farm that day."

Savannah giggled. "It is! It *is* one of those!"

"But . . . how—"

Tenderly setting the pumpkin back in the exact spot she found it, she grabbed her aunt's hand and led her to the stone bench beside the grave. "Remember when we were in the Commons park and I ran back to give Ruby the pumpkin?"

"Yes," Sadie said, waiting to see where this was going.

"Do you remember seeing her bend down and whisper something?"

Thinking back to that day, she did remember that she'd wanted to ask Savannah what the old one had said to her. "I do remember that. I was going to ask you about it, but it slipped my mind. What did she say after you gave her the pumpkin?"

The girl's eyes grew to the size of prize-winning melons. "She asked me if I'd be upset if she gave it to someone she knew. She said he was a very special person."

Both pairs of green eyes shifted to the dab of orange perched on the grey headstone.

"See? Her special person was Daddy!"

Perhaps our paths will cross the next time you two find yourselves in the cemetery. Icy fingers ran up Sadie's spine like a skeletal hand over piano keys.

But there was more.

"And look here!" Savannah cried, reaching into the satchel. The bump in the fabric disappeared when the tiny orange object was extracted and held high. "This is the final pumpkin I brought from the farm. I got it for Daddy!"

She skipped a few steps away from the bench and knelt. As she set her gift beside Ruby's, her voice was clear and strong. "Hi, Daddy. I got this just for you. I hope you like it. I didn't know you knew Ruby, but I guess she knows everybody because she's God. Maybe that can be our little secret . . . between you and me and Aunt Sadie. I wanted to come today—"

Sadie felt a lump form in the throat. It felt like a boulder. She fought back tears. Her niece was being so brave, she didn't want to be the one who fell apart.

"—because I have something I really, really need to tell you." The girl bent to pluck off a shriveled leaf from the engraved stone.

The quiet approach of a woman distracted Sadie's attention from the girl. When she saw who it was, her heart lunged with a surge of apprehension. The woman was wearing *jeans* of all things! *Oh, go away!* she mentally shouted to Mira as she watched the newcomer slowly creep up to her daughter's back.

The sisters' eyes met. They held like the massive antlers of two whitetail bucks locked in battle.

The antlers were released when Mira warmly smiled. "Shhh," she silently mouthed, while raising a lacquered fingernail to her lips.

They both lowered their gaze to the child and listened.

"Daddy? Aunt Sadie and I saw Ruby in the cemetery last week. She was telling somebody to quit hanging around and go home where they belonged. That night, I lay in bed thinking about it. It scared me because it made me think that maybe you couldn't go home because you were waiting for me to get better . . . to stop blaming myself for your accident."

The woman on the bench saw her sister's hand fly to her mouth and muffle the sound of an outcry. Above the trembling hand, eyes began to mist.

"So I want you to be able to go home and be with Ruby, Daddy. I wanted to tell you that I don't blame myself anymore. Ruby said that people die because it's just their time to stop hearing the music. And that's nobody's fault, it's just how it is."

Mira's shoulders were quivering.

"And, Daddy? One more thing. Please don't be mad at Mama. I know she loved you a whole lot. She misses you so much that she has to keep really busy so she doesn't hurt so much. It's okay because I know that deep down, in her very heart of hearts, she loves me, too. She doesn't mean to be crabby all the time, she just—"

Mira dropped to her knees. Arms flung around her child as a torrent of sobs broke through her dammed-up emotions. "Ohhh, my baby!" she cried, while beginning to rock them both back and forth. "Ohh, my sweet, precious baby!"

Surprised, Savannah first looked up at her aunt. Tears were falling in a steady stream over her cheeks. The woman behind her could only be one person. "Mama?" She turned her head. "Mama!"

"Oh, yes, baby, it's Mama. I'm so sorry. I've been such a fool. I've been so blinded by grief that I've been running away from everyone I loved . . . from everyone I should've been running *to*."

The two faced each other. Mira examined her daughter's face so intently it was as though she were seeing it for the first time. Trembling fingers cleared a stray tendril from the girl's eyes. "Oh, God, forgive me, honey. Please, forgive me for shutting you out."

Sadie watched in awe as the shattered pieces of her sister's shell fell down about her. One of Ruby's words drifted to the fore of her mind. *Marinating.* Yes, she thought, Mira had been marinating, looking at the past and examining the whys of her behavior. Finally, she was ready to move on. Seeing the two now, she felt like an intruder in their private moment. It crossed her mind that she should quietly extract herself from the scene.

Small hands cradled Mira's face. "I told Daddy I stopped blaming myself for his accident. You shouldn't blame yourself, either, Mama. Neither of us could help how we felt, but now we know better, huh."

Mira's gaze swept over the mirrored surface of the headstone. Her fingertips dipped into the crevice of the engraved name. "Oh, David," she whispered. "Forgive me, my love. Forgive me for not taking the love we shared and showering our daughter with it."

Seeing her mother cry so hard upset the child. Her small hand tenderly covered the woman's. "Daddy didn't blame you, Mama," she comforted. "I think it just made him sad to see you hurting so bad."

"Don't be sad, my beloved," Mira murmured, setting her palm on the grass below the stone. "We're going to be all right now. Our little Savannah and I are going to be all right." Again, she reached over to trace the lettering. She'd been so involved in the moment of her breakthrough that her awareness hadn't extended beyond the child. Now it was expanding to take note of a greater range of her surroundings. "What? Pumpkins?" she whispered, giving a quizzical glance at her daughter.

Wiping tears from her eyes, Savannah managed a smile. "I brought one of them for Daddy," she said.

"One?" she asked, eyeing the twin orange orbs.

The girl's tousled ringlets bounced with her nod. "Ruby left the other one. I gave it to her and she asked me if it was okay if she gave it to a very special friend of hers. When Aunt Sadie and I got here, Ruby's pumpkin was sitting right there. I put mine beside it."

Trying to absorb the information, Mira again shifted her gaze to the two orange objects on the headstone. "She knew your daddy?"

"Ruby knows everyone, Mama. She's God."

Hearing that, Sadie stiffened. *Oh, Savannah, I wish you hadn't said that right now. Everything was going so well.* She steeled herself for the expected response.

Mira pulled the child closer to her. "I love you, honey. I love you with all my heart. Things are going to be different from now on. We've got over two years' worth of catching up to do." Her eyes went to those of the woman on the bench. "Yes," she repeated, "things are going to be a lot different." Holding her hand out for her daughter, she smiled. "Let's go sit with your Aunt Sadie."

Choosing to sit beside her sister, Mira situated herself between the only two family members she had. Normally, she would have placed Savannah in between, choosing distance as her preferred position.

Mira's choice of positioning was so out of the ordinary, Sadie noticed the uncharacteristic move. She nearly startled when the manicured hand gently covered her own. She looked down at the strange sight, then raised her eyes to meet her sister's.

Eyes misting over again, Mira said, "There's one last person I need to ask forgiveness from. Sadie, I've been such a fool, a real jerk. I've treated my very own sister like a . . . well, like a juvenile delinquent or a suspected criminal." Whether from shame or as an effort to blink and clear the tears, she lowered her gaze to their hands. Her fingers splayed to interlock with those of her sister's.

"I'm not sure how or even where to begin and—"

"Whatever your reason, you have my forgiveness," Sadie cut in. "There's no need to go into every little thing. Maybe it'd be better if we just sat here with David. We don't have to talk right now."

"But I have to say that I'm sorry. I'm truly sorry for acting like such a fool. I'm sorry for ordering you about like a downstairs maid. I'm sorry for being so completely insensitive and crass. I apologize for acting like a conceited, elitist snob." Then a grin lifted the corners of her mouth. "I'm going to get Savannah a puppy."

Savannah hopped off the bench like a jackrabbit and stood before her mother. Small hands rested on the woman's knees as the girl leaned forward, face close to the promise-maker.

"You mean it, Mama? For sure? We can really get a puppy?"

When was the last time she'd seen her daughter's face light up like a Christmas tree? Had it been so easy to do? Oh, how she'd missed that beaming little smile, the twinkling eyes, that infectious giggle. Her heart sank to know that she'd deprived them both of so much over the last couple of years. Vowing right then and there to make her family the highest priority in her life, she laughed through the tears.

"Yes! You and I—Aunt Sadie, too, if she wants—will go to the shelter and pick out a puppy."

A shadow clouded the girl's expression. "But, Mama, what about your carpets?"

"*Our* carpets will survive a puppy," she grinned.

Savannah's eyebrows shot up. "Did you hear that, Aunt Sadie? We're going to get a puppy! And it's okay if it pees on the carpets!"

Sadie, elated over how things were going, tilted her head in warning. "I don't think it's exactly okay, but having those little accidents on the carpet is all part of the training period. I'm sure your puppy will be a very smart one and be quick to learn."

The child was so excited that her fingers twitched with energy. Feeling the rough denim fabric, she curiously eyed her mother. "Jeans? You never had jeans in your closets. You don't wear jeans."

Embarrassed by her former stuffiness, Mira glanced at her sister, who also wore a puzzled expression. "Okay," she said with a sigh, "this is where I need to back up a little." Her voice held more than a hint of humbleness.

"Ever since I blew up at you," she said to her sister, "about being crazy and needing some help, I realized I was jealous of your closeness to Savannah." Her eyes went back and forth between the sister sitting beside her and the daughter standing by her knees. "I know now that it was a selfish and entirely unwarranted attitude. Savannah should love her auntie. There should be love between you two, but I resented it. And I think I resented it because I knew I wasn't being someone my daughter could easily love. I'd created a wall between us and then was full of rancor because I saw her giving you her love. I desperately wanted that love, yet continued to behave in a manner that blocked it." She disgustedly shook her head. "God, what an incredibly self-defeating way to behave.

"Anyway, I talked with Nick about your Ruby. It seems that she was so highly respected by both the homeless and law officers who knew her that I became more than curious." She eyed Sadie and cringed. "I called Tina."

Sadie's eyes rounded. "You called her?"

"Three times," Mira confessed. "I called because I realized that I'd been passing judgment without knowing all the facts. I talked to Nick, Tina, and Caitlin. Caitlin told me about the Haitian woman. And Tina told me about your rune layouts and how things happened with Paul. And lastly," she said, "I sat in the kitchen last night and had a long talk with Greta and Josef. After that I never went to bed. I spent the whole night doing a lot of thinking, fitting the pieces together and coming to the conclusion that—"

"So where were you this morning, Mama?"

Mira squeezed her daughter's hands. "I went shopping," she proudly admitted. "I went shopping for real people clothes." Her eyes lit up. "As a result of my thinking I realized that I was just skimming the surface of life. Business is business, but one's home is where the real living is done. So I bought a wardrobe that I can hike and garden in. One that I can get grass stains on when we play volleyball and—"

"Volleyball?" Savannah questioned. "We don't have a volleyball or net."

Knowing how much her daughter loved playing the game, Mira's eyes glistened. "We do now!"

Dropping her jaw, Savannah cried in disbelief, "We do?"

"Yep. And guess what else?" she grinned.

"What, Mama? Oh, what?"

"I ordered you a trampoline. It's being delivered as we speak and Josef is having it set up in the rec room."

"Did you hear that, Aunt Sadie? A trampoline!" Savannah's gaze happened to graze the surface of the bench. "Mama," she eagerly said, picking up the satchel. "Look what Ruby gave me!"

Mira took the bag that her daughter held out to her. "Was this hers?"

The auburn curls bobbed. "It's magical," the girl announced. "Ruby said it's never, ever empty."

The woman peeked inside. "It's not?"

"Nope. Ruby said that even though it looks empty, it's always full of possibilities. She said that there's always possibilities."

The mother's hand caressed the worn, flowery pattern of the fabric. "Ruby was pretty smart, wasn't she. She was a very special lady, huh."

"Oh, yes!"

"I'm sorry she's gone, honey. I wish I could've met her."

"She's not gone."

Frowning, Mira looked to her sister.

A small hand touched Mira's chin and turned her attention back. Savannah looked deep into her mother's eyes. "There's a secret about her," she whispered. "Ruby's not really gone. She's God, Mama. She just went somewhere else for a while."

Mira blushed. "Honey," she gently began, "I didn't know her. And because I didn't know her, I can't say who she was or wasn't. Maybe she was just a bag lady who happened to have some extraordinary perceptual skills. Or she could've been a wealthy woman who wanted to devote her life to helping those less fortunate than herself. Maybe," she added, "maybe she was an angel . . . or God . . . dressed as a street person. Whoever she was, she changed my life. Somehow, she managed to come into all three of our lives and fix what was wrong. She changed us, all of us, forever. And, for that, I'll be forever grateful to her. I wish I could've let her know how thankful I am."

"You can, Mama! You can tell her in your prayers. Or just talk to her in your mind. God hears everyone's thoughts. In fact," she sparked, "you probably just did tell her. She probably just heard everything you said because—"

"I know," Mira smiled, "because she's God."

Sadie tightened her grip on Mira's hand. "Whoever she was, she was a real lady."

The three talked for almost an hour more, then fell into a companionable silence that was heavy with a new sense of relatedness. Rents in the fabric of their familial bond had been mended. Old wounds were left behind.

A ray of sun escaped from a break in the grey November sky. It speared through the knobby fingers of the oak tree and caught the golden highlights of Savannah's hair before landing on her daddy's headstone.

The light drew Mira's attention to the ground at their feet. "I hope David understands," she murmured to no one in particular. "I didn't mean to close my heart the way I did. It just hurt so much to keep it open."

Sadie squeezed her sister's hand. "This might sound bizarre," she said, "but, in a way, what you did paid a tribute to him. It certainly wasn't the best way to go about it, but it showed that you loved him so much that you couldn't bear to go anywhere near the emotion. We all react differently to grief. We all bear our emotional crosses in separate ways. We, those around you, understand your reaction. I'm sure David also does. And now that you realize that the love you shared with him should've been turned to your daughter, well . . . it shows you've come a long way. What matters is that, in the end, you opened your heart again."

"I never thought you were crazy, Sadie," Mira said softly. "Last night when I was doing all of that deep thinking, I realized that I'd used Ruby as a way to take out my resentment on you. It was completely unfair. So wrong. By doing that I betrayed my own integrity. It wasn't like me to be intolerant, to not respect another's belief. I had no right to criticize and condemn your belief in Ruby like I so viciously did. For that, I apologize."

"You'd reached a point of desperation. At that point you were clutching at anything that you thought would strengthen your wall."

Mira smirked. "Funny," she commented, "that's exactly what Greta said last night. We did a lot of talking. So much became clear." Lowering her gaze to the headstone, she released a tired sigh. "If you two don't mind," she whispered, "I'd like to spend a few minutes alone with him."

Sadie respectfully stood.

The child picked up her satchel. "Okay, Mama. We'll wait over by the cars."

Ten minutes later, Mira joined them. "What now?" she asked.

Savannah knew. She yanked on her aunt's arm. "Today is two days," she smartly informed.

Mira cocked her head. "Two days?"

Sadie leaned down toward her niece. "What do you mean?"

The girl pouted her lips and gave her aunt a disappointed look. "You forgot. Remember when we had lunch with Ruby in that café? You asked her when the big birthday was going to happen and she said in a couple-a days. It's been a couple-a days!" Savannah pursed her lips again. "And remember what else she said? She said that destiny has a funny way of bringing people together—even by a blackberry pie. Today is two days. We should all go have blackberry pie."

When they got to the café, they chose a table for four.

The waitress set slices of the fruit pastry before her three customers. And as directed, a double portion of blackberry pie—warmed—was set in front of the chair occupied by an old, faded carpetbag.

Sixteen

Ten Days Later

On Tuesday morning, Sadie found herself on the final leg of her trip. And although this was the third day of her journey, she couldn't shake the strange sensation that being on the interstates caused. After the dramatic breakthroughs at the Woodward estate, it'd been the first time she'd felt truly welcomed there. Loved. Crossing the country again made her feel torn. Was she driving toward home or away from it? Either way, she reasoned, she was a winner because she had two homes now.

The long, quiet hours on the road had given her golden time to review all that had happened, including the memorable week she'd stayed beyond their party of blackberry pie. Mira had thinned out her work schedule in order to spend the week with family. She'd called in favors from her peers and delegated research among her paralegals. Caitlin worked overtime and went in on her days off so that Sadie and Mira could spend more time together.

It had been a wonderful week, one loaded with myriad strong visuals that stuck in the mind as permanent snapshots of a happy family. The three of them did everything together. They went with Mira to a car dealership and helped her pick out an SUV. "We can't take a Lexus to all the fun places we're going to," she'd said. Then she'd driven off the lot and headed straight for Michael's to load up six carts with autumn and Thanksgiving decorations. She had smiling scarecrows for Josef's gardens, colorful dried arrangements to hang on the doors, garlands, gourds, silk flowers of yellow and orange to brighten every room with holiday cheer. "We're going to be the most festive place in the neighborhood!" she'd vowed.

Merging onto another interstate, Sadie caught herself smiling at the memory of her sister's renewed sense of holiday excitement. She was truly joyful with celebratory anticipation. And little Savannah was beside herself; she'd gotten her mother back.

The driver smirked and shook her head, recalling the afternoon Mira strode into the club wearing her Levis. With chin in the air, she'd held her daughter's hand and proudly walked shoulder to shoulder with her "crazy" sister. What a time they'd had ignoring the snide whispers and catching the gossipers' stolen side glances with head-on glares. Exhibiting uncharacteristic behavior and watching the shocking reactions, Mira quickly learned, was ten times more fun than milling around a stuffy soiree wishing the violinist would break a string to liven up the monotonously dispassionate chamber music.

And when the three of them visited the animal shelter, Savannah had eagerly checked out the rows of cages. Her heart about broke seeing so many four-legged orphans enthusiastically doing their best to be rescued and taken to a real home. Each time she approached a cage, tails wagged like pinwheels on a windy day. She wanted to take them all. After a good hour of narrowing down her choices, she settled on a sweet year-old Australian shepherd mix who immediately acquired the name of Sugar Pie.

Eventually Sadie's thoughts returned to Ruby. *Had I really caught glimpses of her during the last couple of days?* She mentally replayed the separate incidents without reaching a definitive conclusion. Over and over, she took both sides of the debatable issue.

Was it even possible for the old one to be hundreds of miles from Chicago?

You're thinking inside the box. What about possibilities?

But . . . she really had died, hadn't she?

Where's the body?

I must've been nuts to believe she could've been God.

Does God have a photo ID? Who knows what God looks like? Do you?

I'm being egomaniacal to think God would appear to me, talk to me, give me a gift.

Had to be somebody. Why not you?

Because I'm nobody special.

Everybody's a somebody. Everybody's special.

So what's the purpose if the world didn't know God was back?

That was *the whole purpose.*

Why aren't you letting me win any of my points?

Because you can't. All of yours are packed inside that box.

Are not!

Are too!

Oh, for cryin' out loud, this is the most asinine, inane conversation I've ever had.

Is it? Are you sure about that?

"Yes!" she shouted. "Shut up!"

Frustrated with the conversation, she passed the sign indicating that she was leaving New Hampshire. "Home," she said, with a sigh of relief. "Maybe being in Maine will bring me back to Kansas." Exiting the interstate, the van cruised along a secondary road like a dog catching the scent of home.

"Two more hours," Sadie anxiously told herself. "Two more hours until I'm back in the real world." Then, privately vowing to stop thinking of things that were unthinkable, things that had no acceptable answers, she jabbed at the radio button.

The music worked like a charm. After she had conduced her own sing-along for an hour, it was eventually joined by the discordant notes of an ogre. Her stomach growled and groaned a pitifully woeful tune. "Don't think there's much in the fridge," she told the ogre, while keeping her eyes peeled for a place to stop.

The first tendrils of a rolling mist had begun to curl its fingers around the clapboard buildings of the small coastal village of Cooper's Inlet. Spying the welcoming lights coming from the windows of a crowded eatery, Sadie slowed. And by the time the van nosed into the parking lot of the popular roadhouse, droplets of the chilling moisture were gathering on the windshield.

Once inside, she closed the door against the nippy November greyness. Turning, she couldn't help but smile at the familiar local color. It had the ambiance of home.

"Sit wherever you can find room," the busy waitress called from the oversized circular corner table. The six men she was serving were guffawing from a punch line she'd just delivered.

Rowdy voices drew the newcomer's attention to the hallway. It led past restrooms to a dimly lit back room. "Pool room," another waitress explained. "It's open to everybody." Seeing the customer's wary expression, the woman in the apron whispered, "Ladies, too. There're ladies back there. Nice bunch of folks. You like to play?"

"No, I . . . I'm returning from a long trip." She patted her midsection and grinned. "Only an hour from home and I need fuel."

Understanding a traveler's needs, the waitress assured the new customer that their menu offered just about any type of fuel anyone could want. "Sit wherever. I'll be with you in a minute."

Sadie scanned the room. The counter stools were full. The only clear table in the place was a booth by the front window that had just been bussed. She pointed to it. "Is that okay for one? You're busy. I don't want to take up a whole booth if—"

Quickly checking her watch, the waitress flapped her hand in the air. "Nah, the main rush is over. This crowd's gonna start to clear out. Go ahead. That booth's fine." She handed Sadie a plastic-covered menu. "You want coffee while you decide?"

The newcomer nodded and headed for the booth.

Ten minutes later, as the clam chowder was warming her insides, the homey atmosphere of the place was warming her soul. Everything about it shouted of home. Everything from the wooden lobster traps hung on the netting strung over weathered barn-wood paneling to the glossy gymnasium finish on the pegged, plank flooring.

Set into the far wall, a stone fireplace crackled, sending flares of reflection on the slick yellow mackintoshes tossed over chair backs.

Customers' heavy woolen pea coats in various stages of wear hung from wall pegs.

Several oil paintings depicted fishermen in precariously tilted boats as they leaned over to pull in their weighty nets.

Flickering flames danced inside hurricane lanterns hanging from three support beams.

Low conversations of the diners carried the stock Maine accent.

The warmth of the roadhouse was beginning to make her sleepy. As much as she wanted to get home, the thought of driving through the fog felt like a drudgery she wasn't up to. She glanced out the window while draining the last of the coffee. As a wave of thick mist thinned, she froze when eyes locked on the red hat of an old woman.

The cup clanked as it slipped from her grip.

Her head dropped into trembling hands.

"You okay, miss? Do you have a headache?" asked the concerned waitress.

Sadie, fighting the urge to look out the window, tiredly looked to the woman at her side.

"No," she said disgustedly, "I just keep thinking I see old women in red hats."

Instinctively, the server's eyes shifted to the window. She squinted through the wavering haziness. "You mean that old lady in the park over there?"

The green eyes suddenly lost their drowsiness. They shot open like a racetrack's starting gate. "You see her? You see her, too?"

This was one peculiar customer, the woman thought. "If you mean that old lady across the way with the posies in her hat, yes. She started coming to the park every day for over a week now. I'd say ten, eleven, days or so. Don't know where she lives. Heard her name is Violet, like that little sprig of silk flower stuck in her hat. Funny thing though . . ." the woman trailed off, seemingly intent on leaving it at that.

"What?" the seated customer pushed.

"Well, I see her just about every day and . . . oh, nothing."

"No, please. What?"

"It seems to me that that woman's got more shoes than anyone I know. And that knitting bag she carries around is odd."

"Odd?"

"Yeah, there never seems to be anything in it."

Slowly, Sadie's head turned back to the glass.

The elder across the way shuffled to a stop, turned to the roadhouse, and winked.

Blood rushed to Sadie's cheeks. Body twitched with the chill that shot down her spine. She jerked her head away.

"You don't look so good, honey," the waitress noticed, plopping herself down across from her ill customer. "You're a little green about the gills. Can I get you anything? It couldn't have been the chowder because it's famous in these parts. Folks come from miles around for my chowder. I make a new batch every night myself from Michael's fresh . . ." The worried woman stopped talking when she realized her customer wasn't listening.

Ignoring the ongoing prattle, the dazed customer surreptitiously glanced out again.

There was nothing there but the rolling fog.

So much for believing I was safe back in Kansas.

Still feeling the chilling effects of the ghostly apparition, she shoved her hands in her pockets. One hand touched the warm object and she pulled it out. Uncurling her fingers, she blinked from the sparkle reflected by the flickering hurricane lamps.

"What'cha got there, honey?" asked the inquisitive server.

"Ohhh," Sadie wearily murmured, "just some cheap costume jewelry someone gave me once. Nothing, really. No more than a piece of pretty glass."

The woman's interest was piqued. Struggling to lean her abundant bodice over the table to get a better look, she drew in her breath.

"Lady," she secretively pleaded, reaching to place her hand over Sadie's, "don't go anywhere. Please. Sit. Sit right there. I'll bring you more coffee. This is Tuesday, the day my sister has her shop closed. She comes all the way down here from Freeport and helps me out during the rush hour on Tuesdays. Bless her heart. I'll be right back with your coffee. It's on me."

Sadie frowned. *What is she talking about?*

Seconds later, the waitress was back with her sister. She poured from the steaming carafe. "Did I tell you this is my place?" she excitedly asked without waiting for a reply. "Name's Gloria and this is my sister, Ruth. She's a jeweler. Has a going concern up in Freeport. Go ahead, honey, show her your little piece of glass."

Ruth inquisitively bent forward, watching the customer's fingers unfold.

She, too, sucked in her breath. "May I?" she asked.

Sadie held her hand out. "Sure."

The jeweler expertly turned the piece this way and that. It was held up to the light at a just-so angle. It was turned over. It was given a full inspection. After giving her waiting sister a hard look, she nonchalantly scanned the diners in the room, then bent low toward the seated customer. Raising a cautioning eyebrow, Ruth carefully placed the jewel back in the owner's hand and recurled the fingers over it—hiding it.

"I wouldn't go flashing that thing around if I were you," she whispered. "If there's one thing I know, it's gemstones. That's no colored glass. I've never seen a ruby that big. Or that clear. Or color that deep. I'd have to use my loupe to be sure, but it doesn't look like there's a single imperfection in it. The cut's what makes it even more unusual—like nothing I've ever seen before. I'd also have to do research on that cut. A star cut has been generally believed to be impossible to achieve. That's—"

Possibilities.

"—the real thing, though. Yep, that's a genuine ruby."

Sadie turned pale as the color drained from her face. Speechless, all she could do was tighten her fingers and stare at the jeweler.

"You got yourself something you need to lock away in a safe-deposit box," Ruth strongly advised. "It ain't the Hope diamond, but it'd sure cause quite a stir with gemologists. One thing . . . it'll sure enough buy a whole lotta happiness."

An image of the Wealth rune flashed before her eyes. As the sisters left, she slipped the gem back into her pocket. Eyes were drawn back to the window. No, she thought, this bit of wealth will never be used to buy anything. It's already a gem of wisdom, my sign of faith, of possibilities. It's my reminder to always believe in my convictions—to believe in belief.

Leaving the coffee, Sadie rose to look for a phone. Finding one in the hallway, she dialed Tina's number.

"Sadie!" her friend squealed. "Where are you?"

"An hour from home. At a roadhouse in Cooper's Inlet. I have to—"

"Is everything all right? Are you okay? No car trouble or anything?"

"I'm fine. I just called to—"

"Ohhh! Am I glad you called! I'm so excited I can't stand it! Have I got a shocker for you!"

Not likely.

"Paul's back!"

Tina won. It was a shocker. For the second time in an hour, Sadie was struck speechless.

"Sadie! He's got money! Tons of it! His maiden aunt named him as her sole heir because, even though she knew he needed money, he never asked her for any. Sadie, she was loaded! And I mean *loaded!* He's so sorry for being so stupid and taking off, hurting you. He's done a lot of hard, honest thinking, made realizations, and he's back with hat in hand! He's back—"

He'll come back with hat in hand. Isn't that what Ruby said?

"—on bended knee and . . . oh, God, you should see how different he is! Sadie, guess what else?"

Silence.

"Well, of course, you're speechless. You know that cute little place up on the hillside overlooking—"

—the sunlit harbor. The one with flowerbeds leading up to the idyllic rose-covered cottage. The one with the white picket fence.

After Sadie hung up, she returned to the booth. Sip by wonderfully reviving sip, the hot coffee cleared the fog from her mind. She looked out the window, recalling Ruby's words about reality. She'd said that, although people persisted in perceiving different aspects of reality as likened to different worlds, or having differing opinions of what the *real* world was, there was really only *one* real world. There was no separate Kansas. No separate Oz. Both were the possibilities existing in the one reality. And as far as Paul went, Ruby had also called that one.

Sadie got up from the table, paid her tab, and stepped out into the swirling fog. With Ruby's prediction about Paul still fresh in her mind, she raised her face into the mist. After deeply inhaling, she released a long, extended sigh of acceptance. *One day at a time. I'll take one day at a time. After all, who am I to argue with God?*

Hampton Roads Publishing Company

. . . for the evolving human spirit

HAMPTON ROADS PUBLISHING COMPANY publishes books on a variety of subjects, including metaphysics, spirituality, health, visionary fiction, and other related topics.

We also create on-line courses and sponsor an *Applied Learning Series* of author workshops. For a current list of what is available, go to www.hrpub.com, or request the ALS workshop catalog at our toll-free number.

For a copy of our latest trade catalog, call toll-free, 800-766-8009, or send your name and address to:

HAMPTON ROADS PUBLISHING COMPANY, INC.
1125 STONEY RIDGE ROAD • CHARLOTTESVILLE, VA 22902
e-mail: hrpc@hrpub.com • www.hrpub.com